D1525639

Searching For Eden

Love and Justice, Volume 1

Kimberly Ford

Published by Kimberly Ford, 2020.

SEARCHING FOR EDEN

First edition. November 5, 2020.

Written by Kimberly Ford.

To my fabulous kiddos. You are such bright spots in my life. I can't imagine my life without you.

Martin, love of my life, God blessed me the day He brought you to me. I love how you love me!

Chapter One

She rechecked the rearview mirror.
Nothing but darkness.

She'd been driving for hours, since the last water stop. Fatigue made her muscles heavy. A deep breath filled her nostrils with the musty smell of old car and stale cigarettes. The nasty scent had been her only companion for days in her life or death race for Canada.

Ever since her blind dash out of Dallas, she'd run on adrenaline that flowed through her veins like the Trinity River flooding from its banks. The last forty-eight hours were nothing but a blur.

"Gotta stay awake. Get to the border." The words echoed into the empty interior. The same ones that had repeated on a loop for the last few hours, since her life was turned upside down.

She squirmed in the seat, patted her cheeks, and stifled a yawn. There'd been no time for sleep, not since her escape. They'd be looking for her.

Through the focused lens of fear, she remembered hands as they clawed at her shirt, fingers bruising her tender skin as they groped her. Even now, his breath, a mix of garlic and cigarettes, gagged her. The sickly-sweet aftershave still clung to her clothes.

Then the gunshot. Her wrists still ached from the recoil. Her ears had rung for hours.

And the blood... *Oh my God, so much blood.*

And she still didn't know what happened to Jared.

Her lungs refused to expand as if a massive fist squeezed her airway, no matter how much she gasped and pulled. Her tongue swelled to fill her mouth and spasms of pain raked her stomach, bending her over the wheel.

Panic attack.

Again.

Cool metal slid under her fingers as she grasped the compass on the copper chain at her left wrist. Rough texture grounded her, and the terror loosened its hold ever so slightly.

The smallest trickle of air swept through her nose, but it wasn't enough. She would suffocate out here in the middle of nowhere with no one to know. She grunted. No one would *care.*

Breathe. Breathe. Another tendril of air. And then another. Another.

Breathing was the key. Deep lungfuls of oxygen and sheer willpower held the anxiety in check, but a full-on attack still lurked. Still nipped at her heels. She wouldn't reward the fear by feeding it. She couldn't. The price was her life. As usual, there would be no white knight coming to her rescue. Right now, she needed to keep her head clear and focused.

Her brother's young voice sing-songed in her head. *One day we'll go to Canada, Eden. We'll track down Dad and then it will be okay. Everything will be okay. Like it was before...*

Those words, his presence, had been her only comfort on so many lonely nights as they huddled together in dark alleys or abandoned buildings.

She dug fingernails into her arm, desperate to relieve the tingling that raced along her skin—always an after-effect of the panic attack.

Only two hours away from the Canadian border. *So close.*

Lights flared in the thumbprint-smeared rearview mirror, and her heart seized. The chaos threatened to return and battled at the walls of her defenses. The lights inched closer until the car could've kissed her bumper.

She white-knuckled the wheel until her fingers burned with an ache that slithered up her arms like two pythons squeezing their prey.

A street appeared on the left, and she made the impulsive turn, fishtailing onto the dirt road. The other car followed.

Sweat beaded on her upper lip. She drove until the next intersection, made another left-hand turn. Then a right, with the car on her tail, winding farther away from the main road.

That couldn't be them. No one but Jared would know where she headed. Fear crawled through her body. This couldn't be real. She'd driven all the way from Texas to be nabbed so close to freedom?

The other driver angled down a dirt path. Her body went limp as she continued down the narrow road. Tears of frustration clung to her lashes. No friendly glow of a distant city. No streetlights. No lights period. Nothing but inky blackness and relentless despair.

Her phone chirped. "Jared." A sob choked her throat.

"Jared? Where are you? I've been so worried."

The shrill whistle of a nose-breather answered her.

Oh, God.

Time stopped. The chaos that smoldered beneath the surface reignited.

There was only one person she knew who breathed like that. "How'd you—"

"That's right bitch. Do you really think you can hide? There is nowhere you can go where we can't find you."

Jared would never give him the number... unless...

Hang up. Hang up. Her hands shook as she fumbled to turn it off and it slipped from her grasp, springing from the seat to floor. She groped around the floorboard and took her gaze off the road long enough to glance down. The car bounced through a pothole, and the wheel jerked hard to the right. She peered up in time to see the headlights leap from tree to tree, and wrenched the wheel back to the left.

Too little, too late.

Towering trees moved in and out of shadows as the car rolled and flipped down an embankment. One moment she hung upside down from the seatbelt, and the next her head slammed the steering wheel. Over and over again she flipped. Empty water bottles ping-ponged around the interior, and her overstuffed run-bag followed in their wake.

A scream ripped from her throat as the car landed on its side and everything went black.

Chapter Two

S *eventy-two hours ago.*
"Awww, come on, Eden. Jusss one more drink. Never heard last call. You can't send me home yet. Itssss been a loooong week. Need—" he hiccupped. "Need 'nother drink."

Eden Glover sashayed around the bar. She stopped at the corner and leaned a hip against the side. At twenty-nine, this was her life.

Herding drunks.

The boozer slid off the stool in his attempt to stand, and tried to right himself with little success.

She pressed a fist against her lips and bit her cheek, holding back a smile.

After several failed attempts to save his dignity, she took pity and guided his staggering body to the exit. "Sammy, it's two-thirty in the morning. You know the rules. The bar shuts down, and you go home to bed." She unlocked the door and gently pulled him into the humid Dallas night.

"How 'bout you let me come home with ya? We can keep the party goin' in your bed." Flying drops of spit punctuated each slurred word at the same time he tried to waggle the two caterpillars above his eyes.

She bit back a gag reflex. The urge to drop his arm and stalk away overwhelmed her, but she didn't miss a beat. Soon a hot shower would wash away the filth of the world. No matter what, Sammy was as harmless as a June bug. "Darlin', your wife would miss the hell out of you and come hunt us down. Besides, your chariot awaits."

She helped him into the cab, gave the driver the address, and headed back in The Beer Bong for the nightly cleanup.

Selah Fox, bartender and Eden's boss for the last seven years, carried a rack of glasses from the kitchen. She sat them on the counter and began unloading. "Did he go quietly?"

Eden flicked the long, heavy, ponytail off her shoulder and brushed peanut shells into a bucket. "He needs some new material."

"You're a saint for putting up with him night after night."

"Trust me, Sammy Duval is a sweetheart. I've dealt with far worse."

Selah wagged a perfectly manicured finger under Eden's nose. "One day you, me, and a bottle of tequila are gonna have a long sit-down. I need to know what kinda life you led that makes you think a drunken slob is a sweetheart."

"Trust me, there's nothing to tell." Nothing a gentle-woman like Selah—who'd been raised by her family—could ever comprehend. And truthfully, Eden was more at home with the darker patrons of The Beer Bong than with the clean-cut lunch crowd on her day job at Mallory's Diner.

"That's the last of the glasses." Dax, co-owner, cook and Selah's husband, came through the door from the kitchen untying a stained white apron. The quick kiss he planted on the other woman's cheek made Eden smile. Since meeting Selah in a GED class nine years ago, they'd become the only family she could count on. They treated her with kindness, and she repaid them with half-truths. But the less they knew about her past connections, the better.

Dax pointed a thumb to the back. "I put your bags of food by the door. Lots of good stuff left tonight. Too much drinking and not enough eating going on, I guess."

Saturday nights he always made extra food to add to her "bags" since the bar closed on Sundays. They assumed it kept her fed through the weekend.

She didn't correct them.

"Thanks, Dax. I'll finish up here. You two go on."

"We'll see you Monday night."

"You got it. Enjoy your family."

Ten minutes later, Eden grabbed the worn gray backpack and slung it on her shoulder. Her life in a bag. Where she went, it went.

One last glance around the kitchen, before she turned out the lights and hefted the food. He wasn't kidding. They each weighed several pounds.

As she stepped into the alley, warm, moist air settled over her skin. The harsh scent of pot, stale cigarettes, day-old garbage, and urine burned the tiny hairs of her nose. She sucked in a breath and tip-toed around a used condom, a pile of filthy needles, and items of discarded clothing.

Shadows shifted inside the tent-boxes littered between the doorways lining either side of the alley. Eyes highlighted by the lamplights followed her progress onto the street before she turned right and started the four-block trek for home.

The quiet of three a.m. embraced her as she sauntered down deserted streets. Families with their two-point-five kids slept with the misguided belief that bolted doors and guard dogs kept them safe from the riff-raff and gangs that prowled the night.

Her gaze roamed from one side of the street to the other. Ears strained to catch the echo of footfalls or whispers carried with the breeze. Alone yes, but that didn't mean she dropped her guard. Might get a girl a short ride to hookin' with a gold-toothed pimp dogging her every step.

She stopped at the next corner, under the dim glow of the bus stop sign and put the heavier bag of food on the bench. After another quick scan, she crossed the side street and hid in a doorway.

It only took a few minutes for them to come into the light. Six of them swarmed the bag like ants on honey. All ranged in age from five to fourteen.

A thorn she carried deep in her heart, twisted.

Street life was difficult no matter what age. But for these children, danger waited around every corner.

A roaring in her ears preceded images of another group of misfits. In her mind they'd been bigger. Stronger. But, as with this group, very much alone. The only hope any of them had of surviving was to band together. Become a family.

"It must be Saturday. Look at all this food."

"Remember to share. We gotta make it last. Won't be more eats this good 'til Monday."

The oldest admonished the younger ones. A strict hierarchy ruled these makeshift families, and rule number one, never break the rules. Your life depended on your brothers and sisters.

"But I'm hungry."

"I know..." Their childish voices faded in the distance as they took their loot and disappeared.

Eden swiped a tear as it escaped over her lower lid. "Stupid dust. Makes my eyes water." Her feet shuffled as she resumed the path for home.

A light from behind illuminated the black street.

The short hairs at the base of her neck rose. She shivered. A car.

Okay, no need to panic. Probably nothing. Lots of people drove cars.

One by one the seconds ticked by. The light still glowed from a distance, and the whine of the engine had yet to reach her ears.

Without turning or stopping forward motion, she glanced down and to the left. It moved at a snail's pace.

Not a good sign. Whoever sat in the car searched for something. Or someone.

A knot formed in her belly. A new thought took hold. This might be one of those life-altering moments. The kind that made headlines—*Woman found naked and dead face down in the gutter.*

An empty doorway to the right beckoned, and she ducked into the shelter of darkness. Her hand fisted around the mace in the left pocket. The thumb of the other twitched over the button on a switchblade tucked inside a strap around her waist.

Her heart pounded too loud in her ear. Air, instantly dry, sucked all moisture from her lips, but her head was clear and focused. With a pinch of luck, they'd get bored and go on their merry way.

She chanced a peek around the edge and reeled back as the unfamiliar car slowed to a standstill at the corner.

Damn. Damndamndamndamn. Oh, God, had they seen her? Adrenaline boiled through her veins. She abandoned the mace and reached for the doorknob jabbing into the small of her back. Her head dropped against the door and her eyes clamped shut. Locked.

Her lungs shutdown, and her tongue swelled to fill her mouth. No panic attack in months and *now* one shows up? Fingers groped for the bracelet. *Breath in, breath out.* The repeated mantra calmed her mind.

Think. Think. She shoved the fog of panic from her head. She'd been through worse. Quick action always kept her alive. The only way out—straight ahead. Or, she waited for them to corner her. She'd picked up an arsenal of self-defense moves over the years. Take a couple of 'em down. If that's all there was. She didn't have a chance to see how many were in the car.

Run for it. These streets belonged to her. She knew them like a mouse, trapped for eternity in the same maze. If anyone had a chance of escape, it was her.

She laid the second bag of food on the stoop and willed a plague on the douche bags who made her give up Sunday Nachos. But running would be faster without the drag.

With a deep breath, she tightened the strap of the backpack. *One, two, three...* She bolted to the right and didn't look back. The stark glare from the headlights told her all she needed to know. They still idled in the same spot.

She didn't even reach the next street before her name floated from behind.

"Eden! Damnit, stop! It's me."

She froze, back stiff. Eyelids dropped over gritty, exhausted eyeballs. She knew that voice. Turning, she retraced her steps. "Smoke? What are you doing? You scared the shit out of me."

"Sorry. Been looking for you."

Eden waved a hand at the car. "Whose car is this?"

"Does it matter?"

It mattered enough she worked six days a week at two jobs to afford a one-room, rat-infested, hellhole away from the past. Dump? Yes. But it was safe. And warm. And dry. Well, except for the occasional leak. She'd spent years trying to get away, and she'd be damned if anything would threaten that. "Whose. Car?" Her tone held a challenge. She didn't need trouble here. Her territory. Not theirs.

"Jared sent me. Said to tell you, it's time. He's in trouble."

No! Jared made his choice. She'd tried to help him, *begged* him to leave. He'd refused.

So damn unfair he wanted her to toss everything away. Her hard-won freedom. Her friends. Her community. What would Selah and Dax do Monday when she didn't show? Who would feed the kids? Everything in her wanted to refuse.

The bracelet on her wrist burned a reminder. She sucked in a breath and let it trickle past clenched teeth. Jared needed her.

Nothing else mattered.

Chapter Three

"The answer is still no." Liam Conlin gripped the steering wheel and repeated the same thing he had the previous three times.

A barrage of emotions pounced across his twelve-year-old son's face. Anger, hurt, sadness. Disappointment. Vivid blue eyes so like his mother's burned with unshed tears of frustration, and his bottom lip trembled. Noah shouldn't ever play poker. He didn't know what it meant to hold your cards close.

Noah was a carbon copy of Krista, down to his white-blonde hair and the freckles spattered across his cheekbones. Similar thought processes, too. Probably the reason Liam gave him a pass more often than not.

Krista had always worn her emotions like a neon sign around her neck. Some of Liam's strongest memories involved pushing her buttons just to see the glow.

He'd known how to flip her switches, good and bad. Knew what she would say before she opened her mouth. Knew her heart better than his own. Warmth filled his chest. God, he missed being that close to someone.

"Dad." Noah interrupted his musings.

His son's disappointment stung Liam's heart. He hated the role of tyrant, but Noah asked him to take a risk he just couldn't take. "Aren't you sick of this conversation? I know I am. This is the third time in as many days. My answer hasn't changed."

Never one to give up, Noah pinned him with a glare meant to intimidate.

Liam couldn't help himself. He laughed. Had he ever dared look at his father that way?

"Why do you have to be a cop all the time? Any other dad would be happy I wanted to play basketball."

Ouch. That stung. He hadn't been a cop in four years.

Not since the night Krista died instead of him.

When he quit to move his family to tiny Moose Head Falls Minnesota to become the proud owner of J'Emma's Country store. Being the local small grocery, general store, and only breakfast stop in the small community, made for a safer more monotonous life.

The lump of granite that resided in his chest did its job, and the heart beneath kept beating. Liam flicked his signal and guided the black Ford F-150 king cab off the highway onto the two-way county road toward home.

"Well, are you just going to ignore me?" Noah grumbled.

Liam swallowed past the irritation lodged in his throat. "You have my answer."

"Daddy wouldn't ignore you, Noah. He's a good daddy." His daughter, Zoe, offered her two cents from the back seat.

He hid a smile. At seven, she still believed him a hero. The slayer of the boogyman and monsters under her bed. She always had his back.

And he loved her for that.

"I'm not asking to hang out with friends after school. It's basketball. The gym coach and his assistant are always there."

"Enough already. I said no." He bit his tongue. Dammit. Would he ever get a handle on the single parenting stuff?

Noah jabbed his elbow into the door. "It's not fair," he whispered under his breath, just loud enough for Liam to hear. Arms crossed. Bottom lipped shoved out far enough to balance a pencil. The picture of tween rebellion.

For a split second, Liam second-guessed his decision. He wanted to believe Noah would be safe in a more loosely run after-school program. He wanted to believe that riding the activity bus home would be okay. He wanted to believe everyone in the world could be trusted to be who they said they were.

But they weren't. And he didn't know how to let go of the terror that soaked him in sweat every time he tried to be a better father and let them be normal kids.

Moose Head Falls Minnesota, with its roughly one thousand residents, may be one of the safest places in the country. Hell, it's why he'd moved the kids here four years ago. But he still couldn't let down his guard. Old habits never die. His gut said no, and the gut never let him down.

Almost never.

The sun slipped into the horizon casting a golden glow in the twilight. To take his mind off the disappointment he'd caused Noah, he replayed the conversation he had earlier with Sheriff Wilson when the man came into the store.

Moose Head Falls was one of the smallest towns in the county and didn't have its own police force. The county seat was in Two Harbors and the sheriff made his rounds throughout the county showing up every other month. As he did every time he passed through, he complained about old age and needing a break from all the traveling. And as he did every time, he tried to persuade Liam to take the deputy job that had been vacant for over a year. As tempting as the offer was, he turned it down. Just as he had done the last three times.

He'd reminded the sheriff that the county and all its people were his concern. Noah and Zoe were his. A fact Wilson conveniently forgot.

Movement on the side of the road crossed into the beam of his headlights and then disappeared.

What the hell was that? Way too slow for an animal.

Noah sat up straighter and leaned forward, straining to get a better glimpse. "I don't think that's a deer." The tension eased from his face as curiosity got the better of him.

"What? What doesn't look like a deer? I can't see. I hate sitting back here," Zoe whined.

The hairs along Liam's arms rose as if a storm brewed and a warning bell pinged at the back of his skull. He slowed. Whatever it was, he didn't want it to lunge in front of him.

"Up there. It's a person." Noah jabbed a finger just as the figure staggered into the circle of headlights.

What was a woman doing out here in the middle of nowhere all alone? A few years back, a rash of highway carjackings were carried out just like this. A body on the side of an isolated road. A decoy to lure unsuspecting travelers. He sighed and rubbed a hand along his jaw. Nothing but darkness in his rearview mirror. He didn't remember an abandoned car. Then again, maybe his argument with Noah distracted him.

As he debated what to do, the woman lurched and fell.

He pulled the truck onto the shoulder directly behind her and waited. No movement. Shit. Now what? Nothing outside the perimeter of the headlights caught his eye.

Noah unsnapped his seatbelt and reached for the door handle.

"Wait here."

"Awww, Dad."

"Wait. Here." He didn't like this. "Lock the door the second I get out."

"But—"

"Keep your eye on your sister."

He stepped out and waited for the click of the lock. Gravel crunched beneath his boots. The scent of decayed leaves and distant chimney fires hung heavy in the air. His gaze assessed the surroundings for any threat.

A cold breeze rustled the trees, casting shadows just outside the circle of headlights. He closed his eyes and listened, other than the whistle of the wind it was pristine silence. Almost too quiet.

He glanced at the truck to assure himself the kids were still locked inside. An owl hooted, sending him two inches off the ground, his heart in his throat. *Smooth, dude. Real smooth.* A shudder traveled down his spine.

He'd dismissed his inclination to grab the gun from the locked glove box— a decision he now regretted.

He squatted beside the body, shoved the mass of tangled red hair away from her neck, and reached for a pulse. Not dead, but her pulse was slow and weak.

"Hey, wake up." He tapped on the side of her face. "Can you hear me?" Nothing. He noted the dried blood down the side of her forehead, her skin was cold to the touch. How long had she been out here? He shook her again with the same response.

Pulling out his phone he placed a call to the local emergency number.

"Emergency services."

"This is Liam Conlin from Moose Head Falls. I need medical assistance out on Baker Road."

"What is the nature of the emergency?"

"Woman down. Non-responsive. Looks like she's been in an accident, but I don't see a car." Drunk? Still didn't explain how she got out here.

"Is she breathing?"

Liam grunted. "She's breathing, but she's unconscious. Her pulse is weak and her skin is cold."

"I can't get an ambulance there for at least forty-five minutes."

"Forty-five—" He dropped his head and his shoulders sagged.

"I'm sorry, sir. I wish I could help, but both of the local ambulances are in service."

"Thanks for nothing. We're not far from the emergency clinic in Moose Head Falls. I'm going to transport her there." He hung up and slipped his phone back in his pocket.

"Looks like it's you and me, sweetheart." He sighed and rubbed a hand over his chest.

Past training kicked in and he checked her for obvious injuries and determined it was safer to move her than leave her out in the elements any longer.

He smoothed the hair further off her face. "What the hell happened?"

Decision made, he carefully slid an arm under her neck, another under her knees and rocked her into the cradle against his chest as he rose. Long legs draped over his forearms. She was lighter than he expected. "Noah, grab your phone, Doc's number two in your favorites. Call her. Tell her to meet us at the clinic," he shouted as he carried the woman to the back of the truck.

Zoe opened the door and scooted out of the way.

He hesitated. Damn. What was he doing? Putting a stranger, covered in mud, scratches, and bruises in the truck with his young daughter. He should've called the sheriff. But he was too far away by now to be of any help.

"Dad, Doc said she'll meet us there."

He squinted between Zoe and the comatose woman in his arms. Too much time until emergency services arrived. "Zoe, climb up front with your brother and click the belt around both of you."

As Zoe moved to the front, he slid the woman onto the backseat and secured her as best he could then scrambled into the driver's seat.

"Who is she, Daddy?" Zoe craned her neck to catch a glimpse of the stranger. "Maybe she's an angel from heaven."

He glanced back before making a U-turn toward town and gunning the gas. His mind raced. No car. Cuts, scratches. Out cold. No apparent identification. But one thing was certain...This woman had nothing to do with heaven.

This kind of trouble...*her* kind of trouble could only stem from one place. And that place would freeze over before he let it touch his kids.

Chapter Four

Noah opened the door to the local clinic for Liam to carry the woman through.

"We're set up in here." Doctor Abby Logan pointed to the room across from the entry. "How is she?" She followed them into the room.

"I don't know. Her breathing is shallow. And she's been unconscious since we found her." He arranged the woman on the exam table and stepped out of the way. "I didn't think we should wait for the ambulance."

The doctor and her nurse surrounded the mysterious woman, assessing and taking vitals. "You did the right thing. They can take up to an hour to get here."

"Is she going to be okay, Doctor Abby?" Zoe chimed from the doorway. Tears pooled in the bottomless blue of her eyes.

Liam hefted her into his arms. His teeth clenched, and guilt chewed at his insides. He smoothed a hand over her back. Of all the dumb luck. He'd spent four years shielding them from the evils of the world. Then this dropped in their lap.

"We'll do what we can, honey." The doctor didn't look up from her examination. Her movements swift, with the skill of someone used to the daily trauma of the ER, not the routine grind of bee stings, broken bones, and the occasional foreign object stuck up some kid's nose. It occurred to him he didn't know what the doc did before *retiring*, as she called it, to Moose Head Falls.

"Pulse is thready," Doctor Logan's nurse, Viv, offered.

"You gotta help her." Zoe's voice trembled. "She fell from the sky and got hurt. My mommy sent her with a message. Please make her okay."

Liam stuck his head out the door and knocked on the wall to get his son's attention through the earbuds. Hiding behind music was his way of coping. "Noah."

Noah pushed himself from the hard floor. "Yeah, yeah," he said with all the weight of a put-upon older sibling. "Come on, Zo-Zo, I have a new game on my phone we can play."

Liam set Zoe down and crouched so they were eye level. "Listen to your brother. And don't worry. Doc is the best around." He placed a kiss on her forehead. "Noah, sit over there in the chairs where I can see you."

Noah tugged on his little sister's hair. With a gentle palm to her shoulder, he guided her from the exam room.

Viv left the room and came back a minute later with a sealed suture tray and IV kit. Setting them on the counter, she pulled gloves and surgical-grade towels from nearby drawers, putting them all within easy reach.

"Pulse weak, skin is cold to the touch and dry. She had to have been out there for hours." Doc lifted the woman's eyelids and flicked a light in each. "Pupils are responsive."

The nurse took rapid notes as the doctor continued her examination.

Doc pulled the stethoscope from her ears. "Set up the IV. We need to get her hydrated, pronto."

"She gonna make it, Doc?" Liam asked.

She jumped at the sound of his voice. "Oh, Liam. I forgot you were there. She's severely dehydrated. No telling how long she was out in the elements. Cuts, scrapes, hoodie shredded..." Her voice trailed off, concern etched in the wrinkles around her forehead. "She has two gashes to the side of her head. Glass embedded in both. Most likely a concussion. I'll need to do a CT scan to be sure. Was she in a car accident?" Doc turned soft brown eyes on him.

He shrugged one shoulder. "I didn't see a car. Just found her on the side of the road."

Viv gave him a nudge. "Excuse me, Liam."

"Hey, Doc, this has nothing to do with your abilities, but do you have everything you need to treat her here or should I call for an ambulance?"

"I phoned North Shore Regional when Noah called. They're on standby if we need them, but I think we've got it covered. Why don't you go wait with your kids? I'll come to get you when we're finished in here. Unless you need to go, I can call you."

He looked at the helpless woman on the bed. A weighted knot sat in the bottom of his stomach. "We can wait for a bit." He turned to leave and stopped. "When will Max get here?"

Max James stood over six-foot-four. He made Liam look like a rag doll. Early thirties, with a tawny complexion, long sandy hair and green eyes, word on the street was the females in town described him as a Hawaiian God.

He was also Liam's friend. The kind of man who had your back. And he happened to be in town for a few days.

With biceps the circumference of most people's thighs, he looked like he belonged on a stool outside a bar—not in a white doctor's coat. A perfect person to stand guard until the sheriff or one of his deputies arrived.

Doc stopped mid-procedure and glanced up with a stunned expression. "Max? Why on earth would he be here?" She flicked her gaze to the wall clock. "At seven-thirty? He's on vacation."

"No, I get that. But don't you think it would be safer with him here?"

Both doctor and nurse snickered.

His faced heated, and he cleared his throat.

"If you fear we need protection from a comatose woman who can't weigh more than, what would you say, Viv? One hundred twenty-five pounds? Then, by all means, call in backup. Or stay. For now, kindly exit the room so I can focus." Doc dismissed him with a flick of her wrist and turned her attention back to her patient.

Liam rubbed the back of his neck. Properly chastised, he headed to the waiting room to join his kids. With a tired sigh, he sank into a chair next to Noah. Zoe crawled into his lap.

"Is she going to be okay?" Noah asked.

"I think so. The Doctor seems confident. But I need to call Sheriff Wilson and let him know what's going on." He lifted Zoe from his lap, but she slid her arms around his neck and burrowed her face into his shoulder.

"No, Daddy. You can't call the police. What if she has a message from mommy? If the Sheriff takes her, she may get mad and not tell us."

"Why do you think she'd have a message from mommy?" Liam looked from the top of his daughter's head to Noah flashing a *what in the world is she talking about* expression.

The boy rolled his eyes and quirked the corner of his mouth. "She's been going on and on about mommy's message. I keep telling her the woman isn't an angel, but she won't listen."

Those words ripped a hole in Liam's gut. He folded Zoe in his arms and cuddled her beneath his chin. When Krista... He released a heavy sigh. After so many years it should be easier to say. When Krista died, Zoe had just turned three. Other than photos and stories, her memories were vague. Why she insisted the woman had a message was beyond him. Beyond his ability to fix.

"Zoe, you know this woman isn't an angel, right?"

Zoe shook her head in denial.

How did he respond to that? Once again, a dilemma for Krista, she would have known what to say. "Look at me, Zoe."

She pulled back and gazed up with trusting blue eyes and smoothed a tiny hand across his face, offering him comfort.

"Zoe, Mommy is in heaven. I'd bet she's happy there. She looks down on you and Noah every day, but..." He glanced away and stretched his neck. Buying time.

"It's okay, Daddy. I understand. That lady is not an angel. She's my new mommy."

Chapter Five

His mouth opened then snapped shut. Eyebrows shot straight to his hairline. "What?" He sputtered on the word. She could sprout a sparkly tail and unicorn horn, and he wouldn't be any more surprised. "Honey, why would you say that?"

"I've been praying for a new mommy. Every night. And the lady fell from heaven. Who else would she be?"

He stared, incredulous. "God doesn't just send mommies out of the sky, Zoe."

She shrugged and crossed her arms. "We'll see."

He surrendered. Planting her feet on the ground, he handed Noah a couple of bucks. "Go with your brother and get something from the vending machine."

They crossed the room hand-in-hand. Noah wrapped an arm around his sister's shoulders as they took their time making their picks.

Liam smiled in spite of the situation. He seldom allowed junk food. This was a rare treat.

"They would have been better off with you, Krista. It should have been me that night." If he'd been on time, it would've been. He rubbed a hand over his face, and tried to pull himself together before removing the phone from his pocket. Someone needed to report this to the sheriff.

The phone rang twice before Ben's commanding voice rang in greeting. "Sheriff Wilson."

"Ben, this is Liam. I don't know how far away you are, but we could use your services in Moose Head."

"What's up?"

Liam reclined into the chair and crossed his legs at the ankles. "On the way home tonight, I found a woman, nearly dead, on the side of the road. Doc's working on her now."

"Foul play?"

"Don't know. But she's been through the wringer."

A long pause, followed by the rustle of papers. "I can't make it back until tomorrow evening. Afternoon at the earliest. But let me check to see if I have a deputy in the area. I'll call you back." He disconnected before Liam could say anything more.

He sat forward in the chair, elbows on his knees. He didn't like this. His personal radar blasted warning signals he couldn't ignore, but no one else saw a threat. An unconscious woman, while unusual, didn't always spell danger. There could be many reasons for her appearance. Maybe he was overreacting.

Noah's laughter drifted from the other side of the room and pulled him from his pensive mood, reminding him of his priorities. The woman's story didn't matter. It didn't matter how she landed here. Someone else could puzzle it out. Wasn't his job. His kids were.

It was sometime later before the doctor exited the exam room, face drawn, and took the seat next to his. Viv hustled to the back, doing her best to hide the blood-soaked rags as she passed the kids.

Doctor Abby stopped the kids as they headed over to them. "Noah, do me a favor, take your sister to my office and show her the superhero collection."

"That's not necessary," Liam said. "They'll be fine over there."

She placed a warm hand on his forearm. "There is no way in or out of my office except by you. They'll be safe there. I think it's for the best."

Liam's gut tightened. It wasn't good news if matter-of-fact Doctor Abby Logan didn't want to talk in front of the kids. Were the wounds severe enough to cause death? He gave a nod of consent to Noah and then watched them leave his sight.

"Sheriff Wilson gave me permission to fill you in on the details since he couldn't be here. She's in bad shape. But she'll come through," she said as if reading his mind. "I had to stitch up two gashes to her forehead, treated abrasions. Severe dehydration, low blood sugar..."

He waited four beats for her to finish. "But?"

"Something happened to her."

Liam grunted. "Of course, something happened. The question is, what?"

"Some of her nails are broken, uh...*torn*. The surrounding blood is probably her's, but it could be someone else's. I can't tell."

"What makes you think it could be someone else's?"

They stared at each for a long time. "It looks like someone strangled that woman. Contusions circle her throat. They're at least a few days old."

And the hits kept coming.

"Any idea who she is? Do you or Viv recognize her?"

"Sorry, no I don't. This was on her wrist." She handed him a copper chain and pushed to her feet. "I can't tell you what happened to her. But she can when she wakes up."

Old instincts died a long, slow death, no matter how deep he tried to bury them. He examined every inch of the bracelet. Copper chain link attached to a small compass. The engraving on the back read *Eden, may you always find your way.*

So, the mystery woman had a name. "You told me her nails are torn and bloody, did you take samples? Any evidence of skin?"

"I did. I don't know what good it will do. There was no evidence of rape. But we've bagged her clothes and followed all procedures, just in case." She headed to the back. "I'll let you know if anything changes. I called Sheriff Wilson and let him know my findings."

He yanked his phone from his pocket and hit redial as she hustled off.

Ben answered on the first ring. "Talk to me."

"Doc said she filled you in on everything. I think you should get someone out here tonight."

"Slow your roll, Sherlock. Doc has everything under control. This is not her first rodeo. She was an ER doc in LA for many years and before that she was a doctor in the Army Rangers. I think she's got it covered. As far as our vic —"

"What about who did this to her?"

"As I was saying, you've secured our vic for the night. Doc told you the bruises appear to be several days old. Not likely whoever hurt her is in the immediate area. Bottom line, we don't know what happened to her." A weary sigh came through before he continued. "Look, this isn't Minneapolis. We don't have the funding or the manpower to drop everything. I wish we did. Doc has everything under control. I'll get someone out there in the morning if I can. I have no one nearby. That's what happens when you don't have a dedicated deputy in the town."

Did the man just take a dig at him? Now? How could he be so relaxed about this?

"You can't be serious. What about the state patrol?" Liam asked.

"What about them? This doesn't constitute an emergency. My hands are tied."

Liam scrubbed the side of his neck. "An unconscious woman is not an emergency?"

"For Doc, yes. Me, no. The vic is secured. The bruising is old. Doc knows the procedures, she's kept her clothes, all evidence will be there or sent off to the lab. There is nothing more that can be done tonight. I'll head back right after my court summons. In the meantime, if anything else comes up call me. It'll be fine. Probably a domestic dispute originated miles from here. Doubt anyone is after her."

The sheriff hung up, and Liam slid his phone back in his pocket. He didn't like this. His head admitted Ben might be right.

His gut told him the sheriff was wrong.

Chapter Six

He slapped his hands to his knees and pushed himself from the chair. There was more to this story.

Striding into the exam room he froze in the doorway. His trained eye caught every detail, even as his brain logged it away for future use. The stranger, Eden, laid there. Motionless. Skin colorless, as if someone had drained the life from her.

Just like Krista.

He shook his head, dislodging the phantoms, and moved further into the room. Her hands rested on top of the white sheet. The knuckles of the right bruised, skin split. Almost as if she'd punched something. Or someone. Nails jagged and torn, just as Doc said.

A splash of color faded under her left wrist. With a gentle touch, he lifted it to find a tattoo in brilliant shades of red and orange encircling the tender skin. A Phoenix from the ashes. Beautiful, identifiable mark. He laid it back down and continued his inspection.

Someone, probably Viv, had smoothed her tangled hair, and the mass piled on the pillow like fall leaves around her head. He leaned in to get a better look at the marks around her neck. The greenish-yellow a stark contrast to the pale skin around them.

He was so close, her soft exhales swept the hairs at his temple. His gaze roamed to her face. Soft, full lips, high cheekbones, and long, thick lashes that cast shadows beneath her eyes. There was a vulnerability, a softness to her. He fingered a strand of the golden-red hair. "Who did this to you?" The silky tresses slipped over his palm.

One last survey, starting at her feet, working his way up to her face where those dark lashes now framed eyes wide with the cold light of terror.

His breath hitched at the back of his throat. Hairs tickled his neck and time slowed. He lost himself in the most extraordinary eyes he'd ever seen. One light brown, with golden flecks radiating through the amber iris. The other an ice blue, with a navy ring.

His heart flipped as if someone attached live jumper cables to his chest. Flipped again, and then again, before it raced from zero-to-sixty in a blink.

Her mouth fell open, and color bloomed up a slender neck to her cheeks.

Lulled by what he assumed to be a weak, helpless victim, he didn't expect her strength when she slammed her hands against his shoulders, knocked him back two steps, ripping the IV from her arm. She swung her legs over the side of the bed and shot a foot into his stomach hard enough to knock the wind from him.

He had a minute to be thankful for her bad aim before she attempted to dart past him to the door.

Wild terror filled her eyes.

"It's okay, no one's going to hurt you —"

"Get back." She held a hand out to ward him off. "Stay away from me." Her dry voice rasped over the words.

"Stay calm. You're at a clinic, the doctor had to stitch you up."

His gaze scanned the room for potential weapons and landed on the instrument tray at the same time she saw it. *Son of a bitch!*

She didn't hesitate, but snatched the scissors and jabbed them in his direction. Three steps toward him, she herded him toward the door.

"You don't want to do this. Just relax. I told you, you're safe here." He moved out of the room.

"Liam, what have you done to my patient?" Doctor Logan gasped.

He ignored her. "No one will hurt you. Now, why don't you give me the scissors before you hurt *yourself*." He took a cautious step toward her and kept eye contact the whole time.

She wobbled. Those curious eyes glazed over.

He held his breath, certain she would go down, but she held on like a trooper.

Another shuffled step toward him.

"It's Eden, right?" He kept his voice low, soothing. His heart raced, pounding in his ears like a rapid-fire machine gun.

Zoe's squeal of excitement reached him before he caught her from the corner of his eye. She jumped and clapped her hands.

Eden's body quaked, and she swung on shaky legs in the noise's direction. The weapon now pointed at Zoe.

Panic soldered his feet to the floor. Red fog curled at the edges of his vision.

She took one step forward. At this distance, a simple fall, and the silver tip would puncture his baby.

That image was enough to shatter terror's grip. He charged the woman, his arms caging her.

The scissors clattered to the floor, and she struggled for a moment then collapsed against him like a dead cat.

"Zoe, Noah get back." He scooped the woman into his arms and carried her back to the exam room where he laid her onto the table. Fear still racked his body.

Spinning on his heel, he glared at the doctor. "You need to call Max. Now. You and Viv can't stay here alone with her. She's a danger." He should've left after he brought her in. His desire to make sure she was okay put both kids in danger.

"You're just annoyed she got the better of you," Viv mocked, but her voice shook, and the attempted humor didn't reach her eyes.

"She caught me by surprise." No way he'd admit he underestimated her. It wouldn't happen again.

"The poor thing woke up with no idea where she was, with you hulking over her. Do you blame her?" Doc asked. "Besides, how is Max going to help?"

"Max is capable of handling this situation." A furnace burned his insides and his skin itched and tingled with sweat. He needed a cold blast of air. *Need. To. Chill.*

Abby's spine stiffened and her mouth stretched in a tight line. "I've known Max for a long time. We've been through hell together. I'm well aware of what he is capable of, trust me."

Liam took a second to absorb this piece of information. He'd always known there was something special between the two of them. But he didn't expect her to bristle up like a mama bear. "Then you should want him here now."

"Are you telling me you can't handle one lone woman? Why do we need Max here? If you're so worried you can stay."

Liam wiped a hand over his head. "I can't keep my kids here."

Viv put a cool hand on his arm, her eyes huge with concern. "I can call Jim. He can take them home with him. They can have a sleepover with my kiddos."

He looked from the stranger on the bed to the two women waiting for him to respond, his resolve shifting. The scuffle of feet from the doorway reminded him what was important. Noah and Zoe already witnessed too much.

"I've already exposed them to more than I should have." With one last look at the women he stormed from the room. He did what he could for them.

For her.

Now, he needed to do for Noah and Zoe.

HOURS LATER, LIAM TOSSED and turned instead of sleeping. His brain gnawed at the images from earlier. Throwing the blankets to the side, he shoved his legs over the edge of the bed and cradled his head. A heartbeat throbbed at his temples where pain had been a malicious squatter in his skull for hours. No amount of aspirin could boot it out.

He stood up and stretched as he crossed the floor. The hardwood was cold under his bare feet.

First, he checked Noah's room then Zoe's. Both slept peacefully. The same as an hour ago. And the hour before that. Neither of them seemed bothered by the evening's events. Apparently, he was the only one whose sixth sense pinged off the charts. Tucking the blanket under Zoe's chin he brushed the hair off her forehead.

He took the stairs down to the main floor and made the rounds of all the doors and windows, ending in front of the refrigerator. The light from the interior cast an eerie glow into the darkened kitchen. He grabbed a bottle of kale juice, slammed the door and leaned on the counter. No matter how many times he wandered the house, he couldn't dispel the unease that settled into his bones.

For years, the feeling had followed him. A vague sense of impending doom. When he'd uprooted their lives and moved them to remote Minnesota, he thought those feelings were gone for good.

This time was different.

This time, his unease had a name.

Eden.

Chapter Seven

Awareness flirted and ruffled the edges of blackness clouding her mind. The sharp sting of antiseptic burned her nose, noise rumbled from a distance and penetrated the fog of confusion. She groaned. The movement, like shards of glass against her raw throat. The sound ricocheted inside her head. Big mistake.

Her tongue stuck to cracked lips. Not a drop of moisture. Everything hurt.

Something soft cushioned her head and the rest of her body. Might as well have been a cement slab for all the good it did. Every joint, muscle and bone ached with a pain so deep her lungs wheezed in protest with each inhale and exhale.

She experimented with opening one eye then snapped it shut again. *God,* even her freakin' eyelashes hurt.

She raised her hand toward her temple but didn't get more than an inch or two before she met resistance. Eyes flew wide despite the discomfort. A stale yellow ceiling tile with cartoon sea creatures and a mermaid stared back at her. *What the...*

In slow motion, she pushed herself to a sitting position and tugged on her hand. A plastic zip tie, the kind used by police, restrained her left wrist to the rails of a hospital-style bed. A needle embedded in her forearm led to an IV on a stand next to the bed.

Her stomach knotted and sweat trickled down her spine. She tugged against the tie and tried to twist it off or pull her hand free. That earned her nothing but raw skin. Why would someone tie her to a hospital bed?

Where the hell was she? The room was sterile white except for the cartoon-painted ceiling. The back of the room had nothing but a window framed around a black sky. White upper and lower cabinets, a jar of antiseptic wipes and a box of latex gloves next to a stainless sink completed her new prison. Besides the massive waves of pain rolling through her body, fear raised its ugly head suppressing logical thoughts.

With her free hand, she flipped the sheet onto the floor and examined her body for wounds. Wiggled her toes, twitched her legs. Everything worked, but the effort brought a new batch of pain.

She took stock of the rest of her body and came up with tender ribs, raw throat, and bandages on her head. That explained the drummer's solo beating in her skull every time she blinked.

Questions swarmed faster than she could process them. None of which came with answers. Her first instinct was to shout, but with no idea who stood on the other side of the door, it didn't seem like a wise move.

Instead, she lowered the left guard rail in increments careful to avoid any noise. Once down, she swung her legs over the side and dragged in a ragged breath. A sharp stab from her ribs stopped her cold, and she wrapped her free arm around her middle. The pain couldn't be any worse if she'd been run over by a herd of stampeding steers.

As her breathing slowed and the agony receded to a dull ache, she tried to make sense of what happened. Where was she? How did she end up here? The last thing she remembered was...*was...nothing.*

She slid from the bed and stood on shaky feet as the flimsy hospital gown flapped open. Waves of dizziness washed over her, and she reached for the wall to keep upright. The relentless spinning sent her gut into a spiral. Nausea churned in her stomach like the Gulf during a hurricane. *Oh my God.* She slammed her eyes shut and tried to draw as much air into her battered chest as she could. Breathe out. Breathe in. A couple minutes passed before she was almost certain she wouldn't throw up all over the white floor. For now.

The hospital room offered no clues to her location or why she was there. All that was clear was the friggin' pain in her body and the drum solo still beating in her head so loud she couldn't think straight.

She remembered nothing. Her mind a black hole. So why did terror fill her to the exclusion of anything else? Her right hand flew to her left wrist, her fingers tapping, rubbing. A primitive need to *run* consumed her. She had no idea what, but something, some*one* was coming for her.

The tendons in her neck tightened, and cold sweat coated her bare back. *What should I do?* Something in this room had to hold the answers.

A mirror hung on the wall to her right. All it would take was a few steps... She tugged on the bed, but it didn't budge. Her efforts were rewarded by fresh spasms of pain.

The wheels must be locked. Unlocking them might make more noise than she wanted.

The last thing she needed was company. At least not until she understood the situation. Hell, she needed to know who she was.

She scanned the room. Something had to trigger her memory. No clothes, no bag, or purse, everything belonged to the hospital or clinic or wherever she was. The thing in the room that didn't belong was her.

She sat gingerly on the side of the bed. Short, shallow breaths were all she could manage around the sore ribs. The waves of pain needed to stop so she could think clearly. Footfalls echoed twice from somewhere on the other side of the door. The occasional muffled voices pushed her further into panic mode. Couldn't defend herself chained liked a defenseless animal.

Her gaze fell on the counter. Maybe something useful would turn up there. It took some riffling, but deep in the back of one drawer she found a pair of nail clippers.

It took less than twenty minutes to snip through the thick nylon, but by that time sunlight brightened the window she'd tossed the clippers on the bed and pulled the IV from her arm.

She slid to the floor, for the first time aware of the cold tile beneath her feet. A good sign. Her head cleared and her body ached a little less this go 'round. She stood a little taller and took the three steps to the door.

She pulled on the handle.

Locked.

A sob choked off her airway, and she dropped her chin to chest and closed her eyes. The window. She spun around and crossed the floor to the back wall. Dammit, it didn't open.

Fresh out of options. Either she waited for someone else to decide when to let her out, or scream and bang loud enough that someone came *now*. No telling who would walk through the door, but at least it would be on her terms.

It took less than four bangs and two shouts for the lock to click in the door and an older woman in a white jacket stopped in the entrance. Petite with shoulder length dark hair, she had a friendly expression that warmed her honey-colored eyes. The laugh lines around her mouth deepened—but a vein of grit pulsed just below all the fluff.

Mental note, whoever this woman was wouldn't be an easy mark.

"Good morning, Eden. I'm happy to see you up."

Eden. She rolled the name around in her head hoping for a familiar ring. Nothing.

The doctor? Nurse? The woman chuckled as her gaze flicked to the bed. "I see the restraint didn't last long. You're resourceful." She sailed into the room and flicked on the light. "Don't be afraid. I'm Doctor Logan. We've spent most of the night checking on you. I wouldn't have wasted my time if I wanted to hurt you." She motioned to the bed.

Eden hesitated and glanced from the doctor to the door.

"I'm afraid you won't get far in your weakened condition. I want to check your vitals." When she still didn't move, the doctor patted the bed. "Please?"

She skirted the doctor on the way to the bed and perched on the end.

"How are you feeling?"

"Fine. I..." her voice crackled around the words. She swallowed and opened her mouth then tried again.

Doctor Logan waved her off and marched to the door. "Viv, will you bring water, please?" She circled back to the bed. "You were pretty dehydrated when Liam brought you in. It's no wonder you're having difficulty talking." Inspecting the IV entry, she gave Eden's arm a gentle pat. "Can you tell me what happened?"

A nurse, probably Viv, stepped into the room. She handed Eden a glass before moving to the counter by the window.

"Don't gulp it down, just enough to wet your mouth. Any more and your stomach might rebel," Doctor Logan warned.

The cool liquid trickled in and exploded with sweetness. She needed more, but forced herself to stop. "Thank you." The water bathed the tender flesh and made her voice stronger. "I don't know what happened."

"It's not unusual to block out a traumatic event. We assume you've had a car accident. But we haven't found a car. Let's start with something simple. Is Eden your name? I hope so, it's what we've called you all night." She rolled a stool over and sat close to the bed.

Eden's forehead wrinkled in concentration. "You don't understand." She glanced between the nurse and the doctor. "It's not that I don't remember what happened. I don't remember *anything*."

The other women exchanged an uneasy glance. The doctor moved with efficiency as she checked Eden's eyes, inspected the gashes on her forehead, giving her a full exam. "It can happen. You slammed your head hard. You have two areas I had to stitch, but you have a lot of other cuts, abrasions, bruised ribs..." Her voice trailed off, and she pulled out the chart and stared. Her eyes didn't move like when someone is reading. More like she bought time to figure out what to say next.

Eden didn't like where this headed.

"When Liam brought you in—he's the one who found you—you were unconscious and severely dehydrated. You were out there for a while before he came along. Your neck and larynx are bruised. I would guess you've been through a traumatic event besides the car accident. Your brain is probably protecting you."

Eden's heart raced and her fingers played over the column of her neck. Sliding from the bed, she walked across the cool linoleum to the mirror and stopped in front of it. It might as well have been a stranger's image. One blue iris and one brown iris triggered nothing but shock.

She traced the cuts, the stitches, and trailed across her split lip before she craned her neck to inspect the imprints. Her breath came in ragged gasps, her body clammy. Who did this to her?

The echo of a gunshot. Muscles trembled. A flash of blood.

"I need to go. I need to get out of here." She took two steps to the door.

"You can't leave yet." Viv tapped her shoulder, but Eden shrugged her off.

"Eden, does this look familiar?" The doctor's voice penetrated the red haze, and she held up a copper bracelet. "You were wearing it when you came in."

Eden crossed the floor. The cool metal sent a shock of awareness through her the instant her fingers curled around it. A compass attached to a chain. She flipped it over and read the inscription. *Eden, may you always find your way.*

Some part of her recognized it. But an impenetrable wall blocked the memories. Her gut told her it also held back demons better left alone.

"Here, let me help." The doctor took the chain back and attached it to her left wrist.

Eden climbed on the bed. "I feel like it should mean something, but... How long until my memory comes back?"

The doctor shrugged. "It's hard to tell. Once the swelling goes down, we'll know more. Every injury needs to heal in its own time. You might notice bits and pieces or they may rush in all at once. It's hard to know with head trauma. We need to keep you for another day or two." She rolled the stool back and stood. "One thing I think it's safe to assume. With that southern twang you're not from around here."

Eden stored that clue away.

"It's early. Are you hungry? I'll have the cafe send over some breakfast. Meanwhile, Viv, will you bring her two more pitchers of water? I need you to stay hydrated, or I'll put that IV back in. Take it slow." Doc raised her eyebrow in a gesture of sternness.

The thought of food turned Eden's stomach, but when the opportunity came to run, she'd need her strength. "I guess eggs would be nice and a Coke."

"No coffee?" Viv asked.

Eden cocked her head and gave it some thought. "Just Coke."

Viv scurried off.

"Why don't you relax? We'll bring your food in when it gets here."

She laid back, feigning fatigue. Inside, her mind churned and her body tensed, ready to bolt.

The doctor gave her one last glance before she left the room.

"Doctor Logan, the sheriff called," a man's voice boomed as the door clicked shut.

Eden's ears perked up, and she slipped toward the exit. The knob turned in her grip. At least they hadn't locked her in again. She peeked through the crack but couldn't see anyone.

"What did he say?" She recognized the warm tones of the doctor.

"He'll be here around one today to interview the young woman."

"Perfect. That should make Liam happy. How was Mr. Henry?"

Eden let go of the door, the droning buzz of a beehive in her ear rose to a roar.

The sheriff. Here to interview her. Sheriffs weren't a bad thing. Only a criminal should fear a cop. Right? Nerves zapped skin like the thwack of a rubber band as the dark walls of anxiety closed around her. A stab of pain in her gut nearly dropped her to the floor.

She chewed her lower lip. *Run!* She slapped her hands over her ears. What was that voice? Why was she terrified beyond reason? Was it the sheriff? Why would she be so afraid to meet him?

Don't feed the fear, a voice she didn't recognize as her own, sounded in her head. Too much. Too much. Too damn much to process.

She made her way to the bed and continued to push the panic away. Her fingers played over the bracelet at her wrist. By the time calm, rational thought had returned, there was a knock at the door. Aware of the flimsy hospital gown that left little to the imagination she yanked the sheet to her chin and tucked the edges beneath her bottom, seconds before a mammoth of a man walked through.

Good lord, he had to be over six-five!

"Don't be afraid. I'm Dr. James. Max. I have your food." He approached the bed and held out a huge hand. When she ignored it, he dropped it and continued as if it was no big deal. "You need anything, you let me know." His eyes crinkled at the corners and his lips twitched with a smile meant to charm. He held up the bag of food.

"You're one of the doctors?" Her hand trembled when she grabbed the bag.

"I am. Well, not here. I'm in a hospital down in the Twin Cities. Just here helping Doc."

He must have sensed her unease because he walked toward the door. "Enjoy your breakfast. Mae cooks a mean omelet." He winked as he left the room.

Eden opened the Styrofoam container. Two greasy, sunny-side up eggs stared back at her. "Eek." Her stomach rebelled. She grabbed a piece of toast, screwed the bottle cap off the Coke and chugged a huge gulp. So good.

She pulled a packet of plastic utensils out of the bag. As she ripped open the plastic and laid them next to the Styrofoam on the counter, her gazed landed on the knife. Maybe it was time to get the lay of the land.

Removing the gown, she turned it around, so it opened in the front, tied the top, and rolled the two sides together. *Voila.* Nothing like an ass hanging in the wind to shake a girl's confidence.

All body parts secured, she opened the door and peered out. Max sat behind the counter in the entryway but no one else was around. "Psst. Hey, any place a girl can um... freshen up?"

"Ah. Down the hall and to your right." The phone rang, and he turned his attention to the person on the other end.

She proceeded down the hall, glancing in doors as she went. Most of them were exam rooms, empty offices and...*bingo.* The last door on the right appeared to be a laundry area complete with a window and a stack of scrubs. It only took a few seconds to find a pair that looked like they might fit and slipped them on.

The window wasn't big, and it emptied into a parking lot, but it appeared secluded. Best of all, it slid open with ease.

Knife gripped between her teeth, she climbed onto the counter and hooked her leg over the windowsill. It took a few twists and shimmies, but she maneuvered her legs out first and hissed as her ribs scraped against the sill. She hung there for several seconds to catch her breath.

Stars exploded behind her eyes when she dropped the short distance to the ground. She crouched with her hands buried in the colorful leaves that blanketed the area.

A soundless scream lodged in her throat, and a blast of cold air sucked her breath away. She stood up slowly, her left hand pressed into her side. Agony ricocheted throughout her battered body. The damp, cool soil seeped through the bottom of her feet. No shoes. Something she needed to remedy if she wanted to put distance between her and this town.

She took two steps back, and swiveled into a warm, solid mass. Her gaze landed on a row of tan buttons attached to a green shirt molded around perfectly chiseled pecs. She swallowed repeatedly and trailed her gaze up into a pair of dark eyes. Eyes that teased the first real memory she'd had.

"Going somewhere?" A deep masculine voice rumbled through her.

Chapter Eight

S he tipped her head back. Her gaze traveled up to a square jaw shadowed by a day's growth, a mouth drawn into a tight line and, further up, a head of glossy black hair. But his eyes were cold, hard chips of black ice. A shiver that had nothing to do with the weather skated from the top of her head to the bottom of her bare feet.

She'd been taller than both Doctor Logan and Viv. The stolen scrubs stopped above her ankles and wrists, so it was a good guess she wasn't short. This man towered over her.

Alarm bells fought for dominance over the pounding in her head. Her mind might be a blank slate, but it recognized a predator when it saw one. And this man had predator written all over his hard-candy body.

In hindsight, the plastic knife she fisted in her hand seemed silly. Probably snap like a twig if she tried to jab him. His forearms alone belonged on a superhero.

Another step back.

"Now, you wouldn't be thinking of running. Would you?"

The voice. His eyes might be daggers of ice, but his voice, like a smooth, mellow whisky, flowed over her skin. If she wasn't so bent on her getaway, she might stand there all day just to hear him talk. She shook off the hypnotic suggestion. "Easy, big guy."

She held the ridiculous knife between them even though she must be as scary as a homeless kitten. "I don't want any trouble. I'm just going to take my little plastic knife and head on my way. No harm, no foul."

Her request didn't slow him down. She found herself disarmed by a grip faster than a rattler strike. "Lady, what makes you think I'd let you waltz out of here?"

His grip switched to his other hand, and he hauled her to the front of the clinic. Two kids stared slack-jawed at the scene.

A twig jabbed into the tender flesh of her foot, the last wound-free spot on her body. She hopped on one leg and tried to jerk her arm free. "Ow! Slow down you brute. In case you didn't notice I don't have shoes on." The ache in her side was almost unbearable. Tears of frustration and pain burned her eyes. It took every ounce of will to keep them from streaming over the lash line. She would *not* let this surly bastard see her cry.

"I guess you should have planned your little escapade better." But he loosened his grip and slowed his pace.

She dug in her heels and jerked her arm, but rather than freedom, he clamped his hand tighter. "Let me go! Someone, help!"

"Yell as loud as you want, babe. I don't care if you're kicking and screaming, you're going back. Noah, take your sister inside." When neither of them moved he barked, "Now!"

They scampered away, but not before the little girl's face lit with a brilliant smile.

"Do you always treat your kids like mini soldiers?"

"What?"

"Never mind." The man was as soft and cuddly as a bramble bush. Hopefully their mama was nicer. "How did you see me?"

He turned the corner with her still in his grip. "I saw a leg coming out the window as I drove by. Since Viv and Doc use the door it didn't take a genius to figure out who it belonged to."

Opening the door, he propelled her through in front of him. "Max, what the hell are you thinking? She almost got away."

The giant posing as a doctor, stood behind the counter, a chart in his hands.

The hairs on the back of her neck stood on end. She fell back a step. All her confidence and swagger fled in the face of her current predicament. Did this town have any average-sized men?

"I don't think you have a thing you can say. I heard she got the drop on you last night." Doctor Max's expression remained deadpan.

"I told Abby to keep that zip tie on her. What the hell is she doing climbing out the window?"

"Aww, come on, Liam. She's not a threat to anyone. Eden, why'd you do that? And after I brought you some of Mae's fine cooking, too."

"Where is the doctor?" Liam ignored the other man.

His grip at her armpit held her so high she had to hustle on the tips of her toes as he escorted her across the floor and left her in the *room*. The place where this horror began.

"Stay," he barked.

Her teeth snapped together with enough force to nip her tongue. The tang of blood burst in her mouth. She'd been wrong, *that* was the last pain-free place on her body. "Woof-woof."

"What?" His glare drilled through her.

She gulped. "Sit. Stay."

His forehead wrinkled in confusion.

Could he be that dense? "What is...commands you give a dog?"

She answered his blank stare with crossed arms, a raised eyebrow and a cocky tilt of her hip. She'd be damned if she let him see her misery or the fear that raced through her.

"Liam, what are you doing to my patient?" Doctor Logan came through the front door. "I leave to get a change of clothes and breakfast. I come back to find you manhandling the poor woman."

"The *poor* woman was trying to escape through the back window when I got here."

"You probably scared her. She's my *patient.*"

Sarcasm burst from his lips. "I wasn't even here. She was slithering through the window when I drove by."

The doctor flashed that bit of grit Eden had noticed earlier.

Heat seeped up Eden's neck, blossomed over her face. Like a little kid, she dropped her gaze to the floor and shuffled her feet. This is what it must be like to disappoint a parent. "I'm not into the whole prisoner thing."

Doctor Logan rubbed a hand over her forehead. "And Liam here is not a cop. A good, if paranoid man, who seems to be forgetting this woman is a *victim* not a criminal."

"Then why is she crawling out a window?"

"Oh, for goodness sake." The doctor shut her eyes and took a few deep breaths. "I'm not cut out for all this. I'm a simple country doctor that runs the local clinic."

A chuckle drew all their attention to Max. "Oh, sorry, I thought you were trying to lighten the mood with that whole *I'm a simple country doctor* thing. My bad."

The doctor ignored him and continued. "Eden, stay in your room. Drink water and try to rest. Liam..." she stared at him so long Eden squirmed for him. "What happened to the whole innocent until proven guilty stuff you cops believe in? The woman has no clue who she is."

"What do you mean?"

"I mean she has amnesia."

He snorted again, louder this time. "You bought that load of crap? I thought you were smarter than that."

"Liam Conlin, don't make me embarrass you in front of your kids. I thought you were the self-appointed hired gun. When did you get your doctor degree?"

A giggle erupted from Eden's lips and, even when the grouch of a man glared at her, she didn't stop.

Liam turned his stony expression back to the doctor. "Fine. You *think*—"

"I *know*..."

"She's *convinced* you she has amnesia. If she's innocent why is she running away?"

All three of them gawked at her like she was an exhibit in a zoo.

Liam's expression said he had her red-handed. Arms crossed and the smirk of a smug asshole plastered on his face.

When she didn't answer quick enough, he quirked an eyebrow.

She planted her hands at her waist and gave all three of them the evil eye. "I guess waking up in a strange town, in a strange place with your arm cuffed to a bed changes a girl."

"I'm sorry about that. But after you attacked Liam with the scissors, we felt it would be safer for everyone, including you, if we restrained you," the doctor said.

A flare of adrenaline shot through her. She jabbed a finger at Liam. "I held *him* at scissor point?" If she'd held him at knife point not once, but twice, it was no wonder he didn't like her. She strained to catch something, some morsel of a memory. Surely, she'd remember confronting this ogre—but sadly, nothing came to the forefront.

"I can't let you go until the sheriff gives his okay. Besides, I'm not ready to release you yet."

Eden dropped her head. "Agh!"

"I have to get the kids to school. Sheriff Wilson said he'd be here at one, I'll be back. Keep her locked up." He turned and headed for the door. "Noah, Zoe. Let's go." He couched the command in soft tones, and his hands were gentle on each of their shoulders.

Both kids stared at her with undisguised curiosity as they walked by. The little girl, with long black hair just like her father's, smiled and waved. The sweet innocence of the child tapped a place in Eden's heart. Caught off guard by the need it triggered, she didn't know how to respond.

The door closed as she stepped back into the room. She slid down the wall. What fresh hell did this man bring? The most gorgeous piece of eye candy she'd ever laid eyes on, at least that she knew of, and meaner than an angry viper. Then again, she couldn't remember who she was, let alone the people in her life.

She sat up straighter. What if she had a husband or boyfriend? Images of the faded purple, green markings around her neck mocked her with their secrets. Husband, boyfriend— either one might explain this.

He might be Mr. Rugged GQ in flannel with all the charm of a prickly cactus, but Liam Conlin also carried an edge of danger that stood between her and freedom. The voice in the back of her head that screamed *run* clamored louder with every minute she stayed here.

The image of the impish little girl with black hair hovered in her mind as she trustingly did her father's bidding. One thing was certain. Liam Conlin struck her as a man who treasured those he loved.

Chapter Nine

As promised, at one o'clock on the dot, the thick, whiskey-smooth voice of the man who occupied her thoughts for the last three hours entered the building. She'd had nothing to do but stress over the sheriff and anticipate Liam's return.

She still had no idea what was going on. The closer the hands on the clock tick-tocked to one, the more despair gnawed at her guts. To say meeting the sheriff frightened her would be a lie. Pure terror turned her body to petrified stone. For the life of her, she didn't know why. Normal, law abiding citizens didn't fear police.

Despite the fatigue that gnawed at her bones, her body rejected the need for sleep. Shame too, a catnap might've helped prepare her for a rematch with the grouchy mountain-sized Liam when he returned.

After the dust had settled earlier, Max shared the events of her rescue. It appeared she owed her life to the man who rubbed her wrong in so many ways.

She curled her lip. Did that make him her savior or tormentor?

An unfamiliar voice caught her attention, boisterous with warm undertones. That must be the sheriff, the man who held her fate in his hands. Oxygen fled her brain and her skull shrunk around the useless mass.

Fingering the copper chain of the bracelet she sent out a silent plea for Max's friendly face. She slid from the bed when the handle on the door turned.

Hope died a quick, and tragic death the minute Liam's sunny disposition greeted her.

"Oh. It's you."

"The sheriff is here."

"Why are *you* here?" She face-palmed him to stop his reply when she brushed by him into the waiting area. "No, wait. Let me guess, you're the local VIP around here and need to butt into everyone's business?"

Twin lines furrowed between his eyes. "No dignitaries in this town."

She tsked. "Ah, don't sell yourself short. Every town has a Very Important Prick."

A snicker from across the lobby grew into an infectious belly laugh that came out as a cross between the bray of a donkey and the honk of a goose. "You must be the young lady who's got this town all abuzz." The sheriff joined them in front of her pseudo jail room.

With his hat in his hand, he stood just a head taller than Eden. A map of wrinkles, and deep smile lines crisscrossed his worn face. The multi-hued grays of his slicked back hair and close-trimmed beard reminded her of a winter sky.

His fatherly appearance and demeanor put her at ease. The tension she'd been holding on to since learning she was the subject of his investigation released, and her shoulders sagged at the twinkle in his faded blue eyes.

"Guilty as charged."

He didn't seem so bad.

"Eden, right?"

She nodded. "That's what they tell me."

"Sheriff Wilson, call me Ben. Doc offered her office so we can talk without interruptions." He stretched his arm toward the back of the building.

She took two steps and Liam fell in behind her.

"Whoa. She doesn't need a bodyguard." The sheriff flashed her a wink.

Liam crossed his arms. "She's not the one I'm trying to protect. She wields a mean plastic knife."

Oh, what she wouldn't give for that silly plastic knife. She'd aim it straight at the cold block of ice the man called a heart.

The sheriff patted the other man on the shoulder. "While I appreciate the thought, I got it from here. Why don't you wait over there? We won't be long." He spun on his heel and waved Eden to follow.

She couldn't help herself. She blew a red-faced Liam a kiss. Despite the uncertainty surrounding her entire existence, a soul-satisfying smugness settled within her chest. All he could do was stand there and fume. Made her chuckle.

The sheriff took the chair behind the desk, motioned her to the padded one across from him, an amused expression written across his face. "Glad to see you two getting along so well."

Ready to get this over with and be on her way, she gingerly sank into the chair. As the day wore on, some of the stiffness lessoned, but it would be a while until she could move with any degree of grace. "He's got a lot of buttons to push." She shrugged. "What can I say? He invites button jab-bing."

"So, tell me something about yourself, Eden. What about a last name?"

She scrunched her face and tapped the bandage over an itchy patch of liquid stitches. "I'm sure I have one, but I've no clue what it is." The ache in her head throbbed with a new intensity.

All traces of humor gone, the man turned to business. The relaxed atmosphere he created fled in a blink. "What *do* you remember? There must be something."

A crater the size of a football field opened in her chest, and confusion flooded in. As if she hadn't asked herself the same question all morning. Who forgets every detail of their life? "The doctor told me it might be awhile before my mem-ories return. I wish I had more. Sorry. You probably know more than I do right now."

"Okay let's try this, do you know the date?"

She pursed her lips and shook her head.

"How about where you are?"

Another shake.

He sighed. The chair squeaked as he leaned back, crossed his arms and rested his chin in his hand. "You're in Moose Head Falls, Minnesota."

Minnesota? *Was that far enough?* A voice whispered in the back of her mind. Far enough from where? She fought the urge to wrap her head in her hands. God, if this pain would go away maybe she could form a coherent thought.

"The man out there you seem intent on annoying is the man who found you on the side of the road. You might have seen his two adorable kids. He's fiercely protective of them. As I am of my county. Any reason either of us should worry?" He tossed the pencil he held down on the desk.

Shoulders slumped in defeat, she struggled to breathe past the lump in her throat. Why did everyone feel the need to point out Liam's heroics to her? It made it difficult to hold onto her annoyance with him. "I got nothing. But if you'll just have the doctor give me my clothes, maybe a few bucks, and point me toward the closest bus station, I'll be out of your hair and his. No one will have to worry about me."

The shrill voice in her head begged him to do what she asked. One thing, *just one thing,* needed to go her way today. No clue where she would go, but the prickly fear of being hunted consumed all rational thought.

"Afraid I can't do that. I have to investigate whatever happened to you. Doctor Logan already sent your clothes off to the lab, and I have to take your picture and one of that beautiful tattoo. Where did you get that done?"

She glanced at her right forearm, and bit the inside of her cheek. Crafty old devil thought he could catch her in a lie. Her index finger traced the flame colored wings of the Phoenix where they stretched toward her wrist. "It is beautiful isn't it? I assume I went to a tattoo parlor." Her lips lifted in a playful smile.

He wrote a bunch of notes in his little cop book and then took out his phone.

She squirmed in her chair. Okay, playful didn't distract him. "Is this really necessary? The pictures?" Again with the hidden voice, the voice of wisdom that chanted *no! No!*

"No matter what you find out, I don't plan to file charges. I've done nothing wrong. At least I don't think I have..." Stupid. Stupid. Stupid. "What I mean is I'm not a threat to anyone."

"You sure seem to be in a hurry to get out from under our hospitality." He pinned her with a stern glare.

Her stomach hollowed. "I'm sorry. I don't mean to sound ungrateful. To any of you. It's just... I don't know how to explain it."

"Let me stop you there—"

She shoved to her feet and leaned across the desk. "Please. I know I sound crazy, and you have no reason to believe me, but it's important that I be somewhere. Don't ask me how I know. I just do." She choked on the bile of desperation that bubbled from her gut.

He glanced up from his notes, his eyes filled with sympathy. "I would love to let you go. However, the doctor hasn't cleared you. Until I've done a missing person report, run your fingerprints, and completed my due diligence, I can't release you either."

"Fingerprints?"

"All part of the process. I have to make a few calls. I'll be right back." He stepped out of the room. The quiet murmur of his voice penetrated the door. It nagged her that she couldn't make out one word of what he said.

Her brain was fried. A sarcastic laugh echoed in her head. More like scrambled. She flopped into the chair, pulled her knees beneath her chin and wrapped her arms around her legs. The pressure on her ribs eased. For one-second she wished herself into a grain of sand. One among millions on the ocean floor. Her fingers rubbed against the cool chain of her bracelet. How would she find her way out of this mess?

A few minutes later the sheriff came back. "Good news is Doc said she'll probably release you tomorrow. Bad news, I couldn't arrange a place to stay until Monday."

"You mean I have to stay here until Monday?"

A mischievous smile hovered at his lips. "I think I have another option."

THIRTY minutes after the sheriff disappeared behind closed doors with Eden, Liam walked back into the clinic.

He'd grabbed a quick sandwich at the cafe, and tried to forget the infuriating woman who, in less than twenty-four hours, managed to convince otherwise intelligent people to drink her special brand of Kool-aid. She reserved her prickly side solely for him.

Antiseptic and an ocean of white greeted him. Even after all this time, doctors and hospitals still gave him an oppressive sense of hopelessness. And he was here because of *her*. He couldn't wait to stand on the street corner and wave good riddance when the sheriff drove her out of town.

Laughter came from behind the door. What the hell did Ben find so funny? She was a stranger with a hinky story and even more bogus claim of amnesia, and they were laughing? He glanced at the clock on the wall. A victim's statement shouldn't take this long.

Needing a distraction, he went in search of Max and found him behind his desk poring over patient charts. "Mind if I kill time?"

"Sure. What's up?" Max closed the file and took a sip from his drink.

Liam took a seat and stretched out in the chair across from his friend. "Thinking."

"Don't let me stop you."

Max arrived in town when he'd finished college. The same time as Doctor Abby and her husband. Between semesters at medical school, he lived in Moose Head Falls with Doc and her husband. Now, he split his time between completing his residency in Minneapolis and helping here when he could.

Liam rubbed a finger across his chin. "You've spent the day with her. What's your impression?" No need to specify who *she* was.

Max twirled a pen between his thumb and index finger and leaned back in his chair. "We've had a few conversations. Snarky, anxious, wary. Scared. All things consistent with someone who has complete amnesia."

"You buying the amnesia is real?" As a medic in the Army Rangers, Max was trained to sniff out suspicious activity. He had to have his own doubts about her. Liam refused to believe he was that paranoid.

"Yes. You don't?" Max furrowed his brow. "I've seen her chart. You've seen her with your own eyes. Her head's stitched in two places. It's not a stretch to believe her brain is scrambled."

"I don't know what to think. I don't understand why no one else finds the circumstances of her appearance disturbing."

"That's not a fair statement. Ben's in there now. Abby went through proper procedures for a suspected crime. We all understand your concerns. I don't know what happened to her out there. But, if you're asking me if she's lying about the amnesia, no. In my professional opinion, that woman has no clue who she is, and in that regard my gut tells me she's not a threat."

The back of Liam's neck tingled. Krista always called it his spidey sense. But this woman, however innocent everyone else perceived her, was an unknown, outside his control. He didn't like things outside of his control.

His entire world rested in his kids. He didn't know what he would do if anything happened to either of them. It was his job to protect them. His obsessiveness meant he'd never win Father of the Year. A small price to pay in his book.

A few minutes later the door squeaked on its hinges and Eden and Ben emerged from the office. Eden came to an abrupt halt as her gaze locked on him. A soft blush colored her cheeks, her lips parted in surprise. Then the mask of insolence slid into place.

Ben twirled his hat before he placed it on his head. "Well, Ms. Eden, I have all the information I need. Once the doc releases you tomorrow, Liam here will make sure you have a place to go."

"Wait. What?" Liam stood up so fast the chair scuffed against the floor and tipped into the window. "Why would

I make sure she has somewhere to go? Isn't she going with you?"

"Course not. I told you yesterday I'm on county rounds. I need photos and a statement. That's it."

Eden flinched and blinked way too many times as her gaze darted around the room.

What was she hiding?

"She can't stay here. We don't have a jail house."

Sheriff Wilson smothered a chuckle. "She's not a prisoner, Liam. She's been through an ordeal. I would like us to get to the bottom of it, however I don't have a place to take her. Who better than an ex-cop to keep her safe? It's only for a few days. If we haven't found out who she is by Monday, I'll try to arrange other accommodations. Loosen up, Liam. I hereby deputize you."

Liam blazed a hole right through the man, but the expression on Ben's face told him it did no good.

"I *need* your help. I'm down two deputies in the area. Doc isn't ready to release her, and I don't want her to leave until I've found where she belongs. Or what happened to her," Ben said. "This time of year brings out all the leaf-hunters, the festival is in a few weeks, and there are no spare rooms."

Liam scrubbed an agitated hand through his hair and let out a long-suffering sigh. All he wanted was to get rid of her, now he no choice but to babysit her. "Where would you like me to put her?"

"Didn't you buy Jonas's house out by the lake when you bought J'Emma's Country Store from him?"

"Yup." Didn't take a neon sign to figure out where this conversation was headed.

"I happen to know Jonas liked his beer a little too much, and Emma would lock him out. On those nights he retired to the Dog House. The room above the garage."

"It's one room, with no heat. I can't put her there."

"Toss a couple of heaters and blankets up there. Or, here's a thought, put her in one of your spare rooms. Look, Liam, I get your concern, but I don't think there's a threat here."

"Women don't fall from the sky with handprint bruises around their necks."

She cupped her hands beneath her chin.

Guilt scratched the back of his throat. He averted his gaze.

"Whatever happened to this young lady, she's the victim. Doc isn't ready to release her, I gotta run a background check and follow up with missing person reports. She has nowhere to go."

Liam tried to reason with the man one more time. "But—"

"Who knows?" Ben patted his shoulder. "You might enjoy yourself." He opened the door and disappeared around the corner.

Liam stared at the woman who'd turned his ordered life into a chaotic mess.

She splayed her feet, her fingers curled around her hips. "Well, Mr. VIP, guess I'm all yours."

Chapter Ten

Friday afternoon and as promised, Doc released Eden into Liam's care.

When he'd picked up the kids after school, Zoe greeted Eden with an ear-shattering squeal of excitement. Her new best friend. The entire fifteen-minute ride back to the store his baby girl chattered non-stop, confided her whole life story to the woman.

Liam flipped a towel over his shoulder, pulled a heater from the supply room and took another one from behind the counter. Hopefully, they would be enough to keep the little room over the garage warm.

Frustration scribbled over his thoughts. Since they'd come back to the store Eden's new groupie followed her everywhere. The weekend loomed into one, long, nightmarish, obstacle course to maneuver. Guess he should be thankful there'd been no more mommy talk. God, he hoped she'd given up that warm-fuzzy notion.

The sheriff strolled away from the clinic the day before without a care in the world. Without *her.* To add insult to injury, Doc refused to allow Eden to spend the weekend in the clinic, pointing out their license wouldn't allow them to keep her any longer. But her concussion hadn't had time to heal, and Doc needed her to stay in town until she deemed Eden healed enough to move on.

His brain still refused to grasp what had happened. How did he find himself the disgruntled caregiver of trouble with a capital T?

Maybe he worried too much, but life happened. Without warning. The night Krista died had been as routine as any other. No reason to believe life, as he knew it, was about to change forever. One minute he was on his way home for date night with his wife, the next...

He slapped the towel on the teakwood counter. Nope, not going there.

"Did you kill it?" Her voice, husky, almost a purr, brushed with velvety smoothness over his ears. Jolted him from his secret hell to a place made for rumpled sheets and lazy whispers.

The thought rattled him to his core, and he shook it off as if burned. A harsh breath rattled the back of his throat. "I didn't kill anything."

Those two-toned eyes took his breath every time. It was as if two different people stared back at him from beneath thick, dark lashes.

His fingers twitched with the need to brush the soft skin running across the base of her neck.

He wrenched his gaze away and cleared his throat. Max was right. He'd been alone too long.

"My bad. Did the countertop annoy you?" Honeyed sweetness coated each word but the hint of mockery carried the sting of an angry wasp.

A muscle jumped at his jawline. "Do you need me?"

"No. But I'm bored. Can I help?"

Of all the words he expected, boredom wasn't one of them. "This is a one-man gig. Besides, Doc gave me strict instructions. You need to sit around and do nothing for the entire weekend." As if he didn't already have a boatload of work, now he had to make sure she followed Doc's orders.

"I figured your kids were slave labor, I mean *working*, on a Friday afternoon. You must be hard up for help." She arched an eyebrow, waiting for an answer.

Wasn't it bad enough friends offered unsolicited advice? Now a complete stranger felt the need to add her two cents. "They're none of your concern."

She plopped her hands on her hips and pinned him with a smirk. "Don't they have somewhere else they could be? Hanging with friends? Playdates? I'm just sayin' I never see you without them. It's not natural."

"Never see me without them? Lady, you've seen me twice in your life."

"Do you have proof?"

"*What?*"

"I have amnesia, it's possible I've seen you more than twice." A playful glint shone from her eyes and the quizzical tilt of her head would have made him laugh if he were in a humorous mood. "I mean, now that I think about it, this entire thing might be a ruse to get me into your bed."

Heat consumed a path from his neck to his face, eyes widened in shock. He fell back a step, choking on a tangle of words all jumbled at the base of his tongue. He couldn't tell if she joked or not. "You're off your rocker." The words sputtered out of his mouth and sounded lame, but it was all he could muster.

"Well?"

He huffed an exasperated sigh. "Well, what?"

"Anything I can do? If I'm forced to spend the next three days with you, the least I can do is help out."

He waited for the snide remark that didn't follow.

The patina of fading bruises marred the delicate satin of her neck. A smattering of freckles across her forehead and the bridge of her nose gave the peachy glow of her complexion a childlike quality. The depth of sadness in her eyes screamed *broken*. Damaged beyond recent events.

In that instant, compassion swallowed him. Tension eased between his shoulder blades. "Doc would have my head if I put you to work. Go take a nap."

"That's all I've been doing for..." She cocked her head to the side, as if a thought rushed by before she could grab it. "As long as I can remember." Her laughter floated, bubbly, like a feather on the breeze.

Her willingness to laugh at herself surprised him, and his lips spread in the first genuine smile since he'd found the woman two nights ago. "That's a long time, but not long enough."

"Fine. I'll go to the back, stare at the walls, and make up memories to entertain myself." She pivoted on her heel then stopped, swept him with a confident appraisal over her shoulder. "By the way Mr. VIP, a smile looks good on you. You should wear one more often." Her long, red gold ponytail swayed just above the curve of her butt. A butt that filled out the borrowed scrubs to perfection.

Did she walk that way on purpose? Slow, seductive, sway or did it come as natural as a breath? Shivers zipped from nerve ending to nerve ending. It took a monumental effort to force his mind back to work.

A few hours later, the last flurry of customers left the store, and Liam went in search of the kids. They'd been too quiet and conspicuously absent.

Laughter reached him from the back room. He frowned and stopped at the side of the doorway. What were the three of them up to in there?

"Did my shoulder rub help your sore head, Eden?"

"A little. Thank you, Zoe. You're such a sweet thing."

Zoe giggled. "Daddy, says I give the best massages."

He silently cursed himself. Of course her head hurt. Should have offered her an aspirin or asked if Doc had given her anything for pain. She gave him so much spunk it was hard to remember the accident happened less than forty-eight hours ago. Leave it to Zoe to get to the heart of things.

"Why doesn't your dad want you to play basketball? Isn't that what families with two point five kids do?"

"The activity bus won't come all the way into town to drop me off. How would I get home?"

"How far away is the bus stop from your house?"

"We live outside of town, by the lake. The bus comes two miles close. Isn't that right, Noah?" Zoe said.

"Almost. Dad drops us off and picks us up from school every day. That means he would have to leave the store to pick up Zoe then come back to get me two hours later. He says it's too much time away from the store."

A pfft burst from her lips.

Liam imagined the eye roll to go with the sound.

"Is Moose Head Falls part of a big crime wave?" Sarcasm covered every inch of her words.

Noah laughed in response. "Right? It's why we moved here four years ago. It's safer here."

"What—" The color drained from her face when he stepped into view.

Whatever clever reply danced on the tip of her tongue died and her full lips dropped into an O.

"Hi, Daddy. Eden is playing with us, isn't that nice?" Zoe, oblivious to the tension, beamed at him.

"Get your coats. Noah lock up."

"But we still have thirty minutes—"

"Now," he snapped before Noah completed the objection.

"Yes, sir." Noah shuffled from the room, head down, shoulders rounded in defeat.

Liam scowled at Eden. A slow burn started in the pit of his stomach. "Can I see you out here, please?"

To her credit, her expression appeared contrite, but he couldn't tell if it was genuine.

"Let me make this clear. You've been thrust into my life, the life of my kids. You won't be here long enough to be their best friend or their cheerleader. If we're going to get through the next few days, we need to set some ground rules and as far as you're concerned. I have one... My kids are off-limits. None of your business. Questions?"

She bit down on her lower lip until it turned white in an obvious attempt to crush her usual snarky comment. Whirling around, she stomped off muttering a pinched. "Whatever you say, VIP."

"What? No *Mr.* this time?"

"You don't deserve the salutation."

"Daddy, why are we leaving early? Noah said you're mad and we have to leave early. Are we going home? 'Cause I'm ready to go home. I can't wait to show Eden my room." Zoe prattled on and on with no need for an answer, following Liam through the store as he completed his closing routine.

This was going to be a long weekend.

Chapter Eleven

Liam spent a good hour cleaning out the Dog House, as the Sheriff called it, for Eden. Then he set up the heaters and piled several heavy blankets on the air mattress. Early October brought bearable overnight lows, and so far, they'd had unseasonably warm weather. It shouldn't be too cold for her.

He made sure the power worked and gave one last check around the makeshift bedroom. The smallest twinge of guilt pricked at his conscience. Not going there, he shook it off before it took root. At least she had a place to sleep.

On the way thru the garage, he stopped at the jeep buried under the gray car cover—the jeep responsible for a huge fight days before Krista was killed. Relegated to a life under wraps.

As much as he loved his wife, they'd had their problems. Over the years they'd drifted apart. The jeep had been an impulse, an attempt to recapture their carefree lifestyle before kids. The afternoon he'd pulled up with the shiny new car, she'd been furious with him. Instead of seeing the gift for what it was, a way for them to reconnect, she'd ridiculed him for wasting money.

He rubbed his hand across the rough fabric. Too many times he'd wondered, if Krista was still alive, would they even be together? He liked to think so, but after her promotion she'd become preoccupied by work, withdrawn from the family. Not that he was a model husband. The first few years of their marriage he'd been deployed more than he'd been home, and the life of a cop is always chaotic.

Back in the house, he gave the spaghetti sauce a quick stir and set a pot of water to boil. When they'd arrived home, he'd sent the kids to their rooms and Eden to the den in the basement. He'd handed her the TV remote and told her to stay away from the kids.

His intention had been to keep them at opposite ends of the house. Noah didn't need a stranger goading him on for more freedom, and Zoe was too impressionable. The whole mommy issue had blindsided him.

It was Zoe's turn to set the table, which meant Noah had the enjoyable chore of clean-up. He exhaled sharply and released the negativity he'd carted around all afternoon. Zoe may tune out the tension around her, but eventually his pissy attitude would affect her sweet nature.

As he reached the top of the stairs, a childish giggle drifted from Zoe's room.

Lightness filled him. It'd been a long time since the Noah hung out with Zoe. Maybe the events of the last few days had taken a toll on Noah, or maybe he aimed to offset Liam's bitchy attitude from earlier. He vowed to make the rest of the night go smoother.

He froze, hand poised over the door handle. Familiar feminine tones followed by Zoe's girlish giggle overflowed from the room.

Ah, hell no.

Damn woman just crossed his line in the sand without a blink. What the hell did she not understand about *not your business?*

"Thanks for playing with me. I don't get to play with a lot of girls. Just Daddy and Noah. Unless I'm at school."

He leaned in to hear better.

"Do you have a lot of friends at school?" Eden's soft voice held a note of kindness, not the coy, snarky tone she used on him.

"Oh, yes. I have lots of friends. I even get invited to parties after school. My best friend, Kenzie, she asked me to have a sleepover one time, but Daddy said no." Her sigh held the fatigue of an old soul.

"He wouldn't? Seems harmless enough. Why'd he say no?"

The hairs along his neck stiffened.

"He said it wasn't safe. That's why Noah can't play basketball after school. Noah said after mommy died—"

"Zoe." He pushed through the door. "It's your turn to set the table." Cracked head or not, enough with meddling.

One look in his direction and Zoe's baby-blues pooled with crocodile tears. Her bottom lip trembled.

Eyes closed, three deep breaths, he willed the knotted muscles between his shoulder blades to release. Then he knelt down and cupped his hands gently around her shoulders. "I'm sorry, baby. Please, go tell Noah to help you set the table."

"Okay, Daddy."

He waited for her to grab Noah, for the footfalls to fade away before he rounded on Eden.

"You are such an angry man." She said before he even opened his mouth. "Forgive me for saying this, but you always seem on the verge of an explosion. That can't be healthy." She crossed her arms and eyeballed him.

Any words about to spew from his lips died a sudden, awkward death, and left him flapping his gums like a guppy out of water.

She dropped her arms and brushed past him for the door. "You really should think about meditation or... I've heard yoga can help with stress relief. Seriously, you have two kids to think of."

Anger issues? Stress relief? That was rich. She disrupted his neat, orderly life, then told him to meditate?

She made it as far as the top of the stairs before he recovered his composure.

"I will not tell you again, stay away from my kids. You're here a few days, it will only confuse them when you leave. They've had enough loss in their lives." He placed his hand on the small of her back and nudged her toward the stairway. "Let's go, I have your room all ready."

She stepped back and glared at him. "You gotta stop with the bubble wrap around your kids. You're smothering them." Her gaze softened. "You can't shelter them from the world, Liam."

Blood ran thick, pulsed with furious intensity in his neck, and his breath slowed to a labored pace. He could and he would. His kids were happy. Damn happy. She didn't have a clue. He dismissed the unease that curled into a bristly ball in his gut.

He curled his palm around her upper arm and pulled her down the stairs, past the kids as they stood like statues, mouths wide enough to catch flies, through the yard into the garage. The wooden skeletal steps were too narrow for them to go up side by side, so he guided her to the front.

"This is where you'll stay for the next few days. With luck, Ben, the sheriff will send someone out by Monday. The heaters should keep it warm enough and there's a TV. The previous owner used this room, so a cable line was out here. I'll get your dinner."

He left before she formed any reply and returned a few minutes later with a plate of spaghetti, crusty garlic bread, and a Caesar salad.

"Thank you. I see you're a jack-of-all-trades. Dad, shopkeeper, cook, town VIP." Their fingers brushed as she took the plate and dropped it on the table as if scorched. A scarlet flush dotted her cheeks. "So, is this my new jail cell?" She buffed her hand over her shirt.

The movement caught the soft light from the lamp, illuminated her satin skin and turned it rosy. Static buzzed in his head with the image of that same hand pressed into his chest. The small, delicate fingers, explored. Dropped lower...

"Why are you so scared for your kids?" She edged the room, trailed her nails over the walls, casting an occasional glance at him from over her shoulder.

He shoved balled fists deep into his pockets and rocked back on his heels. She goaded him, but he refused to bite. "The door is unlocked. Come or go as you want. But the house door stays locked."

"Why do you look at me like that?"

"Like what?"

"Like you want to rip my head off and devour me or... You just want to *devour* me." The way her voice dropped to a husky octave on the last two words left no doubt where her mind went.

Lust pushed through his veins and settled low in his groin. "I... You..." Son of a bitch, the woman had the ability to leave him speechless. *How the hell was he supposed to answer that?* Being right was beside the point.

"Well, well, well. You want me." Awareness bloomed in her eyes and she gave him her full attention. "Why, sir, I believe you're blushing." She layered the Southern accent on thick. "I have to say, I'm flattered."

"Don't be. I don't have room in my life for love. And if I did, it would be with someone less annoying."

She quirked a brow, the one over the amber-gold eye. "Who said anything about love?"

Chapter Twelve

Dinner was the best thing Eden had ever eaten. Not that she knew that for certain, but she'd bet one of her blankets. Except for the salad, which sat untouched, she ate every last bite then used the bread to clean the sauce off the plate.

She flipped on the TV and mindlessly surfed the channels, then ditched the remote to pace the tiny room. No bigger than ten by ten, the space held an old kitchen table against the back wall, an empty bookshelf and a matching desk and a chair. One small lamp perched on the corner of the desk cast a rosy glow. The air mattress in the middle rounded out the room.

Not bad for a space obviously unused. The heaters made it comfy. She tilted her head and scanned the room again. She couldn't put her finger on it, but something didn't fit.

Then it hit her. For a musty, unused room over the garage, everything was spotless. From the old wooden floors, to the window, all the furniture. Clean. Not one speck of dust on any surface. Which meant someone had taken the time to clean it.

A goofy grin split her lips, and she hugged her arms around herself. An image of Liam The Mighty, mop and dust cloth in hand, tickled her clean down to her toes. Shallow woman. She was helpless to stop the delight that ran through her. The addition of an apron and rubber gloves did nothing to detract from the masculine perfection.

An olive complexion stretched across chiseled cheekbones, along with the day's growth of stubble that shadowed his strong jaw. Dark, intelligent eyes, and the occasional flicker of charm, that he did his best to try and hide. Swoonworthy by any girl's standards.

And that was just his face.

She puffed out a sigh. Yes, he was a hottie. But with concussion-induced amnesia, a banged-up chassis ready for the junk yard, and the sure knowledge someone hunted her, she had no business feeling anything other than terror. And confusion. Lots of confusion. Her personal quicksand sucked her down.

A mirror on the wall captured her attention. Like everything else in the room, it gleamed, no dirt to mask the truth of her reflection. She walked close to study the reflection and wagged her eyebrows. "The better to see you with, my dear." Seriously, who had eyes like that? One blue, one brown. Did anyone else in her family have them? A lonesome melancholy washed over her when she wondered about family.

She moved closer, ignored the bruises and the distracting eyes. Freckles spattered her forehead and nose as if someone took a paintbrush, filled it with tan paint, and flicked it at her face. Red hair hung in a long mass down her back.

Nothing special, nothing that shouted, *notice me.* A girl who melted with ease into the background where shadows lived. Except for those freakish two-toned eyes, that screamed, *hey look over here, you'll never forget me.* Had she ever tried to hide them with contacts?

She collapsed on the mattress and draped the blanket around her. Her head weighed two tons and fatigue came out of nowhere to claim her.

The muffled thunder of a gunshot shoved back the curtain of dreams.

WIDE-eyed, she jerked awake and almost fell from the mattress. Fear crushed her chest and her breath wheezed through dry lips.

A dagger of pain stabbed with methodical thrusts into her skull.

She shot me! The bitch shot me!

She scrambled to her feet and scooted until her back collided with the wall. Who said that? Her gaze scanned the room. Was she alone? The lines blurred between dream and reality. A tide of blood everywhere.

A dream. Only a dream.

Ice-tipped barbs of hopelessness pierced her lungs. The pressure had the same effect as a punch to the gut. She couldn't catch her breath. Her fingers groped for the bracelet.

Crawling to the window, she shoved it open and stuck her head into the brisk night air.

A tall, brutal man hovered at the periphery of her memories.

Friend? God, she hoped not. Enemy? Someone who wanted her dead?

Whoever *he* was, might be out there right now. Waiting for her.

She glanced at the tree line. Emotions, too many to process, splintered and skated down her spine in icy shivers.

Breathe in. Exhale chaos. Breathe in. Exhale confusion. She couldn't just sit here idle. Fear didn't own her.

Time to leave, it wasn't safe. He might not be here yet, but it was only a matter of time until he found her.

The snap of cold, crisp air penetrated the smoke and mirrors her mind kept throwing at her. She flicked her bracelet. Minutes ticked away as she focused on *nothing*.

Composure somewhat restored, she pulled her head inside, closed the window then slipped on worn tennis shoes. Grabbing a blanket, she twirled it like a cape over her shoulders. Too bad it couldn't make her invisible.

The doorknob turned without hesitation. She yanked it open and hustled down the stairs and took a minute to get her bearings. Then made a mad dash for the road.

Deep down, she recognized a cloud of darkness followed her. She couldn't remember the details, but instinctively she understood. This family, the town, would be safer with her gone.

She walked for at least thirty minutes and found the way to the main highway. The adrenaline rush from the dream, flashback, whatever plagued her, dissipated and the fragments of memory faded the farther she got from Liam's place. *Which way?*

No car. No money. No phone. The borrowed scrubs and thin-soled shoes her only clothes. More important, where did someone with no identity go?

The southern twang of her words stood out from the people she'd met. If she was on the run, it made no sense to leave until she regained her memory and figured out her next step.

A frosty wind snaked through the thin cotton of the scrubs, and reminded her, in addition to everything else, she lacked a stupid coat, and a blanket wasn't cutting it.

Bitter acceptance settled over her. Nowhere to go. With a heavy heart, she retraced her steps.

She couldn't have gone more than twenty-feet when lights glowed behind her. Instinct told her to run into the trees, but a familiar voice stopped her before she made it to safety.

"Eden, what in the world are you doing out here this time of the morning?"

Doctor Logan came around the front of the car, stopped in the halo cast by the headlights, her arms wrapped around herself. "Where's your head? You shouldn't be out here all alone in your condition. You still have a concussion."

"I... I needed air and guess I got turned around."

"Well, get over here. Good thing my husband and I drove by."

Eden hesitated long enough for another gust, stronger this time, to push her in the back. Tentative footfalls carried her up the slight embankment. As she neared the car a distinguished older gentleman smiled through the window and waved her to the back. Doctor Logan climbed in the front.

"I've been out on an emergency house call. Kevin always goes with me in the middle of the night. Are you okay? Any problems?"

How could you not like this woman? Gentle, warm brown eyes. Eden didn't want to be the reason for the concern that etched the woman's forehead. "I'm fine. Couldn't sleep. I guess I'm restless."

"You're at Liam's place, right? We pass by there on our way home. We'll drop you off."

"Please, don't." Eden regretted the nervous bite in her tone the instant Doc swung in her direction, an unasked question in her expression. "I mean, you can drop me at the top of the road. I don't want the lights pointed down the drive to wake the kids. It's still early, and it's Saturday. They can sleep in."

She turned her attention to the window where the sun began its day by peaking over the distant horizon. "Doctor Logan, will my memory ever come back?"

"Call me Abby. Simple answer, probably. How long? I can't say. Will it all return? I can't answer that either, but in this kind of case, full memory is usually restored once the injury has had time to heal."

Eden gave her a tight-lipped smile. Did she want them back?

As if she read her mind, Abby pinned Eden with her serious *doctor* face. "A lot depends on you. If something else bothers you, your brain may latch onto it and keep you blocked." Abby's deep scrutiny bore through Eden, dug around for whatever lie she kept hidden. "The brain is a complex thing, Eden. As much as we do know about how it works that's about how much we *don't* know. Your memory will come back when you're healed, and ready. Not before.

And in the meantime, you may not believe me, but Liam's protection is the safest place for you to be."

The car came to a stop at the top of Liam's driveway.

"You sure I can't drive you down there, young lady?" Kevin asked.

"No, thank you. I appreciate the ride."

"Eden," Abby called. "Come see me Monday so I can check those stitches."

"I will. Thanks." She waited for the taillights to disappear from view.

The safest place to be.

Chill bumps raced along her skin. Funny how the image of the fair maiden being offered up as a sacrifice to the monster taunted her as she forced herself down the driveway. Straight into her beast's lair.

Chapter Thirteen

" When do I get to be the proud father? Huh?" RJ Sorell's father mocked him as he took off his coat and hung it on the hanger by the door, smoothing imaginary wrinkles. Seventy-five degrees in Dallas and not a cloud in the sky, but Rudy Sorell, ruthless drug king, wore his Dolce and Gabbana overcoat.

RJ stifled a snort. Wouldn't be surprised to find the price tag dangled conspicuously from the sleeve.

The older man leaned on the edge of the desk in front of RJ and loosened his tie. "You've been a disappointment since the day you came into this world."

Gremlins ravaged RJ's gut. "None of this was my fault—"

Rudy stood and slapped RJ on the side of the head. "You're a pathetic bag of excuses. You had one job." His father bent down until RJ could smell the fish the old man had for lunch. "One job."

"It was a double-cross. Jared and that..." He faltered at the sniveling in his voice. Rudy hated that tone. RJ curled his hand around the arm of the chair, sat up straighter and schooled his face to erase all emotion. Inside, his muscles quivered.

His father fiddled with the Rolex strapped to his wrist. A sure sign the embers of agitation sat ready to explode all over

RJ. "She has my drugs *and* my money. Do you think I care *how?* Your crew is your responsibility, and now a DEA agent is dead. The police have been on us like ticks on a hound. You managed to let Jared and his sister slip through your fingers." Rudy met his eyes and slowly shook his head. "Someone's gonna take the fall for the dead agent. You wanna do that?"

"The cops already have Jared—"

"And the only way he keeps his mouth shut is if we threaten his sister. And she's gone. God knows where."

Rudy paced the perimeter of the grand office before he took a seat behind the monstrous, old-world desk. "I can't believe you let a woman get the better of you. Let her shoot you."

He halted and cocked his head as if a thought just occurred to him. "If cops get to her before we do, what do you think she's going to tell them?" His lip curled. His eyes cold. Dead.

RJ shivered. It was times like this he understood why his mother left. Why all Rudy's women eventually left...or disappeared.

"You're going back into hiding. Tonight," Rudy continued. "Don't come back here until I send for you. You and your no-good crew have put the entire enterprise in jeopardy. Hutch and his men will get the bitch. Then we'll make sure Jared and his sister understand the cost of their little deception."

RJ shoved from his chair. He slammed the desk with the fist of his healthy arm. "You can't do that to me. It's not fair." A tremor rocked through him as he realized the impulsive move would cost him. But the repercussions of Hutch getting to Eden before him would be so much worse.

His father rose from his chair. In slow motion, he placed his knuckles on the desk and leaned into RJ's space. "Remind me when you started telling me what to do? You whiny, lazy..." Without flinching, without warning, he snapped out a clenched fist and punched RJ in the stitches.

Pain blinded him. Warm blood seeped through the bandage. Tears burned his eyes, as he struggled to keep them from spilling over. Tears would only anger the old man more. He stomped his foot once. Twice. Three times. It did no good. His face puckered as he cradled his arm. Air wheezed into his lungs. Experience had taught him to bite his tongue or the violence would escalate.

Rudy sat down, straightening his shirt as if he'd done nothing more than swat a fly. "Hutch will bring her to heel." With that, Rudy pulled out his phone and pressed a button to call his trusted lieutenant.

Talk over.

Dismissed like the hired help.

RJ slithered from the office, kept his eyes down as he stormed through the hallway and out the double doors to a secluded deck. Humiliation mingled with malice and blistered his soul.

This is all that bitch's fault. All his hard work, his plans...ruined because of her. He'd seen the way his father admired Jared. Treated him like a son. But RJ had been the one to pick Jared off the streets. He *owned* him. Him, and everyone he loved.

And that included Eden.

He grabbed his phone. His father could never, ever get his hands on her. At least not while she was alive. Lucky for him he had an ace in the hole.

Because if Rudy Sorell ever found out the truth, he wouldn't hesitate to kill his only child.

Chapter Fourteen

After the walk back from her attempted escape, she'd foraged through the garage, and found a bottle of Coke and a bag of Doritos in the back of Liam's truck. She couldn't face the tiny room, so she took her treasures and wandered out to the lake. The obstacle course had been a pleasant surprise. After she inhaled the chips, she took two swigs of Coke, and with high hopes, got started.

The first round nearly trounced her already battered body. She ignored the pain, not the smartest decision, but the physical exertion helped clear her mind.

Humph. Who was she kidding? There was nothing to clear. She had *empty vessel* stamped across her forehead. But at least the self-inflicted torture gave her something to focus on besides the bogeyman.

It had been stupid to leave, and now she paid the price. If she couldn't get through a simple obstacle course without air wheezing through her clenched teeth, she had no business being on the run.

Life didn't play fair. How was she expected to stay alive if she had no clue what direction or from whom the threat came from?

Midway through her half-hearted second round, a ferocious ache throbbed from the lacerations on her forehead, the skin itchy and tight. But as Liam came into view, she refused to acknowledge the pain. She pushed her shoulders back and stood straighter. *Never show your weakness.*

Dressed in gray sweats, he'd pushed the sleeves of the partially zipped hoodie back to reveal muscular forearms. "Kinda cold out here." His greeting lacked its usual bite.

"Not after a couple of runs on your course." She fanned her shirt away from her sweaty midsection. "I'm pretty steamed up right now."

He swept her with a bold gaze, a brief flash of something lit his eyes before he snuffed it out with a blink. If she didn't know better, she'd call that something...*desire.*

"Should you be out here? I don't think Doc would approve of a strenuous workout. I'd go so far as to say, she'd frown on you doing anything more than sitting on your ass."

She rubbed a hand over the throb in her head then dropped it when she realized what she was doing. "I'm fine. I needed to work some things out." She wouldn't admit to the deep aches that pounded her body. The benefit had been the muscle memory. She was strong, her body familiar with hard work.

"And being physical helps you think. I get it."

Pleasure curled around her, a light caress. That was the first time he'd spoken to her without suspicion coloring his words. An acknowledgment she was more than a threat. Like they might actually have something in common. "Did you have it installed? The course?"

"I started it about a year after I moved in. Not many gyms around here. I add another piece every year." He lifted his foot and stretched the heel to his butt. "When you're feeling better, we should time you." He dropped the foot, pulled out his phone and opened a stopwatch. He took two shorts strides to the bench and put the phone next to her food. "Coke and Doritos before an obstacle run. Fuel with garbage and then work your body into a good, cleansing sweat. Not smart. And not healing."

"No? I suppose you drink a few raw eggs mixed with spinach and apple or something equally disgusting."

"Kale and banana. But not a bad guess." He took off the hoodie and reached a well-shaped arm over his head for a triceps stretch.

The sleeveless white t-shirt hugged every muscle and valley. She swallowed a groan of appreciation behind another long pull on the Coke. Every inch of her body hurt, but he sure was easy on the eyes.

"Mind if I go while you rest up?"

"I'm done. Have at it." Her train-wreck of a body had reached its limit. But it took no sweat to sit back and appreciate Liam's efforts. Besides, the fluid lines and muscle bulge, currently on display helped take her mind off her problems.

He lasted an hour. She'd lost count of the number of times he ran through the course. All she knew was the longer she sat there, the further down she spiraled. Her arms were rubber bands at her side, her shoulder joints tight with fatigue. A spasm from her bruised ribs made her nauseous. And fireworks exploded in her head.

"You don't look, too good. Can I get you a kale juice?"

She wrinkled her nose. "You mean that green stuff you're choking down? I fail to see how that will make me feel better."

"It's good for you and the taste isn't bad."

Taking off the cap to the Coke bottle, she sucked down the last of the dark liquid, her gaze fastened on him from beneath her lashes. "Didn't we already have this conversation?"

He stared at her with deep intensity.

She couldn't get a read on him. "Breakfast of champions, right?"

His Adam's apple bobbed several times. "Something like that."

"I think I'll stick with Coke." She screwed the cap back on the empty bottle and gave him a stiff smile. "I'd love a shower."

"Top of the stairs, end of the hall. There are towels in the closet next to the bathroom."

She willed her body to stand with no outward signs of distress and walk across the yard with her head high, back straight. Relief eased over her when she stepped into the kitchen. A hot shower and a nap—in that order.

LIAM SCRUBBED A HAND through his hair and eyed the icy lake. A watery plunge might give him the cool-down he needed.

Four years without a woman had his imagination in overdrive. No other answer made sense. Either that, or he was stone cold crazy, panting after a woman who threatened the security he craved. It was time to take Max up on his offer to get back in the world.

On that note, he checked his watch and picked up his phone. Time to follow up with the sheriff. Liam needed

Eden gone. The sooner the better. He'd give old Ben a kick in the pants and remind him of his promise to vacate her by Monday.

He punched the numbers and waited for the booming answer.

"Sheriff Wilson."

"Ben, it's Liam. You want to text me an address for Monday?"

Nothing but crickets.

"You do remember your promise to have her out of here by Monday, right?"

"About that... looks like that's not going to happen anytime soon."

His nostrils flared. "How much longer?" It took Herculean effort to force the words out around the chorus of four-letter words dancing on the tip of his tongue.

"Here's the thing. All the hotels in the area are filled and Doc hasn't released her yet."

Liam glanced at the house. An image of her wet, slick body under the shower flashed through his mind. "And when does Doc expect to release her from care?"

"Concussions are tricky. No telling how long until she's recovered."

"There has to be another solution."

"In a perfect world..." His voice trailed into oblivion.

Liam rubbed his thumb and forefinger over his eyelids with enough pressure to shove both eyeballs into his skull.

"I'll keep looking for an alternative," Ben offered. "I give you my word."

What the hell kind of ambiguous statement was that? "Right."

"And Liam. I know this is a hardship. I appreciate you stepping up."

Like he had a choice. What was he going to do? Throw her out? "Sure. Always glad to help." He made no effort to hide the sarcasm.

A soft chuckle echoed in Liam's ear. "Talk to you soon." Ben disconnected with a fateful click.

Liam pumped out triceps dips until his arms shook, and he couldn't lift his weight one more time. Eden herself *may* not be a threat, but he still believed a cloud of chaos surrounded her.

Maybe he could burn off his frustration with another round on the obstacle course. If that didn't work, there was always the lake. Not exactly cold enough for a polar plunge but it should get the job done.

Chapter Fifteen

E den stepped from a hot, steamy shower and wrapped herself in a soft towel. Wiping steam from the mirror she leaned in for a close up. "Damn girl, you'd frighten a scarecrow out of its stuffing."

The whites of her eyes cobwebbed red with fatigue, dark circles ringed her lower lashes. At least the scratches on her face appeared less angry.

The shower had worked out some muscle stiffness, only time would ease the aches that went along with the gaping holes in her memory.

A quick rap on the door startled her right out of her towel.

"Just a minute." She yanked it up around her body before she cracked the door and peeked into the hallway.

A pile of clothes sat folded at her feet.

She poked her head around the door and scanned the area. Empty. Both kids' doors stood wide open. She snatched up the clothes. The temptation of something other than scrubs was too much to turn down.

The pants belonged to someone vertically challenged with the fit of cropped jeans. No bra to be seen.

The sweater on the other hand, was huge. She slipped it over her head and inhaled the warm, cinnamon scent that reminded her of Liam. Another sniff at the collar and warmth hugged her. Silly, but happiness filled her.

She slipped the thick socks on and wiggled her toes. Happy feet. Wherever she came from, her body wasn't used to the crisp weather.

She fluffed the towel over her hair. The finger-comb strategy did nothing for the mass of tangles. A real comb sure would be nice.

While she was clean, dry, and warm, she couldn't walk around like this. She wanted her own clothes, her own stuff. Was that too much to ask?

She sighed. "You need to bite the bullet, ask to borrow money and use his phone to call a cab." *Then what?*

That question could wait until later. Satisfied with her plan she plastered a smile on her face.

The aroma of bacon drew her down the stairs to the kitchen. Mr. VIP, who built an obstacle course, body-guarded his children, and took in strays, even when he didn't want to... belted out Top Forty songs along with the radio while making chocolate chip pancakes. A relaxed Liam, hair damp from the shower, and smelling of fresh air, used the spatula as his microphone.

The kids sat at the table, full of snickers and laughter.

It was all too cute.

She clamped a hand to her lips to stifle her giggles, but not before one slipped out and shocked everyone into silence.

Liam turned down the volume.

Three pairs of eyes stared at her. A flush crept across Liam's cheeks and his free hand swiped the back of his neck.

"Hey, you're wearing dad's sweater," Noah said.

Her gaze flew to Liam's in time to see the flush turn a brighter crimson.

"Sorry about the pants. They belonged to Krista, my wife. I donated all of her clothes after she died. I must have missed those."

"Oh, I'm sorry... I can give them back." His dead wife's pants?

"And wear what? Trust me, she doesn't care." Liam's voice went from laughter to gruffness.

She ran a finger beneath her collar. When she put it on, the heavy sweater had been a hug, now, the wool scratched against her skin. "I'm sorry. I don't want to get in the way I can take a Coke back to the garage." She forced her feet to slide backward, toward her isolated prison.

"No need. It's pancake Saturday." He pointed to the table. "That's your plate."

She really didn't want to go back to that lonely room. "Pancake Saturday, huh? I guess I could hang around for a few."

"Eden! Come sit by me." Zoe hopped from her chair and dodged across the floor to guide her back to the table. She patted the seat next to her before she took her own. "Sit here. Did you have sweet dreams?"

"Did I what?"

"Daddy asks us every morning, did you have sweet dreams?" Zoe glanced at her father. "Dontcha?"

"Every morning, Butterfly."

Eden pulled out the chair and sat. "I guess I did."

"There's coffee over here. No creamer, plenty of sugar."

"Coffee doesn't sound like my kind of drink. I'll take a Coke."

"Dad doesn't let us have that," Noah said.

"I'm not even sure where you got the one you had earlier." Liam flipped a pancake onto the plate with expert precision.

"Under the seat of your truck. It's where the Doritos were."

"Daaad." The kids chorused together.

Liam held up his hands. "Hey, not mine. Probably Max's."

"Yeah, right." Noah grabbed a fresh pancake from the stack his father put on the table.

Eden winked at Liam. "I did find it under the passenger side."

"Who has a good story from the week?" Liam took his seat.

"I do. I got an A on my math test." Noah's chest puffed with pride. He huffed on his fingers and scrubbed the nails across his shirt.

"Nice work. Proud of you." The two fist-bumped across the table. "Zoe?"

"That's easy. Finding Eden." The little girl wrapped Eden's wrist with syrup-coated hands and flashed a big toothy grin. "Your turn, Eden. Pick one good thing you want to share."

Considering the circumstances, she wasn't sure what she could say. Silence stretched while she searched her brain for something good.

"How about I go next?" Liam offered.

The disappointment on the girl's face was too much.

"That's okay. I'm next. I'm sure I can think of something. My brain is just a bit rusty."

Not like she had a huge pool of events to pull from. The warmth and love she absorbed in this picture-perfect Saturday morning routine seeped into her beaten body. Slam dunk. "You guys have been the highlight of my week."

Both kids sat a little straighter, smiles on their faces.

Liam mouthed a silent *thank you.*

Her cheeks burned, and she dropped her gaze to the plate. Her thumb moved in lazy circles over the metal utensils while they dug in to the fluffy stacks of perfection in front of them. It was all so nice. So normal. So not her life.

The banter, the closeness, it all left her uncomfortable. She didn't belong. An intruder gawking from the outside.

She dug deep, tried to uncover a tidbit, even a scrap of memory that revealed a similar experience in her own life.

Were her people out there? Did they miss her?

Over the next twenty-minutes Liam engaged his kids in conversation about school, friends, the coming weekend, and private jokes. Domesticated like this, the worry lines he'd carried between his eyes since they met, dissolved.

This was a good man. She liked him. The way he talked *to* the kids, not through them. Maybe her initial assessment of him had been hasty. She rubbed the space in the middle of her forehead to ease the tension.

"Are you in pain? Didn't Doc give you some medicine?" Liam asked.

She dropped her hand. Touched by his concern all she could do was nod. Not that she would take them. Pain meds left her groggy and she couldn't afford vulnerability. In any form. For any reason.

"You made a mistake when you ran that course. You're banned from further use." Liam carried his dish to the sink. "Noah, Zoe, bring your dishes. Butterfly, you're in charge of Eden's things."

"She doesn't have to do that—"

"It's okay. I'll take care of you." Zoe patted her arm and then stood with her elbow on the table. "Did it hurt when you fell from the sky?"

Noah gave her hair a playful tug. "Dork, help me with the plates."

Eden chuckled in confusion. "I didn't fall from the sky."

"Sure you did. Daddy said you came from nowhere. Everyone knows angels come from the sky." With that she picked up the dishes and walked into the kitchen.

Eden ground her fingertips into her temple. As adorable as all this family stuff was, she needed to get out of there or the pin-prick stars pinging behind her eyelids would explode. "I'm going out to my room. But I have a favor to ask."

Liam cocked an eyebrow and folded his arms over his considerable chest. Skepticism written all over his face.

She cleared her throat, forcing herself to stay humble, and not reach for the snark she wore like a shield. "You've done so much already. I have no right to ask. I appreciate the use of these." She plucked at the heavy sweater. "They don't fit. I was hoping I could borrow a few dollars to call a cab. Buy some necessities."

His eyebrows shot to the ceiling, but he said nothing.

"I'll pay you back."

Liam chuckled. "There aren't any cabs around here. The store you need is a good hour drive."

Her shoulders sagged. "Oh. How about Uber?"

Liam's cheeks puffed out a sigh, and he glanced from Noah to Zoe. "What do you say? Sunday road trip?"

Noah pumped the air. Zoe clapped her hands. "Yes! Play Zone Pizza Palace." They shouted in unison.

He flashed her a dimply smile. "I close the store on Sundays, so we'll drive over tomorrow. That should give you enough time to rest up."

The kids rushed from the room. Liam turned back to the sink. "You. Go get your pain meds. Take a nap. The kids and I leave for the store in fifteen minutes. I don't need Doc on my ass because you don't follow directions."

She wandered out to the room over the garage and flipped on the heaters before she snuggled under a pile of blankets.

Somehow her shopping trip had turned into a family outing with her warden. Mixed emotions whirled through her head. She wanted to analyze them. Take them apart and put them back together, see where that left her.

She just needed a few minutes to rest her eyes. Then she would figure it all out.

ONE DAY DOWN, ANOTHER to go. Liam whistled as he turned into the store parking lot. Eden slept at home and the kids were with him. All was right with his world. At least for the next few hours.

This couldn't have worked out better. Eden running the obstacle course had been the answer he'd needed.

Not that he wanted to see her in pain. He'd checked on her before they left. She'd been nestled under the covers like a hibernating bear, too tired to come to the store with them.

Eden, draped in his sweater, pants entirely too short for legs that went on forever, invaded his thoughts. She'd stood in his kitchen, vulnerable and exposed. The emotions she tried so hard to hide painfully obvious as she struggled with the need to cut and run at the same time he read her desire to stay.

He shifted in his seat and silenced a groan. Distance was a good thing.

Spending a whole day with her on a shopping trip to Whitekeep was another matter.

Chapter Sixteen

S unday afternoon, they trudged through the parking lot of the superstore in Whitekeep.

The hour drive had been tolerable. Both kids sat in the back engrossed in their hand-held gaming consoles. Eden sat with him in the front. She'd been quiet most of the drive. Giving one-word answers when needed. That was fine with him. The less interaction the better.

Yesterday afternoon he'd placed a call to a friend still on the force back in Minneapolis, gave him a full description of their mysterious visitor. If there was anything on the wire, his friend would find it. Liam would breathe easier once Steve got back to him. Not that he didn't trust Sheriff Wilson, but he might not have the same urgency Steve would.

"Hey, Dad, we're going to Play Zone Pizza Palace, right?" Noah asked.

"Yes! You said we could yesterday. Please, Daddy?" Zoe added her vote.

Liam groaned. He had three words for that place. Crowds. Crowds. Crowds. Chaos. Okay, four. But no matter what time of day they went it was a massive wall of humans and keeping up with the kids in that environment proved next to impossible.

"What's Play Zone Pizza Palace?" Eden asked.

Zoe tucked her hand in the woman's and headed down the sidewalk toward the clothing store. "It's the best pizza place around."

Warmth spread through Liam's chest at the pure joy written all over Zoe. Until Eden showed up, it never occurred to him that his daughter missed female interaction. He assumed she was too young to notice. That he did a good job as both mom and dad. Yet, she preened for Eden's attention. Made him question his assertion that anyone outside the three of them would be an intruder.

Zoe skipped along, their clasped hands swinging between them. "They have games, a play area with slides and ladders. You win prizes. Noah always wins way more than me, but he shares."

Eden's steps slowed. "Noah sounds like a good big brother." She came to a full stop, angled a vacant gaze toward Zoe, her head tipped to the side. "I..."

Liam came to an abrupt halt behind them. "What's wrong? Did you have a memory?"

Eden nibbled the corner of her lip. "I don't know. Something Zoe said...grrr. It's so hard." She stamped her foot. "I get these images, glimpses of people, things. But they're disjointed, behind a veil of mist. If I reach out to touch them, they dissipate. My life is a black hole." Her shoulders drooped.

There were a few memories Liam wished to shove into a dark space and forget. Who didn't? But he couldn't imagine the emptiness of not knowing who you are. "Try to let it go. I know it's difficult. Doc said you would get more as you healed."

Her usual cocky, self-assured expression fell away. Beautiful eyes shimmered with unshed tears. She stared at him, a portrait of confusion and hurt all mingled into one messy finger-painted canvas.

He moved his hand toward her face in an impulsive move to thumb away the lone tear that magnified her lashes. Instead, he dropped it to his side. As a father, he'd hugged away his share of cuts and scrapes over the years. But this wasn't something he could slap a princess bandage on and kiss it better. "It's only been a few days. Give it time. You'll get through this." He gave himself a mental smackdown. What kind of lame-ass advice was that? Why was it so hard to find a comforting word?

Her lashes fluttered down, and she sighed. When they drifted open again the unshed tears glittered with defiance. "Of course I'll get through this. I always land on my feet. Come on, Zoe. Let's go find some clothes."

Confidence and spunk were fully restored.

A mask. All that attitude was a mask she used it to keep everyone far enough away they couldn't see the hurt and vulnerability rattling behind the cage she kept them locked in.

SHOPPING bags secured safely in the truck, they were on their way to Play Zone Pizza Palace.

Eden still couldn't believe Liam's generosity. She'd hoped for a pair of jeans, a t-shirt or two, underwear, maybe a sweater with a few personal items. Instead, she came out with an embarrassment of riches. Multiple jeans, t-shirts, a couple of sweaters, enough undergarments to get her through the week as well as some makeup.

When she'd tried to explain it was too much, she couldn't possibly pay him back, he'd shrugged it off. Mumbled something about he knew what women needed.

She shook her head. Liam had more layers than seven-layer cookie bar.

"Dad, come on. You're *so* slow," Noah urged as he turned to walk backward. Blond hair ruffled in the breeze, hands shoved in the pocket of his sweatshirt, he was all boy. An excited grin covered his face.

Another fragmented image crashed through her mind. A boy. This time accompanied by a voice, *Come on, Eden. You're such a slowpoke.* She struggled to hold on to the memory a little longer. This recollection, like the one from an hour ago, was comfortable, wrapped her in warmth, made a smile form at her lips. A name teased the tip of her tongue. But as she tried to pull it in, it shattered into colorful slivers right before her eyes. Damn. All her memories to date had filled her with fear, dread. With the need to run. Not these. These made her feel loved, cared for. Why couldn't she hold on to it?

She'd come so close to a breakdown earlier. Almost allowed Liam to see all the harbored fear she kept at bay. Something about the man worked its way under her defenses. It would be so easy to turn to him.

"We're here, Eden," Zoe shouted.

All three of them waited for her at the door.

She forced a smile and hustled the last few steps.

It took a moment for her eyes to adjust to the dim interior, but when they did her heart rate sped up and her skin buzzed.

In the middle of the room stood a huge playground area with slides, climbing walls and tunnels that wound like a maze back and forth over the space above. Along the perimeter of the warehouse-sized room were games of every variety. Electronic basketball, a shooting range.

Kid nirvana.

Her mouth dropped open. Did places like this actually exist? "Oh. My. Gosh."

"I take it you've never been to a Play Zone Pizza Palace?" Liam's tone teased.

"I think I can say with complete certainty. No. Never."

"Hey, Dad, there's a table over there near the playground, so you can keep an eye on Zoe." Noah weaved his way through the crowd without waiting for a reply.

"Slow down." Liam's lips thinned into a grim line. Tension poured off him in tangible waves, and his gaze darted around the room, alert for any threat. He had a death grip on poor Zoe.

Play Zone Pizza Palace would be a nightmare for a control freak like Liam. Not for the first time, she wondered what made him take the whole protective-dad-thing to such a high level. All good parents wanted their kids safe. But his possessiveness bordered on overkill.

Sympathy for his plight mingled with a dash of humor. It surprised her he'd even agree to bring them here.

The kids slid into one side of the booth and Liam stood at the corner of the other, one eyebrow crocked at her. When she didn't move, he motioned for her to slide in.

Eden cleared her throat and shuffled from one foot to the other, gaze darting from the wall to Liam and back.

Her heart tap-danced in her chest a bead of sweat coating her upper lip. She'd be pinned between the brick wall and Liam's boulder-sized body. Not a place she wanted to be. The lure of her bracelet whispered its promises, begged to be caressed. Instead she squared her shoulders and slid across the bench. No need to let him see her anxiety.

With anyone else, the bench would have been plenty wide enough. Not with Liam, their bodies touched, shoulders and hips.

Damn, if the heat didn't brand her through her clothes. It made her squirm, forcing her to become intimately acquainted with the wall.

A young waitress with short brown hair and a sunny smile materialized at their table. "Good afternoon. My name's Brandy and I'll be your server. Have you ever been here before?"

"Yes," the kids burst in unison. Liam's head bobbed.

"Then you know the drill."

They all put their right hand out and Brandy stamped an image of a fox on each of them. Liam waved her off before she could stamp Eden's. "That's okay. She doesn't need one."

"Oh. Okay." Thrown off her game Brandy hesitated before she picked up her speech. "Would you like to buy tokens?"

"We'll, take forty dollars' worth. I'll take a water and two waters for them." He pointed two fingers at his kids.

Four sets of eyes pivoted to her. She stared back. Oh, right, her drink. "Coke, please."

Brandy gave her the typical waitress apologetic scrunchy face. "All we have is Pepsi."

"That's fine."

"And a large veggie pizza and medium cheese pizza," Liam added.

Once the waitress brought the drinks and tokens Noah took his cup, and after firm instructions to stay within eyesight of the table, dashed off to the games.

"Eden, do you want to go with me?" Zoe asked.

"I would lov—"

"I'm sure, she would rather stay here," Liam said. "Remember, Zoe, you stay right here in the playground until you're ready to play the games then come get me."

"Yes, Daddy." Zoe skipped off, her black ponytail swinging at her back.

Eden squirmed in her seat until she faced the man plastered next to her. "What's with the stamp thing?"

"It makes sure no one leaves with a kidnapper. Before you exit, the manager will check adult hands to the images on the kids' hands to make sure they match."

"Oh." She shrank into the back of the booth. That explained why he'd excluded her. He didn't want to take the chance she'd leave with Zoe and Noah. He still didn't trust her. Not that he had a *reason* to.

"When does Doc want to see you again?"

"In the morning. Before you take me to wherever the sheriff is sending me."

A stone wall descended over his face. "About that. I talked to Sheriff Wilson yesterday. He hasn't found a place to take you. He's still looking. You'll be staying with us a while longer."

"I'm sorry to be a burden to you. I don't know if I...if I thanked you for stopping that night." It took everything she had not to turn away from him. To allow him to see her gratitude. Unfortunately, it allowed him access to the vulnerable side as well.

Now it was his turn to squirm, and the lightest tinge of red hit his cheeks. "Anyone would have."

She cupped his hand with hers before she thought better of it. Goose bumps spread up her arm. "No. Not everyone. Not even most."

His gaze went from their joined hands to her face. Lust flashed in his dark eyes, turning them a stormy gray.

Her breath caught. Everything in her longed for that storm to sweep her away. To stand on the bluff, wrapped in the windstorm of desire. Embraced in the beauty of his strength. She craved it like a dying soul craved salvation.

And it wasn't hers to have. Faced with the reality of her situation, she jerked her hand from his, cradled it in her lap. She needed to explore the reasons for her craving to belong, but not here. Somewhere far from him.

Her brain searched for something to say. A normal topic that would keep her from going places she had no business going. "I... Doctor Logan needs to see how I'm healing. She wants to see if my glue is holding up."

At his blank look, she kicked herself. Stupid joke. "She used glue to hold the cuts together."

"Oh. Right."

Did his voice sound gruff or was that just wishful thinking on her part?

Over the next several minutes the awkward silence grew to the size of a Texas steer.

Wait.

How did she know how big a Texas steer was? Was it a memory? Just something people said? No... definitely memory.

"I remember steers," she blurted. "Well, I remember Texas steers. I think I'm from Texas." Excitement made her voice edgy.

He nudged her. "I told you if you relaxed it would start to come back. Do you remember anything else? Like how you ended up on the side of the road?"

She strained and tried to dig deeper but came up empty. "I wish I did. But no. It's as if I was born the moment I woke up with you staring down at me." That memory burned, forever in her brain.

He grunted in response

A man of so many words. A silent giggle echoed in her head. If she could have one superpower for a day, it would be to read this man's mind. What thoughts rattled around in there? "You're doing it again."

Liam arched one dark eyebrow in question. "What?"

"Staring at me, like you want to devour me."

This time he held her gaze for the span of a breath, before he glanced around the room. Searched out each child. When he'd located them, he turned his attention back to her. "Sorry if I make you uncomfortable. I have a few trust issues."

She let the charged moment pass. She wasn't going to force him to admit to something that scared the living daylights out of her. She knocked a playful punch to his shoulder. "*You*? No. I would never have guessed."

A half-cocked grin spread across his face, and her heart tripped. A tingle zipped along her skin.

And with that one confident look, the storm beckoned her for another dance.

Chapter Seventeen

He opened his mouth, but Zoe interrupted whatever he was about to say when she took a seat across from them. A dramatic, heavy sigh puckering her lips.

"What's wrong, Zoe?" Liam asked.

"A stupid boy's being mean."

Liam sat up straighter, his gaze roamed the area. "Who? Where? What did he do?"

She turned around and leaned over the back of the seat. "That's him." She pointed to a boy a year or two older than herself. "Every time I try to go up the ladder he stands in front and won't let me."

Liam's face crumbled in relief. He pinched the bridge of his nose. "Take your tokens to the games over there." He pointed to the bank of video games right next to them. "The pizza will be out any minute. The boy won't be there all night."

Zoe slumped against the table. "But I want to play in the maze."

Eden slapped the table. "And you should be able to. Don't let fear keep you from things you enjoy, Zoe. Don't let that boy scare you." The words didn't belong to her. She knew they were true, but so far, *she'd* allowed fear to control her every action. It sounded like advice from another woman with another life. Is that who she was? Someone who wasn't afraid? She wished she knew.

"What the hell are you doing?" Hostility roared from Liam's lips.

Zoe and Eden both flinched.

"Butt. Out." He was so in-her-face, the tiny hairs fluttered with his words. "The boy obviously wants to annoy her. Verbal confrontations lead to physical confrontations. She doesn't need to go in the maze right now."

Eden didn't know why it was so important, it shouldn't matter to her one way or the other, but she *couldn't* let it go. Despite the growing glow of anger on his face she persisted. "But she shouldn't be punished because of some bully."

"I'm not punishing her. I've removed her from an uncomfortable situation."

"But you're not teaching her how to *deal* with an uncomfortable situation. Life is uncomfortable. You can't bury your head in the sand and hope it goes away." She narrowed her eyes and went for the jugular. "I would think you'd want to teach her how to handle them. How to keep her safe."

Their gazes locked in a battle of wills. Liam's darkened. "I'm teaching her to remove herself to a place of safety."

In her peripheral, Zoe squirmed in her seat as she stared wide-eyed at the two of them.

Eden snorted. "Yeah. Like that works."

"Zoe, take the tokens to Noah. Now. He's right over there."

"Okay." She sighed and took the cup, her steps slow, head bowed.

Liam's bulk overwhelmed the small bench seat. "I've told you twice. Stay out of my business. I won't tell you again." He spat the words through gritted teeth. Frustration and resentment laced the command.

Her stomach churned. They'd gone from devouring looks to wanting to destroy each other. Eden dropped her gaze, hoping to diffuse the moment. Avoidance was never the right path. "All I'm saying is you're teaching your kids to be afraid. Don't you think they should learn to take care of themselves?"

"She's seven. I take care of her."

He couldn't be that dense. "What does she do when she doesn't have you? I'd think you'd want to empower your kids. Don't make them afraid of their own shadows."

Liam stood up so fast the table shook. "I'm going to check on our food." His nostrils flared, fists clenching at his side before he leaned in and lowered his voice to a growl. "Last warning," he fired, before he stomped off.

Eden fumed, shooting mental arrows at the brute's back. Brute was too good for him. What kind of man didn't want his kids to stand up for themselves? She knew he was overprotective, but this was nuts. Zoe and Noah wouldn't stand a chance at survival in the real world if he continued to shelter them like helpless kittens.

Hollowness swelled in her chest. Who was she kidding? Liam made it clear he didn't give a rat's ass about her opinion. Nor should he. She'd be a distant memory to all three in a week or less. But if that were true, why did what she say rile him up so badly?

Zoe slid into the booth across from her, the cup of tokens still filled to the top. "I'm bored." She draped her arm across the table and dropped her head in drama-queen fashion.

A smiled softened Eden's mouth. My goodness, Liam had an actress on his hands. "Aren't you supposed to be with your brother?"

"He's ignoring me. I like playing on the playground. I'm not big enough to reach the games he plays and he won't go to the other ones."

Eden nibbled the cuticle on her thumb. The gears in her head spun with frantic urgency. There were two paths in front of her. Play it safe, suffer the pouty girl or be a risk-taker and teach Zoe life didn't always play fair. You couldn't wait around for someone else to protect you. Besides, the boy couldn't be more than seven or eight. The odds were low he'd pull out a knife.

The reality of that thought stunned her. What kind of life makes you even question if an eight-year-old carried a knife? She was starting to wonder if she wanted to know who she was before Liam found her.

Decision made, she slid from the booth and held out her hand. "Why, don't you show me the playground. It looks like fun."

LIAM fumed and paced in front of the waitress station.

"Can I help you?" A waiter asked, a cheerful smile on his young face.

"Did I ask for help?" He regretted his tone the instant the kid's smile slid south. *Good job jackass, scare the shit out of the kid because you can't control your emotions around one annoying viper-tongued woman.* "No. Yes, I want to speak with my waitress, Brandy."

The boy eyed him warily. "Ah, sure. I'll find her for you."

Liam wiped a hand over his neck. *God*, the woman had all the charm of a timber rattlesnake. And her venom had him all jumbled up. He refused to believe he was the problem here.

Besides, she didn't know the first thing about him. He would always be there for the kids. He ignored the niggling voice that pointed out the lie. There would come a day when he wouldn't be around—*No!* Not going there.

Get through the meal. Get home. Get the kids settled for the week and ban her to the garage. That was the plan.

"Georgie said you were looking for me?" By her nervous expression Georgie must have told her an asshole waited for her. "Is everything okay? Your pizza should be out any minute."

He forced a smile that probably came across more demented madman than good-guy-on-a-white-horse. "Good. Thank you. That's all I wanted. Good job."

"I'll bring your pizzas to your table. You don't need to wait here."

He maneuvered through the crowd back to the table, his gaze automatically searched for the kids. A mixture of fear and logic raced through him when he couldn't locate them. No one would get out the door without the matched hand stamp.

He stopped in front of the empty booth. No Eden.

"Here you go. I told you it would be right out." The waitress put the large pizza on the table. "I'll be right back with the other. Do you need more drinks?"

"Yes." Maybe Eden had enough of his dictatorship and hightailed it. The Doc would have his head and no telling what the sheriff would do. Shoulda listened. He'd tried to tell them he wasn't the man for the job.

Noah's head bobbed and ducked at the machine as Liam came alongside him. "Food's ready."

"K, almost done." Noah never took his eyes off the screen.

"Where's your sister?"

"How would I know?" Noah jabbed the gun to the left and shot.

Liam's shoulder's tightened. "I sent her over here a few minutes ago." He did a slow 360. He missed nothing. No Zoe.

No Eden. His breath caught. His head swung to the door.

She couldn't have taken Zoe out of the building. What was her end game? Feign amnesia and steal his kid? He'd made his share of enemies while on the force. None big enough or with enough brains to plan an elaborate scheme like this.

"Noah, go back to the table and don't move."

"Awww, Dad, I have one life left—"

"Do it."

He spotted Eden at the same time he reached for his phone to call the authorities. Her face was pale, eyes wide. Zoe clung to her neck.

He met them halfway and took a sobbing Zoe. Relief washed through him.

Eden hadn't stolen Zoe, she'd rescued her. "Thank you." He mouthed. "Tell daddy what happened, Zoe. Are you okay?"

She sniffled and wiped her wet face in the collar of his shirt. "The bully knocked me down. I scraped my elbow." Pulling away she showed him the torn sleeve with the tiny cut. "See?"

He sat down and turned her in his lap.

Eden nudged Noah over and perched on the edge of the bench. Her face white, eyes wide. Almost like she was ready to bolt.

"I thought I told you to go over with Noah and stay away from the playground."

"But Eden said I should stand up for myself." She hic-cupped around the words.

The rush of blood pounding through his veins roared in his head. She was a dead woman.

Swear to God, he'd wring her neck before the sun went down. "Eden said..." Heart hammering in his ears, he glared in her direction. "Why did she tell you to do that?"

"She said if you don't stand up to bullies, they keep com-ing after you. I don't want him to keep coming after me, Dad-dy."

Fury consumed him. He clenched his jaw so tight, the ache spread down the corded muscles of his neck.

For the briefest moment, he thought there was something brewing between them. The way her hypnotic eyes read deep, past his walls. Now he knew it was just the ache of loneliness. There was no possible way a woman who drew this much rage out of him could possibly be part of his life. She stirred the wrong kind of passion in him.

She was a thorn jabbed deeply into his side. If he wasn't careful, she'd leave a scar.

Chapter Eighteen

The second they walked through the door Liam barked orders. All alpha-wolf keeping his cubs safe. "Eden. Living room. Sit. Stay. Kids. Bedrooms. Now."

She didn't have to stay. The tightening in the skin across her chest made her.

She'd messed up. Big time. If he didn't throw her out tonight, she'd be lucky. Didn't matter that she had nowhere to go, that wasn't his problem. The way she'd behaved today she wouldn't blame him. What really baffled her though...Why did the thought of leaving cause her chest to ache?

Her fingers flexed and fisted by her side. But seriously, how could he not see the danger he put the kids in everyday? He sheltered them from the uglies of life while he ignored the fact they couldn't defend themselves.

Eden wandered the room, but its cozy invitation did nothing to bring her comfort.

She stopped in front of the fireplace. The stacked stone drew the eye up to the open ceiling and exposed rafters. Twigs and logs were piled in the center, ready for a cheerful blaze to cast its warmth in the room. A gorgeous hand-hewn wooden mantle spanned the width. Pictures of a younger Liam and a petite blonde as they smiled wide for the camera sat on the two corners. Both kids had her deep blue eyes, but

Noah was her mini-me. White-blond hair, freckles. Must be hard to see the image of your dead wife in your child. A constant reminder of your loss.

Drifting to the bank of windows that faced the back, she unlocked the door and pushed it open. The entire wall moved out over the deck. Her mouth dropped. The outdoor space and the indoor space became one. Now that was freakin' awesome. She wrapped the sweater around herself and stepped onto the deck.

Frost already formed on the grass, the rails, and the cushioned lounge chairs. Crisp, fall air cooled her heated cheeks, and she sauntered out for a better view.

The lake reflected the soft pinks and violets of twilight. Trees, in various stages of fall colors, circled the home and the lake.

Tears stung the backs of her eyes. This had to be the most peaceful place on earth.

"Why are you out here? It's cold. I'm not heating the outside."

She didn't turn. If he was about to kick her out, she wanted one more moment of calm. "I wanted air. Who knew the wall opened?" She shuffled inside.

Liam closed the wall—door, locked it, and then shot a bolt into the floor.

Trapped.

He stalked across the floor, lips pulled into a grim line.

Trapped like dinner in the lion's den.

She gulped courage and slipped into what had become a familiar mask. Then let its power lead her around the room, fingering a picture here, a candlestick there. The perfect appearance of indifference. Silence, sticky and weighted, cloaked the room.

His heated gaze burned through her as he tracked her movements. "Stop touching my things. Sit."

"Woof-woof."

"Would you stop that?"

She arched an eyebrow. "When you stop issuing commands like I'm a dog."

He ruffled a hand through his hair. "Fine." He bit between tight lips. "*Please*, sit."

She wrinkled her nose in protest as she took the comfy chair closest to the fireplace and curled both legs beneath her.

The red turbulent glow of his expression didn't bode well. She braced for the uproar that would follow.

"What the hell did you hope to accomplish back there? I told Zoe to avoid her tormentor because I know my daughter. She can't handle confrontation."

"Maybe because you've never asked her to."

"Why do you care?"

Good question. So what if the girl grew up too weak to help herself? It's not like she'd be around to see how she turned out. "I don't know. Cheering for the underdogs I guess."

"I have my daughter's best interest in mind. You have your own."

The barbed words stung even as they carried the blaring horn of truth. "She had to give up something she enjoyed because of that bully. Doesn't that bother you?"

"Not if it keeps her safe."

Eden rocketed from the chair. "From what, Liam? What are you keeping her safe from? A little boy on the playground? I don't think so. That boy bullied Zoe, he should've been removed. Not her. The message *you* sent said she screwed up. You sat her in the corner while he continued to have fun."

"That's the stupidest thing I've ever heard." For the first time since he stepped into the room his gaze drifted away.

"No, it's the truth." She folded her arms across her chest. "What are you so afraid of? You can probably name everyone in this town. And if you can't, I'd be willing to bet you'd find out in a heartbeat. You're suffocating your babies."

"Zoe knows I won't let anything happen to her. I sent her to the games with a cup full of tokens. Hardly a punishment." He ignored her question. Holding tight to his anger.

"You can't always be there, Liam. What happens to her or Noah when you're not there? They have no clue about the real world."

"What do you know about us? You've spent three days with us."

Pain funneled into her heart. He was right. But, all of this...the home, the kids, him... They were the only world she had for now. "As much as you like to think you're always going to be there, you can't be. You're not helping either of them with this pretense."

His lethal expression stabbed her from across the room. If looks could kill, she wouldn't need to worry about her identity. She'd be flat-out dead on the floor.

"Best you remember you're here for a few days. Let's leave it at that." The barely civil words snapped from between his gritted teeth.

She was the first to drop her gaze. The bags from their trip to the store beckoned her from the kitchen table. Their presence deflated her. He'd spoiled her, provided a home, and she repaid him by getting Zoe hurt.

"Right. Of course." She crossed the floor and picked them up one by one. "I think I'm going to go to bed. It's been an eventful day."

Liam followed her to the door and waited until she reached the garage. "Lock the door behind you."

No need to acknowledge him. He probably wouldn't mind if she disappeared into the night.

She shivered in the cold air and hustled across the yard. Inside, she turned to look back. He'd closed the door without a second glance. Her gaze traced her steps, the surrounding wood. A shiver of apprehension shook her. The bruises on her neck ached. If this happened to Zoe her sweet nature would be crushed. She'd be powerless to protect herself.

"You'll always be there, my butt." She mumbled at the closed door he hid behind before slamming her own. The hollow thunk of the lock as she twisted it into place, echoed in the dark garage.

No matter how much time she had here, she needed to convince him to let go of his grip on those kids. Otherwise, he'd lose them both.

LIAM rolled over, smashed his pillow into a pile and dropped his head. He'd gone to bed early in hopes of catching up on sleep. And to get away from his anger over the Zoe incident. Since Eden materialized on the side of the road five days ago, he could count the number of hours he'd slept on one hand.

She had the nerve to teach his daughter to outright defy him. Responsible adults didn't pull stunts like that. Since becoming a single parent everyone and their mother had an opinion to offer on every subject under the sun. But, no one, *nobody* actually defied him or taught his kids to defy him.

He rolled to his side. Rolled again. Sighed. It was no use. Sleep was not his friend. Time to surrender, catch up on the news. The flicker of the TV flashed colors on the dark walls as the toothy grins of the anchors came to life.

"...the plane managed to land safely. In national news, the hunt for a cop killer has gone national. DEA Officer, Samuel Graham was gunned down last Sunday night outside The Dungeon, a popular downtown Dallas nightclub. It appears off-duty Graham stumbled into a drug deal gone wrong and was shot before backup could arrive. The posh club has come under scrutiny in the last few months when a well-loved employee was found dealing drugs from behind the bar."

Heat boiled through him. A punch to the gut knocked the wind from his lungs in one long whoosh. Another senseless death. He hoped they caught the SOB.

"...Grab those extra blankets and stoke the fires. Our stretch of above averages temps has come to an end with overnight lows expected to dip ten degrees below normal..."

He closed his eyes and shook his head. Damn. The heaters weren't powerful enough to heat the open space over the garage on a cold night like this. Eden would freeze her ass off out there.

He should bring her in. This was exactly why he hadn't wanted her here. She was the sheriff's problem. Not his.

Eden's face right before he shut the door on her tonight teased him. She'd been here for two nights and other than her irritating the piss out of him, no dark, sinister monster had shown up on the town's doorstep. He could see the headlines now. *Ex-cop turned curmudgeon freezes innocent stranger to death in his garage.*

"Ah, hell." He kicked his legs out from the tangle of blankets and flared his arms in the air as his feet landed on the floor.

He colored the air with a chorus of four-letter words and yanked on the sweatpants from the chair next to the bed. Of all the damn luck. Stomping across the hardwoods, he pulled the Henley over his head. Someone out there in the great big cosmos was laughing their ass off at him right now.

At the kitchen door, he jammed his bare feet into boots then punched in the alarm code. "Seriously, the cold couldn't hold off a few more days?"

The second the door opened, a chill slapped him square in the face. The frigid temperature sucked the breath out of him causing him to hunker down in the nonexistent collar of his thin shirt. Dry leaves crunched under his boots, stars twinkled above. Any other time, he might enjoy a walk under a big Minnesota night sky. But not tonight. Unlocking the door, he entered and flipped on the main light. "Eden, wake-up." His boots echoed as he stomped across the floor.

"Liam? You scared the crap out of me." Eden's head appeared in silhouette at the top of stairs. "What are you doing here? Was I breathing too loud? Did I violate one of Liam's Laws again?"

He gnashed his teeth. "I thought you might be cold."

There was a long pause before she answered. "No."

He reached the top of the stairs and brushed by her. "Liar. There is no way you're warm enough up there." She had all three blankets wrapped in a tight wad around her. It appeared she still wore her clothes. The puny heaters did next to nothing, as evidenced by his breath fogging the cold air.

"Come on. We're going inside."

She dropped onto the air mattress. "I'm good right here. I have blankets, heaters, everything a girl could want. I've been out here for two nights. I'm sure I'll survive."

He turned off both heaters and unplugged them from the wall. "And I'm sure you won't. You'll be a chattering popsicle by morning. Bring the blankets."

She struggled to her feet, favoring her right side, and elbowed past him. Plugging both units back into the wall, she turned them on before she shot him a glare. "No, I won't bring the blankets. Because I'm staying right here."

The grimace on her face reminded him again she was injured. A fact he was ashamed to admit he kept forgetting.

"You're not comfortable with me in the house. I don't blame you. Truth be told, I think I've been through worse." She laid down on the bed and smiled sweetly at him. "Turn the lights off on your way out."

He interpreted the clack of teeth as Morse code for *I'm a liar and I'm freezing my butt off.*

"I'm fine." She snuggled her head into the cocoon she'd created like a turtle in its shell.

Fine my ass. Enough was enough. First, he unplugged the heaters, then picked her up blankets and all. She cradled perfectly against his chest. "Woman, I'm cold and I'm tired."

She struggled and kicked her legs. "What the hell do you think you're doing? Get your paws off me!"

"Stop struggling or you're going to hurt yourself. I'm trying to be careful."

"Put me down and we won't have to worry about it."

"It's too late for games. Do you have any idea how cold twenty-seven degrees with a windchill below zero feels? The mercury is just gonna keep dropping, we haven't even hit the peak of the cold." He maneuvered down the stairs, careful to avoid banging her head and feet on the walls or banister.

"Put me down. I can walk myself."

At the bottom of the steps he lowered her gently to the ground. "In case you missed it, I have no coat or blanket. I'm freezing."

She righted the blankets in a dramatic swirl allowing it to cap on at the shoulders. "I told you to leave me be."

"And I would have slept like a baby. But I didn't want my kids to know how callous their father can be. So, I guess we're both doing what we don't want...to make my kids happy."

Once inside he locked the door and reset the alarm. "Don't try leaving the house. It's on lockdown." He left her standing at the base of the stairs as he made another circle of all the doors and windows.

"Paranoid much?"

"Yes. Most definitely." There was no point in denying it. Anyone who knew him knew this was his behavior. And as she already pointed out, anyone that knew the town of Moose Head Falls knew it was unnecessary. He pointed to the stairs. "After you."

She pulled the blankets tighter and proceed before him. At the top, she stepped aside and waited for him to go first.

He led her to the only free room, the one across the hall from him. "I'm right there if you need anything."

"Thank you."

Once in his room, Liam pulled the shirt over his head, and tossed it on the chair. A shiver from the cold air pebbled his skin. He opted to leave the sweats on before he dove under the blankets. He'd take them off once he warmed up.

With a sigh of exhaustion, he tucked his hands behind his head, and closed his eyes. Finally. Sleep.

A whiff of lemons reached his nose and he lifted the collar of his shirt. Her scent. All over him. The image of red hair fanned against a white sheet mocked him. He pulled the pillow over his head and groaned.

He was like that little Dutch kid, trying to block all the holes in the dam. Every time he plugged one problem, another bloomed. His happy, well-ordered life seeped away right before his eyes.

Chapter Nineteen

L iam's eyes snapped open.

Silence.

What woke him?

"Get back! I swear, I'll shoot you where you stand. Jared! Where are you?"

His chest squeezed. Despite being in a sleep-coma, he jerked out of bed and grabbed the baseball bat propped next to the side table. His brain fought to understand what happened even as he knew he needed to get to his kids. He threw open the bedroom door and ran into the dark hallway.

"Don't shoot! Jared..." Terror erupted from Eden's room.

Both kids appeared in their doorways the same time he stopped outside Eden's door.

"What's happening?" Noah yawned and rubbed the heel of his hand into his eye. "Who's screaming?"

"Daddy, Eden is crying." Zoe scooted across the floor and reached for the woman's doorknob.

"...Can't do this. Don't make me do this."

Who was she yelling at? He knew damn good and well no one was in there. All the doors and windows were locked, and the alarm hadn't gone off.

"Zoe, get back." He nudged her toward Noah.

Noah instinctively put himself between his sister and the potential threat.

Liam set the bat down and opened the door.

Eden crouched at the headboard, one arm wrapped around her legs the other up in a defensive pose. Her hand held an imaginary gun, but real terror etched her face. "Don't come any closer."

He reached out a hand then dropped it to his side. "Eden, it's me, Liam."

She flinched at his voice. "Get back. Please, please. You were his friend. You said you'd bring me to Jared."

The desperation in her voice made his heart stutter.

Liam slowed his movements so he wouldn't startle her any further. Inch by inch, he lowered himself onto the foot of the bed. "It's OK, Eden. You know me. I'm Liam. You're at my house. You're safe."

His butt had barely hit the mattress when she jumped to the floor, her gaze locked somewhere to his right. Both hands cupped the imaginary gun. "I don't want to shoot you..." Jumbled pleas mixed with commands continued.

"Does she have a gun, Dad?" Noah's nervous voice floated from the doorway.

"No. She's having a bad dream." Night terror, dream, real memories. Nothing he could do but watch, paralyzed by indecision. Wake her? Leave her to come out of it on her own?

"Get back, Zoe," Noah cautioned.

"But I can't see." Zoe popped around Noah's body despite her brother trying to keep her back.

"You don't need to see this." Liam crossed the floor and moved Zoe out of the doorway.

"Liam?" Eden croaked out the words. "What are you doing here?" She scanned the surroundings, a frown creasing her forehead. "What happened? My throat is super dry. It hurts to talk."

"Noah, get water from the bathroom." He eased closer to her. "You've been screaming for the last five minutes. You've probably strained your vocal cords again."

Eden moved to the side of the bed and took the paper cup from Noah. "Thank you."

"Are you okay, Eden?" Noah asked.

"I think so."

"You were screaming." Zoe came into the room and leaned on Liam's leg.

"Was I? I... I guess I had a bad dream." She passed the cup back to Noah and dropped her head into her hands.

"Headache?" Liam asked.

"Pounding."

"Maybe that's a sign your memories are coming back." From what he'd seen so far, they sucked.

"You tried to shoot my dad." Stress strained Noah's face and freckles popped against his paler-than-normal complexion.

What little color Eden had drained from her face. Left her winter-white. "I did?"

Both kids nodded their heads vigorously.

"And you said you wanted Jared. Who's Jared?" Zoe asked.

Eden's head flinched back as if struck, eyebrows scrunched together. "Jared? I don't know—"

"Guys, it was a bad dream. She wasn't threatening me." Whatever she had locked up in that pretty head wasn't party favors and ice cream. And it sure wasn't something the kids needed to know about. Hell, he didn't even watch the news when they were around. "Okay, time to get back in bed. You gotta be up in a couple of hours for school."

"Awww, that's not fair," Zoe huffed.

Noah laid a comforting arm across his sister's shoulder. "Come on, pest. Let's go. I hope you feel better, Eden."

Liam waited until two doors clicked before giving Eden his full attention. "Do you want an aspirin? It's downstairs." He nodded his head in the direction of the hallway.

"Thank you."

Once in the kitchen he grabbed a key ring off the hook and unlocked the padlock on the cupboard closest to the refrigerator. The temptation cabinet. Medications, lighters, candles, matches. All the fun things that tempted kids to disobey the rules.

A snicker buzzed his ear, the heat from her body permeated the pores along his back as she tried to peer over his shoulder.

"Seriously? What kind of freakin' maniac locks up aspirin?"

An embarrassed grin split his face. "This kind."

He handed her the bottle and opened the fridge for a bottle of water. "I can make warm milk. It might help."

She arched an eyebrow but took the water and the aspirin to a stool. "My God, is there nothing the great Liam can't or doesn't do?" And there she was. Sassy, confident Eden. In all her glory.

Grabbing milk, vanilla, sugar, and cinnamon from the cabinets he headed over to the stove top in front of where she sat, elbows on the counter, head in hands.

"That bad?" He poured milk into the pan and turned the gas burner on.

"Yes," she mumbled.

"What do you remember?"

"Nothing I want to. A chaotic mess." The last was nothing more than a vague whisper.

"Sounds like someone tried to shoot you." *Or, she tried to shoot someone.*

"I don't know. It's all disjointed. What does come through is all dream-like." She averted her eyes. The fingers of her hand fiddled with the aspirin bottle while her other hand drummed a nervous beat in the counter.

"You can't force it. Relax. The memories will come." He poured the milk in the pan along with the other stuff and stirred while it heated. "This is a safe place. You know that, right?"

A hint of a smile tucked the corners of her mouth up. "Of course I am. I have the world's most protective dad around."

The twinkle of amusement in her eyes stirred a fire in him he thought long dead. The white cotton t-shirt molded itself around her shape. *And God help him, what a shape it was.* While the night terror scared the living daylights out of him, the skimpy pink shorts that covered her perfectly round, pert ass, hadn't bothered him.

Now, in the sanctuary and silence of his kitchen, with her long legs swinging, *bothered* was such a weak, ineffectual word to describe the torture that now swept through him.

It took monumental effort to pull his gaze from the temptation she offered. He used the distraction of dividing the warm milk between two mugs to still his traitorous body. Somewhat composed, he slid one across the counter to her.

She took a tentative sip and smiled. "Not bad."

He cracked a grin. "Don't sound surprised. My mom's recipe. She used to make this for my brother and me when we couldn't sleep or had a nightmare."

Sadness darkened her eyes. Her hands switched from playing with the aspirin bottle to tracing the handle of the coffee mug. "We never had food in the house let alone having the stuff for making warm milk." She froze. Her eyes flew wide.

"See, bad dream, or not, it opened the door for more. Anything else?"

Her chest rose and fell faster. Sweat beaded the top of her lip and brow, shoulders hunched. "I... I..."

His cop sense tingled.

Agitation spread across her features.

"Chill. Just let it happen."

She clawed her fingers through the tangles in her hair. "All the images are here." Her palm slapped the center of her forehead. "I can see them, moving behind this dark veil. Shifting just beyond my reach. I keep thinking, or hear a word...soil, or sorel. But don't know what it means."

Liam came around the counter and squeezed her shoulders. Tilted her head back, forcing her to look at him with those spell-casting eyes. "You have to stop. All you're doing is tying yourself up in knots."

She lowered her lids. Lashes creating shadows on her cheekbones. "Doctor Logan told me being here, with you, was the safest place I could be. I know I've given you every reason to send me away. And I have no right to ask if I can stay." She sucked in a big breath, held it, then slowly exhaled as she finally met his eyes only to drop her chin to her chest. "I'm asking anyway."

At that very moment he would have given her anything she asked. Anything to bring back the feisty woman he'd come to respect.

Her hand worked the bracelet on her wrist in an almost absent-minded frenzy. When she finally brought her gaze to his there was a softness to her features.

Liam's heartbeat slowed. His vision narrowed in on the woman in front of him. Something monumental was about to come out of her mouth and he was sure it wasn't going to be anything he wanted to hear.

"I want to stay. Just until my memory returns. Please?"

A ringing droned in his ear. His thoughts swirled with lighting speed. In the short time this woman had been a part of their lives, she'd been stubbornly independent and determined to prove she could take care of herself. Now she asked him for protection. It had to be a hard pill to swallow.

She'd also gotten Zoe hurt, and tried to tell him, several times, how to raise his children. Annoying as hell. Not to mention too damn attractive for her own good. But her worst crime, the one he couldn't get past... The cloud of mystery that followed the woman. "I... But the sheriff is already looking for a place for you."

Her mask slipped, and for the first time her true vulnerable nature came through. Not driven by nightmare, or fear or deceit. "Goddamnit! Stop looking at me like a lost puppy." He had to think. Think about the terrible things that might be behind her missing memory. Think about how he hadn't spent all these years keeping his kids by his side. He had to maintain control.

"Yeah, You're right. It's probably a bad idea." She rubbed her temples one more time and picked up her mug so he couldn't see the disappointment on her face.

He saw it and then some. How many nights had he laid awake, the still photo of Krista's body sprawled in death across their living room floor? She'd been all alone. No one to hear her screams. Her pleas for help. How many nights had he wondered if a neighbor might have heard and brushed it off as nothing. How many times had he wondered how different his life and the lives of his kids would be if one person had stopped, called 911? Eden might be someone's wife, or mother or sister. He couldn't allow someone else to suffer through that.

A weighted sigh pressed from his lips, whistled into the middle of the night. Tiny hairs prickled the back of his neck. She didn't play fair. Cocky, exasperating Eden he could handle. This quiet, scared Eden worked her way past his defenses.

He downed the warm milk in one long pull and then rubbed a hand over the scruff of beard. "Fine. You can stay." Four little words. Four of the scariest words he'd ever uttered.

EDEN fluffed the pillows and pulled the blankets around her waist. The warm milk worked its magic and sleep stirred at the edges of her brain, still throbbing with residual pain from the memory swamp.

Asking Liam if she could stay with him had been hard. The flash of memory that caused the night terror was all too real, violent. And despite what she told Liam...all too clear.

Every last detail, embedded in her brain. She'd shot someone. She didn't know who. Or why. Only that she did.

Chapter Twenty

❝ Maybe we're looking at this all wrong. Jared is in jail, and she's gone—"

"With my money and drugs." RJ slammed a hand on the counter. Did he not understand how deep their problems went? "How long do you think it'll be until my father's men track her down? What then?"

RJ pulled two Shiner Bock beers from the fridge and left one on the counter while he roamed his penthouse apartment. The one perk his father allowed him. Not that it was for him, it was for the impression it made. The place was usually filled with his men, but he'd sent them all out. He didn't need all of them knowing his business. "You need to pull your shit together and figure out where she is."

"How you expect me to know that? Dammit, RJ she could be anywhere. I say let her go."

RJ grabbed the other man by the collar. "Do I need to remind you what happens if Hutch finds her first? I don't go down alone."

"Fine. Just let me think."

RJ released him and handed him one of the bottles. "There has to be something you remember."

"I don't know, dude. They were pretty tight. Except for all the times he got sent to juvie. After that it got easier for him to leave her."

"Great. Did you get close to her while he was gone?" RJ leered. He'd wanted a piece of that bitch since the first time he laid eyes on her. Homeless girls were easy. Especially for him. They always thought he would be their way out off the streets.

Not Eden. Her sneers and body language made her disrespect clear. Would it have killed her to smile at him? Acknowledge who he is?

"I do remember one thing. At night they didn't hang with the rest of us. They'd go off and find their own corner. Acted like they were better than the rest of us. When they first showed up, she'd cry every night and Jared would tell her..."

RJ waited. And waited. "What? What did he tell her, you moron?"

His partner's lips moved without a sound and his lids slid half-mast. "I'm thinking, I'm thinking."

Seriously, he'd hitched his future to an idiot.

"I got it." He snapped his fingers. A smug grin on his face. "He'd tell her they'd go to Canada. A place called...Th... Thunder Bay. That's it. Thunder Bay."

RJ pulled his laptop over and opened to map search. "Canada? What the hell did they think they'd find there?"

"I don't know. Family or something."

It took less than two minutes to find there were two main routes between Dallas and Thunder Bay. I-35 to MN-61 right into Canada. Or, she could have taken the longer route up I-70 into Kansas City where she'd pick up 35.

RJ sat back and drained the last of his beer. If it were him, he'd find the most direct route to his destination. No time for sightseeing. Given the circumstances, she'd do the same thing. "She have a passport?"

"How the hell should I know?"

He'd bet she didn't which meant there was a real good chance she was still in the US.

"We flying?"

"Sure. We can use our binoculars to scan for my car as we fly over the area." He stood and swatted the back of the other man's head. "Driving, you idiot. She could be anywhere between here and there. We take the most direct route and hope to hell that's the way she's headed."

"There's gotta be over eleven-hundred miles between here and there. You can't seriously think we're going to find her. There's a thousand places . She could be anywhere."

"Then we'll comb through every place. If we don't find her before Hutch and his men, it won't matter what we do or where we go. My father will kill us both."

Chapter Twenty-One

L iam whistled while he pulled out mixing bowls, measuring cups, spoons, cupcake pan, and chocolate cake mix, transforming the counter into a bakery. Zoe had come home to announce she needed cupcakes for a school party the next day. He rubbed his hands together in anticipation. Baking with the kids always guaranteed laughter. Good vibes ran through him even as he glanced over to where Zoe and Eden sat on the sofa in the living room. Eden grinned at a lame joke Zoe told. Her smile, infectious as laughter on a cloudless day, did funny things to the pulse that quickened through his veins. He bit back a groan.

Family bake time would also help keep his thoughts off their meddlesome, but bewitching, guest. He wiped his hands on a dishcloth and unwrapped a stick of butter. She questioned him at every turn while constantly urging him to let the kids have more freedom. As if they weren't free. As if she knew what they needed. As if she had a say in any of this.

She glanced up. Their gazes tangled across the room.

Every hair on his scalp tingled. A low hum raced along his skin. He spent his days frustrated at her interference while his nights...well, they were just frustrated. There was no freaking way he was the master of his own castle right now.

Eden's memories coming back couldn't happen soon enough. Unfortunately, there didn't appear to be anything new on that front. Which meant his purgatory burned on indefinitely.

Yep. A night of baking with the kids, without her commentary, without the tantalizing scent of citrus and warm vanilla, would be a welcome diversion.

Ingredients assembled, he crossed the floor to the pantry. One last crucial piece to complete the setup. His hand stilled over the apron on the back of the pantry door.

He swallowed passed the rock-sized lump in his throat. The ruffles along the edge played beneath his fingers before he pulled the frilly, pink, heart-filled material off the hook. Krista's apron. The one used only for baking. When he slipped it over his head, fingers twisting the ties at his hips, he could still picture her crooked smile. A ray of light that shone on those she loved. The ache that coiled around his lungs left him momentarily breathless. For his kids. They would never know the warmth of that ray of light. This is why he did what he did. To keep her memory alive for them.

He grabbed the chef's hat and headed for the living room.

"Zoe." He waved the hat. "We have cupcakes to bake."

She jumped from the couch and pirouetted across the floor. "Yea!" She pointed and giggled through her other hand. "You look funny, Daddy."

He did a simple spin. "What? You don't like my apron?"

Eden swiveled her head in their direction, quirked an eyebrow, and let loose a bold wolf whistle. "What I wouldn't pay for a camera right now." She stood, and in that slow, confident stride that made his temperature pop ten degrees, crossed the room to circle him. Her gaze roamed up and down. "You are one hot baker, Mr. VIP."

"You like?"

"I do." Her throaty reply tickled his ear drums.

Warmth blushed across his cheeks. God, what was he? Fifteen, preening under the attention of a school girl? He coughed, pushing traitorous thoughts from his head. "Noah, bake time. Maybe we'll make an extra batch to keep at home."

"Aw, Dad, do I have to?"

Liam's jaw slackened. "I thought you liked this?"

"I've never liked it. It's for girls."

"Since when?"

A shrug twitched his shoulder before his attention wandered back to the TV. "I don't know."

Noah's words kicked the wind right out of Liam. This parenting gig was like a round of kickboxing without protection.

Eden wiggled onto the kitchen table, her legs swaying in lazy circles. Silky red hair floated around her shoulders. "Why don't you swing by the store on the way to school in the morning? Isn't that what dads do?"

"Maybe some dads. Not this one. The kids and I, well, Zoe and I enjoy the time together. Come on, Butterfly, looks like it's you and me."

"Daddy, I want Eden to help me." Zoe's innocent voice knifed him.

"Ah, sure. She can fill in for Noah." He forced cheerfulness he didn't feel into his voice. So much for time without Eden's presence.

"That's so sweet, Zoe. I'd love—" Eden's smile faltered when she turned to him. "Uh, I don't know the first thing about baking. I bet your daddy here knows exactly what to do."

"We don't need him. Don't worry, I'll show you. Daddy doesn't care, do you?"

Liam glanced from his daughter's eager face to Eden's solemn expression. What the hell just happened? He'd gone from a fun night with his kids, to Zoe, to... being benched for a red-shirt freshman.

His brain raced for any excuse to stop what felt like a hostile takeover. But he came up empty. "No. I guess not." What else could he say without sounding like a petulant child? "Just follow the directions on the back of the box."

He moved toward his chair, numb.

"Daddy, aren't you forgetting something?"

"What's that?"

"The apron, silly. I have the hat and Eden needs the apron."

Krista's apron? He pushed down the disappointment. Zoe'd been too young to understand its significance. Less important than her favorite cartoon character, Krista was nothing more than a happy-faced picture on the mantel. Eden was a warm, walking, talking woman.

Zoe's words from the first night at the clinic slammed his ears. *A new mommy.*

He knelt in front of Zoe. "Why don't I keep this while you and Eden get to work?"

"But, Daddy, you said we can't bake without it. We need it."

He sighed and untied the apron then slipped the neck over Eden's head. There was that damn citrus.

"I'm sorry," she whispered for his ears alone.

Zoe tucked her hand in Eden's. "Come on, this will be fun."

Heart dragging the floor, he headed into the family room.

Zoe scraped a chair over to the counter. With her usual flare of importance, explained the process. He pictured it clearly. One hand on the hip, the other directing the show. Zoe, in her element. Try as he might, it wasn't his wife's face he pictured next to her.

In hindsight, the impulsive decision to allow Eden to stay, made in a moment of compassion nine long nights ago, challenged everything he'd worked so hard to accomplish. Every day, she perched next to him in the truck to drop off the kids at school. She filled the store with constant chatter. Was in his face for something to do. Citrus and Eden were everywhere. Dropping her presence like gems that dazzled in the sun. Building memories that would mark Zoe more than her own mother.

He collapsed into the chair, his gaze locked on the TV while his ear trained on the kitchen.

"Pour the box in the bowl," Zoe said.

"Like this?"

Giggles erupted. "No, no, pour it *out* of the box."

"Oh, I see. Now, what do we do?" Genuine happiness rang from Eden.

Zoe let go an exaggerated sigh. No doubt rolled her eyes. "What does the box say?"

Did the woman really not know how to bake, or was this all an act to entertain his daughter? Of course, she knew, every kid learned how to bake at some point. Didn't they?

Come on, Liam, you know better than that.

Images of the lost and neglected kids from his beat in Minneapolis flashed through his head. Not everyone had the benefit of someone to show them this kind of thing.

Their silly banter, spiced with girlish shrieks, filled the downstairs.

A tingling warmth spread from his chest to his limbs. The tension in his face relaxed. It occurred to him Eden might need this connection as much as Zoe. The childish hurt he'd held onto released. Let them have their fun.

The mixer whirred to life, squeals of excitement burst from the kitchen followed by a muffled, "Uh-oh. Daddy is not gonna like this."

That didn't sound good. He shoved from the chair.

"Look at your hair." Eden's voice held amusement.

He rounded the corner. The mixer in Eden's hand spun, flipping what batter still remained into the air. Flour and cake batter speckled the cabinets. Clumps of thick chocolate splattered across the tile like deer scat on the forest floor. More dripped from Zoe's hair.

How did they manage to make this happen?

Eden's tongue flicked a dollop of batter on the corner of her mouth.

His body tightened.

Wide-eyed the three of them stared at each other. The whir of the mixer filled the quiet kitchen. A half chuckle, half sputter erupted from his mouth, before it turned into an all-out belly-clenching howl. "You weren't lying when you said you didn't know how to bake."

She shook her head. An impish smile tugged at the corners of her mouth. Mischief danced in her eyes.

"Look at me, Daddy. I'm a giant cupcake." Zoe raised her arms to the side and pranced from one foot to the other.

"Yes, you are, Butterfly. Let me get a cloth and clean you up."

Liam approached and took a peek into the bowl. "Let me guess. You've never used a mixer before?"

"No." Her straight-faced expression told him she spoke the truth.

He bit his cheek, lips trembling. "Did it occur to you to start the mixer on low rather than full speed?"

A lopsided grin twitched the corner of Eden's lips seconds before a quick swipe dotted a glob of batter from Zoe's face onto his nose. "Full throttle, baby. That's how I roll."

"What's going on out here? I can't hear the TV—" Noah came to a dead stop and scanned the room. "Whoa. What happened in here?" He moved further into the room.

When Eden flashed the same crooked smile, Liam knew what to expect. He grabbed Noah in a bear hug and held him as Eden smeared chocolate down the side of his face.

"Now, we all match." Zoe chortled.

"You realize you can't use that batter?" Liam asked between chuckles. Seemed obvious, but based on what he just witnessed he wasn't making any assumptions.

"Afraid I've ruined them." The laughter faded, replaced by dismay. "I don't suppose the ever-organized and efficient Liam has another box?"

"Might. There will be stipulations, of course."

She arched an eyebrow over the blue eye. "Oh, really. I'm all ears."

Liam opened the pantry door next to him and pulled out another box. "I always have a backup, but I can't trust you two alone. Last box." He held it up. "Too late to go for more. This time we all chip in."

Eden didn't hesitate. She untied the apron and pulled it off to put it over his head. "I think it works better on you."

A few hours later all cupcakes were baked, iced, and ready for Zoe to take to school the next morning. Noah sent his usual sullen attitude packing and played along.

"Zoe, it's time for a bath or you'll be too tired to present your creations tomorrow." Liam turned to Eden. "I'll clean this up later."

Thirty minutes later he came into a spotless kitchen with Eden wiping down the last cabinet.

He squeezed her shoulder. "You didn't have to do all this."

"Trust me. It's the least I could do. You house me. Feed me. Put up with all my antics and I made a mess. I think I can clean it up."

His chest heated and expanded. Every time he thought he knew what to expect she threw him a curve ball. "You're being summoned."

She cocked her head to the side. A familiar quirk. "Excuse me?"

"Zoe asked if you'd read her a bedtime story."

An inner light lit her eyes. "Me? Wow. I don't know if I ever had a bedtime story. I'd love to." She stopped. "That is, if it's okay with you?"

"The princess has spoken." He took the washcloth from her, "Go ahead. She's waiting."

"Liam. I..." She chewed her lip. "Thank you. For allowing me to share this with your family. I... I've....It meant a lot."

She disappeared up the stairs before he composed a reply.

Liam rubbed his finger and thumb over closed eyes. The idea he couldn't be everything for his kids slapped him full in the face. It was harder to admit Zoe needed a woman in her life. So did Noah.

Maybe he did, too.

"Good night, Eden."

EDEN came down the stairs, damp from her shower. Since the night terrors two weeks ago, there'd been a subtle shift in Liam. The warmth he blanketed over his kids extended to ruffle around her. The pinched expression he'd worn since they first met, softened. And while she basked in all the togetherness, it was also overwhelming. Somehow foreign.

When She'd suggested she stay at the house he'd agreed without hesitation.

Despite what she told him, the dreams or memories, whatever they were, had been all too clear. Terrifying in their violence. But nothing to confirm they were actual events and not just nightmares. As the days slipped by, and nothing more came through, the power they held over her faded. But she needed to think. Something she couldn't do with Liam so near.

A delicious shudder shot through her. Her attraction to the man grew at an alarming rate. Never again would she look at a kitchen cabinet and not see his chiseled perfection leaning with casual ruggedness against it. All the planes and contours of his chest, his tree-trunk arms, shoulders that went on for days... The total package that begged her to run her hands over all that yummy, smooth skin.

Flutters of hummingbird wings beat a frantic vibration low in her abdomen. She charged into the kitchen. "God, you are pathetic. Get a grip. No more muscles and no more yummy skin. Liam sees you as an annoyance at best and a threat at worst."

Distraction. She needed one. *Now.*

She opened cabinets, rifled through the pantry, the refrigerator. No chips, no dips, no baked cheese crackers. No candy, no chocolate. No nothing. Nothing to satisfy a sweet tooth. Not one piece of junk food lived in this house. What kind of monster locked up medicine and banished guacamole with corn chips? She wanted her own food. Effin' frustrating to have to rely on someone else for everything.

She slapped together a ham and cheese sandwich, tossed a few baby carrots onto a plate. At least they weren't green.

Stopping at the door to the family room, her gaze landed on the computer. The box with all the answers.

On shaky knees, she crossed the floor and took a seat in the rolling chair. In between bites of the pasty sandwich and the crunch of a carrot, she stared at the black screen. A war waged inside. On the one hand, she wanted to pull the protective blanket Liam offered over her head and pretend life was normal. And happy. And full of bliss. But the woman behind the steel wall wanted out. Wanted to tell her something. In the end the need for knowledge outweighed the fear of *knowing*.

Using the password Liam gave her, she clicked into the internet, munched a carrot and scanned the headlines. Old news. New news. Politics. A picture of an older man scrolled onto the screen. Thinning gray hair, tall, trim, dark. Fake tan, dark, the kind you get from a weekly tanning-booth date. Rather than hide his face from the cameras he smiled, his hand held high. A wave, a mocking flick of a wrist captured in a still photograph.

Her hand shook when she opened the article. Police questioned *Rudy Sorell as a person of interest in the death of an off-duty DEA agent. The owner of several Dallas hot spots, including The Dungeon, where the shooting took place, Mr. Sorell has been on police radar in the past.*

Sweat beaded along her back. The half-eaten sandwich curdled in her stomach. She knew him. The woman behind the wall sent out a silent warning. The same warning that urged her to run when she'd first awoke in the clinic.

The walls and ceiling crowded her space. Fear squeezed her lungs, restricted her ability to draw a deep breath. *One. Two. Three.* Her fingers played across the bracelet. *Breathe. Four. Five. Breathe. Breathe.* The trickle of air seeped into her lungs. The next flowed through her bronchial tubes. Another coated her cells. Each life-giving inhalation slowed her heart rate, held the shadows in check.

It was several minutes before she could look at the computer screen without the urge to flee. The burning feet of fire ants crawled across her scalp. The need for knowledge outweighed the fear of *know*ing.

Okay, a familiar face. She could work with that. He was a piece of a puzzle. *Her* puzzle. What she didn't know was *how* he fit in her life. Father, uncle. God, she hoped not. His smug, con-man smile showed his open contempt for the people around him. Her hands fisted on either side of the keyboard.

An internet search brought up several pages of articles on the man. She flipped through them all, scribbled notes. Lots of information came up.

No more triggers.

She flung the pen and paper skating across the desk. The pen struck the side of the chair and the paper fluttered to the floor, under the lip of the chair. She dropped her head on her folded arms and fought back tears. Anything would be better than this blackness that taunted her every time she searched her past. At least then she would know what faced her. Was Rudy Sorell the reason she'd been on the run? If so, she was from Texas.

He was in Texas.

She was in Minnesota.

Her spine stiffened, and she pushed from the chair to pace the floor. Doc herself said being here with Liam was the safest place for her, but being in this town gave her the best cover, too. No one in their right mind would pick here to search for her. With every step, the cloud of dread that hung around her twenty-four-seven dissipated.

Unless… Unless everyone, except her, knew her destination. "Dammit! This is so not fair…"

Her gaze drifted to the image on the screen and the photo next to it of Liam and the kids. No. If she *was* on the run, Moose Head Falls was the ideal place to land. A push-pin dot on the map, thousands of miles from Dallas. The chances of Rudy Sorell, or anyone, finding her here were slim to none.

One thing was certain, she needed to get her strength back. Soon. Fight or flight, baby. Didn't want to get caught on her ass. She clicked off the computer.

In slow, deliberate movements, she stretched a body stiff from inactivity. It was time to push the limits. She hadn't been on the obstacle course in over a week. Then, she made it once around before her body failed her. "Liar. You made it halfway before you wussed out." The only thing that kept her going was Liam on the sidelines. Not this time.

After the third round on the obstacle course a side twitch pulled her up short. Muscles quivered with fatigue. She hurt everywhere. A good, deep tissue hurt.

By the time the truck doors slammed in the driveway she was curled up on Liam's chair, an unread book from the shelves open in her lap.

"Eden! We're home." Zoe ran into the family room and threw herself into Eden's lap. Her chubby little arms wrapped around her neck. "I missed you today."

Taken by surprise it took a minute for Eden to think, then she folded Zoe against her. Ever since The Great Cupcake Disaster three nights ago, there'd been a subtle, undefinable, shift in the dynamics between all of them. The kids accepted her without question into their tribe. A toastiness spread from her chest to her extremities. "I missed you, too. Did you have a good day at school?"

"I did. My best friend Kenzie's birthday was today. We had a party for her."

"Must be nice to have parties while the rest of us goobers work." Noah moaned as he plopped down on the couch.

"I'm making dinner. Don't forget to get started on your homework," Liam said as he came in the room. His gaze landed on Eden and Zoe cuddled in the desk chair. Something flickered across his face before his mask fell into place. "Zoe, go get the table set."

"Awww, Daddy, I haven't seen Eden all day. I was telling her about Kenzie's party."

"You can tell her at dinner."

Her eyes lit up. "I know. It's the best to have a mommy."

Liam tracked her as she skipped from the room. The same expression of... worry... flickered across his handsome face before he turned to Eden. "How was your day?"

"Long. Boring. Can I help you with dinner?"

"Can you cook better than you bake?" A smile quirked at his mouth.

She stood and followed him into the kitchen. "I'm sure I can cut stuff."

"Good. You can cut the mushrooms."

Later that night, as Eden headed to her room, both kids bounded out of their doors. "What are you doing up?" She snuggled her arm around Zoe as the little girl settled in next to her. Eden's heart swelled with affection. In the short time she'd been here, the girl had managed to ambush her heart.

Liam appeared from inside Zoe's bedroom. "The kids wanted to ask you something."

She couldn't read his expression. "Sure."

"We're going to the Pumpkin Festival on Sunday. They're a lot of fun. Have you ever been to one?" Noah's animated face glowed.

She pursed her lips in thought. "I can't say I have."

"They have food, a Ferris wheel, and fireworks, and each of us get to pick out a pumpkin." Zoe chimed in.

"That sounds fun. I'm sure you'll have a good time."

"Yeah. Um, do you want to..." Noah's feet shuffled. "Do you want to come with us?"

Startled, her gaze flew to Liam. He shrugged, a partial smile on his lips. "They're fun."

"Well. I, uh, I think I would like that. Thank you both for asking me."

"Yippee! You're going to love it. Good night, Eden." Zoe hugged her around the waist and headed to her bed, brushing past her dad.

Noah stood, awkward in front of her, his gaze down.

He was a lost and fragile little man. And she wanted nothing more than to wrap her arms around him, but didn't know if he would welcome the contact. She settled for a pat to his shoulder. "Sweet dreams, Noah."

"Are you going to the store with us tomorrow?" Liam's warm spicy scent surrounded her.

Why did a simple smile from that man turn her insides upside down?

She stepped into her room. "Sure. I'll be up on time." Then slowly closed the door. "Night, Liam," she whispered into the dark.

Chapter Twenty-Two

The old wooden floors of J'Emma's Country Store squeaked with the sound of age as Eden wandered the perimeter. Liam told her it was named for the previous owners, Jonas and Emma Stout. Built in the forties, it appeared younger, with polished wood that led the eye from station to station. Cheerful red rugs covered the space in front of bins filled with bulk items, like coffee, various nuts, flours, and dried beans. Local jams and sweet-smelling homemade soaps roped with gingham ribbon sat scattered throughout. Warm and nostalgic. Filled with a unique energy all its own. The kind of place that couples stopped to explore on their way to some *place.* Have a coffee. Grab local honey to try on Sunday toast as they chatted about the week ahead or planned the kids' activities. A place that becomes a part of their couple-speak. *"You remember that cute little place we stopped at on the way to..."*

Her throat swelled. Glancing around for witnesses, she swatted at the acid burn of unshed tears. As with all the other useless nudges that flooded her mind like water over cupped hands, she knew this was not her reality. *Stupid woman.* What would she do with that kind of life, anyway?

Thunk, bang. "Son of a bitch."

She peeked around the corner and slapped a hand over her mouth to hold in the laughter. Ever since they got to the store, she'd waited for the perfect opportunity to ask him for a job, but it never came.

He'd been a crazy man all morning. Charged in and out of tasks before completing any of them. Managed to injure himself twice. He'd ignored her the entire time. Now, he maneuvered one of the full barrels filled with ice-cold drinks and ice off his foot, muttering as he moved. He stopped and hobbled over to the counter when he noticed her.

"Everything all right over there?"

"Fine," he snapped.

"You sure I can't help—"

"I told you, I'm fine."

Eden sighed and shoved hands in her front pockets. Two nights ago, when the kids asked her to go to the Pumpkin Festival, he'd seemed okay with the idea. But since then he'd been impossible. "You better be careful, or you'll fall back to Mr. VIP again."

At his blank stare, she giggled. "Don't tell me you've already forgotten my pet name for you? Very Important Prick."

"Pet names are warm and fuzzy—"

She held her hands up to stop him. "Okay, truce. I reached for the laugh, it didn't work. Go on being your grumpy self."

He gave a jerky half-laugh-half-snort.

"What? You think I haven't seen you stomping around here like a bear on steroids?"

A sheepish grin tugged at the corner of his mouth. Muscular arms crossed a broad, solid chest. "Truce accepted." He pursed his lips. "Look, why don't we go to the cafe and start the day over."

"But we brought sandwiches."

"I need a break. It's slow. Come on, I'll buy you lunch."

Not like she *could* buy. This would give her the perfect opportunity to bring up a job.

They locked the doors, Liam hung a *Be Back Soon* sign, and they headed down the street to the cafe.

"You don't have a problem closing up shop?" This was her chance. All she had to do, was open her mouth and say it...

The warmth of his palm against her lower back as he took her place on the curb melted her brain. What was she going to ask? All she could think about was what it would feel like for his hand to slip beneath the hem of her sweater. The way he'd leave a trail of fire as it moved up her spine.

"It's not that busy this time of day. We'll be right down the street. If someone needs me, they know where to find me."

His words penetrated the sensual fog that had her heart fluttering too fast for its own good.

He opened the door, and the background noise of the interior rushed out to greet them.

After being seated, they placed their orders. Nachos for her and grilled chicken for him.

Then the awkward silence settled in. Conversations buzzed around them. Waitresses hustled from table to table and they both craned their heads in every direction to avoid eye contact.

Liam's fingers drummed a steady rhythm before he finally gave her his full attention. "Do you ever eat anything besides junk food?"

"I prefer to think of it as comfort food for the soul."

"Yeah, your soul is going to need lots of comforting when you drop dead. You haven't eaten one green thing in the time you've been here. Your cells can't live on goo."

She laughed. "Junk food is easy to come by and cheap. Veggies, fresh food are more expensive. You eat this long enough, you get used to it. Besides, there are beans, meat, cheese, avocado, and sour cream." She ticked off items on her fingers as she spoke. "Veggie, protein, dairy, dairy. Avocado is green. All food groups covered." After a sip from her Coke, she held the cup up. "Fluid."

A few minutes later, their waitress put plates in front of them, hurried off and returned with a pile of napkins. "Can I get you anything else?"

"Thanks. We're good."

"You know, you can tell a lot about people from the food on their plate." Eden scooped up a chip loaded with a bit of everything and maneuvered her mouth under the gooey cheese trail.

"Yeah? I can't imagine what that greasy mess must say about you."

She smiled around the mouthful and jutted her chin at his plate. "Grilled chicken and a salad. Steady, hates change, needs control, safe." She took another filled chip and gave him a satisfied smile. Then shoved the entire thing in her mouth.

A slow grin spread across his face.

Her heart did that funny little stutter-skip thing it did whenever he smiled. Those deep eyes, usually icy-shards, warmed, and twinkled.

He wagged his eyebrows and waved his fork over her plate. "Total disregard for authority. Reckless free spirit. Doesn't like to walk too far from the line." Now it was his turn to be smug.

"You can't have it both ways. Either I'm reckless, or I walk the line."

"Sure, you can. You want the world to determine you're tough and don't care. You're also quick to point out fake health benefits to fit in. It's all hogwash, of course, but I'll give you credit for the thought."

He dug into his chicken, relishing every bite.

She nibbled at her chips. He'd hit a little too close to home. Like he'd exposed her for all the world to see. She wasn't sure how to feel about that.

"Don't be so glum. Tell you what, I'll try one of those heart-killers if you eat a bite of my salad."

She wrinkled her nose. "You're not afraid the kids will smell your nacho breath?"

"I keep a toothbrush at the store. I won't tell if you won't." Before she answered, he scooped a Texas-sized pile of salad on to his fork and held it up.

He wanted her to eat from his fork? She swallowed, her gaze traveling from the offensive, green glob to his wicked brown eyes alive with mischief. Okay, Mr. Perfect, let's see how you like *this* game.

Her eyelids dropped at the same time she scraped her teeth across her bottom lip, then leaned forward, resting her full breasts on the table. When his pupils dilated, and only then, did she brush his hand and pucker her mouth around the entire bite.

With a stunned expression and fork hanging in the air, he looked lost.

She silenced a giggle. The temptation to hand-feed him a chip flittered through her mind, but a glorious, if wicked, shudder shot through her at the thought of him licking the melted cheese from her fingers.

So, she took the opportunity to pile four cheesy, good chips on top of his chicken.

He plowed into the nachos with gusto, but not before a blush bloomed across his cheeks.

With him hopefully distracted, now was as good a time as any to broach the job subject. Like ripping a band-aid off. "I want to come work with you."

"Isn't that what we've been doing?"

"For you. I want to work *for* you."

A fork-full of chicken stopped halfway to his mouth.

"Just hear me out. The way I see it, it's a win-win for both of us. I have no clue how long until my memory returns. I can't keep mooching off everyone. If I work for you, it gives me more independence." A crisp nod and a mental pat on the back ended her speech. That came out coherent.

He laid the fork on his plate and blinked several times. The wheels turned behind those see-everything eyes. "Not sure how that's a win-win. I told you before, this is a one-man gig. I don't need any help."

Disappointment soured the food. "You've done so much for me already. I have no right to ask but—"

"Why do you need a job?"

She hated the suspicion that still lurked behind his eyes. "I'm a do-it-yourself kinda girl." She snapped her fingers for emphasis. "At least I think I am. I don't like asking for everything. If I want to buy Coke and chips, I don't want to ask your permission."

"You want a job so you can buy pop and chips?"

Fingers dug into her thigh. Okay, the mental pat on the back might've been a bit premature. "That's not the only reason. I can't keep living off you. What happens when my memory returns? I have no money, no clothes, no car. I thought it would be a good way to earn cash. When the time comes, I need to be able to buy a bus ticket. I would think you of all people would be anxious to get rid of me."

He shrugged. "Still not seeing the win-win."

"And it will let you spend more time with your kids." Her ace in the hole.

A thoughtful expression settled over his features. "I get all this has been hard on you. I can't imagine what you must be going through. But I don't need help."

Impulse drove her next move when she reached across the table and covered his hand. Heat zinged along the skin of her arm, hairs dancing in response.

The intense fire that flared in his eyes told her he felt it, too.

She snapped the singed appendage to her lap. Nothing more to be said. Whatever connection they'd shared over their food choices just went up in the smoke of their touch. Consider the subject dropped. He obviously didn't trust her to be a dependable employee, and she wasn't free to act on the attraction pulsing between them.

The waitress boxed up her leftovers. As always, Liam paid the bill. The walk back to the store was silent except for the occasional car. He still positioned himself next to the curb but made sure to keep his distance.

A few hours later, Liam came to the back where she flipped through a magazine. "It's time to go get the kids."

"I'll get my coat."

"That's okay." His lips tightened, and he jangled his key ring. "You want to manage the front while I'm gone?"

"For real?"

"I'm not offering you a job or anything. I mean... Let's see how it goes."

Chapter Twenty-Three

Liam opened the door and let the kids into the store first. Zoe dashed across the floor and wrapped her arms around Eden's hips.

"Hey, guys. How was school?" Eden's face broke into a goofy grin and she hugged his daughter.

Noah slogged in at a snail's pace. "Noah is sick," Zoe stated.

When Liam picked them up from school, he knew instantly something was wrong. His face had been flushed and his eyes glassy.

"Oh, no. What's wrong, bud?" She knelt in front of him and used the back of her hand to pat his cheek then forehead. "You're burning up." Concern crinkled at the corner of her eyes when she stood, fingers folded possessively over Noah's shoulders.

They shared a silent communication over his son's head, the kind of look he used to share with Krista. The kind of look that passes between parents worried for their child.

He stiffened, the cords in his neck so tight by rights, they should've snapped in half. He didn't ask for her concern. Didn't *want* it. That invited open doors. Doors that were better off shut. "Noah, go lie down. I'll come check on you in a minute."

Noah shuffled like a zombie, his book bag scuffing behind him.

"Do you want Zoe and I to lock up?" Eden asked.

"No. We don't close for another few hours."

"You expect him to stay here for another three hours?" Her voice crackled in shock. "The man who protects them from a strong breeze won't take him home when he's sick?"

He hung up his coat and took Zoe's from her. Annoyance scratched at his neck. "He'll be fine. I have a bed back there for this reason. It's not my first rodeo. I'll give him some medicine, he'll rest, we'll go home. End of story."

"But I'm sure he'd be more comfortable at home."

"And we'll be there in a few hours."

Eden scrunched pouty lips and ground her teeth with enough force a muscle ticked in her jaw.

"By your evil eye, I assume you don't agree with my decision. Congratulations, in two weeks you've mastered the fine art of parenthood. Something the rest of us have taken years to figure out." He leaned into her personal space and lowered his voice, careful to enunciate each word. "You are not their mother. Back off."

He pivoted, ready to storm off in an indignant huff. Then, without any logical reason why, he said, "I'm a single parent doing the best I can. We've been here before. Don't worry about it."

Fingers curled around his wrist, the simple touch branding him with its heat. She stepped in front of him. "I'm not trying to be his mother. You're a great father. I thought... I don't know, because he's sick you'd want him home. In his own bed."

He shook off her hand. "You mind your business. I'll mind mine."

The instant the words left his mouth he wished he could suck them back.

Unshed tears glistened at her lashes and the barest hint of a tremble shook her bottom lip. She didn't say another word but followed Noah into the office.

Nice work jackass. You could've kicked a puppy across the room and gotten the same reaction.

He rubbed tired eyes.

Zoe tugged on his pant leg, drew his attention downward. She stood, hands on hips, stormy blue eyes glaring at him. Not an expression his agreeable little daughter wore often. He bit the inside of his cheek. The child was a bucketful of personality, he'd give her that. "What? You have something to add, Butterfly?"

"You were not very nice to her, Daddy."

Seven going on twenty-seven. That was his Zoe. He dropped to a knee, so they were eye to eye. "You're right. I wasn't. Sometimes adults do things that aren't nice, but for good reason. Now, don't you have some chores to do?" He smiled to soften his words.

She narrowed her eyes. Chubby hands squished either side of his face. Her gaze rooted around inside him, searching, for what, he had no clue. Whatever it was she seemed satisfied when she beamed at him. "You're nicer than this." She rubbed her nose against his and leaned into his ear. "That's what you always tell me." She skipped away. Problem solved.

If only all his female problems were that easy. He shoved to his feet and headed toward his office-turned-sick-room.

Eden sat on the side of the bed. With a sure, confident hand she patted a cool towel over Noah's forehead. Bottom lip smashed between her teeth. The boy's eyes were closed. Face flushed.

He knew the instant she sensed his presence. It was the slight hesitation, almost a tremor, in her movement.

"I hope this is okay. I know you think you're the only one that cares about them." Her throat bobbed. "Tell me something. What is it you hate the most?" She turned to pin him with a glare. "The fact someone else can help them? Or is it me?" Her icy gaze froze him from across the room.

Wrong. *Right?* Was he really so uptight that he couldn't accept someone else in their lives?

He shoved the thought aside. She was trying to confuse the issue. "I need to give him his medicine." He took out two pills, a bottle of water and handed them to Noah. "How do you feel?"

Noah swallowed the medicine and handed the bottle to Eden. "My throat hurts, my head hurts. I want to throw up."

Liam tucked the blanket under Noah's chin and brushed the hair off his face. "Try to get some sleep. We'll leave soon."

He stalked out of the office. A few customers roamed the store.

A widow, Mrs. Rider lived alone and ventured into town once each week. No more. No less. Her trip was as much about necessity as human contact. With her eco-friendly bag loaded with enough supplies to get by until the next week, she'd grab coffee, chat with whoever happened to be around, and fill up on the latest gossip. He didn't need this today. "How are you Mrs. Rider?"

"I'm good, Liam. How is that young lady?"

"Zoe is good. She's in the back with her brother."

"That's nice. Um...but I meant the young lady you found. She's staying with you, right?"

A groan rattled in his head and he fought to keep his expression neutral. Everyone in town, *hell everyone in the county,* must know about the mystery woman.

"Her name is Eden, she's fine. I'll be sure to pass on your hellos."

"Word on the street is she's a beauty and..." She leaned forward. "Southern," she whispered. She inspected him with her curious gaze. Waited.

The woman loved a good story. In the past, he always gave her the obligatory nod or, *you don't say,* as she jabbered on. But if she expected him to stand here and fuel the fire of his own story, she was bat-shit crazy.

"Here you go Mrs. Rider. You're all set. Have a good weekend." He forced a smile that twisted into more of a grimace and slid the bag across the counter.

Her mouth dropped open then snapped into a grim line. She took the items and headed for the door without a word. That would give her something to chew on for the week.

Alone again, he latched onto the present problem. Eden and the kids. He had no reason to be so annoyed. She'd done nothing but play Florence Nightingale to his sick child. A move that, on the surface, seemed out of sync with her feisty, it's-all-about-me character. Then again, in the two weeks she'd been with them he'd learned Eden went much deeper than the surface waters she let the world see. Was she right? Could he be as shallow and insecure as she implied? Or was it her?

The image of Eden nursing Noah tugged at him. She and the kids had an obvious connection whether he admitted it or not. He'd flown solo for so long he didn't see it at first. The question of the day—did he trust her?

Resting his palms against the counter, he drummed out a rhythm with his fingers. He tapped his phone and checked the time. Four-fifteen. The bulk of the weekly business came between five and when he closed at seven.

He scrubbed a hand through his hair. If he didn't trust her, he had no business allowing her to stay. "There you go, asshole. You've already allowed her in their lives. Can't un-ring that bell."

He grabbed a pay-as-you-go cellphone out of locked cabinets. Ten minutes later, phone set up and ready for use, he headed to the back. His heart thudded in his chest with every step.

"You know how to drive a truck?"

Eden twisted and stared at him in confusion. She swung her crossed leg and nibbled at a cuticle. "I guess."

"Good." He tossed his keys into her lap. "You'll be alone with the kids. You need this."

She reached for the cellphone, opened her mouth, but nothing came out.

"If anything...*any little thing* comes up, call me. I put my number, Doc's and the clinic's in the favorites. He won't need any more medicine until I get home." Waves of dizziness kept him off balance.

"You want *me* to take him home?"

"If you think you can handle it."

If he wasn't freaked out of his mind he would laugh at her shocked expression.

"Liam, you take them I'll stay—"

He raised his hand to cut her off. "The next two hours will be the busiest part of the week. Customers stop on their way home from work to get weekend supplies. You barely know how to run the register."

His gaze bore into her. Searched for any reason... any, little, thing that might signal she was the menace he first thought. Nothing but worry shone from behind those gorgeous, eyes. For once, an open book.

Eden swung Noah's backpack onto her shoulder. "Do I need to come back for you?"

"No!" *Deep breath.* "Don't leave them alone. I'll find a ride home. Here's your new number." He handed her a folded piece of paper.

The soft pads of her fingers grazed across his palm, but when he didn't let go, she raised a questioning gaze.

"Don't let them out of your sight. So help me if anything happens to them..."

She flinched as if he'd slapped her. Jutting her chin high, she pinched him with a glare. "I would never hurt them. You can't believe that or you wouldn't let me take them in the first place."

Her posture said it all. She spoke the truth. And she knew it. "Liam, I'll keep them safe. I give you my word."

He swallowed hard. "I know."

"You won't regret this." She hustled both of his kids out the door.

She had no clue what she talked about. He already regretted it.

LIAM placed a kiss on his son's cheek. Almost angelic.

He peeked in on Zoe one more time before he stopped outside Eden's door. Citrus and fresh linens. Her scent. It invaded the hall, the stairwell, hell, it was everywhere. His truck even carried her clean fragrance.

Her door was closed and the light out. It didn't surprise him. She'd been avoiding him all evening. Guilt kicked him in the ass.

When he arrived home, Zoe had been more bubbly than usual, Noah tucked safe in bed, fever down. All was well with his world. Thanks to the woman who'd quickly become a part of their daily routine. Now he needed to eat crow. If she would stand still long enough to let him.

His hand poised over the door, but he stopped short of knocking. What would be the point? He'd catch her in the morning.

He stopped at the bottom of the stairs. Curled into his favorite chair as if she belonged there, was Eden. Lost in the fire's trance, she didn't hear him come into the room.

A silent groan hit the back of his throat. Her scent would never come out of his chair.

A low hum pulsated through his blood. The red-orange glow of the flames brought the autumn strands of her hair to life. Her profile etched in marble.

"Finding any answers?"

She jerked, the silken strand twined around a finger dropped to her chest. "Liam, you startled me. I thought you'd gone to bed."

"Checkin' on the kids." He took a seat on the hearth. Close enough that electricity zinged between their knees. He fisted his hands. "Fires have a way of drawing us in."

She cocked an eyebrow. A quirk started at the corner of her mouth, played across soft lips. "I wouldn't know."

Insensitive. Idiot. "I'm sorry. I didn't mean to bring up painful—."

"It's okay." She patted his knee. "I was kidding."

"I didn't mean to intrude."

"It's your home. I don't think it's possible to intrude. In fact, I should leave you to your chair." She made a move to rise.

His hand snaked out to stop her. "What's your hurry? You look comfortable."

She relaxed into the cushions. "I am. I could get used to this. The crackle and pop, the dance of the flames. It's hypnotic. There's an entire population of people out there who never have peace. Don't know what it means to be warm and safe inside a home with people who love them." Her gaze turned back to the fire.

The cop in him suspected she'd regained parts of her memory. The man in him felt her pain. "Sounds like you knew someone like that."

Her eyelids dropped, lashes shadowing her cheekbones. The bracelet over the Phoenix tattoo spun beneath her fingers. A tell.

He recognized it now, a coping mechanism. In moments of agitation and stress her fingers sought the familiar texture. He doubted she even knew she did it. "Tell me a good memory."

She closed her eyes, took a deep breath. "Vanilla and cinnamon. Whenever my grandmother walked into a room, a cloud of vanilla and cinnamon wrapped you in a hug even before she reached you. She'd make me grilled cheese and cut off the crusts." She leaned forward, so close the heat from her mingled with the heat from the fireplace.

A long curl fell over her shoulder and brushed his arm. Logic told him to sit back. Out of the way of danger, but he didn't listen. His hand closed around the hair spun rose gold in the fire's glow. What the hell was he doing?

Her breath hitched and her gaze locked on the space where they touched.

All five senses were in hyper-drive. His brain shut down.

She sank back and broke their connection. "No one else ever did that for me." Glancing down, she rubbed the bracelet. "She's the one who gave me this."

He swallowed hard. "Is she still alive? Do you know how to get in touch with her? Do you remember anything more?"

"No." She shook her head. "I'm not even sure why I thought of her."

That sucked. He couldn't imagine not remembering the people who made his life worth living. His world revolved around those two kids. They were his people. In the two weeks since he'd found her, no missing persons report matching her description surfaced.

Ah, hell. Everyone should have people. "Thank you for today."

She nodded.

"Noah is still running a fever. He should stay here tomorrow. The Pumpkin Festival is Sunday, and I'd hate it if he couldn't go." He paused, his lips pressed into a tight line. "I thought you could stay with them."

DID SHE HEAR HIM RIGHT? "You want *me* to stay here with your kids all day? *Alone?*"

He shrugged. "It wasn't awful today."

A snarky laugh rushed from her. "Wow. Thanks for the compliment."

He had the decency to look contrite before he answered. "They were good. Happy. And..."

"And?"

A sigh puffed his cheeks. "You were right."

She sucked her bottom lip between her teeth. A thrill raced through her. He trusted her. That tiny morsel settled in her chest and expanded. Liam. Trusted. Her. "What do I need to do?"

His face paled.

Did he regret the decision already?

He scrubbed a hand over his chin. "I'll make a list."

More like a book. "I promise to take good care of them, Liam. Nothing bad will happen."

The silence filled the space between them.

"Well, big day ahead. I guess I should get to bed." She pushed to her feet.

He rose with her. They were so close, her nose a breath away from the buttons of his shirt.

In slow motion he cupped the side of her face.

Her brain fractured, and she imagined herself melting, a pool of liquid heat on the floor. She turned into him. Her mouth against the rough oak texture of his palm, his clean, spicy, outdoors scent already too familiar. A delicious shudder shot through her. She wanted more. She didn't deserve it.

After another deep breath of his scent she placed a chaste kiss to his palm then stepped back. "Good night, Liam."

His gaze burned her as she crossed the floor to the stairs. Hand trembling on the rail, she had to drag herself up the stairs.

"Good night, Eden."

Chapter Twenty-Four

Eden slipped another pat of butter into the pan, set up four slices of bread and topped each with a piece of cheese. Once the butter melted, she slapped the pieces together and put them over the heat.

Her internet search for what to do for sick children turned up lots of useful information. Her takeaways—cold cloths behind the neck, on the forehead, and the miracle of chicken soup. And surprise, surprise, Liam had four cans in the pantry.

The man was efficient. She'd give him that.

He was a good mom and only called them twice an hour.

She popped the soup in the microwave, flipped the sandwiches and patted herself on the back. It was all under control. When Liam came home, he'd see he could trust her. She'd been so excited when he asked her to stay with them. There was no way in hell she'd screw up.

After Liam left for the store, Noah came downstairs with his pillow and blanket. His fever near normal and eyes not as glossy. She settled him on the couch and gave him his first round of meds per Liam's detailed instructions. The man must've stayed up all night to write out the book he'd left on the counter.

Taking the sandwiches from the hot pan, she cut off the crust and sliced them on the diagonal. Then piled baby carrots, crackers, the soup and sandwiches onto a large tray. "Okay, guys. I hope you're hungry. Noah, I read chicken noodle is the soup of choice for sickos. I made grilled cheese, too. I cut the crust off like my grandma did for me."

"Did you remember something, Eden?" Noah asked.

Her stomach fluttered, and she cocked her head to the side. The fog was thinning, but so far not much she could share with little ones. "A little. I remember my grandmother used to bake cookies and make grilled cheese sandwiches for me."

"Oh, yummy. Does that mean there's cookies?" Zoe kneeled on the floor next to the coffee table. "Look, Noah, she cut them in a triangle just like Daddy does." The question of the cookies forgotten.

"Noah, do you think you can sit up and eat?"

"Yeah, I'm a little hungry." In slow motion, he pushed himself up before he dropped his feet to the floor.

She fluffed a bunch of pillows behind him and wrapped the blanket around his legs. "Take it slow. Eat lots of soup if you can. I worked hard on it. I had to open a can, pour it in the bowl, microwave it. I'm pretty proud of that." Somehow, she didn't think cooking was in her arsenal of achievements.

A soft blush heated his cheeks, a shy smile on his lips. "You don't have to mother me."

Eden didn't hold back, she hugged him. "I like taking care of you." And she meant it.

"Aren't you going to eat?" Zoe asked her.

She'd nibbled on leftover nachos, but she didn't think it would be smart to bring them out here. "I ate something while I cooked."

A silly cartoon kept them entertained through lunch. Eden relaxed. Noah felt better, Zoe prattled on as her happy little self. Most surprising of all, she'd made a meal. A sense of pride and accomplishment washed over her.

An hour after they ate, Zoe dragged her tiny butt down the stairs, stopped beside Eden's chair and let out a loud sigh. Resting her elbows on the arm of the chair, she twirled a piece of Eden's hair around her finger. "I'm bored. I want to go play."

Eden rubbed a hand down the girl's back. "We can't go anywhere right now, honey. Noah can't leave. Why don't you sit with me and watch TV?"

"I don't wanna."

"A tea party?"

"I already did two."

"I'm tired of laying here," Noah said. "I'm feeling better."

"You, buster, are not moving. Absolutely not. What do you think your dad would do if he came in here and found you up goofing around?" He'd never leave her alone with them again.

"Ple-ee-e-ase, Eden. I want to do something." Zoe had mastered the art of cuteness and used it without shame.

So much for having a handle on everything. What to do with bored kids? She tapped a finger to her chin and scruti- nized their faces then checked the time.

Zoe's eyes lit with excitement. "Let's go outside and play."

Liam wouldn't be home for hours. She reminded herself of the vow to teach these kids basic self-defense before she left. Now that she knew Liam better, she wavered. He'd be furious if he found out. She didn't want to lose the hard-won trust. But she held fast to her basic instinct. He lied to himself if he thought he could always be there.

A flash of unwashed faces and cruel laughter filtered through the haze of returning memories.

Chills raced across her skin, and a weight sank into her chest. The bracelet spun beneath her frantic fingers. *No.* This was the right thing to do. Liam couldn't honestly expect to play guard dog for their every waking moment.

"Okay, I have a game I'll teach you with one condition." She couldn't have them blabbing to their dad about what they'd learned.

"I promise," Noah chimed in first.

"Me, too."

"Okay, I call this...*how to get away from the bad guy*. But this has to be our secret? Okay?" She licked her lips and wrinkled her nose. Guilt had a bitter taste. "Can you keep a secret?"

"Yes!" They both shouted at once.

"Noah. I'm afraid you'll have to watch this time. But we'll do it again. We'll surprise your dad in a few weeks with how good you are." She pictured the moment they released their little bombshell. Then pictured herself on the hunt for a new place to live.

"I call the first move a knee kick. You can both do this, and if you hit with enough force, you'll knock someone down and give yourself time to run away. Shout fire as you run. Zoe, come here. If someone grabs you by the arm, like this, you'll kick them right here in the knee and then twist your arm and pull it down." She demonstrated the move several times and then had Zoe repeat it.

"Fantastic. High-five."

Zoe slapped her hand.

Noah leaned his back against the couch and stretched his legs onto the coffee table. "Nice job, Zo. I can't wait to try it."

"Let's do another one. This is a bear hug." Eden showed them the move, even as images popped in and out of her head.

She stood in front of a plate-glass window, couldn't have been more than ten or twelve. While inside, instructors taught orderly rows of children these exact moves. A ritual from her childhood. Outside looking in, never on the other side of the glass. The emotion attached to the memory, like so many others, left her lonely. Confused.

Zoe finished one last run-through of the move while a brilliant smile spread across her face.

"Remember. Our secret for now. You can't let your dad see you practice." God, she hated herself. "Not until we're ready for the show."

"Pinkie swear. You too, Noah. You have to pinkie swear." Zoe waved her finger in the air and giggled. "This is what friends do, isn't it, Eden?"

The tiny hairs along the back of her neck swayed. "You got it, girl." Hopefully, she'd done the right thing.

Class time ended well before Liam came through the door a few hours later. Everyone was chilled and content in front of the TV.

"Looks like you guys had an awesome day." Liam hung his coat on the hook.

"Eden took real good care of me, Dad. She put cool cloths on my forehead like mom used too, and she made chicken soup."

Zoe bounced on her toes in front of him. "And she cut the crusts off the grilled cheese."

He cocked his head at her. Instead of the annoyance she expected, he smiled. "I guess I made the right call."

LIAM PULLED OUT CHICKEN, salad ingredients, and frozen cauliflower mash for dinner. His mind buzzed fast and furious with too many questions and not enough answers.

If Eden hadn't broken contact the night before, he would've kissed her. *Wanted* to kiss her.

Rather than the guilt he expected, exhilaration warmed him. He wanted more. He'd raced through the day, excited to get home. Not because of his fear over the kids. No. For the first time in four years, that fear was static in the background.

He seasoned the chicken and put it in the oven.

Eden was an enigma. A mixture of toughness, sass, and attitude that bristled under his skin. And she had an endless supply of opinions on matters that didn't concern her. Or that she knew nothing about.

He grabbed a big bowl and added the salad ingredients.

She was also funny, full of energy, and wonder at the simplest things. In moments of solitude, when she thought no one noticed, all that bravado she carted around cracked, and her vulnerability blinked like a beacon. Despite her independence or maybe because of it, she nagged at his instinct to protect.

He put the cauliflower mash in the microwave and tossed the salad. Hands busy, but mind firmly on the spunky woman currently playing Connect Four with his kids.

Eden's appearance in their lives was a monkey wrench he was ill-equipped to know how to handle. He was in uncharted territory.

He didn't know whether to grab the kids and book a quick retreat, or pack his supplies and embrace the adventure.

Chapter Twenty-Five

"Are we almost there, Daddy?" Zoe kicked her feet and strained to see around the driver's seat. The cutie's enthusiasm was contagious. Eden's own excitement mounted the closer they came to the festival grounds.

"Turning into the parking lot now."

Eden slanted a glance from beneath her lashes at Liam. All his worry lines were gone. It was as if she sat next to a stranger. Wrist relaxed on top of the steering wheel, he tilted his head to the side in laughter. Not a care in the world and so damn sexy.

Was this the real Liam Conlin? The one that lived and breathed before she'd come into the picture?

She itched to palm the side of his face. The day's growth along his jaw would be scratchy against her fingers. If their lips brushed, she wouldn't complain. She'd close her eyes, feel the pounding of her heart as it raced to meet his. Strong arms would circle her waist, hands molding her against him, as her own twined around his neck.

Heat flushed through her. Ever since the near-miss of a kiss in front of the romantic glow of the fire Friday night, she'd thought of little else. She'd been a bundle of fear, excitement, and hope all rolled into one. It had taken every ounce of willpower to get up and walk away.

Far better to allow the emptiness that swallowed her than the stain of regret Liam would carry. And he would regret the kiss. Kisses led to cuddles. Cuddles led to...well, more, and he was too honorable. Too noble for something as base as a one-night stand.

As long as she carried the status of woman-without-a-past, she'd never be able to offer him anything more than one, blissful night.

She didn't want to be a regret.

Liam pulled the truck into a parking space, and everyone piled out. A crisp promise of fall floated on the breeze. The ashy scent of wood fires blended with old leaves. Hot chocolate and a whiff of apples and cinnamon warmed the chill in the air.

"What do we do first?" he asked.

Images, disjointed, and unprocessed, blinded her to the present. *Boots. Bright yellow tie, a cowboy hat.* Yes... They all belonged on a huge statue called... She cocked her head to the side. Did she know the name? She did! Big Tex.

Did she remember anything else? She slowed. *Spread the Love, Y'all* in bright yellow against a red backdrop. A familiar city skyline wrapped her in a sense of *home*.

Like pieces of a jigsaw puzzle, they all slid into place to form the first complete picture of her past.

That day had been as cloudless as the current one, but hotter. Sticky. It had also been the best day of her childhood. She and a group of kids snuck into the Texas State Fair. She'd been with Jared and Smoke.

A burst of giggles stirred her belly, bubbled through her like the fizz of sparkly wine.

"Hot chocolate," Zoe shouted.

"Rides." Noah and Liam fist bumped.

Her gaze took in their actions, the words, but her brain was three steps behind. Lost in a memory that didn't leave her breathless with fear. She had a brother. Jared. She was not alone in the world.

"What's your pick?" Noah asked. All three stared at her.

She pulled her mind from the past. Her movements were almost robotic as she turned to Noah. "Excuse me?"

Liam's warm hand cupped her shoulder, his eyes filled with concern and questions.

She pulled herself together and reassured him with a wink. "I remembered something. I have a brother."

"That's great. Anything else? A way we can contact him?" Liam asked.

For once, her brain threw out a jewel she could embrace. One that didn't leave her wondering what kind of life she'd led. She smiled. "No. But I have a brother. It's enough for now. So, what did you ask me?" She turned her attention to Noah.

His shy expression melted her. "You've never been here. You pick what we should do first."

"Me?" She scrunched her face, tried to recall the options. What was it Zoe said? Something about marshmallows. "I say hot chocolate first." She gave Zoe a thumbs up. "With tiny marshmallows."

"Yeah! Take that boys, another girl in the house."

Liam's gaze lost focus as if he chased a whisper from the past.

Zoe grabbed her dad's hand and slipped the other into Eden's.

Sensory overload slammed them when they entered the festival area. Bales of hay stacked on either side of the entrance held bushels of apples and small pyramids of pumpkins. Straw-filled scarecrows stood guard at more fall displays scattered around benches and trees. Colorful tents dotted the field, with more evidence of the season outside of each. Baked goods, spiced apples, and BBQ filled the air.

Hot cocoa in hand, Noah requested they go to the pumpkin-carving booth. That didn't hold Zoe's attention for longer than five minutes.

"I wanna get my face painted." Zoe tugged on Liam's leather jacket.

"We'll go there in a few minutes—" Liam stopped mid-sentence and turned to Eden. "Unless Eden wants to take you?"

Eden straightened, eyes blinking too fast. It was one thing for her to watch them in the safety of the house. But out in public? Where anything could go wrong? "Seriously?"

He nodded at the line forming outside the tent. "If it gets me out of that long line, I'm all for it. We'll be over shortly." He handed her a wad of orange tickets.

Bewildered, she took the little girl's hand, and they trotted over to the tent a stone's throw from Liam. They waited for a good fifteen minutes for their turn.

"I want a butterfly. What are you getting, Eden?"

"I'm too old for face painting." She chuckled around the words.

"You should. It can look like the picture on your arm."

"That would be pretty," the artist offered.

Eden contemplated the Phoenix tattoo on her wrist, the bright orange and yellows blending in with the themes of the day. "You're right. Why not?"

While the artist painted Zoe's face with a butterfly, Eden flipped through the options and settled on a parrot for her cheek requesting the colors match her tattoo. The young lady used artistic license and threw glitter—that would be everywhere in a matter of minutes—in the yellow.

Eden pointed to the white plastic bag in Noah's hand when they met up with the boys. "What did you get, Noah?"

"A pumpkin-carving kit. Dad said I could carve my own this year." His chest puffed with pride. "I see dork got a butterfly. How original." A nudge to his sister's shoulder bought him a shove in reply.

"Look what Eden got." Zoe tugged on Eden's arm, turning her to the side.

Liam's eyebrow quirked. "You got one?"

Heat crept up her neck. The crimson blush no doubt clashed with the orange and yellow paint of the parrot. "Yes."

"Cool! It matches your tattoo." At least Noah seemed impressed.

"So, what's next?" Eden grabbed Zoe's hand.

"Petting zoo."

Mayhem. Nothing else could describe the craziness of the petting zoo. Animals and humans mingled in a free-for-all of hay, feed pellets, poop, and squealing and crying children, all punctuated by the bray and grunt of four-legged creatures.

One persistent, speckled goat nibbled at her ankles, chewed on shoelaces and mouthed the cuff of her pants. She brushed him off, scooted out of the way only to find him back for the next course.

Liam took pity on her and whisked her to freedom. His whispered *I'll protect you* tickled the hair around her ear. Three little words that swept her breath away and made her insides quiver. Had anyone ever said that to her before?

The warm spiciness that was Liam blanketed them, and she relaxed into his side. His arm, weighted and secure, settled across her shoulders. The happy couple waiting on the sidelines as their kids played inside.

After lunch, they wandered into a costume booth. Witches, zombies, knights, princesses, unicorns, superheroes. Something for everyone.

"Okay, Zo-Zo, what are you going for this year?" Liam asked.

She scrunched her face. "I don't know."

"What about you, Noah? You need more time?"

"Nope." He held up a football uniform and grinned. "This is it."

Zoe yanked on Eden's hand. "What was your favorite costume when you were little?"

"Oh, well, I... um..." She was pretty sure she'd never dressed up. Or knocked door-to-door with the words trick-or-treat on her lips. But that sounded pathetic, even to her own ears.

Liam searched her face. Something he'd done regularly since day one, always judging her, but in the last couple of days, he'd been less annoyed and more...intense in a different way.

He seemed to read her discomfort. Something else he was good at. Reading her. "Zoe, find a costume so we can go hit the rides."

Eden's heart sank at the flicker of disappointment on Zoe's face, and she hunkered down to the little girl's level. "You know what, I don't think I've ever dressed up. At least I don't remember. And this seems like so much fun, I'm sure I'd remember. Don't you?"

"Yes! You would." Chubby little hands patted Eden's cheek. "I think you should dress up this year. Don't you, Daddy?"

Eden stood up so fast she backed into Liam's warm, solid body. "I don't think so. I'll just share in your fun."

Liam's laughter rumbled through her back before it reached her ears. "I think you're right, Zoe. Everyone should dress up at least once in their life."

Eden licked her lips and stepped from the shelter of his heat. "I don't want you to waste your money on me."

"It's my pleasure." He waved his hand to encompass the contents of the booth. "Take your pick."

Tempting. A mischievous idea teased her with its genius.

She tilted her head and flirted with him from under her lashes. "I will if you will."

He gave her a lopsided grin.

They stared at each other, weighing the challenge with both the kids goading them on.

Liam crossed his arms and rubbed one hand over his chin. "I'm betting, *you're* betting, I won't do it." He stared a fraction longer. "You're on. Pick whatever you want, and we'll meet back here. Zoe, you're with me. I need your expertise."

Eden laughed. "Noah, you up for the challenge?"

"Oh, yeah." He grabbed her arm and pulled her off to the women's side.

"So, what do you think?"

"How about a lady warrior?" Noah held up a red, white, and blue costume with very little material.

Eden inspected it and shook her head. "I don't think so." A scantily clad fighter wasn't the look she was going for. She wanted to find something different. Something that pooled over her skin to puddle at her feet. Something that made her feel soft.

Liam's three little words floated through her mind. *I'll protect you.* She wanted feminine.

They searched for several minutes and then she found it. The beautiful blue gown of a fairytale princess, white cape, and glittered white gloves. Elegant. Sophisticated. "This." She held it in front of her and twirled.

Noah wrinkled his nose. "It's so girly." He sighed. "I guess you are a girl."

She held it up in front of the mirror, pictured Liam's expression as she came down the stairs. Would he light up when she walked to him?

Once back at the register, they did their best to hide their choices from each other. Liam handed Noah cash. "Here. You pay for these. We'll both be surprised on Halloween."

Zoe clapped her hands. "You're gonna love Daddy's, Eden."

"And Dad will probably love hers."

They took the secret packages back to the truck and spent the rest of the afternoon on the rides, stuffing themselves on vendor fare. When it came time to pick their pumpkins, Zoe took her own sweet time, explaining the finer points of the process to Eden.

By the time the sun sank into the horizon, they'd begun the trek to the fireworks field, looking for the perfect spot to spread their blanket. Eden's face hurt from all the laughter, and her feet ached from the miles they'd walked.

The wind shifted, the breeze a cold chill over her skin.

She shivered.

A sickly, sweet scent, mingled with stale cigarettes, choked her. Coated her tongue.

The air in her lungs burned. A painful weight crushed her chest. She spun, gaze searching the faces of the crowd. *He's here.*

He'd found her. But who was he?

"Liam, run." Ripped from her throat.

He didn't hear. They were too far ahead.

Lewd laughter, hoots, the voices of boys swirled round and round. Teenagers came from behind. Circled her, closing her in. No escape.

Darkness narrowed her vision. She came to an abrupt halt and turned in slow motion. Liam and the kids were nowhere to be found. They hadn't even noticed she was gone.

Why would they?

Shouts and obscene jesters poured from the group of teens surrounding her. The cloying aftershave hit her nose again.

Cigarettes. Familiar. Yet not.

Laughter rang in her head, bodies crushed against her.

"No, please, let me out..." Her voice, no more than a whisper, choked her.

No one would hear.

They never did.

She was on her own.

Always.

Strange hands grabbed her elbows, dragging her along with their tide of chaos. Shouts rang in her ears. "Party time." Hot breath smothered her face. "Come on, pretty lady." Followed by raucous laughter.

"Let go of me." A reserve of steel filled her and she jerked one arm loose then the other. A kick to the shins of one partier brought a yelp. "Leave me alone."

"Out of the way." A firm voice penetrated the fog. She knew that voice. It was her safe place. She wanted to crawl into the arms it belonged to. Hide from the memories that made her too weak to fight off a bunch of drunk frat boys.

Strong hands pulled her from the group leaving a rush of cold air after the crush of bodies.

"What's wrong with her?" A male voice asked.

"We didn't do anything, man. I swear," another said.

"Just keep walking." The voice held an undercurrent of fury. Protective. Of Her. She never expected that.

That smell again. Darkness and fear surged. *Breathe. Breathe. But she couldn't.*

"Come on, honey, let's get you somewhere private." Liam anchored his hand at her waist.

"No," she wheezed. "Go... I need to be alone." She took two steps before her knees gave out.

Through the cobwebs of panic and the terror that gripped her, one thought kept repeating. Not the one she wanted to hold close. Not the one that promised a home. It was the one that told her she would never be safe again.

He found her.
And he wanted her dead.

Chapter Twenty-Six

Eden's feet tangled, and she went down hard. It took two attempts to push her feet flat to the ground, and she ignored his outstretched hand, but she righted herself. A glimpse of tear tracks glistened in the street lights before the braid curtained her face.

Liam had never felt more powerless. People stopped or pointed as they walked by, and both his kids stood wide-eyed, trying to figure out what happened. The sight of her panicked and defenseless stirred a protective need so strong he didn't know how to hold it all in.

The Eden he'd come to know over the last month would have plowed her way through that group like a fiery badass.

His gaze roamed over the gawkers. Some stared openly, others tried to be discreet as they slowed and craned their necks. But no one stood out as a threat. Still, instinct clawed at his gut.

Satisfied no immediate danger shadowed them, he brought his attention back to Eden. She'd collapsed against a rock, legs pulled tight against her chest, head resting on top of her knees. Her fingers tapped and twirled the bracelet in a frantic dance he hadn't seen from her since she first came to live with them.

The sight made the skin along his neck itch. This wasn't right. He couldn't stand by while she went through this alone.

"Zoe, take Noah's hand. Stay close."

He squatted in front of her. "Come on, honey. I'm gonna get you out of here."

"No. Leave me alone." The words came out in a strangled mess.

He slapped his hands to his knees. The male need to do something, *anything*, sat like a weight in the pit of his stomach. "Eden, let me at least take you over to the bench. You'll have more privacy."

She didn't answer for a long time. "I... don't want... the kids or you to see me." She gasped between gulps of air.

"No one cares." Nervous whispers and snickers hung in the night air. "*We* don't care. But the ground is too cold. I'll get you to the bench, and we'll leave you alone."

He exhaled a sigh of relief when she placed her hand in his and allowed him to pull her into the shelter of his arms. Music blared over the speakers, marking five-minutes until the fireworks show. The gathered crowd lost interest, drifting off to find their place in the grass.

He handed Noah the blanket and moved them from the main path to a secluded bench where she dropped with a deep exhale. The wood shook with tremors as she inhaled great gulps of air.

Without asking, he took a seat and scooped her onto his lap.

"What... What are you doing? You said you would go." She squirmed and twisted in his grasp.

"I lied." His hand rubbed up and down her back, murmuring endearments only she would hear. Much like he did for his kids when they were young and frightened from a nightmare. "You're shivering. I'm not leaving."

She peeked from beneath those long, thick lashes as they fluttered over pale cheeks.

Deceptively innocent.

Breathing calmed, the muscles along her spine lost some of their tautness. Her side sagged into him. "Why are you doing this, being nice to me?"

"Because you need me."

The bracelet moved back and forth under practiced fingers. As a distraction, he pointed to the metal chain. "This helps?"

"Yes. It blocks the noise of the world."

"Is that why your grandmother gave it to you?"

She cocked her head to the side. "I guess so." An aura of frustration hovered around her. "I hate how weak all this makes me. Breathe. It's simple, in out, in out."

"You're stronger than your fears, Eden. You have too much fight to be weak."

Lashes fluttered in a rapid blink. "What kind of person can't remember their life? I'm afraid..." Her eyes flew open. "What if I'm not a good person?"

The same fear that ran through his head. Before.

Before she became the woman who tried and failed to make cupcakes because a little girl idolized her. Before she became the woman whose laughter dazzled like sunlight sparkling along the waves of lake Jackson. Before she became the woman who cared for his sick son like... He swallowed past the hurt in his heart. Like a mother.

He cupped the side of her face, the tear-damp skin cool against the warmth of his palm. His thumb traced a lazy path across her lips. "That's not possible."

"How? How can you know that?"

"I just do. I follow my gut. Always have."

A tiny smile twitched at the corner of her mouth. Once again, her lashes lowered. "And you've never been wrong?"

The first echoing boom of fireworks sent a shudder through Eden that vibrated in his lap. A flash of red and green filled the air with an electric current shot straight through his heart. "Only once."

Zoe moved in and rubbed a hand down the Eden's braid. "Are you better?"

"Yes, sweetie."

His daughter beamed and snaked her arms around Eden's neck.

"Noah." Liam motioned him over and pulled out his wallet, handing the boy a twenty. "See that vendor right over there?" He pointed across the field. It wasn't far, and he'd be able to keep an eye on them. "Take your sister, go over to that vendor, and get us three bottles of water."

Eden startled, eyes wide. A man could lose himself in those eyes. So beautiful, unique. "You're sending them off alone?"

"I can see them. You need me right now."

Lips parted in a silent O. A stray hair broke loose from the braid and danced in the breeze.

He brushed the curl behind her ear. A thought nagged at him. This woman, with her unique brand of seductress and innocence—all soft vulnerability—plucked him from the darkness he hadn't even realized he'd been living in. Made him feel things he never wanted to feel again.

And he didn't hate it.

"When the kids get back, we'll leave. Do you need me to pull the truck closer?" She'd had several attacks, but this was by far the worse he'd witnessed.

"No. Let them finish the fireworks. I need to sit here for a while, anyway."

Laughter greeted them before the kids. He took the bottles of water and sent them back to the blanket to finish up the show.

He handed one to her. "Do you want to talk about what happened?"

"No." She curled the corner of the label from the plastic bottle.

His arms tightened across her mid-section. A perfect fit for him. Resting his chin on her head he pretended not to notice the aftershocks that quaked through her. "Panic attacks are not a sign of weakness. They make you a fighter." Lame words, but the only ones he could find to offer some kind of comfort.

She winced, her gaze trained on the sky.

"Those boys back there... They brought up a memory. One I wish I could keep locked away. I was young, I don't know, maybe ten, I was attacked. Molested."

Four rockets exploded in the air.

"I think I got separated from...my brother. I remember wandering for a while. Out of nowhere, a group of boys came from behind. Surrounded me. Hands yanked me into an abandoned warehouse."

Liam's body stilled. But his mind raced with questions. First and foremost, who allowed a ten-year-old to wander alone in abandoned buildings?

"There were five. Two of them...ripped my clothes...touched me. I screamed until my voice was raw. Someone came along. They scattered. But the person just left me there." Her feet twitched, ready to bolt from his lap. "I ran away. Hid. I was weak. I should've fought harder, screamed louder. Something other than being a helpless victim." She spit the last two words through tight lips.

"Stop. You were one little girl against five boys. Your parents should have protected you." Anger at the faceless adults who'd let a child stray from them, raged through him. "You can't blame yourself. This happened all the time when I was on the force. You. Are. Not. To. Blame." He tilted her head, his thumb caressing the soft skin of her chin. She had no choice but to look him in the eye. "I'm sorry someone wasn't there to protect you. You deserved better than that."

She jutted her chin from his grip and looked away. "We're always alone. There's no white knight or superhero on the horizon. You either learn to fight, or you die." She brought her attention back to him. "You can't protect everyone, Liam."

Their disagreement over the pizza palace incident came to mind. It all made sense, now. No one ever had her back.

Never protected, never sheltered, she assumed the entire world operated like her irresponsible parents.

Time for Eden to learn she wasn't alone.

EXHAUSTED, Eden crawled into the warm bed and pulled up the blankets to block out the cold of the room. Nothing would cure the chill in her heart. Her brain hurt. She closed her eyes but the colorful events of the day kept prying them open. Flipping over, she shot a silent scream into the pillow. So many good memories she would hold on to forever.

And guilt. So much guilt.

She hadn't lied to Liam. The assault happened, just as she said. But it wasn't what triggered the attack.

The aftershave, the cigarettes could belong to anybody. But one person she *knew* did wear that smell. *RJ Sorell.*

But Jared was the only one who knew where she'd been heading.

And he'd never tell.

RJ melted into the crowd, his gaze locked on Eden and the man intent on sheltering her. He'd kill to know what they talked about. But he couldn't risk it. Not yet.

Over the last few weeks, they'd crawled up highway 71 to interstate 35, stopping at every little podunk town along the way. They'd finally caught a break three days ago. He'd been in line at the last gas stop when some old lady yapped about a mystery woman with two different colored eyes in Moose Head Falls.

She'd clicked her tongue and sympathized. "The poor thing has amnesia. No idea who she is."

They'd arrived in Moose Head that night only to find it was so small they stood out like a sore thumb. For the last three nights, they'd slept in the car on the outskirts of town while they tracked her down. And *bingo*, here she was. Under the protection of some local country boy. He didn't believe for one minute the bitch lost her memory. She'd played these people just like she always did.

What would Jared think about his precious baby sister now? All those years, he'd pampered, protected, treated her like a china doll. First chance she got, she'd run off and let his ass rot in jail while she found a new protector.

Adrenaline and hatred mixed in a lethal combination. Not that it would matter. By the time they were through with her, there wouldn't be much left of the wench. But he'd still relish the look on Jared's face when he shared her fate.

"Are we gonna take her?"

RJ glared at the other man. "What? Here, in the middle of this crowd, with her lackey guard dog sniffing around her? We're going to follow them and find out where she's staying. I gotta figure this out."

She must've stashed the cash and the drugs close by. Even if they could take her now, she wouldn't give up without a fight. If she died accidentally, he might never get his stuff back.

"Go get the car. Pull it up over there at the end of the sidewalk. Stay low. Don't let her see you."

"You said she has amnesia. She's not gonna recognize me."

RJ whacked his right-hand man on the back of the head. God, he was all kinds of stupid. "She doesn't have amnesia, you moron. She's working these people. That money is stashed somewhere, and we need to find it."

"Why would she do that, RJ? I told you, she's headed to Canada. That's where she and Jared always talked about going. She wouldn't have stopped here for no reason."

"Use your head. You're on the run and need a place to hide. What better way to do that than convince a town full of idiots you can't remember shit?" Brilliant actually. Maybe he wouldn't kill her right away. She was a beautiful woman. Might prove helpful. Lust made him hard. It might be fun to toy with her a while.

"I don't think she'd do that—"

"Did I ask you to think? No, I asked you to get the car. And call the boys. Tell them to get their asses up here, pronto. Make sure they know to keep their mouths shut—to everyone. They can't trust a soul. You got me? I'll take it out of your hide if anyone else shows up. Meantime, I need to find somewhere we can hole up without drawing gossipy eyes."

Chapter Twenty-Seven

L iam's laughter as he joked with one of his customers brought a smile to Eden's face. He'd changed over the last few days. Less bitey.

Remnants of nerves that refused to fully dissipate curdled in her stomach. She wanted, no *needed,* the old grouchy, stick-up-his-butt Liam. She hadn't earned his kindness. Didn't deserve the gentle way he cared for her while she'd recovered from the paralyzing fear two nights ago. Guilt strangled her. She stretched and pulled the turtleneck that constricted at her throat. It'd be so much easier if he still treated her like a leper.

The entire picture was still shadowy, but she had to come clean. There were ugly things in her past. And he had a right to know.

The morning sprinted by as she'd worked up the nerve to tell him only to have a customer come in or the phone ring. Then the cycle repeated itself.

When the current customer left, she took a deep, fortifying breath, and pulled out one of the barstools. "Hey, can we talk?"

"Sure." He came around the counter and took a seat, his knees cradled around her's. "What's up?" The heat from his palms seared through her jeans in a possessive touch.

She stared. The words jumbled and refused to come out. "Um... I wanted to talk about Sunday. But I'm not sure where to start."

His phone rang. "Hold that thought."

A mixture of relief and annoyance washed over her. Finally got up the courage to tell him and another damn call.

"Hi, Viv. Yeah, she's here." He winked. "I think she'd like that. What time?"

The hairs on the back of her neck bristled. She didn't like the idea of anyone making plans for her.

"Five minutes? She'll be there." He hung up, a mischievous grin split his face.

"I hope the *she* you're referring to is Zoe."

"Viv and Abby want you to go to lunch with them."

A pulse sparked in her neck. "I can't do that."

"It's lunch."

"For starters, I don't know how to lunch with the ladies."

Liam chuckled and patted her leg. "It's not a job interview, Eden. I think you can handle this."

She hopped from the stool, no longer able to sit still. Easy for him to say. Lunch with the ladies, dinner at the club, double dates, kids to soccer practice... Those events were for real people. Not ghosts. Ghosts floated through life unseen, ignored. Props for the main feature. They existed without existing. "I have no money. I have nothing interesting to say."

"Don't kid yourself. You have opinions on everything. I'm confident you'll figure it out."

"Why do they want to have lunch with me, anyway? What do they want?"

He slid from the stool and stopped her mad pacing with two hands to her shoulders. "It's not a conspiracy. They like you. They want to get to know you better. And I'll give you some cash."

She shook her head. "No. I've already taken too much from you. I can't ask you for anything more."

"You didn't ask." He pulled out his wallet and shoved two twenties into her front pocket. But rather than beating a hasty retreat, he paused. A flash of something close to desire brightened his dark gaze, and he took a step closer.

A shudder shot through her. His fingers kindled a need as they brushed against the thin strip of material over the sensitive hollow where thigh met torso. She imagined herself melting into the stool, hormones a liquid flow of lava through her veins.

She hissed in a sharp breath. *You want me.* The words she'd used to taunt him weeks ago, now haunted her.

"That should cover it." With the agonizing speed of a sloth, he walked his fingers across the outer pocket, knuckles kneading their way out. A wicked grin curled his lips.

Her breath hitched. *Damn him.* Arousal made her brain fizzle, her cheeks burn. He didn't play fair.

He abruptly reversed directions and steered her toward the coat rack and gave her a gentle push. Grabbing a vest, he slid it over her arms.

Her body still purred like a cat. She'd never think clearly again. "But I needed to talk to you."

"And you can. Later." He nudged her out the door. "Right now, they're waiting. Go have fun."

She spun herself under his arm and back into the store. Hands on hips, she tapped her foot. "And for the record I don't appreciate being manhandled."

Liam laughed, his playfulness written in every line etched around his eyes and mouth. In one move he pushed her out the door, in the second move he closed it, and in the third, he locked it. A wave followed. "Bye-bye."

Eden smacked the thick glass. "Fine. I'll go, but don't count on me having a good time." She turned down the street, the crisp air a welcome slap to her hot skin.

She approached the cafe and paused outside. *Pfft. Doing lunch.* Friends gathered around tables, shared food, good conversation. It was as foreign as small towns, or Christmas carols around a cheerful fire. As foreign as the security she'd experienced under the umbrella of Liam's protection.

On cue, all heads raised in curiosity when the bell above the door announced her presence. And with the same fluid motion, returned to their conversations without missing a beat. Except for the two ladies in the back table who waived for her attention with genuine smiles on their faces.

Lightness, like fizzy bubbles, filled her chest. A sense of belonging brought a smile in answer. Is this what true friendship felt like?

"Hi, sweetie, how are you doing?" Doc greeted her.

"Healing nicely, thanks to you."

Viv pulled the chair out next to her. "Have a seat, I ordered you a Coke, is that right?"

Eden raised an eyebrow. "Good memory. Also, much appreciated. Liam's house is devoid of anything on the junk food spectrum."

Both women chuckled.

"Tell us, what have you been up, too? Scuttle-butt is, you, Liam and the kids were spotted at the Pumpkin Festival Sunday. Together." Doc winked. "Are my facts right?"

Heat burned a trail up her neck and ears. Note to self, nothing was sacred or private in small towns. On the one hand, there was reassurance in that. People cared about you. On the other, to an ex-street kid, overlooked by everyone, it suffocated her.

"Yes. I told them I'd never gone to a pumpkin festival before. The kids wanted me to experience it."

"Afternoon, Doctor Logan. Viv. Here you go." The waitress put a Coke down in front of Eden and flashed her a huge grin. "My name's Maggie. It's a pleasure to meet you, Eden, right? You're the woman, the one that dropped from the sky."

Eden hated the way her nervous chuckle sounded harsh when she'd shot for carefree. Fists curled around the glass, her fingers slicking over the condensation. "Does everyone know who I am?" The last word whistled through a pinched throat.

Maggie's face was open and honest. No negative vibes. Simple, honest curiosity. "Drawback to small-town life. Everyone knows your business, and when someone new comes in, they are the hot topic."

The muscles between Eden's shoulder blades loosened. There were no threats here. She was an oddity. A new face. "That's me. Minus the fall from the sky, of course."

"It's a pleasure to meet you. And they're right, your eyes are stunning." She squeezed Eden's shoulder, her perky smile swept to include Viv and Abby. "Are you ladies ready?"

After they placed their orders, Viv leaned in and put her elbows on the table. "Let's get back to the festival and details."

They wanted details. She had a lot to choose from. Nixing the unsexy panic attack, of course. "We had fun. The kids talked me into face painting, Liam had to rescue me from an amorous goat in the petting zoo. We all picked out pumpkins. They're going to teach me about carving."

"I can't believe you've never carved a pumpkin," Viv said.

Eden shook her head. She was pretty confident pumpkin carving had never been a part of her childhood. "At least not that I remember."

The next few minutes, they discussed fall and the festival in general before Maggie brought their food.

Eden took a big, cheesy, chip loaded with crunchy goodness Spicy ecstasy exploded in her mouth. God, she missed good Tex-Mex.

Giggles caught her attention.

"What? I'm allergic to anything green."

"And as a doctor, I should tell you to eat more of them."

"Perfect place to change the subject. I have a question. Liam challenged me to a costume throw down. I'm not clear where we're going to wear them."

Both women stared at each other with their mouths open. "Liam Conlin challenged you?" Abby didn't even try to hide the disbelief.

"Yeah, he took Zoe to help him make his selection, and sent Noah with me. We picked out costumes, and we're keeping them hidden until the big night. Only, I don't know what the big night is."

Viv snapped the napkin and dropped it on her lap. "It's a parade down main street. He let you walk off with his son. And he wasn't with you?"

"And *challenged* you? Meaning, he was being playful?" Abby's voice carried a ring of doubt.

"Very playful. All day." A shot of adrenaline coursed through her. "Besides, it's not like I left the tent or anything."

"When was the last time you saw Liam Conlin have fun, Viv?" Abby asked.

"I can't say. But I'm intrigued he let you out of his line of sight."

Eden nodded. Warming to the topic, she leaned forward, arms folded on the table. "I can do better than that. I stayed home with the kids all day Saturday while he went to work."

"Get out!" Viv gasped.

"No way," Abby said at the same time.

Eden puckered her lips, and nodded. The conversation was surreal. She could say the wrong thing or do the wrong thing. This was something she'd never done. Everything told her girlfriends were not a thing of her past. But she liked it. Relaxing with friends, sharing their lives. Sharing hers. "Truth."

"What prompted that?" Viv asked around a mouthful of food.

"Noah came home from school on Friday with a fever. I suggested he would recover quicker in his own bed. You can't mean to tell me he's never left those kids alone. Certainly, he trusts them with someone here. What about you, Viv? You're married with kids of your own. I can't believe he wouldn't leave them with you."

"Eden, there's been no one, other than you. I offered to have my husband come pick the kids up from the clinic the night he found you. He didn't want to leave until he learned if you were going to be okay."

Eden snorted. "He wanted to make sure I didn't attack anyone."

All three laughed at her joke. Goosebumps pranced across her skin. A feeling of being a part of something other than herself steamrolled through her and the last of her guard dropped.

It gave her the courage to ask the one question she had no right to ask. Liam's voice rang in her head, *none of your business, Eden.* "Why is he so protective? He won't even allow them to ride the bus."

Abby glanced down and fingered an imaginary piece of lint from her silk shirt. "In the four years he's been here, I've never seen Liam without the kids." She sighed and turned soft brown eyes to Eden. "It has something to do with his wife. I don't have details. All I know is she was brutally murdered while he was on patrol."

That would have torn a man like Liam in two. A stab of pain slammed her chest and a weight settled in its wake. The man who believed he could protect his family from the big, bad evils of the world, lost his wife to murderers.

The two women continued talking as she processed the illicit information. Liam would be furious if he knew she'd asked. That she held this piece of his life in her head. Would he hate her for it?

He'd glued himself to those kids for the last four years to guarantee their safety. What would he do if he found out the woman he brought into their home had ties to criminals? And not the petty theft kind.

"Are you sure, Steve? You found nothing?"

"I've checked all the databases. She's clean. Now, tell me why you called me? Why not the local sheriff?" His old partner from the Minneapolis police force called to update Liam on the background search he'd requested for Eden.

"He's involved. Good guy. Doesn't move as fast as I would like."

A rumble of laughter reached his ear. "Same old Liam. Get the info and get it fast."

"Things move at a slower pace up here. It's taken some getting used to."

"When are you going to tell me what this is about?"

"I told you. We needed to know who she was. I thought we could get the information through you."

"Na. Don't try to lie to me. I know you better than anyone. Something is up and you're not getting off that easy. Who is this woman?"

"That's why I called you, jackass. I don't know."

"Look. You're the best cop I've ever worked with and you have the gut-sense to know when something's off. You can't let what happened to Krista make you doubt yourself. Trust your gut."

Sweat pearled along Liam's forehead. Could he do that again? Go all in?

He thanked his friend and promised to send pictures of the kids to appease Steve's wife.

He wasted no time in calling the Sheriff. It rang so long he thought it would end up in voicemail.

"Sheriff Wilson."

"Ben? It's Liam."

"I was going to call you this afternoon. I have some updates for you." Papers shuffled in the background followed by a bang as something dropped. "I got nothing."

Liam pinched the bridge of his nose. "That pretty much confirms what my buddy back on the force said."

"What? I'm crushed. You went behind my back and called in someone else?" Sarcasm ran through every word.

"Sorry, but yeah. You had to see that one coming."

"Yes, my friend, I did. And I wouldn't have expected any less."

"Now what?"

"I don't know. That's up to her. We've done all we can to try and track down who she is."

Liam's shoulders drooped with a heavy sigh. "Where's she going to go? She has nothing. No one." Every inch of Eden's face, already so familiar, floated before him. How could someone be so alone? Not one person missed her?

"She could always stay in Moose Head Falls. I'll let you know if anything new surfaces." He preempted any further conversation with a click.

Liam had been so worried the chaos would follow her. Instead, she came alone.

The next two hours passed with a handful of customers, stocking the shelves, and any other busy work he could find to distract him from what he really wanted.

Eden to walk through the door.

The creak and pop of old building his only companions in the empty store.

Eden needed to be told no one searched for her. *And somehow it fell to him.* Fingernails scratched through the scruff on his jawline as he dug deep for the right words. Not that he believed any words would be a comfort.

When Eden strolled in a few minutes later, all the blood in his head spiraled to his feet like water swirling down a drain. Sunlight filtering in the window behind her struck auburn gold as she stood before him. Oxygen evaporated and he didn't care. Breathtaking.

She mumbled a distracted greeting on the way to the back room to drop off her coat.

"How was lunch?"

She took the stool on the other side of the counter from him, her fingers tip-tapping the teakwood. "Okay, I guess. It was fun."

"If you had a good time, why do you look like you're mooning over a lost puppy?"

"Hmmm?" She rested her elbow on the counter and dropped her chin onto her hand.

"The weatherman is calling for a flood of cats and rabbits tonight." He wasn't sure what was going through her pretty head, but she certainly wasn't listening to him.

She sat up straighter, head tipped to the side and scrunched her nose. "He said what?"

"I use that line on Zoe when she is not paying attention to me."

A kiss of pink swept over her cheekbones as white teeth nibbled her lips. "Sorry. I guess I'm processing. Lunch with friends is not in my wheelhouse."

"How do you know if you can't remember? It might've been something you did all the time." He grabbed her hands in his, the need to take all the hurt away too much.

"I just know." Seconds passed. "I just know." The last statement barely a whisper.

After the panic attack on Sunday, he'd suspected more of her memories had returned. He hadn't pushed, instead hoped she would trust him. But it couldn't hurt to nudge. "What do you remember?"

Her lips sealed tight before she spoke. "I didn't have girl-friends. I had..." The gears behind her eyes spun as she struggled for the right word. "Colleagues. Acquaintances that came in and out of my life."

That explained the sheriff and his buddy coming up with no missing person reports.

"I'm sorry, Eden. But that kind of gives me a lead-in on something I need to tell you. I talked with Sheriff Wilson while you were gone. The good news is there are no warrants out for you." He let a smile soften his words.

Something akin to relief flickered over her expression.

"The bad news is there is no missing person report either. I'm sorry." He sounded like a broken record with *I'm sorrys.* Nothing he could tell her right now could soften the blow.

Her eyes stared with a shattered, hollow look. "I don't matter to anyone." Sadness laced her words.

"You matter. Maybe..." He scrubbed his hand through his hair. "Maybe, you have no family."

"Yeah."

A vice clamped around his heart. How does a person reconcile the thought that no one cared enough to even look for them? Her hurt broke the last barrier he'd held on to like a shield.

He missed the snappy comments delivered on velvety tones and the slow, fiery grin she usually paired with them.

Coming around the counter, he sat next to her, cupped her hands in his.

Eden was not a threat. She was alone in the world. After three weeks, no one looked for her and the world still spun at the same speed it always had. Resolve settled in his bones. She needed help and he wasn't ready for her to go anywhere yet.

He took a deep breath and let it rush out before he could change his mind. "I have a favor to ask you. Well, actually it's more of an offer than favor."

"Go for it. I owe you for everything you've done for me."

"I've been thinking about what you said, about the kids. They would benefit from going home right from school rather than sitting or working here at the store."

Her mouth open and closed without a sound.

"I'm serious. When Noah got sick, and you took him home, I could see it in his face. I'll pay you."

Her nostrils flared. "I should be paying you. You supply everything for me."

"True. But, if it was a job and I pay you, you can buy your own junk food and your own colas. And you could do lunch once a week with Doc and Viv. You wouldn't be sponging off anyone then." He didn't stop to question why it was necessary that she feel at home.

"Let me get this straight. You, Liam Conlin, want me, Eden...whoever, to take your kids home every day after school?"

"Yes. That is the plan."

She batted her eyelashes. "Why, Mr. Conlin, I do believe you are starting to trust me."

His brain buzzed, blocking out everything but her voice. The velvety tones he'd craved moved in a slow, leisurely spiral down his spine. His world bubble expanded from three to four, and it became harder to remember life before Eden.

A stray hair fluttered in the space between them, and he smoothed it back, his hand brushing the pulse at her temple. "And I do believe, Ms. Eden you are settling into Moose Head Falls nicely."

Chapter Twenty-Eight

Liam leaned against the tool bench in the garage, one arm crossed over his stomach, the other propped on top, staring at the gray cover over the Jeep Wrangler. He'd stood like that for at least ten minutes, thinking, arguing with himself.

Since he'd asked Eden to take care of the kids every afternoon, and he agreed to let them ride the bus to the store, they'd all fallen into a routine. After taking the kids to school, he and Eden spent the day at J'Emma's. If she didn't have lunch with Viv and Abby, the two of them walked down to the cafe or lunched on leftovers. Once the kids got off the bus, she took the truck and drove them home for the afternoon.

The biggest drawback had been how he got home. He either got a ride from someone, or Eden and the kids had to come back for him.

But the new system worked.

Both kids were both happier, more relaxed. Instead of the nightly, mad-dash from the time they got home until bed, he could enjoy his time with Noah and Zoe. Somehow in her short stint with them, she'd become part of the team rather than an outsider.

And nothing terrible had happened with this new turn of events.

Noah meandered into the garage, his puffy, Land's End vest opened, ball cap twisted to the side. "Whatcha doing?"

"Something crazy. Wanna help?"

Noah's eyes lit up. "Sure. What are we doing?"

Liam cranked up the radio. "Slide the doors closed and turn on the heater."

His son scrambled to follow directions. "Are we going to work on the car?"

Liam whipped the gray cover off, exposing the cherry-red Jeep Wrangler. He ran his hand over the fender.

Still in beautiful condition. Then again it should be, he only drove it once in a blue moon. Just enough to ensure the engine ran smoothly. The Jeep represented a piece of his past he couldn't part with, but it was time to put it to good use.

Noah took off his vest and tossed it on a box, a wide grin of expectation spread across his freckled face. "Now what?"

"Let's get the supplies together for an oil change."

They went through the steps, one by one as Liam showed his son the ins and outs of the engine.

"Did I ever tell you grandad took me to my first car auction when I was fourteen?"

"Nope." Noah pulled the oil pan from the shelf.

"I won a 1970 Corvette Stingray."

"You had a Corvette? That's cool."

"I did. Two flat tires, the other two missing, no windows." He chuckled. "It was a hot mess."

"How's this?" Noah held up the filter for inspection.

"Here like this." As Liam showed him what to do next, he continued. "It took us two summers to rebuild that car. But it was a beauty when we were done." They solved all the world's problems, discussed girls, grades, careers. Life in general.

No matter how busy, his father never missed their scheduled time. Everything Liam knew about his dad, as a cop, a husband, a father, he learned in the shop one weekend at a time.

"Granddad taught Uncle Jim and me everything we know about cars." Until this moment he hadn't thought of Noah driving one day. Didn't want to think about it. "I thought we could do the same thing when you turn fourteen. Go find an old car. Fix it up." Talk about life.

Noah stopped what he was doing and gave Liam his full attention. "That would be too cool. I'd like that."

Grease smooshed across Noah's face, baseball cap flipped backward, flannel shirt tied at his waist, and the pink tip of his tongue shoved between even, white teeth as he worked to unscrew the top of the air filter housing. The tiniest hint of a smile played on his lips, features relaxed.

Liam wiped his hands on the grimy towel.

Happy. The boy looked happy for the first time in a long while. A mixture of joy and shame tangled in his chest. Shame that it took a stranger to come in and turn their lives upside down for him to see how he'd been suffocating his children.

He slid under the car and unscrewed the oil plug and set the drain pan beneath.

"How's it going at school?" He asked sliding out and sitting up.

Noah fiddled with a screwdriver. "Good. Thomas's birthday is this weekend."

"Nice, how old?"

"Twelve." The screwdriver clanged at his feet and the old familiar pinched expression returned.

Liam tossed the wrench into the tool chest. "Spill it. What's up?"

"He's having a party, Friday night. It's a sleepover. I know I can't go. But all the guys are going to be there. You know his father..." The words rushed out in one long gush of excitement.

Liam opened his mouth, the word *no* on the tip of his tongue. Then something clicked in his head. He'd spent so much energy protecting the kids, that he forgot to let them *be* kids. A fact that Eden pointed out at every turn. The whole reason he'd moved to Moose Head Falls in the first place was to give them a better life. Holding them hostage to his fear was not the better life he wanted.

Hoped etched the crease between his son's eyes when he made his last pitch. "His mom is the PTO secretary. How bad can they be?"

What the hell was he doing? All the times he'd taken off on his bike to go play a pick-up game or the nights spent at a friend's house or hiking around some of the best lakes in Minneapolis shaped him into the man he was today. He wanted Noah to be resourceful, brave and adventuresome. None of that was going to happen as long as he kept coddling the boy.

Noah's chin trembled. "Couldn't I go? Just this once?" He jammed his hands in his pockets and hung his head. The joy deflated right out of him. All the fun of the afternoon, the connection they'd made, gone.

Liam took a deep breath. It was time. There wasn't a person in town he didn't know. "What time does it start?"

Noah stared. His eyes blinked rapidly. "Seven?" A question. Spoken so softly, Liam had to strain to hear it.

"Okay. Do you need a birthday present? Sleeping bag?"

"Yes. Wait a minute. Are you saying I can go?"

"I am."

"To a sleepover. I wanna be clear... You, *my dad,* are saying I can go to a sleepover? At a friend's house? Without you?"

Liam laughed and ruffled Noah's hair. "Yes. Yes. And yes." He took a deep, steady breath. "That's what I'm saying."

"Yeah!" Noah jumped a foot off the floor and punched the air before hugging Liam. "Thank you. I can't believe you said yes."

Neither could he. Uncertainty already plagued him, but the joy on Noah's face made it all worthwhile.

"I'm gonna go call, Thomas." He ran for the door and skidded to a halt. "Are we done? Cause I want to call, him."

Liam nodded. "Yes. Ask Eden to come out here before you get on the phone. Please."

He was on a roll. He'd made Noah a happy camper. Now he hoped to do the same for Eden.

A few minutes later, she came through the door that Noah left open in his haste to get out. "Noah said you wanted to see me."

Make-up free, long hair tied into a high ponytail, jeans, boots with a cardigan pulled tight against the cold. Fresh, wholesome. His heart tap-danced in his chest.

Her eyes lit up when they landed on the Jeep, and she stopped short. "Nice." She ran her hand along the lines.

"It's been sitting here for a while. Unused. I try to clean it up, run it through its paces a few times a year."

She peered inside. "I've never seen you drive it." An innocent statement.

The dagger in his chest, while not fatal, left him breathless. He swallowed hard. "It was a gift. I bought it for Krista, my wife. Before she died."

Eden shot away from the vehicle like a bullet from a gun. Her gaze darted around the room before landing on him. "I'm sorry, Liam."

A thickness lodged at the back of his throat. "I had a Jeep when we first met. We traveled all the time in that thing. She drove it while I was deployed, but after Noah came along, it was no longer practical. We traded for a minivan. I bought this one to recapture some of what we'd lost over the years. A week later, she was gone. I couldn't bring myself to drive it, and I can't get rid of it."

She leaned against the back of the car and played with the ends of her hair. "I understand. It's a reminder you don't want, but one you can't get rid of." She chewed her bottom lip and peeked from beneath long lashes. "What happened to her?"

The dagger twisted. He picked up a rag and wiped his hands, but the guilt would never be wiped away. "During my time on the force back in Minneapolis, there was one house we got called to all the time. Domestic issues. They had this kid. A boy." He wiped the beads of sweat from his forehead. "I don't know. Something about him spoke to me. He looked lost. This went on for a few months. I got the brilliant idea I could be a mentor for him. Make a difference. I made a decision to take him under my wing."

He paused for a breath. For so long he'd held it in. Told no one. This was so much harder than he anticipated. What would she think of him once she knew?

"We started doing little things together. Lunch and basketball. Then Dad ran out. Mom had no money. I thought I could teach him about hard work. I had him...offered to pay him to cut the grass, do yard work. He could practice on me, you know? Then he could start his own lawn business." He carried the oil pan to the recycle bucket, his brain numb.

"Don't stop. I want to hear what happened."

"Yeah, well that may change. I screwed up. The first chance he got, he told his buddies where he was, what we had, and they showed up when I wasn't there. Krista was alone."

"Oh God."

"They didn't have to kill her. She would have given them anything they wanted."

Silence settled between them.

He turned his back and squeezed his eyes shut. It used to be a way to block out the images. Now, he didn't want to see the condemnation he knew would be on Eden's face.

Protecting his family was the only job that meant anything. And he'd failed.

The heat of her reached him first. She'd made no sound as she glided across the floor, but it surrounded him. She pressed into his back, wrapped her arms around him and rested her head between his shoulder blades. A perfect fit.

"Liam."

Nothing more. Everyone always tried to fix it, excuse it away. Sooth his guilt.

Eden simply embraced him.

This was what he needed. The sweetness of her arms cradled his disgrace and offered comfort. He covered her arms wrapped around his middle and leaned into her embrace. His entire universe condensed to music, the pounding of his heart as it mingled with hers.

After a few minutes she moved around to the front of him. "Thank you for sharing that with me. So many things make sense now. I'm really sorry for butting between you and the kids—"

"Don't be. It's been four years. There's always going to be *what if,* but nothing changes the past. I've been holding on to emotions I should've released a long time ago. It was easier to hold onto them."

The unexpected release of tension startled him. It was time to move on.

He cleared his throat. "*That* was not why I brought you out here." He pulled the Jeep keys from his pocket and dangled them in front of her.

"What's this?"

"I realize the story I just told you might tarnish this, but I wanted you to have a way to get around. It's not right that you're trapped here or at the store all day, every day."

Her eyes flew wide. "I couldn't possibly."

He placed the keys in her palm, curled her fingers around them. "You can. It needs to be used. If it makes you feel any better, you have the kids out here every afternoon. What if something happens and I can't get to you guys?"

She stared at her fist without a word.

What went through that beautiful mind?

"The sheriff pushed me on you, and you didn't deserve that." Shoving the keys in her sweater pocket, she cupped his cheeks. Hands warm. She stretched on toes and kissed his temple. "Thank you. I appreciate everything you've done for me."

Her lips were velvety, as he'd imagined they would be. She molded perfectly against him, all soft and satin just as he'd fantasized.

His knuckles skimmed down the side of her face to rest at the base of her neck. A pulse beat an erratic rhythm too fast to ignore.

Her bold gaze held him hostage. He tumbled into the pools of amber and navy with the absolute knowledge that his life would be forever changed.

HIS hands slid from her shoulders, her spine, to rest at her waist. They stood so close a puff of air couldn't come between them. Christina Perri's *A Thousand Years*, crooned in the background. Slow. Sensual.

She nestled into the protective cage of his arms. Safe. She envied the woman who would one day win Liam Conlin's love. To know that every morning and every night, he belonged to her.

She belonged to him.

His fingers tucked a hair behind her ear. He always did that. "What are you doing to me, Eden?" His voice cracked on a whisper.

"What are you doing to *me*? I'm supposed to be finding out who I am, and instead, I'm content just to be here."

"Don't think." His body swayed to the music filling the garage. "I don't want to think beyond this. Beyond now."

Thoughts of real life, the darkness that hovered on the edge of her memory, fled. Pushed away by the man who held her like a treasure. This was everything she'd ever wanted.

The song came to an end, but neither moved. Time hung on their mingled breaths as he lowered his head.

Everything slowed to a crawl. The skin at the back of her neck tingled.

Her lungs ceased to function. Her lids closed as their lips touched.

"Daddy. You in here?"

Like ice water, Zoe's voice splashed over them from the other side of the wooden doors, and they jumped apart. Eden's insides quivered, her knees shook. The heat of desire had to be a neon sign on her flushed cheeks. Thankfully, Zoe was too young to understand the look.

"I've been looking all over for you. Oh, hi, Eden. Daddy, I think Noah is confused."

Liam picked up the towel, put it down, and pushed back the hair on his head. "What's up with Noah?"

"I heard him on the phone telling Thomas he could come to his sleepover. I tried to tell him you wouldn't say yes, but he told me to mind my own business." She cocked her head. "Is that a nice thing to say to someone? I don't think so. I was only trying to help him."

Liam laughed and picked Zoe up. "Noah's not confused. I told him he could go to Thomas's for a sleepover."

"You did?" Zoe and Eden asked at the same time.

"Yeah! When can I go on a sleepover?"

"Whoa, whoa cool your jets, Zo-Zo. You're seven, he's almost twelve. We'll talk later."

She thrust her lower lip into a pout. "Not fair." She squirmed to get down and stomped off to the house.

Eden laughed. "So, when is Noah's sleepover?"

"Friday." He dropped his arm on her shoulder, and they followed Zoe into the house. "Someone recently told me I was holding on too tight or something like that."

Eden's heart pitter-patted. He'd listened. She fell into step next to him. The voice of caution shouted at her with each step, *guard your heart, guard your heart.*

But it was too late. She was falling. And falling hard.

Chapter Twenty-Nine

Zoe stood at the kitchen door, a sullen expression darkening her face as Liam turned the truck down the driveway. Eden knelt behind her and wrapped the little girl in her arms.

"It's not fair, Eden. Kenzie had a sleepover for her birthday, and I couldn't go. How come Noah gets to go to Thomas's?"

Eden spun her around and pressed their foreheads together. "I know you're disappointed, Butterfly, but Noah is older, that happens. My brother is older, and he's always done things before me." That was an understatement.

Zoe wrinkled her nose. "What was he like?"

Eden inhaled sharply and shoved to her feet, inches from her head slamming the doorknob.

Her mouth dried. Much of what she remembered wasn't fit to share with a seven-year-old. "I... He was good to me. Took care of me when no one else wanted to." Always made sure she had food, even if his methods were south of legal. "How about we do something fun?" Anything to change the subject.

"Yes, please." Zoe pounced on the balls of her feet and closed the door. "What do you want to do?"

Eden tapped her chin with a finger, ticking off potential activities and dismissing them as fast as they formed. She needed something Liam sanctioned, no more self-defense, but also Zoe-approved.

She snapped her fingers. "I have it. Your dad said it was going to be a while before he came home. He always makes dinner, right? How about we cook for him?"

"Yeah! What should we make?"

Good question. A quick forage through the pantry and the fridge turned up the ground beef he'd sat out the night before and a bag of potatoes. "How about we search the internet for some recipes we can make with this stuff?"

Zoe scurried off to the kitchen to grab an extra chair while Eden settled at the computer, jiggling the mouse. Luckily, Liam didn't turn it off. His home page with current news popped up. Eden typed into the search bar, finger poised to click enter when a headline caught her eye.

Texas-wide manhunt for suspected cop killer, RJ Sorell, has gone nationwide.

A low hum grew to a thunderous roar, and blackness tunneled her vision. Everything froze, like a TV screen after someone hit pause. Her hands curled around the side of the desk. Nationwide. He could be anywhere.

He could be here.

Her brain played through the scenarios.

Zoe bumped and nudged Eden's chair, trying to get close enough to see the screen. "Sorry."

Get it together, Eden. You can't afford to lose it right now.

Liam trusted her to keep Zoe safe. She couldn't, *wouldn't* let him down.

What if that had been RJ the night of the Pumpkin Festival? Fear tried its best to choke out logic, but she couldn't allow it to consume her. She pulled in deep, ragged breaths until she had control again.

Moose Head Falls, Minnesota was eleven, twelve-hundred miles from Dallas. She was a needle in a haystack. This was probably the safest place to be. No way the Sorells had found her. It was paranoid to think they'd tracked her down.

She wrestled the jitters, because that's all they were, *jitters*, under control. Another deep breath and she forced her fingers to look up recipes. They searched for something good over the next few minutes, but a sense of dread sat like a boulder in her stomach.

After settling on meatloaf and mashed potatoes, she printed out the recipes, and they headed into the kitchen. Even so, she couldn't keep her gaze from the front window. *There's nothing out there.* The road leading to the house was empty. No signs of movement anywhere on the property. Still... "Honey, I'm going to lock the front door. Be right back."

"Hurry. Daddy won't be gone too, long."

Deadbolts helped the feeling of unease, but she kept a phone nearby just in case. Zoe was right about the timing.

Hopefully, Liam stayed gone long enough for them to pull this off. After a few minutes with the silly girl, the worry retreated to the back of her mind. The heaviness didn't leave her, but she was able to enjoy herself with one eye to potential threats. She shouted out the ingredients while Zoe pulled what she could. "We got this."

"Yeah," Zoe squealed. They high-fived and started mixing.

Eden put the potatoes on to boil. She had no clue what she was doing, but who cared? She was cooking a meal for someone who'd done so much for her. It was all she had to give.

They tossed the chopped onion into the ground beef. Too late, she realized the oats container was empty. "Oh well. We don't need them, right?" She asked Zoe as if the little girl was the authority on meatloaf.

A shrug was her answer.

The first indication that the missing oats might be a problem, was when they shaped the mixture. The meatloaf was more meat-blob.

"That doesn't look 'xactly right." Zoe folded her arms across her chest and glared at the offending mess. "Daddy's doesn't look like that."

Eden nudged the sides into a loaf only to have it ooze back to the messy circle. "I guess we needed those oats. Let's put it in the oven and see what happens. Maybe the heat will help."

They popped it in the oven and cleaned up.

"Does your dad have any candles around here?" Doubtful. It might cause a fire. His gruff voice echoed in her head, and she laughed.

"I don't know. Maybe in there." Zoe pointed to the cabinet next to the refrigerator.

Of course, the locked one. Eden found a set of keys on the hook and fumbled through three before the door opened. Way in the back, sat a set of candles and a box of matches.

"Last steps, get the table set, and then we'll go get ready. He should be home soon."

"Get ready for what?"

"Well... We're making a special dinner for your dad, we want to look nice, don't we?"

"I can wear my party dress." Zoe's expression sparkled at the idea.

They set the table and put the candles out, and headed upstairs. Eden didn't have anything nice to wear, but she did purchase some makeup at the store. Zoe asked if she could wear some, too. Somehow Eden didn't think Liam would appreciate a makeover. She added enough blush to appease the child who preened and twirled in front of the mirror, but not enough to annoy the overprotective father.

Liam came home a few minutes after they removed the meatloaf.

"It smells good in here." He smiled as he took his coat off and hung it up.

Zoe pranced in front of him. "We made you dinner, Daddy."

"You did?" Surprise registered in his voice.

Eden carried the platter to the table. Still a blob. A well done, cooked blob.

"Wow. It's..." He peered at the plate and wrinkled his nose. "What is it?"

"It's meatloaf and mashed potatoes." Eden went to the kitchen and brought out the bowl of potatoes. She'd followed the directions to the letter, but somehow, they didn't look quite like the picture.

She pulled out a chair and took her seat. "Let's eat."

Liam cut into the meat and scooped some onto his plate and Zoe's. "Want to hand me yours?" He gave Eden a lop-sided grin.

Her insides turned to jelly. The candlelight danced shots of orange through his dark hair. Five o'clock shadow dusted his jawline. Strong shoulders, broad enough to carry the weight of the world, but soft enough for a child's head to rest. How could she have ever feared him?

She handed him her plate. "Yes, thank you."

He loaded all three plates with meat and potatoes then scanned the table. "Where's the green?"

"The green?"

"He means the veggies. We don't have a meal without veggies, Eden." Zoe shook her head and stuck her tongue out with a gagging noise.

A frown tightened her forehead. "Aren't potatoes a veg-etable?"

"I guess one meal won't kill us," Liam said.

Eden wanted to pop him right in his self-righteous nose. They'd worked hard on this meal, so what if they didn't have a green?

He scooped a forkful of meat and winked at Zoe.

Eden held her breath expectantly. Maybe it tasted better than it looked.

The expression on his face dispelled that hope. "That is..." His lips pursed and swallowed. "Tasty." Bless his heart, he tried to recover, but it was too late.

Eden took a tentative bite and gagged. "It's slimy! What did I do wrong? I followed the instructions."

Liam laughed out loud. "My guess is you didn't use enough filler and too much liquid."

"Filler..."

"You know, breadcrumbs or oats..."

"Oats, of course." She slapped her forehead. "You didn't have any."

He spooned a heaping mouthful of potatoes. "I bet these are awesome."

She took back the nose-punch comment. He was a good sport. She took a mouse-sized nibble of her own and realized the chunks of partially cooked potatoes were not mashed and ice-cold. Epic fail.

"Oh, Liam. I'm so sorry. We wanted to do something nice for you. Take your mind off leaving Noah for the first time. I ruined dinner."

He squeezed her hand. "You didn't ruin anything. I love it. It's been a long time since someone cooked for me. Thank you." He sat back and gave Zoe a mischievous grin. "I say we skip ahead to dessert."

"Yeah! Wait. Really?"

"Yup, I have some ice cream hidden in the back of the freezer. Why don't you go get it?"

Zoe slid to the ground and skipped to the kitchen.

"Why, you sly dog. You had ice cream all this time and didn't share?" Eden pinned him with an accusing glare and wagged a finger at him.

"Can't give away my secrets." Laughter laced through his words. He grabbed her finger and engulfed her hand with his.

Warm tingles shot through her body like fireworks on the Fourth. "I'll forgive you. This time. How's Noah?" Eden asked.

Liam didn't answer right away but stared at their joined hands as his thumb traced lazy circles over her skin. He lifted a bold gaze. "Thank you."

"For what?"

"For reminding me what it means to be a kid. For helping me to remove the VIP stigma before it was too late."

Heat rose up her neck and blossomed across her cheeks at her earlier reference to his Very Important Prick status. "I didn't do anything." But she preened under his approval anyway.

They stared at each other.

"You've done more than you think."

The dark pupils of his eyes dilated, and she swore she glimpsed a piece of his soul.

"I got it. Let's eat ice cream." Zoe ran in with three bowls, spoons, and a container of mint chocolate chip.

And shattering the moment with all her sweet excitement.

It didn't matter. Nothing could ruin this evening. Eden's cheeks were tight from the constant grin she'd been wearing since Liam came through the door.

She pinched her leg under the table.

Yup. All real.

She was here, he was here... This wasn't a dream. The corner of her mouth lifted higher.

Liam filled the bowls.

"HaHa dessert for dinner, and Noah isn't here." Zoe's joy bubbled over, and instead of resenting her brother's good fortune, she delighted in her own.

Mission accomplished.

Eden held up her spoon. "Cheers."

They clinked spoons and dug in.

After they cleaned up, Liam offered to start the fire pit on the deck. "I know it's chilly out, but the full moon over the lake is beautiful. The fire will keep us warm."

"I'd like that."

He turned the lock and pushed the partial glass wall out. Piling small sticks into the copper bowl, he lit the fire and pulled a couple of lounge chairs next to it. He waited until a good blaze was going then excused himself to put Zoe to bed.

A few seconds later, Zoe came flying down the stairs and grabbed Eden around the legs. "I can't go to bed without telling you goodnight."

"Awww, thanks, Butterfly." Eden knelt for a hug.

The little girl circled her neck and squeezed, right before she whispered, "I love you, Eden." Then she smacked a kiss on her cheek and skipped upstairs like she hadn't just rocked the center of Eden's universe.

How could one tiny sprite of a child cause so much turmoil with four little words? She clung to the euphoria of the sentiment and let her heart take charge of their safekeeping.

Eden touched the side of her face where Zoe's lips still tingled, and grabbed a blanket from the back of the couch.

Stretching out under the stars, she inhaled the scent of dried leaves in the crisp air. Dancing flames with sparking embers created a cozy mood, as she snuggled under the blanket's warmth. A large pale moon cast shadows over the trees. Peaceful. Beautiful. Safe.

Her lids fluttered and slid closed.

A cold breeze blew in and leaves crunched in the grove of trees just beyond the yard. She sat up straighter, turned her gaze toward the noise. Squirrels... Rabbits... Did those animals come out at night?

A scent... Smoke. Cigarettes? Or bonfire? It was faint but gone before she could be sure.

Phantom eyes crawled over her skin. Compulsive itching took over and she clawed at her arms. Damned anxiety. Night creatures. That's all they were.

More leaves crunched, this time closer to the lake. A muscle ticked along her jawline.

Impossible.

She moved to the end of the lounge chair and scanned the area. After five minutes, she huffed a breath she'd been holding for too long. Nothing there. She sighed and sank into the chair. Overreacting over a news article.

"I brought another blanket."

"Oh." She jumped. "You scared me. I thought I heard something out there."

He stopped by her chair. "Raccoons. I find evidence of them in the trash cans all the time. But, if it will make you feel safer, we can share the chair and the blanket." He nudged her to the side and slid into the chair, their bodies touching from knee, to thigh, to hip and shoulder.

All fear, worry, and thought fled under the warmth off his body next to hers. He draped the second blanket over them and dropped his hand to her leg where it seared through the jeans to brand the sensitive skin of her hip. There was nothing but Liam above her, around her... He filled her senses. There could be no fear. Only the love that settled like a seed in her heart. There was no going back.

LIAM squirmed under the blankets and pulled her into the circle of his arms. Vanilla-citrus floated between them.

She might as well be an illusion. Like the morning mist over the lake, she could be gone as soon as her memory returned. What nagged at him the most was why he cared.

She'd started as a thorn in his side, a problem he couldn't get rid of, and turned into a woman his family considered one of them. Noah was renewed, and Zoe smiled every day.

And there was no denying his strong attraction. It had been present from the beginning. Eden was beautiful. Feisty. A raw sensuality that ignited a flame in him. Physical chemistry was not a mystery.

Her compassion for his kids. The failed attempt to make him a meal. Her ability to add sparkle to any room. *Those* were a riddle.

His need to get home every day just to be around her. That was a mystery.

He rested his chin on her head where it snuggled on his chest, and forced himself to focus. "Any more memories?"

She stiffened. Her fingers stilled on the corner of the blanket. The pause almost a beat too long. "No. Well, fragments, I guess. Nothing big."

"Have you talked with Doc?"

She wiggled against him, her leg sliding along his. A pulse of attraction hummed between them.

Desire burned in his brain and he lost all rational thought as she nuzzled her mouth behind his ear. The soft tickle of breath a temptation he couldn't ignore.

He shuddered and reached for his words. This needed to stop. "Maybe you need to see a specialist. It seems like you should remember more."

She sighed. "I've talked to her. She said it could take a while for everything to come back. And it's possible..." She leaned back and gazed up at him. "She said there may be parts that never return."

What if... What if her memory never come back? She could choose to stay and leave the past behind.

Start over.

His skin prickled with guilt. Was he hoping she'd stay broken and confused forever? Forget about whatever family or friends might be out there? Only a selfish prick would wish that on someone. "I still think it might be a good idea to go into Grand Marais or Two Harbors and have an MRI done. It can't hurt."

"What if... I don't know what I'll do if they never come back." Stillness settled over her. "Who will I be?"

He flipped her so she nestled beneath him, his hand seeking the contour of her waist. Blood roared through his veins and echoed in his head.

Her presence awakened him to life again in ways he hadn't even known he needed. "You'll be Eden. Always

Eden. And there's no rush. You can stay here as long as you want."

She curled into him, exposing the creamy skin beneath her shirt. Of their own accord, his fingers caressed the silky curves, every touch a promise.

Like a pampered kitten, she purred contentment. "What are we doing, Liam?"

He swallowed. "I don't know." His voice sounded raspy and unfamiliar. "Whatever it is, we should stop."

She glanced up again. The blanket tumbled from her shoulder exposing the collarbone beneath.

He licked his lips. The shadowy hollow begged him to graze his teeth along the edge, to dip his tongue into the candied sweetness. This was madness. What was he thinking?

His gaze traveled the long expanse of smooth neck, the soft plains of her face, and rested on her beautiful eyes. Each so different yet, both glowed with the same desire. Huge dark pupils swimming in a sea of navy and amber.

He *wasn't* thinking.

She traced a fingernail along his lower lip. "You're right. We should stop. Before it's too late. But... Whatever happens, I want to remember this moment. The way it feels to be held like a precious gem."

He groaned. Not nearly strong enough. He cradled the back of her head, lowered his mouth to hers. Telling her all the things he couldn't say. Didn't know *how* to say. For now, it was enough. It had to be. It was all he had.

A powerful force of need burst between them. She was forbidden fruit, and he wanted it. All of it. All of *her.*

With her tongue, she teased, with her teeth she nibbled, and with each move, he lost himself a little further in the magic she wielded over him.

Sweet Eden.

Not a description. A declaration.

No.

A mantra sing-songed through his head. *My Sweet Eden.* He took the last step and tumbled into the abyss.

Chapter Thirty

Eden smoothed the white overlays on top of the blue princess dress, the imitation silk slipping under her palm. She'd never worn anything other than second-hand jeans and t-shirts or the occasional blouse. The crisp fabric was luxurious and rich, with every move it swayed against the skin of her legs. The illusion of wealth.

The brush glided through her hair until it shone before she piled it all into a messy bun. A hint of makeup completed the look.

She couldn't wait to see Liam's costume. Zoe had been beside herself for the last couple of weeks, bursting to spill the beans. Shoving the hiking boots on, she laughed and dropped the dress in place. The brown tips showed just beneath the beautiful gown. Too bad she didn't have a pair of glass slippers.

A soft knock on the door broke her train of thought. "Eden, are you ready? Dad's downstairs waiting, and Zoe is prancing around like some fancy horse." Noah's amusement colored his tone. Since coming back from his sleepover, he'd been a different kid.

It was now or never. "Ready as I'll ever be." She opened the door, and Noah's mouth dropped.

"Wow. Wait till Dad gets a load of you." A crimson blush stole up his face.

Eden kissed his cheek and stifled a chuckle as he turned even redder. "Not too shabby yourself, Football Dude."

Noah headed down the stairs first. Zoe's joy reached Eden before she hit the bottom step.

"Move Noah, I can't see her. I've waited so long to see her costume. Ooo..." Zoe breathed out the last as Noah stepped out of the way. "You're a beautiful princess, Eden."

Liam stepped into view. Everything good and pure in her world stood at the bottom of the stairs, waiting.

Dressed all in black and silver with swords on each side, there was no doubt what he was. Her Knight in Shining Armor.

Dark hair curled beneath a silver helmet, his brown eyes twinkling behind the visor. Shiny chainmail layered a black turtleneck that molded across broad, muscled shoulders, hugging solid biceps.

Laughter burst from her lips. The man wrapped black jeans with foil.

Foil.

The playfulness of the costume and the moment was not lost on her. That he was willing to walk around town wrapped like leftovers, for her, for the enjoyment of his kids, was remarkable.

Her heart stopped, knees buckled. She hovered on the edge of a cliff. One step, and she'd fall, helplessly lost and willing to follow this man anywhere.

She corralled the fantasy and brought herself back to reality. "No weakling white knight for me, I get the rare and elusive black knight," she teased.

"You're... *perfect*." He paused. "And for the record, honey, black knights have way more fun."

The way he lowered his voice, shot ripples of dreamy desire through her body. She might *be* a princess because she was living in a fairytale world.

"Look at me, I'm a princess too." Once again, oblivious to the energy going on around her, Zoe twirled in her brown fringed dress with tan tights. Her hair hung in a thick, messy braid down her back. Long strands dangled willy-nilly, and tiny hairs spiked from the twist.

"Gorgeous as usual, darlin'." Eden winked at Liam and whispered for his ears only, "Haven't mastered the braid yet?"

"I can take down the bad guys, cook, fold laundry, I can even do ponytails and barrettes. But these fingers were not meant for braiding." He waggled his hands in the air.

Eden pulled a brush out of her bag. "Mind if I offer to fix it?"

"Be my guest."

She pulled Zoe over to the couch and stood her between her knees. It took a few minutes to untangle the mess and brush it to a glassy shine before she started a French braid.

The boys talked about the night ahead, their voices a gentle hum in the background. Zoe prattled as per usual, not even caring if someone listened or not.

Eden's fingers stilled mid-twine and surveyed the room. From an outside observer's eyes, they were a picture-perfect little family. Her chest swelled, an almost painful squeeze.

She swallowed, tears clogging the back of her throat. "There. Perfect. I think we're ready to go."

They left the house single file and piled into the truck. Liam's fingertips brushed against her hand. Their pinkies linked and not even wild horses could drag her gaze away.

Maybe it was too many nights huddled in cardboard boxes or dank, smelly old buildings. Too many nights longing for something more. Too many nights dreaming of her hero. The one who would one day whisk her from street life, and carry her off to the castle.

Maybe it was simply the magic of the night.

Whatever it was, Liam Conlin had it in spades.

It had taken her a long time to accept no one would ever come to her rescue. But here was a man capable of doing that. A deep sigh rattled her chest. So much love for his kids. He'd made it clear from the beginning, his kids were everything. She knew she was a simple distraction.

It made her want him all the more.

By the time they reached town, the brilliant sunset faded into the horizon, and fun Halloween-themed music blared from speakers placed strategically around the center square. Shopkeepers up and down both sides of the street had gone all out decorating for the event with fog machines, inflatable figures, and tables filled with bowls of candy, cookies, popcorn, and drinks. A half-inflated bouncy house sat in the middle of the street surrounded by trees wrapped in orange, purple, and green twinkly lights.

Little monsters, ghosts, witches, firefighters, and princesses swarmed the sidewalks. The chatter almost drowning out the music.

All the wholesome family fun made Eden giddy. "Who is manning J'Emma's while you're out playing King Arthur?"

"I asked Viv's husband if he would hand out the candy while I'm with the kids." Liam opened his arms and turned. "What do you think of your first Halloween parade? Is it all you dreamed of?" The laughter in his voice was contagious, and she giggled.

"Exciting. It's all so spooky and merry at the same time. Do you people go all out for every holiday?"

"Wait till you see Christmas. A veritable winter wonderland around here."

Her breath hitched. Christmas was two months away. A lifetime.

They started around the shops talking to everyone. Eden was surprised at how many of the townspeople knew her and treated her as one of their own.

Stabs of guilt nagged at the back of her mind. A flash of faces. Selah and Dax. Of course, the bar. So much slid into place with that one niggle of guilt. She'd kept so much from them, too. Seemed she lived her life on a repeated loop of deception and half-truths.

"Look, it's Doctor Abby." Zoe dragged Eden over to the clinic with Noah and Liam close on their heels. "We all dressed up this year. Even Daddy."

"Well, look at you. A princess and a knight. How appropriate." Doc winked at Eden and hugged her. "Are you having fun?"

Eden scanned the street. "I've never seen anything like it."

Doc grabbed her arm with interest. "Does that mean you're getting more of your memory back?"

"She's not," Liam jumped in. "We were just talking about that a few days ago. Maybe she should go into Two Harbors for an MRI or something."

Panic seized Eden. "No, no. He's worried, but I told him you said it would come back in its own time. I... I'm getting jagged pieces, but nothing big. I thought I'd have more by now." She hated herself for lying to these people.

"Come on, Dad, I see the guys." Noah tugged on Liam's arm.

"In a minute. Doc, what do you think? Should she go or wait it out?"

Doc's scrutiny made Eden squirm, and she dropped her gaze.

"Come see me tomorrow, and we can chat," Abby said.

"Okay, now can we go?" Noah tugged on Liam's arm and pointed toward his friends.

"You got Zoe?" Liam asked her.

She nodded.

Doc stared open-mouthed at Liam's retreating back. "You've worked some mighty powerful magic on that stubborn man."

"I think he's just realizing it's time for them to have some freedom."

"Thanks to you." Abby dropped a handful of candy into a child's bag. "You can fill me in tomorrow. I think there is more to this story than you are dishing right now."

"Don't let your imagination go crazy. At least not until we talk." Eden squeezed Zoe's hand, and they stepped out into the street with the parade flow and scanned the crowd for Liam. Laughter competed with music as costumed people danced and passed each other in the street.

Someone grabbed Eden from behind and twirled her to the music. At the same time, she lost her grip on Zoe.

The masked man danced and spun her over and over, his hold so tight on her wrists she couldn't break free.

Beneath the chaos, something more sinister bulldozed its way through her. The same sour odor as the other day at the festival clung to the air around her. Her stomach heaved from vertigo.

Zoe's laughter bubbled around her, but she couldn't find the girl in the crowd. Panic knotted at the base of her spine. The man wore a werewolf mask that blocked even his eyes from view. She never saw what happened to Zoe. How would she explain this to Liam? Where was he?

"Let me go. Get off me," she snapped.

"Such a fragile bond," a hoarse voice rasped from behind the mask. "It can all be ripped away in an instant."

She yanked her arm from his vice-like grip.

Then the man was gone.

Zoe stood inches from her. A huge grin on her face.

Eden cleared the two steps between them and dropped to her knees, hugging the girl to her chest.

Icy fingers of terror gripped her, freezing her feet in place. Crazyland just around the bend. She reached instinctively for the bracelet.

Not going there. No way. Her nails dug into the palm of her hand. She was a fighter, dammit. Liam entrusted her with Zoe, that was her priority. She scanned the crowd for the man, but they'd disappeared into the throng of trick-or-treaters.

"Are you okay?" Eden squeezed the girl's shoulders.

Zoe smiled from ear to ear. "That was fun. I saw you dancing with a werewolf. Wait until I tell Daddy and Noah."

Somehow, she didn't think Liam would see the humor in any of this. "You know girlfriends share secrets, right? Maybe we let this be our secret. What do you think?" It was probably all harmless, but the fact she'd lost the girl's hand in the crowd, even if only a moment, would not sit well with papa bear.

"Sure. Let's go." She slipped her hand in Eden's, and they skipped off to find the boys.

Eden's skin crawled with heat, pushing the cold straight through the top of her head. All the sparkle and joy of the night left her. What was she thinking? Yes, the odds were against being found, but who was she kidding? She'd bring nothing but heartache to this town.

"We've been looking for you. Having fun, Butterfly?" Liam's tone was slow and smooth, with a hint of amusement. The muscles around his kissable lips relaxed.

"This is the best Halloween parade ever. Eden and I danced in the street. Didn't we? And look at all my candy." She held out her hot pink pumpkin already over half full.

So much for girlfriend secrets. At least she didn't say who they were dancing with.

Liam held his arm out for Eden. "Can I buy you a hot cider? I reserved a couple of tables at the cafe. The kids can look over their loot and suck down cocoa. And you can get warm."

Two hot cocoas and two ciders were ordered as they settled into their seats. Eden excused herself and headed to the bathroom. She needed a few minutes to think. To breathe. To process what had happened.

She'd broken away from the gangs and stood on her own two feet. Turned her back on the likes of the RJ Sorells of the world. Her heart rate slowed to manageable levels. She would die before she let them anywhere near Liam and the kids.

But no doubts, that smell was RJ's. She'd recognize it anywhere. Once, could be a coincidence, twice...maybe. But it didn't make any sense. There was no way he could have tracked her here. Of all the places in the US, he happened to land in the exact spot she had an accident? If he was here, how? Something was missing.

She shook her head. She was being silly, he didn't own that scent it was sold in every mall in the country.

After convincing herself it was nothing, she grabbed a paper towel and dried her hands before tossing it into the trash.

She flinched as if slapped. *Do You Know This...* floated over a crumpled, damp picture of her face. Stunned, her hand shook as she pulled the local paper from the can. *Four County Weekly*. It was dated five days ago.

A cold worm of fear spiraled around her ankles, up her legs, and gnawed its way along her spine. Why didn't anyone tell her they were going to plaster her face all over the county?

She exited the restroom, steps heavy. A condemned woman on her last walk. She was out of time and needed to give Liam all the information. This still didn't explain how they found her in Minnesota. But coincidences piled higher and higher with each day.

She couldn't wait any longer. Either tell Liam of her suspicions or move on. But she had no right to stay here. No right to bring the ugliness of her past to this town. To Zoe and Noah, and Liam.

Liam pulled out a chair for her. "Everything alright?"

"Fine. Why?"

"You've been distracted ever since we left the clinic. Did something happen?"

"No. Doc asked me to come in tomorrow. But I..." Just spit it out. "I need to talk to you about something."

He cupped her hand where it lay on the table. "Sure, what's up?"

Her mind turned to mush as his fingers massaged the sensitive skin of her palm. For the life of her she couldn't break the connection. The impulsive need to fluff her fingers through the thick, dark, hair matted around his face from the helmet was too much to ignore. It was soft and silky.

And so unfair. All she'd ever wanted was a family. Friends. *Real* friends. Not survival buddies. "I've never known a knight before. You're very handsome."

"I'd have to say you're my first princess." Lips so warm they branded, replaced his fingers at her palm. "What do you need to tell me?"

How did he do that? Infuse everyday words with all the coziness of warm milk and blazing fall fires?

Nerves zinged, and her chest rose and fell too fast. She alternated between desire and shame.

Shame, because despite knowing what needed to be said, the desire thrumming from every cell screamed at her to keep it to herself. To hold on to the moment for a while longer.

She pushed the cowardly thought from her head. "I haven't been exactly upfront—"

"Liam, Eden! Good to see you both together." Max pulled out the chair next to them. "Mind if I join you?"

"Not at all." Liam waved to the third chair.

Damnit. There was always an interruption.

"Things are winding down out there." Max turned his bold, green-eyed gaze to include her. "You're looking healed. How you feeling?"

"Better."

"Looks like you two found some middle ground. That first day in the clinic, I wasn't sure who'd come out of this alive. But you both seem..." An eyebrow shot to the sky as he scanned them. "Happy."

From there, the conversation droned around her. Liam asked Max when he headed back to Minneapolis. Max listed off how much time he had left in his residency.

It was background noise for the screams in her head.

By the time they reached home, Eden's skin tightened and itched like the aftermath of a wasp attack. Everything was heightened and on alert. She knew she needed to come clean with Liam, but once he knew the truth, he would demand she leave. She wouldn't blame him.

Eden exited the bathroom, her princess costume replaced with a pair of jeans and pink t-shirt.

"Good night." Zoe ran down the hallway and wrapped her arms around Eden's waist. "I had so much fun with you tonight. Thank you."

Tears stung the back of Eden's eyes. God, she would miss them so much. She lowered her arms and hugged the little girl. "It was fun, wasn't it?"

Noah stuck his head out of his doorway, a shy smile on his face. "It's funny how you and Dad had the same kind of costume."

"That's enough, you two." Liam came from his room, pulling a shirt over his head. The glimpse of rippling abs sent a shot of longing through her, and she swallowed hard.

"Finish your goodnights. Time for bed." He stopped so close to Eden they were in the same space. His eyes smoldered as he looked down at her. "Are you going to be up for a while?"

She gulped. "Yes." A hopeful sound floated out of her.

Twenty minutes later, a ruffle in the air raised the tiny hairs on Eden's neck. She closed the refrigerator and turned.

Liam stood in the doorway, his eyes dark and hooded, expression filled with hunger. There was no mistaking what he wanted. What he'd come to claim.

The cola in her hand was not cold enough to cool the fever that ignited like a wildfire. Every atom in her body answered that primal call, but a flutter of fear rippled down her back. This man had wedged himself so deeply into her soul, she would never be able to walk away.

He roamed the room, hands clasped at his back like a man on a Sunday stroll. But, his sexy-as-hell gaze never left hers. When he finally stopped in front of her, she struggled to breathe. Heat pooled between her thighs and a pulsating throb began deep in her abdomen. No man had ever made her feel this way with a simple look.

"I've been thinking of you, of us, since the other night. By the fire." A calloused finger trailed up her arm, drawing lazy circles on overheated skin.

Desire challenged all reason when his hand gently closed around the back of her neck. He leaned forward and nipped the tender flesh of her earlobe shattering the last coherent thought.

"I—"

His lips crushed hers, his clean masculine scent surrounding her. She melted into the solid wall of chest and lost herself in the protective circle of his arms. Deliciously stubbled jawline chafed against her chin. All of her senses were on overload.

No slow burn. That time was past. This kiss was fireworks, bottle rockets, and champagne all rolled into one.

He lifted her against the refrigerator and she wrapped her legs around his waist. "That's right, sweetheart. Hold on tight." His panted words were dry and gritty.

Liam's body became her lifeline. She tightened her grip around his waist, the drive to become one with him so powerful she moaned in frustration against his mouth.

A little voice in the back of her head told her there would be no more interruptions. The time for caution had come and gone.

Now, she wanted to live the fantasy.

THERE was nothing awkward or unfamiliar between them. It was as if they'd done this a million times and knew every little trick to elicit pleasure.

She held nothing back.

But then, he knew this would be how it played out. No shy flower, his Eden. Her lips sought their own pleasure even as he found his. A soft desperate whimper escaped her as he dug his hands in her rounded backside to bring her even closer. A fury of desire consumed him. He was mindless. The tight leash on his control nearly snapped. And he didn't care.

Lost in the power of the moment, it took several seconds to realize she'd shifted away. A shadow flickered in her eyes before lashes shuttered closed.

"Eden?" Another long breath followed by a shudder. "What's wrong, sweetheart?" *Please God, don't let her have changed her mind.*

"I... We didn't get a chance to talk earlier. When Max interrupted us." Her lips, plump and red from his kiss, opened then closed over white teeth.

His hands gripped her hips, pinning her flush to his body. God, she fit him to perfection. He rained kisses from behind her ear to the hollow at her collarbone. "Do you really want to talk? Now?"

"I don't *want* to talk—"

"Then just feel." To emphasize his point, he nibbled the spot at the base of her throat. A hum of satisfaction vibrated against his mouth in answer.

Swallowing his own hungry groan, he willed his needy body to take a step back. This couldn't be rushed. Their connection, their passion, was like a summer storm. Raw in power, wild in intensity. Unpredictable as the woman herself. He wanted to feast on every moment.

A need to savor every inch of this woman took over. He wanted to discover what made her whimper. His pulsed quickened. What made her scream.

He leaned back far enough to continue the stream of kisses down her arm to the Phoenix tattoo at her wrist, where he paused to pay homage to the image. Teasing and nibbling to his heart's content.

"I had something much more pleasant in mind for the rest of the night." Her gasp made his body hardened.

"Yes." Her arms snaked around his neck and she dropped a bone-tingling kiss that nearly brought him to his knees.

This is what he needed. He wanted to howl. She made him think of possibilities. Things he had banished from his life. His hand tangled in silken hair and smoothed over warm flesh while her tongue met his stroke for stroke.

His fingertips slipped over the petal-soft skin hidden beneath her girly-pink t-shirt.

He pulled her off the refrigerator, carried her to the top of the stairs and stopped at her doorway. With slow, deliberate intent, he slid her down his body, prolonging their connection as long as possible. If she really wanted to stop, he would walk away. He was a puppet on a string and she was the master. Hers to command.

God, he hoped she didn't want to stop. It might kill him, but he'd find the strength. For her.

She batted her eyelashes, gaze flickered from her room to him. "You have a bigger bed..."

Five little words.

Five of the sweetest words.

A slow, confident grin spread across his face. "I like how you think."

The distance from door to door might as well have been a canyon. Every step an eternity. Her floral shampoo triggered images of soft summer days, sunbaked bodies and oil. His heart clamored in his ears, blocking any sound but his own thoughts. He yanked his shirt above his head and tossed it on the floor. No finesse, only desperate urgency. *Breathe Liam. Don't screw this up.*

With her back to him she followed suit, the t-shirt rising in slow, mind-blowing increments to expose the long line of her back.

His breath stilled. "You're so damn beautiful. I could lose myself in you." Not wanting to take his eyes off her, he groped for the doorknob and gently closed the door.

He crossed the room and stopped inches from her. Heat simmered. Electricity arced between their bodies branding him a lost man. There was nothing he could do to stop the relentless pulsing of need through his veins.

With one finger he traced the line of her spine from her neck to the waistband of her jeans. Delighted in the silk of her skin. "I want to devour you," he teased in her ear.

He smiled as a fresh wave of tremors rocketed through her.

Circling her waist, he splayed his hand flat against her belly. Fingers tickling beneath her jeans. They needed to go.

Now. He wanted nothing between them. He popped the snap, tasted the curve of her hip as he pushed the pants to the floor. The black satin of her panties nearly drove him over the edge and he cupped the sweet roundness of her ass, his thumbs sweeping back and forth. The crushing need to see all of her drove him, as satin met denim on the floor.

In seconds, she stood bare, with nothing to stop his hands and mouth from exploring her. As he came around the front she glanced down and draped her hair over her breasts.

"Look at me. Please? I need to see those beautiful two-tone eyes."

Slowly she raised her head. Pain and vulnerability, a physical touch between them.

"Please, don't hide from me." He fluffed her hair down her back and tilted her chin.

The tip of her tongue teased her lip. "I'm afraid."

"I would never hurt you."

Tears pooled in her eyes as she boldly met his. "What if I hurt you?"

So much fear and heartache in those words. He wanted to take away all the hurt that caged her in loneliness.

But he didn't know how to answer her. Instead, he silenced any other worry with a searing kiss designed to remove the stain of doubt from both of their minds.

This night would be hers. He would worship her until she knew nothing but the pure intimacy that came from being one with another person.

Little by little the tension eased from her body, and she became an eager partner in their desires. No tentative touch of lips. No asking for permission to explore, only hunger. Raw. Honest. Hunger.

She stretched up on her toes and circled his neck. One leg hooked around his, opening herself to him. His to touch. His to pleasure.

The power in that one move shattered the last of his control and melted the ice that surrounded his heart. A kernel of truth took hold in his soul.

He would lose himself to this woman.

EDEN CURLED ON THE edge of the bed where Liam had placed her. A sense of empowerment swelled in her chest, driving her arousal deeper. Never had a man made her feel so cherished.

Others had wanted a warm body. Liam wanted *her.*

Tremors fluttered through her belly as he dropped his jeans and stood in all his naked glory before her.

He placed one hand next to the sensitive skin of her hip, his face inches from hers.

She couldn't take her eyes off him. Fascinated by the knowledge that at this moment, this strong, kind, heroic man was all hers.

A mischievous smile curved his lips. "Are you going to sit there like a cat curled in the sun, or are you going to share this big, soft bed?"

She slid up the mattress until she leaned against the pillows, and his weight settled over her. His heartbeat pounded a relentless rhythm so fast, so hard, her own heart had no choice but to follow.

A breeze pebbled her skin as he rolled to his side. There was nowhere to hide from his mouth and hands as they explored and roamed where they would. Not that she wanted to. Her body came alive wherever his lips touched. Where his fingers brushed. An urgent pressure built between her thighs until blood turned to an ocean of magma searing her from the inside.

He was her fantasy made flesh. Her hopes made real. Maybe they were both victims of some powerful Halloween madness. She didn't know. But with each graze of lips, each caress, each murmured endearment, she fell further under his spell.

His right hand coasted down the side of her arm and he laced their fingers. His knee nudged her thighs apart as he positioned himself above her.

His mouth nuzzled her breasts, first one then the other. Each kiss sent licks of electricity to heat the pleasure centers of her body.

She was helpless to move as he held her hands pinned to the mattress.

"God, Eden." His voice thick, his breath hot in her ear.

Their bodies rocked, first in a slow, steady rhythm, a heady friction building. Her world narrowed to nothing but erotic sensitivities. He filled her. Surrounded her. Sweat coated their bodies, she was so close, her body tensed, and... and...

He stilled.

She swallowed a groan, her breathing so fast stars danced in her vision. *What the hell?* Opening her eyes, she found his smoldering gaze burned straight through her. "Why did you stop?" Her voiced pleaded.

"What's your hurry? We have all night." The caviler sentiment couldn't hide the tension lining his face. It was obvious he was close to his own release. All it would take was a little coaxing.

She squirmed against him. "Please..."

His hands flew to her hips, halting any movement. "Oh, no you don't." He swayed his own hips, just enough to give her hope. Then he stopped.

"You can't do this. I won't let you." She snapped her teeth over her lower lip. Her nails digging into the muscles of his back. "How long do you think you can resist?"

Holding his gaze, she gave him a playful grin, reached for his hand and sucked his fingers into her mouth, teasing them along her tongue. Nipping at the tips.

She delighted in her power as his body quickened inside her. His guttural sounds music to her ears.

"Eden, I warn you..."

Her arms circled his neck. "What, *darlin'*?" She breathed in his ear. Nibbled the spot behind his ear. "Is this what you want? For me to taste you until you lose your mind?"

His grip on her lessened and she swirled her hips. Luxuriated in the sweet fire that rolled through her.

"You, don't play fair," he ground between gritted teeth.

"Liam, please stop this madness... I *need*..."

"What? What do you need?" He gave a quick, short thrust. "Tell me."

She growled. "I need you to stop playing games. I need *you*. Finish what you started."

When he moved, it was hard, and fast, relentless.

Wave after wave of ecstasy crashed over her until she didn't know where she ended and Liam began. And it didn't matter because in that moment her mind splintered, her body reduced to blissful, crippling sensations.

He thrust deeper, faster, a hiss of satisfaction pushed from his lips and he stiffened.

Her back arched, legs tightened around his waist. Body clenched around him. A moan floated on a long, breathy rush of air, the sound silenced when Liam crushed her lips with his.

Every cell exploded, and white stars twinkled behind Eden's closed eyes.

Liam's head dropped to her chest. Both panting. A warmth tingled throughout her body. He slid to her side and pulled her into the curve of his chest. "Beautiful." His whispered word ruffled her hair.

Later, as their sated bodies curled around each other and his smooth even breathing let her know he slept, she ran her gaze over every inch of his body. Willing it all to memory for the day he demanded her to leave.

She still didn't understand why she feared people may be after her. But she knew her life had been one of loneliness. And loneliness was where she'd return when this fantasy ended.

Chapter Thirty-One

Eden pulled the jeep into the parking lot of the clinic and turned off the engine. A few short weeks ago, this cozy little town trapped her in a stranglehold. The blind urge to run, overpowering. Now, she wanted nothing more than to carve out a niche for herself and stay. To make this her home.

She looked down the street to J'Emmas.

To make *him* her home.

She sighed and climbed out of the car. Last night had been beyond her wildest dreams. Nothing in her imagination prepared her for the beauty of being with someone like Liam. He'd been gentle and passionate. Playful and intense all at once.

They belonged together, and in another life, she'd do everything in her power to show the world the truth of that. But all she had was the crappy life fate handed her. Did she even have the right to wish things could be different? She had nothing to offer but fragment memories and a questionable past.

She walked into the clinic. Max sat behind the desk. "What's shaking, Max?" She cocked a hip on the corner of the desk and swung her leg. He seemed to always be in the front.

"Not much. How you doing? Doc said you might stop by. I was beginning to think I wouldn't see your smiling face today."

"And miss an opportunity to see you? I don't think so. What's the story here? Are you a doctor or a receptionist?"

"Small-town hospital with limited funds means, limited staff. Whoever has time sits at the big desk. Besides, I'm just here on vacation from my real job in Minneapolis."

"Vacation? I thought you worked here."

"Nope. I'm a surgical resident. But I like to come help Abby out when I get a chance."

"Well, I guess it's the town's win. You're so pretty it would be a shame to keep you locked away in some dark office."

Max laughed and picked up the phone. "Doc, Eden is here to see you. Sure will." He hung up the phone. "She'll meet you in exam room two."

"Thanks, Max darlin'." She sauntered into the exam room. The room where it all began. Her first glimpse of Liam. The hulking tiger. He'd scared her to her toes that day. But now... Warmth spread from her core. Now, she couldn't wait to see him every morning. Couldn't wait for him to come home. Loved the way he tucked his kids in at night.

Loved the way he'd made her feel the night before.

"Hello, Eden. Nice to see you today," Doc said as she came into the room.

Eden hopped onto the end of the exam table. "Hey, Doc. Thanks for seeing me."

"There is something different about you."

"Really? And you can see that with your back to me?"

Doc turned around, a mischievous smile on her face. "You have a glow about you. It's the same one I noticed on Liam this morning when I stopped for my morning espresso."

Heat crept up Eden's neck blooming on her cheeks. "You saw Liam this morning?"

"I did. Fun fact, he wasn't his usual grumpy self." Abby proceeded with her exam.

Eden's heart raced so fast she was sure the stethoscope would pick it up.

Ten minutes later, she patted Eden on the leg and removed her gloves. "You've healed up nicely."

"That's it, I'm healed? Everything back to normal?" Then why did she still feel like there were too many cobwebs in the belfry?

"Your cuts and bruises are healed. But how do you feel? No big revelations, I guess."

Eden feigned a fascination with her nails and thought about her reply. "I've had... glimpses. Fleeting colorful images with just enough to draw me in, then they fade away." She raised her gaze to Abby's. "Is it possible they'll never return?"

That was as close to honest as she could get. Little pieces of her life had returned. Unpleasant as it was. How she got here and the events before were still a blur.

"I feel like there is more you aren't saying. How much has returned?"

A single drop of sweat slalomed down the slope of her spine. "Nothing that matters." True enough. She'd give everything up to stay with Liam.

Abby pulled up one of the chairs and sat in front of her. Her hand warm through Eden's jeans. "You know, if you're in trouble, this is a judgement-free zone."

Temptation hung on a sliver of hope. She wanted to share with someone. Wanted to believe that this town she'd come to love would accept her. "I know my name, I know some of my history. I have a brother." At least she did when she'd fled Dallas.

"That's wonderful. Have you contacted him?"

"No. I don't know how." She still didn't understand what she ran from. What Jared's role in all of this was, and until she knew, she couldn't allow even a hint of risk to Liam and the kids or the town.

"Okay, it's a start. Do you remember what happened the night Liam found you? That might help you work your way back."

"No. I don't." That part was true. "His eyes looking down at me are my first memories." A knock at the door drew their attention.

"Is it safe to come in?"

Eden's heart tripped as Liam's voice came through the crack of the door. "Liam." A strangled laugh bubbled uncontrollably from her pressed lips. How much had he heard?

"Come in, Liam." Abby winked.

"Just stopped by to see if you wanted to have lunch at the cafe when you're done."

She breathed a sigh of relieve. Relaxed, and amiable, he probably didn't hear anything.

"Why Liam, I'm honored. You've never asked me to lunch before." Abby said.

Liam's mouth dropped open, and his head swung from Abby to Eden like he observed a tennis match.

"Oh, relax. I was kidding. Give us a few minutes, though. We were right in the middle of something. Eden?"

Her tongue slicked across dry lips, but all it did was parch her mouth. She needed something quick. They both waited for her to say something. "No. I... I didn't have anything more to say. I'm good. It's all good."

Abby scrutinized Eden, concern wrinkling her forehead. "I guess we're done then. I hope you both have a good lunch. Remember what I said, Eden. My door is always open for you."

"Ummm, right. Thanks."

Liam offered his arm and led the way out of the exam room. "See ya, Max." He waved as the other man came out of the second exam room.

They walked across the street to the cafe and took a booth near the back and placed their order.

Eden rubbed her hands up and down her arms. "It's getting colder out there."

"We'll have to find you some warmer clothes. Maybe we can do that this weekend. Head over to the superstore in Whitekeep. We haven't been there since our first weekend."

Eden took a sip of tea before she answered. Her time here was limited. She didn't know if there would ever be any place she could go that she would be safe.

Liam reached across the table and flicked the tips of his fingers across hers. They'd just discovered each other. She wasn't ready to leave him. Not yet. Wherever she ended up, she just wanted more moments to cherish.

They made small talk through the meal, and Liam paid the check. "You were very quiet during lunch. Is everything alright? Did Doc give you bad news?"

"No." She shrugged off the hint of doom and reached for the euphoria from last night. "I've been thinking. Where do I go from here? It's been a month. I have no job, no income..."

He held her coat as she slipped her arms in. "No one says you have to rush into anything. Why not wait a little longer? Maybe more of your memory will come back."

"And do what? Keep living off you?"

"I'm not complaining." He winked and held the cafe door open for her. They walked back to her Jeep at the clinic shoulder to shoulder.

"Not what you said a few weeks ago."

He stopped and turned her to face him, tucking a hair behind her ear. "I've had a change of... heart. The other night, by the fire, you asked me who you would be if you didn't remember. What if we just took that off the table? You can stay with us as long as you want. Maybe your full memory will return. Maybe it won't. It doesn't matter."

She swallowed past the guilt.

Liam stopped abruptly, his gaze on the Jeep.

"What's wrong?"

"What the hell—" He bent down and poked a finger around a slit in the tire. "Who would do this?" He stood up and glanced around.

"What happened?"

"It looks like someone punctured the tire. Come on." He gently tugged her arm, leading her into the clinic. All senses fired at full alert, and he scanned the area.

"I didn't expect to see you two back." Max's smiled faded. "What's wrong?"

"Have you seen anyone around here since we left?"

"No. It's been pretty quiet today. But then I haven't been policing the outside either. What's up?"

"Her tire's been punctured."

Max jumped up to his feet and stalked around the counter.

"Stay here." Liam followed Max out the door.

"Who would do this?" Max's voice flowed from the other side of the car.

"I don't know, but I don't like it. I haven't noticed any strangers in town. Have you?"

"No. Can't say as I have." Max stood to his full height, dwarfing Liam in the process.

Liam opened the back and pulled out the jack while Max removed the spare tire from the back door. "It's a few days after Halloween, maybe we have some pranksters around."

He scanned the handful of other cars in the parking lot. All suspiciously unscathed.

Liam shut down the active cop side of his brain and focused instead on the physical. He wasn't ready to exam the why behind this act.

He and Max worked together and had the tire changed in a matter of minutes.

Liam threw the torn tire in the back for the authorities and held out his hand. "Appreciate the help."

"You got it. Things like this don't happen around here." Max scrubbed a hand over his face. "I have some connections we could call in if you think we need it."

"What kind of connections?"

"Let's just say I can have them here in twenty-four hours."

Liam wiped his hands on the ratty towel he grabbed from the floor of the backseat. He knew Max was ex-military. Whoever he had in mind would be badass. "Good to know. But not my call."

"Maybe not, but I would feel better if it was. Ever thought of being sheriff? Not that I have anything against Sheriff Wilson, just be nice to have someone close by."

Liam groaned. "Not you, too."

Max chuckled. "What's that mean?"

"Ben's been trying to get me to take the deputy position for the last year."

"Shoot, I bet the town would pay you to be sheriff."

Lightness filled his chest, and he mentally ticked off a list of the first five things he would do. He sighed and closed his eyes. That was no longer his path. "Come on. Eden and I need to get back to the store. The bus will drop off the kids any time now."

Eden stood at the door, a long strand of golden-red hair twined around her finger. She stepped aside as they came in. Her eyes darkened and skated away for just an instant. The smile on her lips forced. "All fixed?"

"We're good." He turned to the other man. "Thanks again, Max."

"Any time. Just remember what I said. Twenty-four hours."

"The school bus should be here any minute. You and the kids will stay at the store today."

"I'm about done here for the day. I don't mind going out to the house with them until you get home," Max said.

Liam hesitated, but in the end, he nodded his head. "Obliged."

"I'll finish up and be back in a few." Max headed to the back of the clinic.

Eden wrapped her arms around Liam and hugged him. "I'm sorry about the Jeep."

"What are you sorry for? Not your fault."

"What if it is? Liam, I still don't remember everything, but I *still* have a sense of danger when I try to look beyond the vail in my head. What if someones—"

"It's not you. It's vandals, or kids being stupid." And he wanted to believe that. This woman who wiggled her way into his life, and his heart, couldn't be mixed up with something like this. But a niggling little voice in the back of his head latched onto the fact that in his four years living here, they'd never had a case of vandalism.

He looked down and answered her smile.

Not one.

LIAM locked the store and headed to his truck. He had hoped to leave a little earlier, get home before Eden attempted to cook again. A chuckle rumbled in his chest, and he twitched his head.

While he appreciated her attempts, the meals were not edible, and her aversion to anything green bordered on comical.

"Damnit." He reached across the windshield and yanked a folded piece of paper from beneath the wiper blade and tossed it in a crumpled heap on the passenger side. Why anyone would put ads on vehicles was beyond him. They served no purpose but to blow through parking lots.

A push of the button and the engine roared to life. At the same time, his cell buzzed from his pocket. He switched to Bluetooth and answered.

"Liam, it's Ben."

He turned the truck left onto the road. "Thanks for calling me back. Needed to tell you about an incident that happened around here today. I've been letting Eden use my old Jeep to get around, and when we came out of the cafe this afternoon, her front tire was slashed."

"Are you sure it was slashed?"

"Seriously? I think I can tell the difference between slashed and natural puncture." He didn't try to hide the sarcasm from his voice.

"Sorry, habit."

"Have you seen a rise in vandalism around the area?"

"Hmmm. Not that I'm aware of. But that doesn't mean there haven't been incidents that haven't trickled up to me yet. Why? Are you concerned? Have there been other issues I need to know about?" The humor and playfulness the man usually displayed disappeared, replaced with the all-business sheriff.

Liam thought about the question but couldn't recall anything. "Not that I've heard. Could be some leftover Halloween pranksters still messing things up, I guess."

"I'll file a report in case other incidents come to light. How's Eden doing?" And back to pleasantries.

Eden's laugh, the way she curled next to him in sleep. The way she rubbed the bracelet on her wrist without even realizing it. The way she giggled with the kids. All sprang to mind. "She's good. Doc gave her a clean bill of health earlier today." The same day as the tire mishap. He shook the thought off. "Have you heard anything more? Any hits on her identity."

"Not a one. Nothing from IAFIS, so no fingerprint hits. Still no response to any missing person information. It must be heartbreaking to know that no one is searching for you."

With both his parents still alive and his brother and his family... He couldn't imagine what it must be like to be all alone in the world. "Keep me informed if you learn anything. She's getting antsy."

"You think she's ready to move on? There is nothing more we can do. She has no criminal record, she doesn't remember what happened to her, and if Doc has released her, I guess she is free to go." Ben paused. "Unless she has a reason to stay?"

Liam chose not to answer that. "Thanks for your help, Ben. I'll let you know if anything else odd happens around here." Ben's laughter buzzed in his ears long after he hung up.

There hadn't been so much as a piece of graffiti on a brick wall. Or a malicious broken window. An occasional firecracker under a seat at the cafe, yes. High schoolers 'stole' the mascots of opposing teams from time to time. All harmless kids' pranks. Slashed tires didn't fall under that heading. That crossed the line into violence.

A few minutes later, Liam pulled into his driveway, turned off the engine, the lights, and rested his elbows on the wheel.

Eden's figure stopped in the middle of the glow coming from the window, her face soft with laughter, her shoulders relaxed. Noah came from behind and hit her over the head with a pillow. Her arms circled his son. He presumed to tickle him based on the boy's body language. Zoe came from the other side with her own pillow. Then the three were gone.

The only odd thing to happen was Eden showing up on their doorstep. And now the car he'd given her had been vandalized.

In the last couple of weeks, his house had been transformed into a home.

Heat flushed beneath his skin, ran along the nerve endings, and hollowed his breathing. Eden had warmed his frozen heart. Something he never expected to happen again.

She'd managed to work her magic on all of them. And he couldn't remember a time when she hadn't been a part of their lives.

How could he think she had anything to do with this?

If an occasional bullhorn blared in his head, it had everything to do with his distrust. He knew that now. It would take him a while to fully let go of old fears. Moose Head Falls was a safe environment.

It was time he realized that.

Chapter Thirty-Two

Driving home after a fun Sunday in Whitekeep, Eden wanted to wrap herself in contentment. Joy. Even indifference would be a welcome relief. Instead, the setting sun made the broomstick-branched trees appear hostile against the gray horizon. Feeding the gremlins that had tormented her since finding the tires slashed two days ago.

Kids laughed in the backseat.

A handsome man at her side.

All was right with the world.

Except it wasn't. Never would be.

And this...wasn't her world.

It was an illusion. *They* were an illusion born from the empty shell of her life.

Corralling memories into a cohesive picture was like trying to catch leaves that swirled in a Texas dust storm. But it was enough to know that before waking in that exam room, ugliness had shaped who she'd become. She had nothing to offer a family already marked by tragedy and loss.

Eden stole a look at Liam. Thick lashes fanned eyes that, depending on their mood, could either freeze a body with cold, dark chips of ice or warm it, like a cup of hot milk on a cozy night.

A flutter churned in her abdomen. Which expression would he flash when she told him the truth?

Maybe he already suspected something. He'd been distracted all day. Attentive to the kids and to her, but distant.

She rubbed a fingertip across the door handle. "Is everything okay?"

"Sure. Why?"

"You've been distracted. Like a man plagued by too many thoughts." She tried to force a laugh to lighten the words but failed miserably.

"Not really. Just thinking."

About her? Good? Bad?

Silence stretched into minutes. Even the chatter from the back disappeared.

"I talked to the sheriff the other day. I told him about the tire being cut." The sharp edge in Liam's voice knifed through the silence.

A pounding sounded in her ears and grew to a crescendo as her heart raced too fast. "What did he say?"

Liam shifted in the seat.

The tight grasp of his hand over hers startled her.

"He said there hadn't been any other reports of vandalism, but he made a note of it. Agreed with me, it might be leftover Halloween pranksters." The anemic smile didn't bring the crinkles around his eyes that a real one would have.

It also did nothing to squash the queasiness that rolled through her.

She choked past the nettles that seem to form in her mouth. "What do you think?"

His gaze stayed fixed on the road, his thumb swept in a frantic arc across the side of her wrist, but he didn't answer. Instead, he shifted again, replacing the hold on her hand with a white-knuckled grip on the steering wheel. "He's probably right."

The empty longing of loneliness battered at her newly found security, and guilt robbed her of oxygen.

He made the final turn. A block from home. Then it would be the nighttime rush of dinner, homework, bath time, bedtime. The flurry of activity that made a house a home.

"I... I appreciate everything you've done for me." The words dried her lips like a grape lost to the sun.

"It hasn't been as painful an experience as I first thought." His lips curled, and this time she caught the glint in his eyes before he turned his attention back to the road.

How could she do this? Stand by and watch the light die a quick death at the ring of truth. Maybe it would be better to say nothing and walk away. Leave the three of them to their lives. If she left, any danger would go with her. And they'd never know what kind of monster she was.

Pulling into the driveway, Liam maneuvered the truck to park, and the kids jumped out.

"It's not your fault, you know."

"What?"

He turned toward her and rested his forearm on the steering wheel. "The tire. It's not your fault."

With all her heart she wanted to believe him. Wanted to hold onto the reality Moose Head Falls offered.

Liam pushed the power button and lowered her window. "Noah? What's wrong?"

"The door is opened."

"Get back here now." He reached across Eden for the locked glove box.

Both kids climbed in as he pulled out his gun.

Opening the door, he dropped to the ground. "Stay here with Eden." His dark eyes didn't waver from hers as he mouthed final words before he ducked and rounded the bumper.

His final plea tugged at her heart. *Keep them safe.*

Fear snapped her jaw closed like a clamp. She climbed over the center console to the driver's side and elbowed the lock. "Put your seatbelts on."

Neither child argued. Nothing moved outside the truck. Nothing moved inside the open door. Liam, hunched, and ran towards the house. Her fingers clawed at the bracelet when he disappeared inside.

What if someone waited for him? She should be in there with him. She reached for the door and caught a glimpse of her two charges in the back, faces drained of color. Huddled together.

The fog lifted from her head, heart shattered. With perfect clarity, she understood the dilemma Liam faced every day. If she left to help him, what would happen to the kids? If she stayed here, he faced the threat alone.

Her entire life, she'd had only herself and Jared to worry about, and she'd lost him to his chosen profession years ago. An empty heart was so much easier than one overflowing with...

Her spine stiffened. Overflowing with... *love.*

Dear Lord, what had she done?

LIAM came down the stairs after he canvased the house. A twenty-pound boulder sank into Liam's gut at the same time his breath whistled from flared nostrils. The scent of danger hung everywhere. He slipped the gun into his waistband and surveyed the chaos.

Anger clenched his jaw until grinding teeth punctured his tongue, flooding his mouth with sting of copper. "Dammit. What the hell was going on?"

Every room had been trashed. No idea what the intruders had been looking for, but they left nothing unturned.

Who would do this? More importantly, *why* did they do this? Anything of value was still accounted for. Broken, but still there.

Raw fear snaked down his spine and bulldozed through rational thought.

Think, Liam. Think. Whoever had been there had a reason. It wasn't robbery. What could they have been looking for? Was it some kind of twisted message? Someone dared to enter his home... and do this? None of this made any sense.

Outside, he gulped fresh air.

Eden perched in the driver's seat of his truck, her wild, autumn hair lifting with the cross breeze that came through the open windows. Her eyes closed, and her head dropped to her chest when she saw him.

As he approached the truck she opened the door, and threw herself at him. Arms encircled his neck, and she burrowed into him. Her body so familiar and perfect. How could she have anything to do with this?

"I was so worried."

He slid her to the ground, their bodies still pressed together.

"Are you okay? Is it safe? What happened? Is anything missing?" The words were rapid-fire, the pitch of her voice high, boarding on shrill.

"Whoever it was is gone, it doesn't look like anything was taken." He searched her expression, willed her to look him in the eye, to register shock or disbelief. Anything to acknowledge she didn't know the reason behind the attack.

Instead, she cupped the back of his head and pressed his forehead to hers. Her breath mingled with his, brushed the tip of his nose. "I'm glad you're okay. Good thing we weren't home." Her body quaked beneath his hands, and she broke contact, stepping back, instantly grabbing for the bracelet.

"One of the deputies is in the area and will be coming by. I don't want to touch anything until he's completed his report."

"I understand. What about the kids?"

Both faces pressed into the back window, eyes wide, but for once both silent.

"Do you mind taking them into the room above the garage? Let them watch something. I'll come get you when the deputy leaves."

"Of course. Kids, let's go." She herded them out of the truck and toward the garage like a pro.

A war waged inside, pummeled him until an aching wound festered in his chest.

In the weeks since Eden showed up on their doorstep, she'd become a vital part of their lives. Feisty, annoying, frightened, funny, sweet... she'd never been anything but *there* for his kids. If she'd wanted to harm them, she could have many times over. But the detached, rational, cop that would always be a part of him knew none of this was a coincidence.

No matter how much he wanted it to be.

"Eden?" He had to trust her. Needed to believe he wasn't wrong about her. Because if he was, what did that say about him? He didn't want to exam the need behind the belief. For now, it was enough that he believed in her.

She turned, eyes sad, complexion whiter than a fresh layer of snow.

"Lock it. Don't let anyone in."

She nodded and crossed the threshold, the door locking shut behind them.

A few hours later, the deputy pulled out of the drive, a full report in hand but not much hope of finding the person or people responsible.

Liam led Eden and the kids into the house.

"Wow! Who did this, Dad?" Noah asked.

"I don't know. But the police will look into it. We need to start cleaning this mess up. Both of you can start in your rooms."

"Oh, no! My room!" Panic lit Zoe's eyes, and she ran for the stairs. "My stuff."

A soft huff hit Liam. "You, too, Noah. Just get as much as you can done tonight. Whatever isn't finished, we'll get to it tomorrow."

"Yes, sir."

Eden surveyed the room. "I can't believe someone would do this." Her whisper so low Liam barely caught it.

Tears glistened in her eyes.

Damn. Angry, belligerent, cocky Eden he could handle. Even the softer side she liked to keep hidden...but he'd never been good at tears.

He crossed the floor until they stood toe to toe.

She twisted her hands in his shirt and leaned her head on his chest. "I'm so sorry, Liam. This is a mess."

"What are you sorry for?" He tipped her chin, so she was forced to look him in the eye. "You didn't do anything. Did you?" He didn't realize how much he wanted to hear her answer until the muscles around his shoulder blades shook under the forced constriction.

"No, but you lived a quiet life before me..."

Not a confident declaration of innocence. But he'd take it. For now. "Stop. We don't know how this happened or who did it. No point going down that road just yet. Want to help me clean?"

"Well, I got nothing else to do."

He grabbed a box of trash bags from under the sink, pulled out the last one, and handed it to her. "If it's ripped or broken, toss it. If it's not and you're not sure where it goes, put it on the kitchen table. I have another box of trash bags in the truck. I'll be right back."

Once he reached the truck, he opened the passenger door and reached under the seat for the bags he kept for easy cleanup. A rolled-up piece of paper came out with it. He moved to shove it into his pocket when something stopped him. It was the piece of paper from his windshield the day the tires had been slashed.

Smoothing out the wrinkles, his gaze locked on one word. *Girlfriend.* His hand shook as the rest of the words came into focus. *Do you really know your girlfriend?*

The night closed around him and the cold seeped through his clothes.

Folding the piece of paper, he slipped it into his pocket. Fingerprints were unlikely at this point. Too many questions and not one crappy answer.

His cop's instinct wanted to shine the bright light of interrogation into the room. To question her until she broke. But he wasn't a cop anymore. She wasn't a suspect and his heart wasn't ready for the truth. He slammed the truck door and drew in deep breaths of air.

Once inside, he forced himself into motion. The computer area sustained a lot of damage. The shattered monitor laid on its side, keyboard crushed as if someone pounded it in a fit of rage.

He took a photo of the mess for the insurance company, then started through all the paperwork. Scraps of it covered the carpet. Under the desk calendar, he found more. He recognized Eden's handwriting on most of them.

RJ? If she hadn't remembered anything else... Then who or what was RJ?

He looked over at Eden. Who was she? Was she everything he'd ever wanted? Or was she everything he'd been running from?

Chapter Thirty-Three

The next morning, Eden stared at the ceiling waiting for the night-that-wouldn't-end to make its final bow. She never realized how desolate a bed could be with only one body.

Prior to closing his bedroom door the night before, Liam made it clear it had been a long day, and they needed their rest. He tried to act like nothing had changed, but it was written in the lines of his body. *Everything* had changed.

Tremors rocked through her. The mechanical way he moved through the nighttime rituals. The overheard comment to Zoe that Eden was too busy for a goodnight kiss but he would pass on the message. It was in the smile that didn't crinkle the edges of his eyes.

Her knees wobbled when his words continued to drape her in shame.

He didn't need her at the store in the morning, would she mind finishing the clean-up here at the house?

With the hollow click of the door, her knight had done the unthinkable... He'd closed the drawbridge with her marooned on the other side of the moat.

Alone.

He blamed her. And he was right.

As the morning sun tried to warm her face, Eden curled into a ball to contain the pain that punctured her stomach.

Muted voices penetrated her one-woman pity-party, and she flipped to her knees to peek out the window. A poisonous thread of despair pierced her hollowed chest, as Liam and the kids headed to the truck. Zoe skipped in the protective spot between Liam and big brother. Noah tugged playfully at the messy braid down her back.

Pressure surrounded her once beating heart, turning it to nothing more than petrified rock. She would miss them.

The truck rounded the dirt drive before she settled crossed-legged on the bed. Why couldn't she put the last pieces of the puzzle together?

So much of her memory had returned. Dallas, her world. A petty thief in her youth. A con. She'd been a waitress. She'd lived in a dump because, despite working two jobs, that's all she could afford. Her family consisted of Jared.

Selah, Dax, the homeless kids she took food to every night. Who cared for them now? Did any of them miss her, or was she a blip on their radar?

"Enough. All this feeling sorry for yourself. A few months ago, you thought this kind of life was for starry-eyed fools. You're a bonehead for pining after someone who put his faith in a fantasy." She snorted at her own stupidity, and jumped from the bed, tore the sheets to the floor, and headed to the bathroom.

Not knowing when the next chance would come for such luxury, she entered the shower, cranked it to hot, and turned her face into the spray, letting the scalding water melt the tears. Until her mind became a blessed blank.

Until her heart went numb.

After she dried her hair and stuffed her few belongings into a garbage bag, the sheets went into the wash, the bathroom got a full clean, and she wiped down everything else in the house.

A sob grew at the base of her throat. All trace of her gone with a swish and swipe.

With her pitiful bag of clothes at her feet, she stood at the kitchen counter, pen poised over a blank sheet of paper. Words refused to form. Nothing would be good enough.

Thank you was something you said when someone passed the ketchup or opened a door for you. Not for people who taught you about life and love.

It occurred to her she had no clue how to say goodbye. People in her life just left without a word.

One day her father went to work and never came home. Her mother overdosed not long after. She and Jared lived with their grandmother until they didn't. Jared breezed in and out of her life as he pleased. The way he lived, she never knew if it would be the last.

Heat burned behind her eyelids. She dropped the pen, grabbed her bag, and crossed the kitchen floor for the last time. At the door, she stopped. The urge to turn and gaze on it all one last time almost destroyed her.

But it would hurt too much.

The old familiar loneliness seared her insides the instant the door slid closed with a hollow *thunk*. This ache went far deeper than in the past.

Always on the outside looking in.

Dragging her garbage bag luggage across the gravel, she tossed it in the back of the Jeep. She'd find a way to get the car back to him. Find a way to repay Liam for all he'd done. Right now, she needed a get-out-of-dodge free card.

She shoved her hands into her coat and walked to the obstacle course. It was the first time Liam had looked past her faults. Maybe even respected her in his own gruff way.

Everywhere her gaze landed, there was a reminder of the last couple of months. She dropped her chin and shuffled her feet before she pivoted to walk away when something caught her eye.

A cigarette butt?

She scanned the area. There were so many of them. The night by the fire pit. The smell. The noises.

Someone *had* been here.

She dropped her arms to her side and took two steps back, searching the trees for any sign of life. They could be out there now. Waiting. She executed an about-face and dodged for the Jeep.

A tsunami of adrenaline surged through her veins.

She didn't belong here. Never did. Jared and Smoke were the only people she had left.

Smoke. Her feet slowed. Of course. He would know where Jared was. Her brother's warning rang in her head. *Trust no one.*

She put the thought aside for now and climbed in the car.

At the end of the driveway, she paused. Which way? No ID, no passport, where does someone like that go? It really didn't matter. Her only goal was putting as much distance between herself and the Conlins.

She turned right.

West seemed as good a direction as any other.

Chapter Thirty-Four

L iam wound his way through the parking lot of Wild-wood Elementary. His heart rate accelerated with each repeated loop of the strange phone call from the school secretary. It fell into the *no parent wants this call* category.

No disclosure of what the problem was, no idea which kid was involved, just "we need to see you as soon as possible." The cryptic *everyone is fine* did nothing to appease the dread settling into the nooks and crannies of the muscles bunched between his shoulder blades.

The fact he'd just started his search for the initials he'd found in Eden's chicken scratch the night before heightened the drama barreling through his veins like a tank down main street.

His eyes took a few seconds to adjust to the dark interior of the old building after the bright glare from the morning sun. Typical, old school smells mingled with the cloud of cologne floating from the guy in front of him at the secretary's window.

She photocopied the man's license and had him sign the log.

Liam rocked back on his heels. While he was happy about all the precautions, he could do without all the chit-chat that went along with it. After thorough directions to get to the cafeteria, the man left, and Liam stepped up to the plexiglass window.

"Liam Conlin, to see the principal."

The chit-chatty smile contorted into a frown, followed by a mumbled *pfft*. She buzzed him through the door without a greeting.

Zoe squirmed in a chair outside the principal's office. With her feet on the seat, head crumpled against her knees, she didn't see him.

A gentle breeze could have knocked him over. Neither of his kids had a history of trouble in school, but his money had been on Noah.

Zoe glanced up and scrubbed the heel of her palms into tear-soaked eyes, blinked three times, then launched herself from the chair. "Oh, Daddy, I didn't mean to do it. It was an accident."

He knelt down, and she wrapped him in a suffocating hug. "What happened?" He pulled her back and wiped a tear.

Her eyelids dropped, refusing to look at him. "I didn't mean to do it," she repeated.

"Mr. Conlin, thank you for coming."

Liam stood and extended his hand.

Principal Barrett was a tall, slim woman in her mid to late fifties. Usually, a warm, friendly smile greeted parents. Today, her mouth pinched into a tight slash. "Zoe. Wait here while your father and I talk." She motioned to the bench outside her office. "I'll call you in a few minutes."

"Yes, ma'am."

"Please have a seat." Ms. Barrett waved him into her office and closed the door behind them. "I'm sorry to have to call you like this. Zoe has never been a problem before, and I'm sure it's as she said, an accident. But we can't let something like this go unaddressed."

"Exactly what happened?"

Ms. Barrett pulled out a chair and sat. "It seems she decided to show her friends one of her new self-defense moves during PE. The teacher was busy with another student, and Zoe used the time to hold her own class. I'm all for kids taking martial arts, but they should be taught the importance of discipline. They can't use the techniques on their friends."

Liam shook his head. "Wait, you lost me. What self-defense moves? She isn't taking martial arts classes."

"I just assumed since she said she's been learning self-defense that you took her to classes. If you've been teaching her, then I would object. It's been my experience that something like this should be left to professionals. They know better how to train the young ones."

Liam shrugged off the slow burn that warmed his neck. The fact this woman thought him so irresponsible was a secondary issue. Zoe hurt *someone*? "Let's try this again. My Zoe, the little butterfly sitting outside your office, attacked another child? She must have landed a punch, or I wouldn't be sitting here. And, just spit-balling, but based on your attitude, you must think I condone this kind of behavior."

She busied herself shuffling a stack of folders and nodded. "No need to be defensive, but yes, that sums it up."

"I'm sure this must seem like the end of the world but, my daughter doesn't know self-defense. Maybe she flailed her arms or something and caught another kid by mistake. I hardly think this warrants a visit from me."

"Mr. Conlin, I assure you, the entire thing was witnessed by several children. Zoe was teaching the girls how to get away from someone when attacked. In the process, she punched one of the boys in the eye. When he left with his parents, it was already turning purple." She primly folded her hands on top of the folders and pinned him with a scowl.

He quirked an eyebrow. "*My* Zoe? Blackened another kid's eye?"

"Why don't we see what she has to say?" Ms. Barrett called Zoe into the office. "Zoe, tell your father what happened."

"It was an accident."

"Okaaay. Why don't you tell me what you were doing to cause the *accident*?" He tried to keep his voice level and calm, but the tenuous hold on his control slipped with each minute that ticked by. None of this made any sense. His happy, bubbly little girl didn't even like it when Noah stepped on a spider.

"I wanted all my friends to be safe, too. It's not fair if I know how to defend myself, but they don't. I asked Dylan to pretend to be a bad guy. I wasn't going to really hit him, I just got too close."

"But Zoe, you don't know anything about this. Why would you do that?"

"Yes, I do. Eden taught us, and I've been practicing."

Everything slowed to a crawl. He had no idea how much time passed as he processed this new information. "Eden?" He managed to ground out from behind clamped teeth.

"Yup. She's been showing Noah and me..." Zoe's hand flew to her mouth, her eyes wider than an innocent fawn. "I wasn't supposed to tell."

"You weren't supposed to tell..." Liam's jaw locked, and a muscled ticked under his ear. "Ms. Barrett, I am sorry for what happened today. Zoe will write an apology to Dylan and his parents."

"While that's a nice gesture, I'm afraid that won't be enough. She'll have a week of in-school suspension for the violence."

"Violence? She's seven—"

The principal jutted her chin high, and her eyebrows crinkled across her forehead. "I understand you're upset, but a little boy ended up with a black eye. He's going to be fine, but his parents are understandably angry. We have a no-tolerance rule at the school. She'll spend today thru next week sitting with the teacher in the detention room. Recesses and lunches will be on the sidelines. Hopefully, she'll take the time to think about what is appropriate and what isn't. Starting with afternoon recess, she'll be sitting on the bench at the side fence."

Liam held back the snappy retort he wanted to throw out. He hated to see his butterfly's wings clipped over an accident, but he needed to remember how he would feel if the tables were turned. A boy ended up in the nurse's office. "I understand. Zoe and I will have a long talk about this at home."

Ms. Barrett stood and crossed the floor. "I'll give you two a minute. Normally, we would send her home for the rest of the day, but given her exemplary history and no blood was drawn, we'll start the detention this afternoon."

Liam waited for the door to close, then knelt, eye to eye with Zoe. "What were you thinking? You know better than to use violence to solve your problems."

"But I wasn't trying to solve a problem, Daddy. I didn't want to hurt Dylan. He didn't do anything to me. Eden said you won't always be there to protect us. She was trying to make it so we can take care of ourselves, or we could get hurt." She flung her arms around his neck.

All the anger he'd been holding onto rumbled to life as his innocent daughter burrowed her sticky face into his collar. What kind of person told a child something like that? Better yet, what kind of father allowed that kind of person near his kids?

He pulled back and wiped the tears from her face. "You never have to worry about that. You understand me? I'll always be there. Eden... Eden had a different life than you and Noah."

Zoe sniffed and ran a palm over her nose. "You mean she didn't have a daddy to take care of her?"

"Maybe. Look, you have to go with Ms. Barrett. You messed up, now you have to pay the consequences. At recess, I want you to sit quietly where they tell you, too. Don't cause a scene. Are we clear?"

She nodded her head.

"We'll talk more about this tonight."

First, he needed to clean house.

LIAM slammed his cell phone on the counter after yet another failed attempt to reach Eden.

He'd gone straight to the house after leaving school. The wise voice in the back of his head cautioned about confronting her while the need to throttle something, *anything* still consumed him.

He'd squashed that wimpy voice like a bug on a windshield. But in the end, it didn't matter. When he'd pulled in the driveway, the Jeep had been gone. Maybe she was out running errands. The urge to wring her graceful neck made his fingers ache.

She hadn't answered any of his calls or returned his messages. With no idea where to find her he headed back to the store.

As the day wore on, he vacillated between fury and uncertainty. The weak, sage voice prodded him to remember she probably had good intentions. *Probably.* Not being familiar with kids, didn't realize what would happen.

Like that, the ignition flipped. He *did* know what would happen. Which is why he told her to butt out. But she couldn't mind her business. And then he let her past his fortresses. Given her permission to butt in. To be part of his family.

His life had been orderly, neat, planned. Maybe a bit bland. But it was safe.

Then Eden came along. What was it about her that made him ignore his instincts?

Made him forget the life lessons he'd learned the hard way.

"Howdy, Liam."

He'd been so steeped in his own misery he never heard the bell over the door. "Sheriff, what brings you by?" The smile cracked the skin across his cheeks. He wore his foul mood like a billboard.

Ben's grim expression reinforced the dark atmosphere Liam had been stewing in all afternoon.

Warning bells in his head clanged and drowned out the other man's response. When Ben swung a camo backpack onto the teak counter, Liam knew nothing good would follow.

A heartbeat bellowed in his ears. "Going with a new look?"

Despite the fall temps, a sheen of sweat coated Ben's cheeks. "'Fraid not. Deer hunting season started two days ago. A guy out by Silver Bay has a box stand off Two Pines Drive."

"Middle of nowhere."

"It is, and not easily found." Ben removed his hat, putting it next to the bag. He scrubbed a hand through his hair, the thin skin around his eyes fatigued. "He showed up to find a flipped car crashed through the legs of the building. The whole structure collapsed on top of the car."

Liam kneaded the back of his neck. "Is it hers?"

Ben sighed. Unzipping the bag, he took out a wallet, a key ring, and cellphone. "The cellphone was loose in the car. There is only one number saved, no name."

"I suppose there is no answer when you call the number."

"And it's the standard voicemail greeting. We're tracing it now, probably a burner." Ben paused. "Like hers."

Liam's fingers itched to rip through the contents of the bag. Pulling out anything that might answer the million questions firing in his brain all at once.

"Her name is Eden Glover, she's twenty-nine years old from Dallas, Texas."

Sweat trickled from Liam's hairline over his brow. "She's going to be relieved you found the car."

Unless she didn't want it found.

Ben took a deep breath and reached into the bag. The sad glint from the corner of his eye did nothing to lesson the turmoil seething through Liam's blood stream.

"I'm gonna go out on a limb and say finding this car was the last thing she'd want." Ben pulled out an evidence bag and laid it on the counter. A 9mm Glock stuffed inside.

Paralysis froze Liam to the spot. Bile churned into his throat. The sheriff's lips moved, but no sound penetrated the ringing in his ears.

A gun.

He couldn't reconcile *his Eden* as someone capable of firing a weapon, let alone a gun favored by most criminals.

"That's not all. The trunk contained a duffle bag full of cash, and another full of drugs."

Liam groaned, teeth clenched until the metallic tang of blood exploded on his tongue. "Holy shit."

"It gets better. Heard about the DEA agent killed in the Dallas drug bust?"

A quick nod. Of course, he'd heard. Have to be dead to have missed the story plastered all over the news every night.

"The car matches the description of the one seen racing from the scene. Now, I don't have forensics back yet, but I suspect that gun was used in the killing."

A sucker punch to the face hurt less than this. He laced his fingers behind his head and stared at Ben. "This can't be happening."

"I'm real sorry, Liam."

"Sorry?" Liam slammed both fists on the counter and leaned into the sheriff. "You're sorry? A cop killer stumbles into our little town, and not only do you do nothing, but you pawn her off on me. My kids." The bit of his brain that still operated on a rational level recognized the ridiculousness of his statement.

None of them could have known.

No one told him to trust her.

To open the door to his heart —

No.

She'd fooled them all.

It made perfect sense. Her notion that a ten-year-old boy in a pizza parlor might have a knife. The fear his kids would be defenseless. The nightmares that still plagued her most nights. She lived in a dark world. The kind of world he'd done everything in his power to insulate Noah and Zoe from.

Liam had no one to blame but himself. He chose to believe the house of lies she constructed.

He'd been a fool. "That was uncalled for, Ben. This isn't your fault."

Ben's shoulders sagged. "We don't know the details. Let's not jump to conclusions—"

A sarcastic laugh burst from Liam's lips. "You're joking, right? What other explanation is there?" *Damn.* After the appointment at school, he'd forgotten all about the scribbled notes.

He patted himself down, trying to remember where he put the scrap of paper. "What is the guy's name? The person of interest in the shooting?"

"Sorell?"

Liam pulled the note from his back pocket. "The first name? Rudy?" He pointed to the initials doodled onto the paper. "RJ. I found this last night after the break-in. I didn't write that, and neither did the kids."

Ben chafed his fingers through his goatee. The wheels cranked behind pale blue eyes clouded with questions. "I don't know. I'd like to hear her side before we condemn her. Where is she?"

Standing in his kitchen, curled into his chair, laughing with Noah on the couch, tea party with Zoe. Draped in his blankets, hair covering both pillows.

Everywhere.

Then he flashed on the slashed tires the ransacked house. Alone with his kids. All the madness from the last few hours wrapped like shackles around his heart. Held him powerless over this new impotent rage that burned brighter than a road flair in his belly. "I left her at the house this morning. But I haven't been able to reach her all day." He grabbed his wallet and keys out from under the counter and strode to the door. He glared back at the sheriff. "Well? Are you coming?"

"Liam, you need to cool your jets, or I will restrain you."

He cocked his head and stared the older man down. "Right now, I'd like to see you try. Give me someplace to put all this energy."

Ben caved first, and the stare-down ended. He focused on packing the bag and slung the strap over his shoulder.

Both men exited the store, and Liam took extra care in locking up. Before he laid eyes on that woman, he needed some kind of zen moment to take over. If he saw her right now, he wouldn't be responsible for his actions.

She knew how he felt about his kids. Knew what happened to Krista, and still took advantage of him. Knew she was a threat. At the very least, knew she wouldn't be sticking around and let the kids get attached to her.

As they pulled into the drive the Jeep was still gone.

Now, he knew before even stepping inside.

She was gone.

He took the stairs two at a time anyway. Opened the door to his room. The bed made, the scent from freshly laundered bedding filled the room. All trace of her gone. He crossed the hall to her room but was met with the same emptiness.

As he reached the bottom of the stairs, he found the sheriff waiting by the door. "You can add grand theft auto to your long list of crimes. She and my Jeep are gone."

Chapter Thirty-Five

The hours passed, as the tires rolled Eden farther and farther from Moose Head Falls. And still no clue about her destination.

No matter how far away she got, the heaviness that had settled around her when she walked out of Liam's house for the last time, wouldn't go away. She glanced at the glowing clock on the dashboard. Right about now, dinner prep was underway and the kids would be sharing their day. Would they be upset she hadn't said goodbye? Or would Liam smooth it over as he did everything else?

As darkness encroached, she pulled off the highway, found the closest gas station, and parked in the farthest corner. Away from all lights.

Tired, she turned off the engine and prepared to hunker down for the night. By the time she was done, clothes covered the windows, interior lights were dim, and the outside world disappeared. With any luck, no one would notice her in the dark recesses of the parking lot.

A decision had to be made. If anyone knew where Jared was, it would be his best friend. The last time they'd talked, Jared told her something was wrong, but he couldn't put his finger on what. He'd given her the phone and told her to trust no one.

Certainly, the dire warning didn't extend to Smoke.

The curtain over the dark corners of her mind fluttered. As if the secrets behind it were ready to show themselves. Then the veil settled again, without one morsel revealed.

No, Smoke had been like a brother to both of them from the first week they turned up on the streets of Dallas. She'd tried to call Jared, but he wasn't answering his phone. Smoke was her only avenue. Either that, or wander an aimless path across the country.

It took three rings for him to answer. "Yeah, who 'dis?"

"Smoke, it's me—"

"Eden?"

She sagged into the seat. "I've never been so happy to hear your raspy-ass voice."

"Umm... where are you?"

"You're never going to believe it, Minnesota. Well, I was, now I'm halfway through South Dakota."

"Ooookay..." His voice rose in question.

"Do you know where Jared is? He doesn't answer his phone, and I've been trying for hours."

"Jared?"

"Yeah. You remember, my brother, tall guy copper hair, bad jokes." Snark edged into her tone.

"Umm."

"Smoke? What's the matter with you?"

"You really don't know?"

"I don't remember anything. All I know is I woke up in some clinic with no idea who I am."

"But you're calling me now..."

"My memories are coming back in bits and pieces."

"You have no clue how you got there?" Muffled conversation followed like someone holding their hand over the mouthpiece.

She shrank into the seat. Why was he acting so strange? "Smoke, who's with you? What's going on?"

"He's… here…I…sent someone to get him, we've been looking for you."

Relief washed through her. "Let me talk to him. Where are you?"

"You can't. I… don't know where he is. Right now. You need to meet us. We're in Two Harbors, Minnesota."

"Is she coming?"

"Yeah. Tomorrow afternoon."

"Call Pete and Marcus, tell them it's time."

"Awww, come on, RJ. She's coming of her own free will. That won't be necessary."

RJ grabbed the other man by the throat, nostrils flared, lips curled in a snarl. Reduced to a worthless pile of shit his whole life by his father, he refused to allow one of his own men to treat him that way. "Don't. Ever. Question. Me again. Do you understand?"

His muscles quivered as he fisted his grip tighter, fingers digging into tender flesh. The power he wielded more intoxicating than the drugs he peddled to bottom-feeders. His victim swatted at RJ's forearms, his face turning red. A jerky nod was the only reply the other man could manage.

RJ let him go and strolled to the deteriorating desk.

Smoke found his voice around gasps for air. "I'll call them... I'll make sure they know it's important."

"Good. And Smoke..." RJ glanced over his shoulder. "Make sure they're careful. I don't want my merchandise damaged."

Chapter Thirty-Six

L iam sloshed the last dregs of his coffee into the store-room's small sink then slammed the mug on to the counter. The way his muscles twitched beneath his skin, more caffeine was the last thing he needed.

Not a soul waited for him at the front of the store. This time of the morning was notoriously quiet. The time of day reserved for restocking or ordering. All tasks he usually relished.

But not today.

Today, he needed something to quiet the angry man banging around in his head.

After dropping the kids at school, he'd opened the store and lost himself in the morning foot traffic along with the occasional conversation, even though Eden's absence was everyone's favorite topic.

Now, his stomach churned with the bitter acid oozing down his throat. For years he'd tried to keep the world from touching his kids. And in the space of inhale-exhale, he invited a cop killer into their home. Was he so hard up for a woman that he'd thrown years of training and caution to the wind?

It was good she ran. Better, had she gone before the attachments. Best, if she'd left his Jeep behind. Visions of clenching his fingers around the beautiful neck, that once inspired his kisses, haunted him in the hazy twilight between reality and dreams as he'd tossed and turned the night before.

Doubts clawed at his insecurities. Had he missed it? The signs every criminal waved like a neon flag if you were just alert enough to see them?

His mind raced over every word she'd voiced, every detail of her movements. Tried to wrap his head around what a fool she'd made of him.

A deep breath did nothing to allay the oppressive weight sinking into his chest. Zoe had cried herself to sleep. Noah's silence through dinner spoke volumes. Eden shot a damn hole in the protective dome around his little family.

Liam stomped the perimeter of the store, snagged a walking stick out of the bin by the door, and with more force than intended, chucked it across the room. The scatter of glass hitting the floor echoed through the building and mingled with a flare of satisfaction then disappointment at his loss of control.

The bell above the door jangled at his back, a pair of women's brown shoes stopped next to him. The white doctor's coat hanging at the knees told him everything he needed to know about the ill-timed visitor. He didn't bother to lookup. "Abby."

"Liam. I hate when that happens."

His gaze snapped to hers. "What?"

"When walking sticks run amok."

The stale air clogging his lungs rushed from him in one long exhale. His shoulders deflated.

The morning customers had been circumspect in their comments. He didn't expect the same from Abby. "What can I do for you?"

"I think the better question is, why are you here? You could be home beating on a tree or running that obstacle course of yours until you can't stand."

His body stiffened in anticipation at the idea of physical release. Why hadn't he thought of that?

"Instead, you take out a defenseless..." she leaned forward and squinted. "What is that? A lemon drop candy jar?"

Liam staggered to the backroom. At least now he had something to do. He grabbed the broom and dustpan and started sweeping up the mess. "Does the entire town know about this? I've had long, lingering stares and vague questions all morning. I've had enough for one day."

She shrugged one shoulder. "How are the kids?"

"How do you think? I let them get attached to someone with no plans to stick around. I knew better. But I didn't use my head."

"We always knew she'd be gone when her memory returned. You can't hold that against her."

Her words stirred the raw emotions he'd fought all morning. "*If* her memory was lost. And let's not forget that *one* pesky detail. She's a criminal. How about the fact she used us? The whole town became her hideout. Can we hold her accountable for that?"

Abby had the good graces to lower her lids. "We don't know the entire story, Liam." Her voice barely above a whisper, she glanced back at him. "Doesn't she at least deserve a chance to explain? Maybe we're jumping to conclusions. I haven't seen one news report that mentions a woman at the scene."

Liam inhaled sharply at the sucker-punch. But then what was her connection in all this? He shook his head. *No!* He would not allow her back in. "If she was innocent, why leave?"

"I can't answer that. But I do think the Eden *I* came to know deserves to have her side heard."

EDEN pulled the hoodie further around her head and slouched into the back of the car's seat. She'd arrived thirty minutes earlier and parked a block from the address Smoke had given her. Thumbnail gnawed to a ragged edge, she waited, gaze darting from one corner of the intersection to the other.

No cars passed. No late afternoon pedestrians hurried by on their way to someplace else. Just an empty street. A big, dark, skeletal building hulking in the background.

This was where Smoke said he and Jared would wait for her. A rundown warehouse in the worst part of town.

Arrgh. She shouldn't be surprised. The current scenic-view reeked of the dilapidated buildings they'd lived in from the day Smoke found them hiding like wet rats under a park bench twenty-odd years ago.

Apprehension she'd carried for the last hour, bloomed into a full-on flash flood.

She didn't like this one bit.

While most memories had returned, the specific ones, the events she freakin' *needed*, still tap danced just beyond her reach.

Her brother, Jared. Their best friend, Smoke. Two people she grew up trusting with her life. So why the tingly, *mayday, mayday* crawling over her now?

Movement from the corner of the building caught her eye. She strained to make out the image. Willed it to be someone familiar, but the figure was too far away and hid behind their own hoodie.

There was always the possibility the whole thing was a trap. She grabbed the tire iron from the seat next to her and opened the door. A girl couldn't be too cautious.

Whoever it was, hadn't made her yet. The person ambled in front of the building with what appeared to be a cigarette in his hand. She took the opportunity to slink around the Jeep and darted behind a tree.

This was total stupidity. What the hell had she been thinking? Should've kept driving west. Her heart bashed against the confines of her chest cavity. She had no idea what she was doing out here. Would she even recognize them when she saw them?

He chose that moment to drop his hood. Instant connection raced through her. The platinum blonde hair wasn't her brother's.

She sagged, the crusty tree bark digging through her jacket to the tender flesh of her shoulder. The tire iron slipped from her fingers. "Smoke." On wobbly legs, she took the first two tentative steps then ran the rest of the way. Their bodies collided, almost toppling them both to the ground.

Her arms clutched at his neck. All the mystery, fear, the not knowing of the last couple of months melted from her and she collapsed into him.

Smoke fell back, arms stiff at his side. "Huh... Eden..." His voice cracked. Rising to a question.

"Yes, it's me. God, I'm so happy to see you. Where is Jared?" She craned her neck. Excitement bouncing through her.

He pulled back and pushed her an arm's distance away. "He's, huh, waiting inside. Jared is... is waiting for you." His eyebrows squished together, his upper lip sucked between his teeth.

"Quit acting weird. Wait..." The muscles surrounding her mouth froze. The smile died a slow, bitter death. "Why are you acting weird?"

An image stabbed behind her eyes and she stumbled. A slight shake of the head couldn't clear the images that jumbled in one long black and white reel of out-of-sync photos. Another warehouse, surrounded by cars, men.

She squinted and tipped her neck. Whose men?

Familiar. Yes. But...*not.*

Fevered, dry lips parted. Words died on her tongue. A simple *No...* burned, as it whispered through teeth nailed shut. She cushioned her temples to block the pain of what she saw. Smoke, dragging her through a darkened doorway, the steel gate screeching, as it slammed into place.

He snatched her wrist.

"Don't touch me." She wrenched her arm, but his hand clamped tighter.

Like a comet streaking across the sky, glowing brighter as it pulled closer, images raced through her, too fast to process. But it all began to make sense. "*You*... you told me Jared was in trouble. I *believed* you." A sob ripped from her throat. Blinded to everything but the memory that bloomed from grayscale to full color.

"You stopped me on the street, said Jared needed me. We needed to run and then...Oh, God. You lied." She spat the last phrase like a dagger.

"Quit acting like the victim, Eden. You're the one that took off with RJ's property. You knew exactly what you were doing."

Her chest rose and fell with each labored breath, but even without access to her bracelet, the panic stayed blessedly under control. She notched her head high, found her strength. "That's right. I remember everything you did, you back-stabbing son-of-a-bitch. You betrayed us. Why? You were our friend." She turned to run but smacked into a solid wall.

RJ's arms encased her, crushed the air from her lungs, and held her immobile. "Because he wanted to hitch his train to a winner."

Her struggles were useless. The harder she fought, the tighter his grip. "Let...me...go..." Three little words, but they cost her dearly, hysteria chose that moment to join the party.

"In time. We have a little business to discuss first."

Before she could react, he cocked back a fist. Her head snapped back, pain exploding in her cheek. Sparklers flared behind her eyes, dimmed to gray, then haziness as she struggled to stay conscious.

"That was for the gunshot, bitch." He shoved her to the ground. "Bring her inside."

Smoke hauled her to standing, but her knees buckled. "Dammit, Eden. Why did you have to go and shoot him?"

Dizziness from the blow, sent crashing waves of nausea straight to her stomach. She struggled to keep her greasy breakfast down.

He hissed in her ear. "All you had to do was be patient, and I would've gotten you out."

His words passed through her eardrums, but didn't register.

The tips of her shoes scuffed as he dragged her across the pavement, up concrete steps, through a gaping doorway. The dank, moldy stench from the old building assaulted her, seconds before he kneed her into a chair across from a small desk. The rolling clang of metal shuddered down her spine when the garage doors slammed shut.

"Seems we have a little unfinished business. You owe me." RJ towered over her, waves of danger pouring from him as he passed by.

"Owe... nothing." She spewed, the tang of blood hot in her mouth.

"Where should I start, Smoke? The gunshot? Humiliating me in front of my men? My father. You stupid, bitch. You ruined everything." He lunged across the rickety desk, but there was too much distance between them for the threat to feel real.

The pain that hammered at her head frightened her more than his theatrics.

"I spent weeks planning that operation. The drugs, the money, it was all going to be mine. And the beautiful part? Your precious brother would have taken the fall. Dear old dad would have gone after *him*."

Eden let her chin drop to her chest in a show of weakness. She wanted to weep. Instead, she let Liam's words from that night of the festival ripple through. *You're stronger than your fears, Eden. You have too much fight.* The panic that threatened to pull her under, wouldn't win.

She focused on the echo of RJ's steps as he paced the perimeter of the room. His rambled monologue faded to an almost hypnotic hum, the rhythm providing the mantra she needed to quiet the chaos and gain her wits.

Smoke stood two steps behind her left shoulder. From beneath her right arm, two men stood guard at the door. Her brain worked to remember anything Jared ever mentioned about RJ's crew. Which was very little. He always told her it was for her protection. The less she knew the better. She cursed under her breath. Jared and all his damn secrets might just be her death.

"Once I have the money, the drugs, and you, they will be returned to him."

What did he say? "I can't hear... too much pain."

He came around her blind side, grabbed a fist full of hair and yanked until she was forced to stare at the ceiling.

A whimper escaped her lips.

"I'll return your boyfriend's brats as soon as I have my property, and your pretty little ass in my hands." He pressed her face so close their noses touched.

Bile ebbed at the back of her throat. "You're bluffing." As tight as Liam held the reins, there was no way a screw-up like RJ had the kids.

"Show her." He snapped her head loose and took a seat on the desk.

Notgoodnotgoodnotgood. She needed a way out. Now.

Smoke grabbed her under the left arm and hauled her to her feet. "Don't provoke him any more than you already have."

"I'm the one with a split lip and whiplash. You're lucky my ears are still ringing, or you'd be an oily smudge beneath my shoe. Where's Jared?"

Smoke pulled her behind a pile of shredded paper and spun her around until they stood toe to toe. "You have no idea how much trouble you're in. If you're smart, and I always thought you were, you'll shut up and do what RJ tells you."

The walls closed in around her. Tears burned the back of her eyes. *He's dead.* There was no other explanation. "Smoke, where is Jared?" Her eyes pleaded with him.

He stared and then dropped her shoulder and rubbed a hand behind his neck. "He's in jail. There was this drug deal. Only it wasn't supposed to go down. It was all fake. Set up to fool his father. RJ has a hard-on for Jared. Something about his dad liking Jared more. He was going to take the drugs and the money and frame Jared. But then some off-duty cop stumbled into the middle of everything."

Eden sucked in a breath. "Wait a minute. Are you talking about the story that's been all over the news? The dead DEA agent?"

"Yeah. And Jared got nabbed for it. But the cops are searching for RJ as an accomplice."

She scrunched her eyes and willed the tears away. How many times had she begged Jared to get out of that life? "Did he do it?"

Smoke shook his head. "RJ killed the guy. But his dad wants Jared to take the fall. And they need to be sure he doesn't blab everything he knows."

And with those final words, the steel door that had kept her memories locked away, thundered open. "I was the insurance Rudy needed to make sure Jared did what they wanted."

Smoke nodded. "RJ promised me once it was done, he'd let you leave with me. But then you went all ninja on him and shot him with his own gun."

"He tried to rape me. What was I supposed to do?"

He rocked back as if she'd slapped him. His face paled. "I didn't know." Barely a whisper.

"You were Jared's best friend. You were a brother to me." Smoke's chest caved.

"How did you find me?"

"I remembered all those nights when you used to cry yourself to sleep. Jared would tell you about your dad in Thunder Bay. It was a long shot, but it paid off."

"Why are you doing this? Help me. It's not too late. You know as well as I do if RJ takes me back I'm dead as soon as Jared complies. Or worse." She trembled at the images of zombied hookers from every grungy back alley or inner-city street corner across America.

"I can't. You know that."

She made a pretense of frustration and used the seconds to get the lay of the land. If he wasn't going to help her, she needed an escape route.

And there it was. One story up. A broken window.

It wasn't much, but it was a start.

"Knock it off, Eden. I see you casing the place. Don't try gettin' away. He'll hurt those kids."

Her heart stopped. She swung her head back to Smoke. "Wait. You're not telling me he actually has them? That wasn't a bluff?"

Smoke pointed to a door hidden behind stacked crates.

He removed the chair shoved beneath the knob and stood aside.

Eden stepped into the room and gave her eyes a second to adjust to the pitch black. But everything else stopped when the mass in the corner came into focus.

She pressed her fists into her temples, a primal scream clawing at the back of her throat. Every fear that ever plagued her couldn't compare to the sight of Zoe and Noah huddled together on the floor in front of her. "No. No. No." Her whispered plea filled the tiny space and they faces lifted in her direction.

"Eden!"

Chapter Thirty-Seven

L iam pulled his t-shirt over his head and used it to wipe the sweat from his face as he entered the house. Fatigued muscles quivered with each step.

After Abby left the store, the idea of working out his frustrations on the obstacle course was too much to resist. He put a *Be Back Soon* sign on the door, locked up, and went home.

Now, an hour later, the glacier-sized knot in the pit of his stomach thawed enough that ice no longer jammed his veins.

Movement at the curve of the drive caught his attention, and he ducked his head to get a better view through the window. The red hood of his Jeep rounded the corner. *Son-of-a-bitch.*

She screeched to a stop and jumped out the door. Hurried steps carried her to the house, hair billowing around her head in a cloud of autumn. *Enough.*

Silky skin, laughter that filled his empty chest...all fake. All lies. She was a cop killer.

She crossed the threshold and stopped in her tracks at the sight of him. "Hey."

He crossed his arms and leaned against the counter.

"I've been looking for you." The words floated on a whisper.

His pounding heart stilled and he stared.

"I went by the store. You weren't there." One tear magnified a lower lash before it slipped down her cheek.

His back stiffened. "I thought you left."

"I did. I mean, I didn't mean for this to happen." She waved at an imaginary object between them. "Like this."

"You're done here. We've reached our conclusion. Or at least my family is no longer of any use to you."

"I had to come back—"

Snorting, he pushed away from the counter. "Don't do me any favors, lady. You left. It would be better for everyone if you stayed gone."

She grabbed his arm, the heat branding his skin.

He cursed.

She turned her head to the side, the movement fluttering the hair away from her face.

Air hissed from his lungs at the swollen lip. The deep purple bruise along her jawline splotched up her cheek.

He tucked the strand behind her ear, cupping her chin in the palm of his hand. "Who the hell did this?" What magic did this woman weave that people kept beating the shit out of her? And even after everything she'd done, he still wanted to snatch her into his arms and kiss away the tears?

She jerked away, but the sharp intake of breath bent her over a protective arm cushioning her ribcage.

"Dammit, Eden. Tell me who did this?" His thumb stroked over the bruise before he released her and opened the freezer. He pulled out a bag of carrots, focused on easing her pain. His hand froze halfway to her face then he tossed them on the counter. "Put it on the bruise."

"Why are you doing this?"

"What?"

She placed the bag over the wounds. "Being so nice to me. I don't deserve it."

"No, you don't, but I can't turn *my* feelings on and off."

Eyelids slid closed, she took two steps back. "I don't think you'll have any problem turning them off after I tell you why I'm here."

The skin along his scalp tightened.

She swallowed repeatedly. "I need your help. I need to find my car. The one I had my accident in—"

"Can it, Eden. The sheriff was already here."

She startled, her gaze darting from one window to the next. "What? When?"

"How stupid do you think we are? Just because we're a small town doesn't mean we're a bunch of dumb-ass bump-kins."

"You can ridicule me all you want later. Right now, I need my car. And I can't do it without you."

He placed his hands on the table and leaned in until their breath mingled. "Then let me make this real easy. The owner of the deer stand you crashed in to reported it to Sheriff Wilson yesterday."

"Oh, no." She sagged into the table. "No, nonono. Liam, where's the car?"

He shrugged. "Couldn't tell ya. But if I had to guess, I'd say locked in police impound in Two Harbors."

She spun from the table, hands snarled in her hair, carrots forgotten on the floor. "Liam, listen to me. I... *We* need that car. You don't understand. There is something in the trunk. Something some very bad people want. I need to get it to them."

"How? How did you get tangled up with people like that, Eden? The police have already gone through the car, found everything. The gun you used to kill that agent."

She reeled like he'd punched her.

"Yeah. I'm well aware of what you're looking for. You need to leave before I call the sheriff." Not sure why he hadn't already done it.

"You think I killed him?"

He shrugged. "You had the gun."

She shook her head. "Liam, if I don't get that money, and the drugs to those men within twenty-four hours... they... They're going to hurt Zoe and Noah."

His blood froze. Every atom in his body went still. "No... *How* would they hurt my kids?"

"Because..."

"No more lies, Eden. I don't know what game you're playing, but nothing will touch my kids."

"They already have them. I need to exchange what was in that car for *them*."

"Impossible. I dropped them at school myself. They're in class."

"Did you see them go into the building?"

"No, but..." He strained to see them going in, through the hustle of busses and teachers, carpool. He hadn't worried. School was safe.

That's what everyone drilled into him, day after day.

After day.

He yanked out his phone and punched in the number for school. After two rounds of automation directing his call, he got the Attendance Clerk. "My name is Liam Conlin. I'm checking to see that both of my children are in class today. Noah is in seventh grade, Zoe is in first grade. She's in In-School Suspension."

The tippity-tap of nails on computer keys echoed, and he held his breath.

"It looks like we have both marked absent. The robocall will go out this evening. Is there a problem?"

Neck muscles corded so tight they threatened to burst beneath his skin.

He advanced on Eden in slow, methodical steps, a murderous rage darkening his vision. Venom replaced the blood in his veins.

"Where are they, Eden?"

AS HE PASSED THE COUNTER he swept everything to the floor. Scattered mail, shattered pottery, a bowl of coins. "Where are they?" The pain behind the roar stabbed Eden through the heart.

She'd done this. Reduced this controlled, methodical man to an enraged monster. She deserved whatever he did to her.

In one Hulk-like move, he scattered kitchen chairs and flipped the table standing between them into the family room.

She shivered. Took two steps back.

The hailstorm of emotions filled the room with its energy. His body shook. For the next few minutes, he demolished the rest of the kitchen. By the time his rage was spent, cabinet doors were strewn in broken pieces across the floor.

Despite the brutal hatred that hardened his eyes, he hadn't laid a finger on *her.*

Even in the beginning, he hadn't looked at her like that. There'd been distrust. Doubt. And that didn't come until after she pulled a knife on him. Now, his hostile glare lashed across the distance and burrowed through her shoddy defenses. Sucked what was left of her shitty life right out of her.

The irony? Before Liam, she'd kept her heart encased in ice. Nothing touched her.

Even the lowest of lowlifes understood betrayal. And she'd committed the worst kind.

The bruise on her cheek burned from the punch RJ dealt to prove his point. This house of cards fell under *his* jurisdiction. And she'd just made the man she loved, and the children she'd come to adore, a pawn in RJ's sick grab for power.

He wanted his property. Property she hadn't known she'd taken. No idea where to find it. But the biggest takeaway? She'd sorely underestimated the disease that was RJ Sorell and his capacity to poison those around him.

"Eden," Liam snarled.

She shuddered. "He's been watching me. *Us* for weeks." She traced the edge of the Phoenix tattoo beneath her bracelet.

A reminder that anyone can rise above the destruction of their lives. But, if anything happened to those kids, her life meant nothing.

She sighed and continued. "RJ thought I would eventually lead him to the money. But I didn't know." Would Liam see the truth of her words? Or was there too much hate between them now? "You have to believe me. *I didn't know.* Until I woke up in that hospital bed and saw you staring at me... It was as if my life began in that moment."

Liam scrubbed a hand through his hair and crossed to the counter. Putting as much distance between them as the small room allowed.

It might as well have been the Grand Canyon.

Everything she'd ever wanted, everything she never deserved, shone from his eyes that night. It just took her too long to recognize it.

"When did the memories come back?"

She dropped her gaze to the table.

"How much do you remember?" His voice snapped like a whip.

"They've been trickling in almost from the beginning. A scent here, a sound, jagged pieces that didn't mean much. Until I saw Smoke today, I didn't remember what happened that night."

"What the hell is a *smoke?* Never mind." He paced the kitchen, stepping over the evidence of his fury.

Blood pounded at her temples until she feared they would explode. Ignoring him, she continued. "I kept hoping I was wrong and the signs were just a coincidence. But when they broke into the house, I knew I couldn't stay any longer. I didn't remember Smoke until I was on my way out of town. He is, was, my brother's best friend."

"Just tell me one thing."

"Anything."

He stopped so close his heat surrounded her. "Where are my kids?"

She recoiled. "I'm trying to make you understand—."

"*No*! You're trying to justify your part in their kidnapping. Just tell me where they are."

Her shoulder's sagged. "In a warehouse in Whitekeep."

He lunged for his keys and the door all in one move.

"Where are you going? You don't even know the address."

"There's only one abandoned building like that in Whitekeep."

Eden threw herself in front of the door and grabbed his arm. "You can't. You need to hear me. This isn't some...some penny-ante crook. RJ Sorell is the son of one of the nastiest drug cartel leaders in the country. His father owns Dallas. As much contempt as he has for his son, RJ has his father's full backing in this. You can't just storm in there alone and think you're going to get you and the kids out. I didn't even get a chance to see how many men he had with him. They'll kill you. All of you. Please, we have some time to figure this out."

He glared at her hand like an offending rodent and shook her off. "And what do you suggest I do? Trust you? Follow your lead? Guys like this won't leave loose ends. You might as well have put a gun to their heads."

Her stomach heaved, and bile choked off any response.

He deflated into a kitchen chair, head swaying from side to side. "I ask you again. How did you get tangled up with people like this?"

She scraped another chair across the floor and took a seat. "My father left us when I was five. My mother overdosed a few weeks later. That's when we went to live with my grandmother. We were happy, or at least I was. Jared got into trouble. A lot. A few years later, she started having health issues, and one night we overheard her tell a neighbor she couldn't do it anymore. She called CPS to come get us. Jared said they would split us up."

Tears burned a trail down the side of her face. She closed her eyes to block the memories she wished hadn't returned. "We'd already lost everyone we loved. I couldn't lose Jared, too. So, when he came to my room that night and said he was leaving, I left with him."

"You ran away? At eight? Zoe's age." His voice rose.

"Don't sound so shocked. My story is one of thousands. Just different faces."

For the first time since it all started, he had the grace to look contrite.

"Anyway, Smoke found us under a bench in the middle of a storm one night and took us in. He and Jared became best friends. You were a cop, you know what happens next. You do anything and everything to stay alive, and the wrong people get their claws in you. End of story."

"How long do we have?" Liam broke through her thoughts.

"Twenty-four hours."

"Are they safe?"

Her heart lurched. So many things could go wrong. "Yes. RJ is a ruthless son-of-a-bitch, but he won't touch them, for now. They're worth more alive."

Liam pulled the phone from his front pocket and punched in a number. After the person picked up, he said, "Are you still in town? I need your help. Now. And you can't say anything to anyone." There was a short pause. "Yeah. It's like that."

"The sheriff can't go in there guns blazing," she said when he hung up.

"I didn't call the sheriff." He rose and crossed the room. At the doorway, he stopped but didn't turn around. "Don't even think about leaving. I will track you down. And trust me, any pain you think you've experienced up until now will be nothing compared to what I'll do to you." Then he stormed upstairs.

With a heart too heavy to beat a regular rhythm, she picked the bag of carrots from the floor and headed to the couch. She eased onto the soft cushions and stretched her legs out. Her ribs screamed in protest.

Horrible images paraded across her mind. When Smoke had opened the door, and Noah and Zoe scrambled across the room to wrap shaking arms around her waist, it had nearly killed her. When their tears soaked into her shirt, she'd snapped.

The brain had shut down, and her body flew into action. A swift right to Smoke's face knocked him off guard. Another well-placed kick to his knee took him down and gave her just enough time to herd both kids out of the room.

RJ's men stopped her before they'd gotten ten steps. The kids were carted kicking and screaming back to their cell. In that ten-seconds, Noah tried to use one of the defensive moves she'd taught them before a bloodied Smoke dragged her back to RJ. With two strategic punches, one to the face, one to the ribs, he reminded her, she was powerless.

An hour later, a knock on the kitchen door brought Liam rushing down the stairs. She mustered the last bit of energy and pushed to sitting. No need to let the world see weakness.

"Took you long enough," Liam snapped.

"I was on my way to Minneapolis." Max? The rest was undistinguishable, but it was definitely Max and Liam talking.

"Eden." Expression grim, Max gave a quick nod and took a seat next to her. "You're becoming one of our best patients." He smoothed the hair off her face and inspected the bruise. "Please?" He pointed to her shirt and had her lift it to examine the ribs. "Probably bruised. May I suggest you give up your role as human punching bag?" He pulled out gauze and began to wrap her midsection. "As you know from the last time, there isn't much we can do, but this will stabilize you through the next few hours."

"We don't have time for this. We'll drop her at the clinic. But we need to go. I need to get to my kids. *Now*." Liam stood in the space between the kitchen and the family room, keys in one hand, gun holster dangling from the other.

Max stood and gave the other man his full attention. "While I like what you've done to the place, I think you might want to dial it back a notch or you won't be of any use to anyone. Least of all your kids."

"I called you because I can't do this alone. Not to be my conscience"

"I know you're upset. But, think. You've had too many years on the force and in the military to go off half-cocked. You know what happens when you make it personal."

Hesitation, fear flashed across Liam's face.

"I know you want to bolt for the door. But let's come up with a plan."

Liam gave the hint of a nod and left the room.

After Max finished patching her up, the two men spent the next thirty minutes on a plan that involved duping RJ with a bag of cash, sans the drugs.

"I hate to be the bearer of bad news, but this isn't going to work. You don't think he'll count the cash before he lets them go or notice the drugs are missing?" She offered as a voice of reason.

"You have a better idea?" Liam snapped.

"Yes. You do what the crazy madman wants. Give him the drugs, the cash..." She leaned back and stared at them both. "And me. Then you get the hell out of there."

Liam unfolded his arms. "Two flaws. No cash. No drugs."

Max cleared his throat. "Remember I told you I knew people?" He looked from Liam to Eden but when neither answered he continued. "This is their kind of party. I have no doubt they would love an invite. They have certain, shall we say *skills*, that would allow them to retrieve the bag of goodies from the police impound before they meet us."

"Do you trust them?"

"I did. With my life."

"Do it."

Chapter Thirty-Eight

Eden was right. As plans go, it not only sucked, it was dangerous to boot.

First, they had to steal the drugs and the money from the evidence locker in Two Harbors. Felony number one. Then, they were taking on kidnappers without police involvement. Felony number two. They were using a civilian as bait. Felony number three. And, possible felony number four, their only backup was a group of mercenaries who manipulated the legal line.

The cop in him shrieked in protest. But, none of that mattered. He would do whatever it took to get his kids back safe.

He hadn't been able to take a deep breath since Eden told him RJ had his kids. His brain must be oxygen-deprived. That was the only explanation for why their entire plan hinged on a woman who'd proven to be unworthy of his trust.

Not to mention, it left her vulnerable to the scumbag that had treated her like a walking, talking, piñata.

Don't feel sorry for her. She was a big girl, made her choices. Lived the life that gave the RJ Sorells of the world control over her. Noah and Zoe weren't given a choice.

That was his focus.

Eden would distract RJ and his men while Liam and Max got the kids out of the building. Then they would get her out. Once they were all safe, he would alert the authorities to RJ's presence.

It was the only plan that he could control. The only way his kids would come out of this alive.

He launched from the chair, swiped the rumpled blanket from the floor, and pressed it into a messy fold then tossed it on the hearth. The need to *do* something pounded through him.

All the talk, the waiting, made him nuts. He crossed to the sliding glass door, hands clasped behind his back, spine stiff. The serene lake view was the same as it always was, but its magic was lost on him this time.

Echoes from the night his wife died tormented him. Hideous images mocked him.

Once again, the world still lived and breathed. Once again, his universe shattered. Once again, he failed to heed the warnings and see the wolf in sheep's clothing before it was too late. "What made you pick this town?"

"What?" Eden asked from her spot on the couch.

"Did you pick us off the map? Did you drive by and think it looked welcoming? What was it that said *let me destroy this town?*"

"Liam, I didn't mean for any of this to happen."

Electric currents zinged through his body, the short hairs along his skin shot to attention. He spun on his heel, grabbed the blanket from the hearth and refolded it before tossing it back down.

Eden cleared her throat. "I... I was running scared. Get to Canada. Find my father and wait for Jared. That's all I thought about."

"You expect me to believe you stole the car with no idea what was in it?"

"I'm not proud of my life, but I did what I had to do to stay alive. I found the first car and ran. That's it."

He attacked the blanket again.

She sighed. "If you fold that blanket anymore, you'll wear a hole in it."

"I can't just sit around and do nothing. God knows what's happening to them."

"There's nothing you can do. We need to wait for Max's friends."

He rolled the blanket into a ball and then fluffed it out.

Eden pushed from the couch and approached him but stopped short of touching him. Instead, she took the blanket from his hands and dropped it onto the couch. "I'm so sorry about all of this. If I'd known, I wouldn't have stayed. I know you don't believe me, but I love them, Liam. I don't want them hurt."

Tears turned her eyes to pools of amber and navy as she silently pleaded with him.

Tiny seeds of guilt tried to take root in his soul. She hadn't had it easy— *Damnit! I'm doing it again. Letting her under my skin.*

Why was that so hard for him to remember? He didn't care about her, her past, or her future.

The lie burned in his gut.

He summoned the rage from earlier. Wrapped it around his chest like a bulletproof vest. The only protection he could find. "That's what happens when you live in the gutter."

"You self-righteous... I won't apologize for the choices I made in the past. I left that life." A sob choked over the words.

"Too bad you didn't leave it sooner."

Max came into the room. "I gave the guys the address of the impound lot and the warehouse. They can meet us by ten a.m."

Liam jabbed a finger in Eden's direction. "Don't let her out of your sight. I gotta get out of here."

EDEN sat crossed-legged in the middle of the bed, dressed in comfy jeans, insulated shirt, and her puffy vest. She stared at the crack beneath the door, counting to a hundred in slow, steady beats. The hall had gone dark thirty minutes earlier with the soft click of Liam's door closing. She'd gnawed her cuticles to a bloody mess waiting for him to finally go to bed.

She glanced at her watch. Five o'clock. *Dammit.* Sunrise was only a couple of hours away.

Stepping into the hall, she checked to be sure no light shown from his room. The urge to run in and comfort him so strong she found herself in front of his door, fingertips resting against the smooth wood. She closed her eyes, imagined him lying next to her. His spicy scent surrounding her. He'd given her something no one else ever would. For a glorious time, she *belonged.*

She'd been part of a family.

She'd *loved*. And been loved.

It wasn't enough to last forever. Then again, if her plan failed, forever wouldn't last past sunrise.

A silent goodbye echoed in her head.

At the bottom of the stairs, Max's rhythmic breathing came from the family room, where his bear-sized body overflowed the couch.

Eden took a duffle bag from the floor by the entrance and filled it with sugar, plastic wrap and a box of baggies from the pantry.

She reflexively reached for the key hooks. Her fingers found only air. All the keys were gone.

Damn him.

She jerked the kitchen drawer open and froze as the silverware shuffled against the sides. When Max's breathing remained constant, she sagged in relief, hand closing around a paring knife. If Liam thought lack of keys would stop her, he was sorely mistaken.

Max's car sat just outside the door, the truck angled behind. She'd parked the Jeep farther from the house. She prayed it was far enough away the engine wouldn't wake the men.

She tossed the bag on the passenger seat, reached beneath the steering column, and yanked out the panel. Functional memory kicked in, and nimble fingers sliced and spliced the wires until the engine roared to life.

The drive to Whitekeep normally took an hour with traffic. Given the early morning, she hoped to shave some time off that.

Her plan was simple. Divide the sugar into the baggies, wrap them in the cling wrap, and add them to the duffle. It wasn't ideal, but the weight might buy her time. Hopefully, she wouldn't even need it. *If* she could get the kids out quietly, they may all get away with no contact.

This was all her fault. Her mess to clean up.

If something happened to Liam, there'd be a permanent seat in hell with her name etched in stone. If there wasn't one already. What would happen to the kids without their father? Too much risk. She stood a better chance going in alone, under cover of darkness.

They wouldn't expect her.

Flutters rippled her belly. A slimy worm of fear gnawed at her spine. It *would* be good to have Liam at her back right about now. She slammed the brake on that thought. *No, it wouldn't.*

She'd always been alone. Fought her own battles. Jared had been in and out of juvie so many times, she'd had to learn to stand on her own two feet. Besides, Liam wasn't a knight. Certainly not her knight anymore. He was a man that wanted to keep his world safe from people like her.

Positive thoughts. That's all she needed. Positive thoughts. And a hell of a lot of good luck.

She arrived in good time and slid the Jeep into the same park she'd used the day before to case the place. Plenty of trees to give them cover as they made their escape. If they got separated, the kids should still be able to find it.

Her fingers trembled so much, a snowfall of sugar dusted her shoes as she prepared the bags before trotting off in the direction of the warehouse.

The cold morning turned her breath to fog. Crystalized air burned her lungs. Mind blessedly clear and focused, she stopped at an old oak directly across the street and waited. Watched. No movement anywhere outside, no lights inside, but then RJ and his men were squatters, they wouldn't advertise their presence.

Crouching, she crossed the parking lot to the side of the building with the broken window. *Damn.* It was higher than she remembered. Just above her fingertips. She stashed the bag under a pile of trash and went in search of something to climb.

Precious minutes of darkness ticked by as she searched for anything strong enough to hold her weight. About to give up, her gaze stopped on some broken cinderblocks on the East side of the warehouse.

She stacked the blocks side-by-side and four tall. Once on top, she pulled the few pieces of jagged glass loose from the frame, threw the bag in, then pulled herself through.

The big, abandoned space held a quiet hush that echoed with a tangible vibration in her ears. A shiver raced along spine, hand frozen halfway to the bracelet.

No more fear. She jerked her hand to her side.

They needed a hero, not a heaping pile of useless flesh fighting for each breath.

With renewed energy, she hid the sugar behind a stack of old crates and surveyed the area. RJ was arrogant enough to assume no one would come after him. Which made this easy for her.

Convinced they all slept, she scurried in a half crouch from metal pillar to discarded boxes, to a set of stairs, until she reached the room where the kids were jailed. With slow wiggles, she pulled the chair from under the knob.

Her heart swelled. Noah and Zoe curled on the hard, concrete floor, arms wrapped around each other for warmth and safety. She'd miss them. Assuming she made it out alive.

Their eyes flew wide the instant she covered their mouths. Lifting her hand from Noah's first, she put a finger to her lips before releasing Zoe. "Not one sound. Follow me." The hushed whisper sounded calm and in charge. She only prayed she could keep it together long enough to get them all out. Noah took the phone she pressed into his palm along with a crumpled piece of paper with directions to the car. Her lips settled against his ear. "No matter what happens, get your sister to the Jeep, lock the door, and stay on the floor. Call your dad. I'll be right behind you."

She waited for them to shake their heads in acknowledgement. "Let's go." She mouthed.

Time crawled as they made slow progress across the same path Eden had maneuvered moments before.

Any minute, the pink and violet-blue of sunrise would crack the horizon, casting its sunny glow through the dingy windows, killing their cover.

Dainty, pinpoints of light floated in her vision. The walls closed in, and bloated tendrils of panic shackled her ankles, threatening to hold her frozen in place. The palm of her hand convulsed with the need to rub the bracelet. *No. They need me more.* Her new mantra repeated itself with every step.

She climbed to the top of the bins, pulled Zoe up behind her then lowered her out the window. *So far, so good.*

Next, she motioned Noah to hurry when footsteps from around the corner caught her attention. *Damn.* Their luck ran out.

"Hurry," she hissed between gritted teeth.

"Hey, what are you doing?" A sleepy-faced brute came into view below them. "Aw, shit, RJ, she's got the kids," he yelled at the same time he placed one foot on the teetering stack of boxes.

Noah slid through the window just as a spray of bullets showered the wall where he'd been. One tore through her shoulder, and Noah slipped from her grip. "Go! Don't look back."

She had a second to register the *thunk* and groan when he hit the ground outside the building.

"Don't just stand there," RJ bellowed from behind her. "Get them."

The boxes swayed with the force of RJ's foot against them. A scream ripped from Eden's throat when cement slab met skull at his feet. Pain blackened her vision, and for a moment, consciousness flitted in and out.

Feet pounded around her, but one thought managed to play through her mind. They were out... They were out. The family she loved would be safe. It didn't matter what happened to her.

Somewhere, buried deep within her, a reserve of strength pushed her to wobbly knees, useless arm hanging like a limp rope at her side. Blood seeping into her eye from the open wound at her temple gave her a strange sense of courage. "RJ, stop. Leave them alone." It was more croak than command.

What more could he do to her?

Everything that mattered was already beyond his reach. "You have what you want. You have me. I have your supplies from the car. Leave them out of this." She couldn't think about what he would do once he realized she didn't have his stuff.

"You don't need them, RJ. It's a distraction." Smoke's voice penetrated from somewhere behind her. "We have Eden and the money. You can go back to your dad as the one who fixed everything, not Hutch."

RJ paused, his eyes darting around the room. "Let the brats go. Bring her."

Two men pulled her from the ground. One grabbed the wounded arm and pain swallowed rational thought. She held back the urge to throw up at their feet, but the image of a pile of vomit on their shiny shoes forced a psychotic giggle past her dry lips.

She'd crossed into crazy town. The look they gave her confirmed it.

Seizing the opportunity, she tried to land a kick into her captor's knee. Useless. Nausea heaved again.

They dragged her to the office and dumped her in a chair where RJ perched on the corner of the rickety desk.

A smug look painted his rat-like face. He finally had what he wanted. King of his own castle. His throne.

A snort racked through her. King of dust and junk. She pushed her back straight and sat as tall as she could. Wiping the blood from her eye, she took the time to get her bearings.

All the swagger of the previous minutes melted under his murderous gaze. Her insides quaked.

Reality sank in. If Daddy Sorell didn't want her alive, her life would be forfeited. But he *did* need her. At least for now. Once they convinced Jared to do what they wanted, all bets were off.

"You're a major pain in my ass, you know that?" RJ stood and came so close the sweaty, unwashed odor triggered her gag reflexes.

She sniffed. "What? No showers in your kingdom?"

The last thing she remembered was him kicking the chair out from under her.

Chapter Thirty-Nine

The fitness watch on Liam's wrist vibrated, startling him awake. He glanced at the time. Six o'clock. Guilt stabbed through his sleep-fogged head. *How the hell had he managed to sleep?*

Still dressed from the night before, he swung his feet to the cold hardwood.

He'd wanted to go last night when he returned home, but he let Max be the voice of wisdom. Backup wasn't available, and they needed help. He couldn't take them all on. Someone needed to make sure the kids got out.

Then there was Eden.

Adrenaline ricocheted through his body, the urge to pound something into oblivion a physical ache when he thought of her. Damn her for the lies. The way she'd manipulated them. Allowed Noah and Zoe to become attached.

Damn her for all of it.

He and Max had hashed over the plan until there was nothing left to discuss, and Max declared, in his doctor's voice, they needed sleep.

His heart rate had been on fight or flight overdrive ever since Eden walked in his door the day before. The fact he'd slept even one minute in the security of his comfy bed was unforgivable.

He'd let his kids down. Promised them he would always be there. Taught them to rely on *him* but not how to defend themselves. There was no redemption for that kind of arrogance. And no other word but arrogance described his behavior. He'd done everything wrong.

God help him, if they got out of this alive, that would all change.

Crossing to the closet, he shoved the clothes aside and input the code to the safe he'd installed the day they'd moved in. He grabbed his holster, gun, backup, and knife. The Glock 22 slid into place at his shoulder. The weight of the weapon, familiar. Reliable.

He collected the rest of the armory and headed downstairs. Max's friends would have their own supplies. Between them, they should have enough to take on an army.

If it came to that.

He paused outside Eden's door, hand raised to knock. When he decided the phony wide-eyed innocence was more than he could handle, he moved on. Max could come get her when they were ready to leave.

"Max, let's go," he bellowed from the kitchen. He tossed the ammo bag on the table, and grabbed a bottle of juice from the fridge. Body antsy, he leaned against the counter across from the window, willing everything inside him to calm. He took a long swig and froze.

Something was wrong. He bent down to get a better view of the whole yard.

A sick feeling curdled his empty stomach. Miles sprawled between him and the kitchen door. His mind shut down as each step took him closer and closer to the ugly truth he knew waited for him.

Bare trees silhouetted the pre-dawn morning. The truck and Max's car stood right where they'd been the night before. But the empty spot where the cherry-red Jeep should be mocked his continued gullibility where this woman was concerned.

He took the stairs two at a time, storming Eden's room. Gone.

Son-of-a-bitch. How stupid could he be? Like the simple act of hiding the keys would contain her.

He backtracked to the family room where Max sat on the couch stretching.

"She's gone." Liam threw the half empty bottle against the wall sending a shower of green liquid in every direction.

"What? She went to bed. I saw her go up."

"The Jeep is gone. Her room is empty."

"I've seen the way she looks at you. The kids. She wouldn't do that."

"Yeah, well, add actress to her laundry list of talents. She fooled everyone into thinking she's an angel. Give her an Oscar."

Max puffed out a hard breath and rubbed a hand through his hair. "Why bother coming back if she was just going to leave? Doesn't make sense."

A few hours ago, he'd wanted to believe there was more good in her. Not now. He wouldn't make that mistake again. She didn't give a damn about his kids.

"Maybe it's time to call the sheriff." Max's face was grim. An expression so out of character for the man.

"Are you crazy? They'll kill them the minute they see the cop cars. We go through with the plan. We don't need her."

"You're the boss."

"When are your friends meeting us?"

"Ten."

"Not soon enough."

Anger spiraled his spine to claw the back of his head like a rabid dog. He fantasized about what he would do if he ever saw Eden again. Those mystical two-toned eyes would go dark with fear when he found her.

THEY were about fifteen minutes from their destination when Liam's phone vibrated in his pocket. He pressed the Bluetooth button to answer without looking at the caller I.D. "What?"

"Daddy?"

Liam jerked the wheel hard to the right. Tires screeched as the truck careened to a stop on the shoulder of the road, a spray of gravel pelting the undercarriage.

His heart burst and fluttered into confetti, the air painful in his lungs. "Zoe?" Voice thick, he swallowed and tried again. "Butterfly, where are you? Are you okay?"

"I'm okay, Daddy, but Noah is hurt. Eden dropped him out the window. His leg made a funny sound when he hit the ground."

"Eden?" His scalped tingled. "Is Eden there? Put her on." She hadn't left.

"She's not here. She helped me out first, but when she was helping Noah, I heard loud bangs and then she screamed, and dropped him. His leg is really bad, Daddy."

Noah was hurt. Eden screamed. Saving his kids. "Zoe, where are you?"

"Eden told us to go to the Jeep and wait. She wrote down the address and told us to give it to you. But Daddy, Noah doesn't look good. His face is white."

"Tell me the address."

Max took down the address as she read it off.

"Zoe, listen. Max and I are not far. Stay in the car and wait until I get there. Make sure the doors are locked."

"They are. And we're hiding under a blanket. Please hurry. I'm scared."

He jammed the truck in gear and gunned the engine. "Don't hang up."

He turned to Max and lowered his voice. "Give your guys that address. That's where we meet."

Max gave him a curt nod.

"Zoe, can I talk to Noah?"

A soft ruffle and murmurs followed.

"Dad. The bone... it's sticking out of my leg."

The agony in his son's voice was almost more than Liam could take. If he didn't shut his brain down now, remove all emotions like he'd been trained, he'd be no use to anyone.

"Eden was great. She was like an angel rescuing us. She needs help. Hurry."

"Don't worry. Max and I are going to get her out of there."

His skin burned hot and tight. A litany of curses flew through his head. How could she be so stupid? If she went and got herself killed before he could wring her neck, he was gonna kill her.

Chapter Forty

Despite the freezing temperatures, sweat pebbled Noah's forehead, droplets sliding down the bridge of his nose. He inhaled a sharp, startled breath between clenched teeth, his hand spasming around Liam's.

"Jesus, Max, be careful. You're hurting him." Liam massaged the fevered skin on Noah's arm. The rest of the ride to Whitekeep had been the longest fifteen minutes of his life. But both kids were alive.

"I'm sorry, Noah. I have to stabilize this leg before you can be moved." Max sliced Noah's jeans to his upper thigh and shimmied the material gently from beneath his leg.

Every moan and groan cut through Liam. He wasn't a praying man, but right this minute he had God on speed dial.

Max gave him a quick glance. "What are you going to do?"

Million-dollar question. He couldn't get his brain to think beyond his kid's pain. He scrubbed a free hand over the stubble along his jaw, gaze fixed on Noah's sickly yellow complexion.

He *should* call the sheriff. He *should* be the dad Noah needed him to be. He *should* be the hero Eden deserved. Ride in and rescue her like she'd done for his kids.

"Let me take Noah and Zoe to the hospital. You do what you do best," Max said.

The offer was tempting.

Eden's face merged with Noah's. The problem was still the same. If the cops came in, there was no guarantee Eden came out alive.

Max's calm, confident moves made short work of rolling a ripped blanket into two splints. The last strips were tied above and below the break.

The Ravens, four men and a woman, Max's friends, all badass and the right kind of scary, stood guard around them.

"Noah. I've got to talk to these men. I'll be right over there." Liam nodded for the group to follow just out of earshot. "Max puts a lot of stock in you."

The biggest dude nodded. "Feeling's mutual. Name's, Eli. This is Finn, Domino, Trav, and Kade."

Liam appraised the group. Battled, hardened, and ready to fight. There hadn't been time to break into the impound at Two Harbors and steal the drugs and cash. One felony, gone, but they'd need a new plan.

Thanks to Eden, Noah and Zoe were safe. *Eden. Oh my God, how bad was she hurt?* He closed his eyes, slowed his breathing, and quieted his mind. Called on his training.

Noah needed something Liam couldn't provide. Expert medical attention.

Max could.

Liam knew what to do with trash. And RJ was trash.

He wouldn't let another woman he loved die at the hands of a monster.

Decision made, they quickly hashed out a new strategy.

He circled back to Noah. Taking a deep, pained breath, he closed his eyes. "Max is going to get you to the hospital." Guilt sat like a boulder in his chest.

"You gotta save her, Dad." Noah stuttered over the words, but he put on a brave face.

Zoe scooted forward and placed her hand on Liam's arm. "Don't let that bad man hurt Eden, Daddy. Please."

Pride swelled his chest. He smacked a kiss on each kid's cheek and focused on Max. "If anything happens to them..."

"Yeah. Yeah. I know. Death, destruction, ruin. Got it. Go save your woman."

"My men are in position," Eli interrupted.

Liam stared at his kids one more time. Committed their faces to memory, then stalked off before he could change his mind.

"Once you're in, we'll give you five minutes to get into position. Don't act until you hear my signal." Eli tugged his rifle sling into position.

"What's the signal?"

A slow, casual grin split the big man's face.

Liam got the distinct impression the guy loved his job.

"You'll know it."

EDEN squirmed on the cold floor of RJ's stolen office, trussed like a Christmas turkey. Not that she'd ever seen a *real* Christmas turkey. And given her current circumstances, doubted she ever would.

A grunt vibrated inside her skull. She was out of her mind. Any minute could be her last, and she contemplated her relationship with turkeys. At least it kept her mind from traveling down the dark, ugly road of fear.

After her third escape attempt, RJ bound her hands and feet and dumped her in the corner. His gaze scraped over her skin like sandpaper. The triumphant leers stole her power. Humanity. Left her a hollow shell, stripped bare. God, the pervert was turned on by her helplessness.

He was vile, and if it weren't for the gag shoved in her mouth, she'd gnaw her arms off to get away.

For years he'd made it clear he wanted her. Took every opportunity to make a pass, attempted to entice her with his status and wealth. With each rejection, he became nastier and more bitter.

The choice to leave Jared behind had been as much about wanting something more than stealing cars and running from the law, as it was about getting away from RJ.

Right now, he and Smoke were in the middle of another debate over their next move. Smoke clearly fell on the side of caution, wanting to take her and the money to RJ's father.

The fact none of them had bothered to check the contents of the bag just confirmed RJ was one margarita short of a party.

Smoke continued to push for them to leave, arguing that *her boyfriend* would show up any minute.

Grief oozed into her chest. Before long, the hole would be large enough to swallow her and end the pain that flamed whenever she pictured the hate on Liam's face. Smoke couldn't be more wrong.

Liam was the least of their worries. Once he found the kids, she'd be erased.

RJ twirled a pencil between his fingers. "What's your hurry? I kinda like it here."

"I don't understand. I thought you wanted to be the one to bring her in. Be the hero and prove to your father you're just as capable as Hutch."

RJ swirled in the ratty old chair. "I'm having a change of heart. Being here, in this place." He waved his arms. "It makes me wonder. Gives me ideas."

"Is getting killed one of them?"

"My friend, you of all people should have more faith in me. Look at all I've accomplished. I like this. I like it here."

Smoke's ankles were so close, Eden could count the frayed strings on the hem of his worn jeans.

He cleared his throat and shuffled from one foot to the other. Waves of apprehension poured off him.

She blinked the sting of sweat from her eyes. *What the hell have you done now?* They had a long history, betrayal or not, Smoke was the only one left that *might* be persuaded to help her get out of this mess.

"What about her?" Smoke stammered.

"She's mine. I'll keep her until I'm bored and then turn her out."

A shudder ran down her spine. She knew exactly what that meant.

"What if your father finds us before we get her back?"

RJ answered with a dry laugh, and jabbed the pencil in his direction. "And how would he find us? You were the only one that had a clue where to find her."

Smoke inched closer to the door. "I'm just sayin'...someone might've, you know..." He paused. "Made a phone call to your dad."

The pencil clattered to the desk.

Eden dropped her chin into her chest to get a glimpse at RJ. *Oh no.*

RJ rose, his lips compressed into a tight slash. Eyes narrowed. "Now, why would someone do that?"

Smoke's steps faltered. His face devoid of color. "I... I—"

"What did you do, Smoke?" Poison dripped from RJ's voice.

Smoke froze. "Hutch told me to call him when we found her. I thought I did a good thing."

Rage erupted from RJ. He flipped the desk to its side. "You think I'm stupid, don't you?"

Eden tilted her head back and struggled in her bonds. Smoke stood, feet cemented to the ground.

Her screams to run died behind the gag.

"No. Course not. Alls I told him was you found her, and we were coming home." The raw horror on his face told her everything she needed to know.

He was already dead.

RJ's angry steps devoured the distance between them. An abrupt halt brought the two men toe to toe. One's legs trembled in the face of death. The other trembled with a murderous wave that filled the room.

Eden ignored the pain in her shoulder and rolled on to her side.

Cocking his head, RJ contemplated the man before him. Without warning, he pulled the gun from his holster and fired a shot into his knee.

Smoke squealed and grabbed his leg. "Ow! Oh my God, why'd you do that?"

RJ squinted down the barrel and fired another round into Smoke's foot.

A gasp of pain followed. "Please, RJ, I'm sorry..."

A third shot echoed in the room.

Eden screamed behind the cloth as blood showered off Smoke like scarlet rain before he dropped with a thud.

She squeezed her eyes shut.

Blind panic consumed her. She'd finally lost the battle.

She was at the mercy of a madman.

RJ crossed the floor. Kneeling next to her, he jabbed the barrel of the gun into the side of her head.

The skin of her temple blistered and the smell of scorched hair filled her nostrils as he trailed the hot tip down the curve of her face and over her collar bone to stop just above the wound in her shoulder. "Just you and me now." He ground the muzzle through the congealed mass. Fresh blood welled and began to flow.

Her eyes rolled back in her head, oblivion one breath away.

He jerked her head toward him. "How does that feel?" His gaze rose to hers.

She prayed for it all to end.

"Freaky eyes. Pathetic. You're no better than all the other street rats out there. I can't believe I ever thought you were hot."

The now cooled metal of the gun landed in the middle of her forehead. "I should put a bullet right between your eyes for all the trouble you've caused me."

A gunshot fired as Liam reached the warehouse.

Instinct begged him to storm the door, but he held steady.

A second shot boomed.

Every muscle quivered. He sucked in air. He couldn't charge in like a rookie. He was a seasoned cop, for Christ's sake. He knew what to do.

Another shot.

She could be dead and he stood out here wrestling with his control. He pounded on the door.

The goon at the door pointed a gun in Liam's face and guided him inside.

Liam's heart slowed and his chest hollowed. He laced his fingers behind his head.

Every muscle twitched in protest when the guard took his guns. Surrendering without a fight was detestable, but he couldn't risk a gunshot or struggle alerting anyone to his presence. He needed in. To buy time for the others to seize their moment.

Besides, he was no use to anyone if he was injured or killed.

They crossed through a small hallway and down a set of stairs through a door.

"Ah, Boss, you have a visitor."

Liam stopped, feet planted wide, shoulders squared, chin thrust forward in a show of power.

Relief raced through his veins at the sight of a bruised, bound and gagged, Eden, slumped in the corner covered with blood, shirt ripped.

He wiped all expression from his face. This couldn't be personal.

Battered. But alive.

His tenuous hold on his control shattered.

Who the hell was he kidding? This was as personal as it got.

Liam's fingers flexed with the need to pummel the bloody hell out of the trash who did this to her.

"The boyfriend. Text the others, tell them to be on alert," RJ barked at the man standing behind Liam. "What brings you here?" His gaze landed everywhere but on Liam.

The maggot was right to be afraid.

There would be no mercy.

"I came for what's mine." Liam's direct stare at Eden made it clear why he was here.

Tears streaked a path through the grime over her cheeks. The gunshot wound oozed a red trail. The pain of her arms being tied behind her back had to be excruciating.

A painful pressure built in his chest. He soaked it all in. Let it fuel his anger.

"I think you're mistaken. This..." RJ waved the gun in Eden's direction. "Belongs to me. She owes me. Your brats ran when she turned herself over to me. It was a generous moment on my part."

"*You* let them go?" He quirked an eyebrow.

The man squirmed. "I could've stopped them."

"But you didn't. Release Eden. I'm here to take her home. You're free to go, once she and I leave."

RJ yanked Eden up by the hair Liam loved. "Why would you want this bitch? She'd as soon cut you as look at you." He wiped the barrel of the gun over her neck. "I've known her and her brother since they were kids living on the streets. She was a hellcat then. Still is. Isn't that right, sweet-thang?"

Liam's fingers tapped rhythmically against his thigh. A soothing tactic he'd learned years ago to help focus his mind. "She takes a strong man. A weak man needs violence to tame her," he goaded.

Crimson blotched RJ's face, and a tremor racked his hand.

A ghost of a smile curved Liam's lips when he looked directly at Eden. "You seem to find yourself in need of rescuing again."

"Stop. Just stop talking." RJ's Adam's apple bobbed.

"I came in here, all friendly and ready to do you a solid. Take Eden and go. You could've left before the cops got here. But, now, I'm getting a real negative vibe from you."

"The cops?" RJ pointed the gun at Eden's head.

"You hurt her anymore, you die." Liam's voice was feather-soft and sharp as a steel-edged sword. "I guess I should have listened when you tried to tell me something was wrong."

"That's it. This little convo is over. Shut up. I ain't telling you again." RJ shuffled away from Liam.

Eden lost her balance and nearly fell.

They'd taken all his weapons, but he just needed his escort disarmed.

A rebel yell sounded, followed by a crash from the back of the warehouse. The cavalry had arrived.

Liam whipped his elbow around and drove the bony point into his guard's jaw. Two well-placed punches, and the man crashed to his knees. A kick to the face, and the brute was down for the count.

At the same time, Eden rocketed her head into RJ's face. His cheekbone cracked. Off balance and reeling from the blow, she fell, knocking the gun from his hand on her way down.

Liam wasted no time. The dirt bag didn't stand a chance. Fury drove him.

"This is for every time you used Eden as your personal punching bag." Lighting blows pounded ribs, jaw, temple.

Pent-up rage made him careless, and RJ landed a lucky punch, snapping Liam's head to the side.

He barely had time to shake off the stars before the hairy fist split the thin skin above his left eye. Liam retreated, wiping the trickle of blood before it blinded him.

Rookie mistake, letting his emotions get the better of him. Wouldn't happen again.

Taking advantage, RJ pulled out his switchblade, thumbed the trigger and lunged across the floor.

The cold tip of the blade nicked Liam's forearm as he blocked a stab meant for his heart.

A demonic grin spread across RJ's face. He arced the knife between them. His other hand taunted Liam closer. "Not so brave now, are ya?"

Shit! The guy lacked skill, but he was unpredictable enough to make him just as dangerous. Liam dropped back.

In one swift move, he pulled off his shirt and wrapped it around his right arm.

Then he circled, using his covered arm to block the knife swings. His opponent was reckless. All Liam had to do was wait for his opening.

When it came, he was ready. A side kick to RJ's gut. Followed by a vicious left hook.

The knife clattered across the floor. Liam had him and they both knew it. "You son of a bitch. No one hurts my family."

Shouts from the back of the warehouse grew louder. It was time to end this. Liam knotted his fists and launched a pair of brutal blows before hooking his leg around RJ's knees, taking him down. He ground the heel of his boot into the asshole's throat, chocking off the air supply.

RJ clawed and swatted at the foot until he lost consciousness.

Liam reached for Eden, ripping the gag from her lips.

"Place is secured." Eli came through the office door, gaze circling the room. "Looks like you have things handled here."

"Find some rope —"

"Watch out!" Eli shouted.

Liam swung Eden sideways. A small-scale sonic boom blasted the room, and a yellow-orange light flashed behind them.

A quarter-sized hole opened on the front of RJ's shirt. He swayed back and forth on his knees as a trickle of fatal red spilled from the wound. Life faded from his eyes, and he fell face-first into the floor.

Eden's sobs penetrated the slow-motion action, and she dropped her head onto Liam's shoulder. "I'm so sorry. So sorry."

"I stopped him. He was awake, getting up. Rudy can't know," Smoke sobbed from the corner where he'd dragged himself, a trail of blood behind him. He threw the gun at Liam's feet. "I saved you. You have to protect me." His hands frantically tried to stop the flow of blood from the wound in his upper thigh.

Eli crossed the floor. Kneeling, he checked RJ for a pulse. He glanced at Liam and shook his head.

"Everyone drop their guns." A new voice brought all their attention to the door.

Smoke stuttered. "Ahh, shit. I didn't do it. I swear, Hutch."

The man named Hutch stood in the doorway. His own gun pointed at all of them.

"Shut up," Hutch snapped.

Eli slowly lowered his gun and stood with his hands in the air.

"My men have yours under control right now. No one's been hurt. Let's keep it that way."

Eden pulled away from Liam. "I know you. You work for Rudy Sorell."

Liam's heart quaked in his chest, and he shielded Eden with his body.

Hutch kicked RJ's leg. "I'm going to take this pile of shit back to his father. Leave that one here for you." He waved his gun at Smoke. "You're going to tell the entire truth about all this. Isn't that right?"

"Yes. Yes, I am," Smoke babbled.

"You know Jared had nothing to do with any of this. RJ killed that agent. You're going to tell the cops Jared is innocent. Right?"

"But I..." Smoke's voice trailed off at the glare coming from the bigger man. "I mean, yes. I'll tell them."

"Good. Because if you don't, I know where to find you."

"Why are you doing this?" Eden asked.

"Tell Jared we're even." Hutch barked an order as he left. Someone came and hauled RJ's corpse out of the room.

Sirens whined in the distance. "Liam, I hate to party and leave a mess, but I have to get my crew out too."

"Go. And thank you."

Liam untied Eden's arms then her ankles. He examined the bullet hole. "Are you okay? Abby's not going to be happy with you."

"Are the kids all right? Noah? I tried to get them out." New tears washed over her lower lids.

"They're with Max. He took them to the hospital. Noah's leg shattered when he fell from the window. But he'll be okay. They both will, thanks to you."

Eden squeezed her eyes shut.

"I should've listened to you. You knew something was wrong." He dropped into the closest chair, and pulled her into his lap. His hand roamed her body. Making sure she was okay.

Police poured into the building, surrounding them, guns drawn.

Liam raised his hands where they could be seen. "Officer Liam Conlin, formerly of the Minneapolis police department. Call Sheriff Willson, he'll vouch for me. The pile of shit sobbing in the corner was a witness to Agent Graham's shooting in Dallas. And we need a paramedic here. Now."

As the chaos and commotion milled around them, Liam's mind raced with one thought. This time, the enemy hadn't won.

Eden was alive. His woman was safe in his arms.

"Liam—"

He claimed her mouth in a kiss, telling her in the only way he knew how, she was loved.

Chapter Forty-One

E den sat on the edge of the hospital bed, legs dangling over the side, a cool breeze chilled her back where the flimsy gown didn't close all the way.

The irony of the moment played with her head. Moose Head Falls, the kids, Liam...losing her heart. This chapter of her life opened in a similar fashion weeks ago.

Only this time, she *knew* who was missing.

"You're healing well." The nurse finished with the fresh bandages and pulled the hospital gown back into position.

Eden mumbled an empty reply.

It'd been three days since Liam's kiss erased her doubts, eradicated fears, and filled her with promises. She traced the outline of her lips, where the heat from his mouth still burned.

Even though she hadn't deserved his compassion, he'd sat beside her in the ambulance, despite being told he'd have to find his own ride. His wide hand, knuckles battered and bloody, crushed hers in tender warmth. It wasn't until they wheeled her through the emergency room doors that he left her to check on Noah.

Since then, he'd ghosted.

She'd been interrogated by a parade of local cops, DEA agents and even a Dallas PD representative. Under round-the-clock guard until this morning, when, in all their wisdom, they finally declared her innocent of all charges.

Sheriff Wilson and Abby came to see her the night before. Max, with his sweet grin, stopped by earlier to say goodbye on his way back to Minneapolis.

But not Liam, and the pain of his absence funneled into her soul like a worm through an apple, leaving the surrounding flesh to blacken and die.

He might have forgiven her for all the terror she'd brought into their lives, but he wouldn't forget.

She didn't blame him.

There'd been enough testosterone and adrenaline flying around that warehouse to keep everyone jacked up and ready for some kind of release. That's all the kiss was, and she was foolish to take it for anything more.

No idea where she went from here, but she could never go back to her old life. They'd changed her forever.

The nurse fluffed her pillow and fussed with all the tubes and wires. "Why don't you rest for a while? You look tired."

"A word to the wise, you might want to keep all sharp instruments as far from this one as you can get."

Liam's silk-covered words danced like musical notes over her eardrums. A shot of heat caressed the skin of her neck.

The heart monitor went off in a frenzy of beeps.

The subtle rise of the nurse's knowing eyebrow, followed by a sly smile, sent twin flames to scorch Eden's cheeks.

Stupid monitor.

A pair of tan shoes stopped on the other side of the flowered curtain.

The nurse winked and pushed it across the metal track. "I have to get your last bag of antibiotics. I'll be back."

Eden fought the urge to look directly at him. Sorta like gazing directly at the Texas sun at high noon. It would hurt too much. In the end she lost the battle.

His eyes, dark with concern, roamed every inch of her. Then the corner of his lips tugged up in a devilish smile.

Oh, dear Lord, the man's all kinds of fine.

The pain meds must've messed with her hormones because at that moment she couldn't remember her left from her right or how to swallow.

His chest, sculpted by hours at the obstacle course, stretched the seams of a white button-down shirt.

Sleeves rolled to the elbows revealed strong, corded forearms. Thick, black hair combed to curl just behind his ears. And a day's growth of beard dusted his squared jawline.

All she had to do was close her eyes and the delicious scratch of that beard would scrape against her chin.

But it wouldn't.

Never again, and she was a fool.

Liam was an honorable man, and was probably there to check on her out of a sense of duty.

"I've been trying to get in to see you for days now. But your guards wouldn't let me." He rubbed a finger in the crease between bottom lip and chin.

He'd been trying to see her? "You must not have tried too hard. Abby and Max made it through." She wanted the statement to come off as flip, but it sounded as wounded as she felt.

"After they questioned me, they wouldn't allow me to see you until they were sure you were innocent, and we weren't somehow working together."

A flicker of hope flared in her heart. *No.* She wouldn't get her hopes up again. It hurt too much. She stretched her spine long. "Why?"

"Why what?"

"Why have you been trying to get in here?"

"I wanted to see for myself you're okay."

She tried to lift her arm and swallowed the grimace of pain that came with the effort. "Now you see. I'm fine. You can leave with a clear conscience."

"I was checking on Noah. He's doing fine by the way."

Eden's resolve softened a fraction. "Is he? I've been asking for updates, but no one would tell me how he's doing. I couldn't even get a room number from them. And heaven forbid they let me out of this room." Guilt still chewed at her over his poor leg. "I feel like all I ever do is apologize. I never meant to keep secrets. I just... I couldn't always tell what was real and what wasn't—"

"Stop. I can't begin to understand what it's like to have my mind completely erased. But I know you love the kids. The Eden I've come to know, to trust, wouldn't have intentionally hurt them."

The tightness in her chest lessened as relief washed over her. "Sorry is such a lame word... but I'm sorry for what happened to the kids."

"I am too. His doctor said he came through with flying colors. He'll be in a wheelchair for a while, but he'll make a full recovery."

Tears scalded her eyes and she looked away. "How about Zoe? I hope none of this scarred either of them too much."

He chuckled and pushed away from the wall. The maddening grin was sexy as hell and caused a calamity of emotions to collide in her chest.

"Zoe is holding court at school. She's turned this into a total win." He paused. "I talked to Dallas PD. They've taken Rudy into custody. Smoke has been talking a blue streak and the entire cartel has been effectively shut down."

She puffed out her cheeks on one long exhale. It was over. All the years of worry. Gone. Wiped away. Freedom. "Any news of my brother?" It had been so long since she talked to him.

"Good news. They've cleared him of the charges in the death of the agent. Still looking at jail time for his part in the drug deal. It's odd though, they wouldn't tell me where he is."

Eden dropped her shields in the face of this distressing news. "Why would they do that?"

"I don't know. We'll keep trying."

We'll?

What did he mean? Too afraid to ask, she fumbled with her bracelet. Gaze everywhere but on the man standing in front of her. "They're releasing me today, so I guess I'll figure that out when I get home."

Only Dallas was no longer home. She had no home.

"Not so fast," the nurse said as she bustled into the room.

Both of them jumped.

"Were you standing outside the door eavesdropping?" *Dammit.* This place was a revolving door of people. What did a girl have to do to get some privacy?

"As if I have time. The doctor asked if you had someone to take care of you. You said no. We can't let you go without someone to go home to." She removed the empty bag from the IV stand and replaced it with the new one.

"And I told you, I'm leaving. With or without approval." Crossing her arms the best she could around the medical junk, Eden narrowed her eyes and snapped off a glare. She couldn't afford to stay here any longer. It sucked that someone else could shoot her full of holes and *she* had to foot the bill.

"You can crow all you want. Unless you have family, you're not leaving." The nurse shot her a quick glare and left the room.

Liam waited for the woman to leave, shut the door and prowled toward the bed. He moved with the grace of a predator stalking its prey. Fluid lines. Mouth-watering ripples of lean muscle.

Like typical prey, she froze under the spell. The hum of anticipation started low in her belly. The vibrations flowed outward. Was this real? Or would she wake up in a dark, muggy room thousands of miles away, and find the entire last months were nothing but a figment of her lonely existence?

His lashes lowered over dark eyes. "Why are you giving her a hard time? She's just doing her job." His voice rumbled across the distance.

"I..." She licked her lips. "I'm ready to leave."

He stalked a few steps closer.

What *was* he doing?

"You heard the nurse. You can't leave unless you have people to take care of you."

She huffed. "Liam, don't you get it? There's no one. No home, no family. I don't deserve *people*. All I do is hurt the ones I—" *Love*. She swiped at unwanted tears. "Go home. Your kids need you."

As if he heard nothing she said, he advanced another step. "I might know a place you could go. A place someone would take care of you 'round the clock." His voice dropped another octave.

"Where is that?" That breathy sound couldn't be her voice. And he wasn't suggesting what her heart wanted him to mean.

"I think you'll like it there."

"Yeah?" There it was again, a voice that wasn't hers coming from her mouth.

"Absolutely. Three people to care for you." He stood close enough to fill her space. He brushed his knuckles across her cheek. His thumb softly rubbed the places where pale, yellowish-green bruises still marred her skin.

Zoe's laughter, Noah's shy hugs. Images of the family she'd come to love floated through the pain and fear. She swallowed. "Three people to care for me?"

"Are you kidding? Zoe is going to be waiting on you hand and foot. You're her hero. She's already asking to take karate."

Eden laughed. "Give it time, she'll outgrow it."

"Sadly, no. She wants to be a *kick-butt princess*, her words not mine. I'm afraid I will have to fight my seven-year-old for your attention."

Calloused hands maneuvered over the top of her thighs. His hip nudged her legs wide enough for him to stand between them. Those yummy, roaming hands settled at her waist, the flimsy hospital gown doing nothing to shield her from the lick of flames.

She finally gave in and stared into his eyes. Dark with desire, they held her gaze captive.

He was her whole world and she couldn't remember a time when she wasn't truly, madly in love with him. "Do you want my attention? After everything that happened?"

"Hell ya, sweetheart. I want it today, tomorrow...fifty years from now." Hands cupped her chin. "I love how you call me out when I'm being too hard on the kids." He lowered a soft kiss to her forehead.

"I love the way you say my name with that sexy as hell southern drawl." His lips brushed across the tip of her nose.

"I love dancing with you in a musty old garage to whatever pops up on the radio. Just to have an excuse to hold you close." He nuzzled the hollow where neck met collar bone.

"And I'll spend every day, for the rest of my life showing you all the ways I love you."

His lips claimed hers, one hand laced into her hair, the other gripped her hip and pulled her closer.

She reached her good arm up to circle his neck and gave herself completely to him. Desire and love crashed into her heart like a tidal wave against the shore.

When he pulled back, there was no mistaking his sincerity. "I love you, Eden Glover. What do you say? Are you ready to go home?"

For so long she'd watched the families that passed on the sidewalks, oblivious to how lucky they were. She'd spent a lifetime searching for a place to call her own.

Far from the streets of Dallas, she'd found it, in the wilds of Minnesota.

In the arms of a Knight-in-Tarnished Armor.

"Liam, darlin', I love you with all my heart. And I'm already home."

I HOPE YOU ENJOYED Liam and Eden's story. If you'd like to join my community and learn of upcoming releases please follow me on Facebook at https://www.facebook.com/ Kimberlyfordauthor/?eid=ARBZi6-v3AIgVz76zwwQdndW- PW70bqbd5boCOKZvs2EpANetHHdxz5enFvlHJVk3fkzGdcT- pApt05Nyd

And if you want to keep the party going, click below for a bonus scene, After the homecoming. Candlelight, nachos, and a game of war. What could happen?

https://dl.bookfunnel.com/r7dm1ireo0

If you want to learn more about Dr. Max James and his story, Betraying Teyla will be out this summer.

Thanks for reading!